THE CHAPEL IN THE WOODS

Dolores Gordon-Smith

**SEVERN
HOUSE**

First world edition published in Great Britain in 2021 and the USA in 2022
by Severn House, an imprint of Canongate Books Ltd,
14 High Street, Edinburgh EH1 1TE.

Trade paperback edition first published in Great Britain and the USA in 2022
by Severn House, an imprint of Canongate Books Ltd.

severnhouse.com

British Library Cataloguing-in-Publication Data
A CIP catalogue record for this title is available from the British Library.

ISBN-13: 978-1-4483-0645-9 (cased)
ISBN-13: 978-1-4483-0647-3 (trade paper)
ISBN-13: 978-1-4483-0646-6 (e-book)

All Severn House titles are printed on acid-free paper.

MIX
Paper from
responsible sources
FSC
www.fsc.org   FSC® C013056

Typeset by Palimpsest Book Production Ltd.,
Falkirk, Stirlingshire, Scotland.
Printed and bound in Great Britain by
TJ Books, Padstow, Cornwall.

Dedicated to Elspeth,
Who wanted a story with a pirate in it!

ONE

Extract from Lamont's *Rambles in Sussex and Hampshire Byways*, published by Rynox and West, 1922. Price: one shilling and threepence.

Birchen Bower

Situated near the hamlet of Croxton Abbas, Sussex. The property and chief residence of Alexander Cayden, Esquire. The house, built *C.* 1620 by William Cayden, probably derives its name from the birch woods which grow in abundance in the surrounding valley. 'Bower' can be taken to mean a dwelling in the woods. However, another derivation of the name, taking the secondary meaning of 'bower' as the bow anchor of a ship, can be seen in the central projecting porch which is decorated with a large stone anchor. This carving, certainly as old as the house, is a testament to William Cayden's career as a distinguished sailor, a privateer and his rumoured activities as a pirate.

The house, a fine example of Jacobean architecture, with four gables and large mullioned windows stands in a substantial estate (approx. three hundred acres) chiefly devoted to woodland.

The grounds feature a chapel, of the same age as the house, where the tomb of Anna-Maria Cayden, wife of William Cayden, may be seen.

Anna-Maria Cayden (1597–1638) born Nusta Anahuarque, a native of Peru, was rescued by William Cayden from a Spanish ship off Port Royale, Jamaica. The tomb is ornamented with a jaguar, which is the probable origin of the many superstitions surrounding Anna-Maria Cayden, who, according to legend, haunts the chapel and grounds, sometimes taking the form of a jaguar.

Nearest railway station: Croxton Ferriers (mile and three quarters)
Admission: By invitation only.

With a sigh, Constable Ernest Catton heard the bell clang in the outer room of the cottage that served both as his house and the police station for Croxton Abbas, Sussex. That meant official business.

His wife, Annie, looked at him sympathetically as he quickly wiped a piece of bread round his plate, mopping up the last of the gravy from his steak and kidney pudding. 'Who's that?' she demanded rhetorically. 'It's too bad. You can't have your dinner in peace.'

Dinner, to Mrs Catton's way of thinking, happened at one o'clock sharp. Everyone should know that. It certainly shouldn't be disturbed.

'Duty calls, Mother,' said Constable Catton, draining his tea. 'It's probably something and nothing. Although they're impatient beggars,' he added as the bell rang again.

He scraped back his chair and, standing up, buttoned up his tunic, smoothed down his moustache, and walked ponderously into the office.

Mrs Enid Martin, her hand halfway to the bell, looked up sharply. 'So there you are, constable.'

She was obviously agitated and, what's more, added Constable Catton to himself, looking at her flushed face and narrow eyes, angry.

He sighed inwardly. He didn't hold with women who made a fuss, particularly at mealtimes, but he knew better than to tell her to calm down. 'Now, now, ma'am,' he said soothingly. 'I can see you're upset. Why don't you take a seat and tell me all about it?'

Mrs Martin gave an impatient snort and, pulling up the hard wooden chair, plumped herself into it, holding her handbag like a defensive shield. 'I'll tell you what's wrong,' she said, her voice cracking. 'A pack of lies is what's wrong. They might speak English but they're foreigners in my book. I mean, they're not English, are they? That makes them foreign and it's all wrong for a pair of foreigners to come here spreading lies. That they should come here and say such things about my poor Derek is what's wrong!' She glared at him. 'Or don't you think so?'

'I'm sure I would, ma'am, if I knew more about it,' said Constable Catton. Who the dickens was Derek? He pulled up a chair and sat down, facing her. He didn't have a clue what she was talking about but whatever it was, it didn't sound as if there'd been anything that called for immediate action. He thought of a tried and tested remedy. 'Would you like a cup of tea?'

Mrs Martin dismissed tea with an impatient wave of her hand. 'Don't be ridiculous, man! Tea, indeed!'

'Well, what seems to be the problem?' asked Constable Catton, trying to keep the resentment out of his voice. 'It's Mrs Martin, isn't it?'

He had known Mrs Martin by sight, as he expressed it, for some years now. A very superior or, as some unkindly said, toffee-nosed woman, who lived in a neat, respectable house overlooking the green. What else did he know about her? She was a widow and had lived in London before coming to Croxton Abbas. A leading light of the village Literary Society, and a stalwart of the Croxton Abbas Players, she was a regular attender at church. She had a son who lived in America, and who was, apparently, very successful.

'Mrs Martin?' prompted Constable Catton.

She drew a deep breath, gathering her thoughts. 'It's about my son, Derek.' Her face softened. 'A fine boy.'

'I did hear as he'd done well for himself.'

'Indeed he has. He's the private secretary and agent for a very rich man.'

'And his name is?' said Constable Catton, pulling a notepad towards him. 'This rich man, I mean?'

She shook herself impatiently. 'His name is Jago. It's *because* of Derek that this Mr Jago is so very well off. Derek acted as his agent in Florida and accumulated a large fortune on his behalf. I would like you to bear that in mind, constable.'

'Very well, ma'am,' said Constable Catton woodenly. He'd never heard of Florida but knew better than to demand details now.

'This man, this Jago, wanted a country estate in England and asked Derek to find a suitable property. Ideally it should be a small estate, on the south coast and near the sea. When he mentioned the fact in a letter to me, I suggested Birchen Bower.'

'I see,' said Constable Catton, sitting up. He might never have heard of Florida but he knew all about Birchen Bower.

The last owner, old Mr Cayden, had died – was it four or five years ago? A fair while anyway. It had passed to his sister, or some such, an old lady now, who didn't want to live there. There had been the occasional tenant but for the last couple of years it had been up for sale and, to all intents and purposes, abandoned.

Albert Burstock, the local small builder and handyman, went in once a week to keep an eye on the place and to do any running repairs necessary. A lawyer in London paid him five shillings a week to do it, which was money for old rope in Constable Catton's opinion.

Old Burstock had announced one night in the Cat and Fiddle that the place had been sold, to the general astonishment of everyone in the pub. After all, who would want a rundown, out of the way place like that? Apparently an American with a hatful of money, this Mr Jago, that's who.

'Derek and his wife arrived a fortnight ago,' continued Mrs Martin. 'Naturally, his first action was to come and see me. I had, following Derek's instructions in his letter, obtained a set of keys from Usborne and Coverton, the solicitors who had administered the estate.'

'Ah,' said Constable Catton knowingly. They must be the lawyers in London who paid Albert Burstock his five bob a week.

'Derek took the keys and left. He warned me that I would see very little of either him or his wife for the next week or so, as he had a huge amount of work to do, up at the house.'

'Ah,' repeated Constable Catton. From what he knew of Birchen Bower, that was only too likely to be true.

Mrs Martin leaned forward, her eyes narrowed in anger. 'So you can imagine my astonishment – my absolute distress – when Mr Jago and his wife – if she *is* his wife – turned up at my house this morning, demanding to know where Derek was and accusing him . . .' Her voice broke off and she gulped. Opening her handbag she pulled out a handkerchief.

Constable Catton shifted uneasily in his chair. He never knew what to do with a woman in tears. 'Accusing him of what, Mrs Martin?' he asked gruffly.

She dabbed her eyes and sat up straight. 'Accusing him of theft!'

'Of theft?' repeated Constable Catton. He couldn't for the life of him think what there could possibly be to steal up at Birchen Bower. If there had been anything, old Burstock would have made off with it months ago, if he knew anything about it. He'd always managed to stay on the right side of the law, had old Burstock, but he was a bit too sharp for his own good.

'What's been taken?'

'Nothing!' snapped Mrs Martin. 'It's all a wicked plot.' She was about to say more when, with a jangle of the bell, the front door opened.

A tall, square-built man, an elegantly dressed woman beside him, stood framed in the doorway. Mrs Martin turned round and gave a little gasp. 'This is Mr Jago,' she said in acid tones. 'And his wife. I'm sure they're only too anxious to tell you more.' She stood up and glared at them. 'I refuse to listen to any more lies.'

Mrs Jago looked shocked but Mr Jago was more conciliatory. 'I'm sorry you've taken this attitude, ma'am,' said the stranger politely, raising his hat. 'I guess we all want to get to the bottom of what's really happened.'

She sniffed. 'That's as maybe,' she said, drawing herself upright. 'I'll leave it with you, constable. But remember what I said.'

With a stiff nod of her head, she flounced out, the Jagos standing aside to let her go.

Mr Jago shook his head as she left, then, ushering his wife in before him, came into the police station. 'Are you the chief cop round here?' he asked.

'For the village, yes I am, sir.'

Mr Jago gave a swift glance round the tiny room with its old deal table, the telephone on a stick, the fireplace with a vase of daffodils perched on the mantlepiece, and shrugged. 'I guess you don't have much crime in these parts.'

'We have some, sir,' said Constable Catton, feeling oddly defensive. After all, Albert Burstock for one, couldn't be trusted near anyone's chickens and was more than happy to help himself to the odd rabbit, whoever it was supposed to belong to. There were always drunks, of course, and the occasional tramp to keep an eye on, but he didn't suppose that would count with this American gent. He and Annie enjoyed their weekly trip to the pictures, the Electric Theatre in Croxton Ferriers, and the way they carried on in America, what with gangsters and tommy-guns and so on – well, you couldn't imagine it in Croxton Abbas, no.

'We're pretty peaceful in these parts, sir,' conceded Constable Catton.

'I'm glad to hear it,' said Mr Jago, pulling out a chair for his wife. 'That's one of the reasons we decided to settle here, isn't it, Rosalind?'

'It is,' she said dryly. 'And as soon as we step off the boat, we find we've been robbed to the tune of twenty thousand dollars.'

Constable Catton gaped at her. 'How much?' he asked incredulously.

'Twenty thousand dollars,' she repeated. She looked at her husband. 'How much is that in English money, Tom?'

'Between four and five thousand pounds, I guess.'

Four or five thousand pounds? Ernest Catton couldn't begin to imagine that much money. 'But . . . but how?' he managed to say. 'And what? Pound notes, you mean?'

'Of course not,' said Mrs Jago. 'Diamonds. My diamonds.' She sighed impatiently. 'Tell him, Tom. I was a fool to be taken in, but I thought I could trust them. We've supported the pair of them for long enough.'

Constable Catton looked enquiringly at Tom Jago. 'What's this about, sir?'

'It's about my former employee, Derek Martin and his wife, Jean,' said Tom Jago heavily. He jerked a thumb at the door. 'That was his mother, right?' Constable Catton nodded. 'Well, I guess she's only sticking up for her boy, but the facts are the facts.'

'And the facts are?'

'You know I've bought Birchen Bower?'

Constable Catton nodded again. 'Yes, sir. We'd all heard an American couple had bought it.'

Tom Jago smiled thinly. 'I'm Canadian, as a matter of fact, but that's beside the point. My great-grandfather came from these parts and I always fancied owning a country house. Derek suggested Birchen Bower and I told him to get in touch with the lawyers and go ahead.'

'It's a bit tumbledown,' said Constable Catton, unable to help himself. 'You'll need a heap of money to bring it up to scratch.'

'That's not a problem,' said Tom Jago dismissively, much to Constable Catton's secret admiration. 'I don't mind spending money if I'm getting something in return.' His eyes narrowed. 'What I do mind is being robbed. Especially by a guy who had every reason to be grateful to me.'

'You took him out of the gutter, Tom,' put in Rosalind Jago bitterly. 'That's what really hurts.'

'That's not important right now, Rosie. The point is, constable, that Derek worked for me for a good few years as my agent in Florida and elsewhere. He did well. He had the handling of some considerable sums and was always honest.'

'He was honest with you, Tom,' put in his wife. 'You know there were rumours.'

Tom Jago thrust out his hands in a dismissive gesture. 'I know. I didn't believe them,' he said wearily. 'But . . . I trusted him.' He sighed deeply, then shook himself. 'What you've got to understand, constable, is that my wife was worried about travelling on board ship with her jewellery.'

'I said as much to Jean Martin,' put in Rosalind bitterly.

'So you did,' agreed her husband. 'And it was Jean who came up with a plan. It was just crazy, she said, to keep the diamonds in a jewellery box, even if it was lodged in the purser's safe. All that did was advertise there was something inside worth stealing.' He smiled wryly. 'And what you've got to remember is that I'm known to be a rich man. We've always had to watch out for thieves. Well, Jean Martin suggested that she should take my wife's diamonds. After all, they were travelling second class and wouldn't be supposed to have thousands of dollars' worth of jewels with them. More than that, if she sewed them into the lining of her coat, no one would know they were there.'

'And I agreed,' said Rosalind in disgust. 'Like a complete fool, I agreed.'

Her husband reached out and squeezed her hand. 'Don't blame yourself, Rosie. I thought it was a good idea, too.'

He glanced up at Constable Catton. 'Well, you can guess what happened. We got off the boat in Southampton this morning, expecting to find Derek Martin waiting for us. When it became obvious he wasn't going to show up, we hired a car and driver to take us to Birchen Bower.'

'Was anyone there, sir?' asked Constable Catton.

'No, the place was deserted. And, I might say, unlocked. Anyone could've strolled in and made themselves at home.'

'And had they?'

'Well, no,' admitted Tom Jago. 'As far as that goes, I guess we should count ourselves lucky. However, the Martins had surely been there, because their trunks were in the hallway, but most of the things had been taken – including the coat with my wife's diamonds.'

Constable Catton gave a slow whistle. 'So what did you do then, sir?'

'I didn't know what to do,' admitted Tom Jago. 'I was sure there must be an innocent explanation, but I was damned if I could think what it possibly could be. You see, what the Martins *should've* done was make the place habitable and it was obvious it hadn't been touched.'

'The place is filthy,' said Rosalind, curling her lip.

'We can fix that,' said her husband patiently. 'Anyway, I knew Derek's mother lived in the village and thought she might be able to tell us what the hell had been going on.'

'We'd been robbed,' said Rosalind. 'It was obvious.'

Tom put his hands wide. 'That seemed the simplest explanation, but I thought he might have been taken ill or something and removed the diamonds for safekeeping.' He ignored his wife's dismissive snort. 'I didn't know Mrs Martin's address, but the driver was still there and he suggested we ask at the post office. So we drove back into the village and did just that.'

'And Mrs Martin went nuts,' said Rosalind. 'All we did was ask her if she knew where her precious son was.'

'Well, you did more or less accuse Derek of taking the diamonds,' said Tom.

'You were just beating about the bush. I asked her what we wanted to know and she hit the roof. She flew off the handle and threw us out, then came marching out of the house after us in a fine old temper, shouting she was going to the police. I wanted to stop her.'

'And I thought we'd better let her have her say with you, constable, then come and put the record straight.'

'You didn't want to confront her, Tom,' said his wife with a sniff.

He grinned reluctantly. 'That's true enough.'

Constable Catton felt a surge of sympathy for him. A woman in the sort of mood Mrs Martin had been in wasn't someone to be crossed lightly. 'That's probably very wise, sir.'

'So we allowed her enough time to see you – we didn't quite manage that – then it was back to the post office. We were told to look for the blue lamp over the door and that would be the police right enough and here we are.'

Constable Catton shook his head. It was a sorry tale but for the life of him he couldn't see what he was meant to do. After all, by the sound of it, this Derek Martin and his wife had had at least a fortnight to get clear.

London, that's where they'll be, he thought sagely. And under an assumed name, if he knew anything about it. London? He couldn't deal with cases that involved London. This was a case for more senior officers than him, without a doubt. He wouldn't be surprised if Superintendent Ashley himself took a hand. At the thought of the superintendent, he brightened. It would be out of his hands. Yes, the superintendent would know what to do. And the first thing he'd want were details. He pulled his notepad towards him. Proper routine, that was the ticket.

'Now, sir,' he said, sharpening his pencil with his penknife, 'if I can just take down a few facts . . .'

TWO

Jack Haldean waved cheerfully to Ashley, then nosed the Spyker to a halt beneath the tree-lined shade outside the Cat and Fiddle.

Ashley, who had been enjoying a quiet pipe and a half of bitter, got up from the bench.

'Hello, Haldean,' he said warmly, as Jack swung himself out of the car. 'It's good to see you again. How's married life suiting you?'

'It couldn't be better,' said Jack. 'Betty's the absolute tops.' He stretched his shoulders and looked appreciatively at the village high street running down to the beach, with its weathered cobbles, half-timbered houses, little shops and geese grazing on the green. In the distance he could hear the murmur of the sea and there was a whiff of salt in the air. He turned to Ashley with a smile. 'It's good to see you. I feel as if I'm playing truant.'

'Truant?' questioned Ashley.

'Betty and Isabelle have been shanghaied by Mrs Dyson to help her plan the village fete. You remember Mrs Dyson, the vicar's wife?'

'I do indeed,' said Ashley warmly. 'She was a great help last year.'

'But persuasive. I only narrowly avoided being sucked in. I had my fingers crossed that you'd say you were free this lunchtime when I telephoned this morning.'

'I was delighted to hear from you. I didn't know you were around.'

'Yes, Betty and I are having a few days with Arthur and Isabelle.'

'And how are they?' asked Ashley.

Ashley liked Arthur and Isabelle Stanton very much. The first time he had met Jack and his cousin, Isabelle Rivers, as she then was, was at her parents' house, Hesperus, in Stanmore Parry in connection with what the papers called the fortune teller's tent mystery.

He'd been a bit intimidated and more than a touch defensive at the prospect of interviewing the local gentry in their big house. In his experience, hardly anyone, rich or poor, enjoyed being interviewed by the police.

He'd also, he remembered, been puzzled by Jack. With his dark hair and gypsy-ish face, he'd stood out like an orange in a basket of apples amongst his solidly Anglo-Saxon relations. More to the point, though, he'd been really puzzled by how friendly everyone was. There was, as he found out, a reason for that. Jack, the detective story writer, was aching to be involved in solving a real-life mystery and the rest of the family were backing up his bid to be taken into Ashley's confidence.

Well, that had worked. The mystery of the fortune teller's tent had been resolved and Ashley was generous enough to acknowledge that without Jack's help it would still be a mystery. As, indeed, would a number of other cases.

'They're both doing well, I hope?' said Ashley. 'And how's the baby?'

'Little Alice? She's got Isabelle and Arthur twisted round her little finger. Mind you, Betty's as bad.'

'You're impervious, I suppose?' said Ashley with a grin.

'Well, you know how it is,' said Jack sheepishly. 'She is our god-daughter, after all. But Betty goes completely soggy at the sight of her.'

'Well, that's women and babies for you,' said Ashley tolerantly. 'I remember when we were expecting our first . . .'

More family reminiscences followed as they strolled towards the pub.

'I must say though,' said Jack, 'I was surprised when you asked to meet up in Croxton Abbas. I expected I'd have to motor over to Lewes. What brings you here?'

'I've got to see a chap here this afternoon,' said Ashley. 'I don't know if you've heard of the case? It's that big diamond robbery at a place called Birchen Bower.'

'Of course I've heard of it,' said Jack with a laugh. 'Isabelle's been full of it. I don't know what's surprised her most, whether it's that someone's actually bought Birchen Bower at last or the fact that the diamonds were sewn into a coat.'

'It was a damn silly thing to do with thousands of pounds'

worth of diamonds,' said Ashley. 'Some people are so sharp they'll cut themselves. Why not take it on board the boat, give it to the purser, and get a receipt?'

'Well, to be fair . . .' began Jack, when Ashley put a hand on his arm.

'Quiet, Haldean,' he warned in a low voice.

A tall, well-built, fair-haired man had come out of the news-agent's two doors down from the pub. He stopped and raised his hat as he saw Ashley. 'Why, hello there, Mr Ashley,' he said pleasantly.

Jack looked at him curiously. The American twang was unmistakable, an odd accent to hear in the tiny Sussex village. He knew from Arthur that a Canadian called Jago had bought Birchen Bower. This had to be the same man.

'It's good to see you,' continued the man. 'I'm expecting you up at the house later.'

'That's right, sir. Three o'clock we said.' Ashley half turned to Jack. 'May I introduce Major Haldean?'

'You must be Mr Jago,' said Jack, shaking the outstretched hand.

'That's right. Tom Jago,' he added, looking understandably surprised, then laughed ruefully. 'It's the voice, isn't it? I sometimes feel like an exhibit in the zoo, the way people stare, but I guess everyone'll get over it soon enough.'

'I'm glad we've met,' said Jack. 'I believe you're coming to dinner at the Stantons' tomorrow. My wife and I are staying with them,' he added.

Tom Jago brightened. 'Arthur Stanton, you mean? It was real kind of him to extend an invitation. I'd like to reciprocate, but we've got a heap of building work going on and we aren't up to visitors yet. Still, my wife and I will be mighty glad to make the acquaintance of the neighbourhood.' He tipped his hat. 'Nice to meet you, gentlemen.'

'He seems a pleasant enough chap,' said Jack, once they were inside the pub and armed with a pint of bitter apiece. He looked at Ashley shrewdly. 'Do you want to pick my brains about the case?'

Ashley laughed and put a match to his pipe. 'To be honest, there's hardly anything to worry anyone's brains about. Mr Jago

– he's really Captain Jago, but doesn't use his title – had his diamonds pinched by a man he thought he could trust.'

'That's this chap, Derek Martin, is it?'

'And his wife. I've sent a cable to the police authorities in Florida to see if they know anything about our precious pair. Mr and Mrs Jago moved around the States and North America quite a bit but the Martins seemed to have stayed mainly in Florida.'

'D'you think they might have been up to dodgy business in Florida?'

'Mrs Jago does,' said Ashley, nodding in agreement. 'Her husband doesn't, but she's probably got more of a grudge, as they were her diamonds.'

'She might be a better judge of character,' suggested Jack.

'That's very possible,' conceded Ashley. 'The thing is, although the facts seem as plain as they can be, Mr Jago doesn't really believe that Derek Martin's a wrong'un. Apparently Martin had control of a fair whack of Jago's money and he always found him to be perfectly honest. He liked the man, as well. He liked him very much. However, granted that the diamonds have vanished and so have the Martins, I think he's whistling in the wind.'

'Probably,' said Jack slowly, lighting a cigarette. 'I must admit that, granted it was apparently Jean Martin's idea to sew the diamonds into the coat in the first place, I just assumed that the Martins rolled up to the house, swiped the diamonds, and made off as fast as they could.'

'To London, most likely,' said Ashley. 'Yes, that was my opinion, too. I still think it's by far and away the most likely thing to have happened. I'm prepared to bet that the diamonds are now safely in Holland, where they can be cut so they're unrecognisable, and our Mr and Mrs Martin are considerably better off.'

The slight hesitation in Ashley's voice made Jack look at him shrewdly. 'You're not a hundred per cent convinced though, are you?'

Ashley looked uncomfortable. 'Well, no. Even though that more or less must be what happened, I have wondered about it.'

'Why?'

'Well, there's Mr Jago's attitude for a start. That made me think a bit.'

'Does anyone else agree?'

'Nobody else knows Derek Martin,' said Ashley. 'There's his mother, of course,' he added with a smile. 'She gave me a photograph of him, which is something. She thinks he's innocent, of course, and is saying so loud and long. I've seen her. More to the point, she insisted on seeing me. She thinks her son is a real blue-eyed boy, but that's to be expected. But Mr Jago . . . surely his opinion is worth considering. The trouble is, if the obvious explanation isn't right, what did happen? I'm blessed if I can think of an answer.'

'Could it all be down to Jean Martin?' asked Jack. 'Derek Martin's wife? Or does Mr Jago think she's wonderful, too?'

'No, that's not so. Mr Jago liked her well enough, but I don't think he knew her very well. Mrs Jago liked her as well, but she's in no doubt that the Martins are guilty.'

Ashley picked up his beer and looked thoughtfully at Jack. 'What are you saying? That Derek Martin was harried into stealing the diamonds on his wife's say-so?'

'Maybe. Or maybe – and you must remember that I write mystery stories for a living – the truth is a lot more sinister. Derek Martin's disappeared. Where's he gone? Has Mrs Martin taken the opportunity to make herself a lot richer and get rid of an inconveniently honest husband at the same time?'

Ashley looked puzzled. 'I don't see . . .'

'Murder,' said Jack succinctly.

Ashley spluttered into his beer. 'You're joking,' he gasped hoarsely, once he had stopped coughing. He took out his handkerchief and dabbed his chin. 'Good grief, Haldean, no one's suggested any such thing. That's an appalling idea.'

'So it is,' said Jack with a shrug, 'but it's another explanation and you said you couldn't think of any.'

'I can't go crying *murder*,' said Ashley in an urgent whisper. 'There's no evidence.'

'Don't agitate yourself, old thing,' said Jack kindly. 'As I said, it's just an idea.'

'But where would the body be hidden?'

'There probably isn't one,' said Jack. 'It's nothing more than speculation.'

Ashley leaned back against the oak settle and let his breath out in a long sigh. 'Just remember it is speculation,' he complained. 'This robbery has caused quite enough upset without you making melodramatic suggestions.'

Jack grinned. 'Fair enough. But you asked where a body could be hidden—'

'It wasn't a genuine question,' interposed Ashley grumpily.

'And from what I've heard of Birchen Bower, you could probably hide a hundred bodies in the woods without anyone being any the wiser.'

'No one's done any such thing,' said Ashley firmly. 'And do me a favour. Don't mention this to anyone else, Haldean. Keep your ideas to yourself. This case is bad enough without you inventing headaches. Without the luckiest of lucky breaks, I don't think we've got a cat in hell's chance of recovering the diamonds or laying hands on the Martins and I've had to put up with more than a few sharp words from the chief constable on the subject already. If the rumour of murder took hold . . .' He shuddered. 'My life wouldn't be worth living and that's a fact.'

'All right,' said Jack with another grin. 'I'll keep stumm. But don't be surprised if you hear some dark rumours about Birchen Bower.' He held up his hands pacifically. 'Not from me. I won't say a dicky bird but the place has quite a reputation locally. A bad reputation, I mean.'

'I'm not surprised,' said Ashley. 'The house is all right, I suppose. It's been looked after, although it probably needs bringing up to date, but I wouldn't like to live there and that's a fact. There's far too many trees. They're encroaching on the house. It's like a jungle clearing up there. From what I've seen of the estate, I don't think those woods have been touched for years.'

'It's not just trees,' said Jack. 'You know it's meant to be haunted?'

Ashley laughed. 'You don't say. Of course it's meant to be haunted. It's exactly the sort of place that everyone thinks is haunted, but that's nothing more than village tittle-tattle.'

'There might be a bit more to it than that,' said Jack.

'You're kidding,' said Ashley blankly. 'You don't believe in all that rubbish, do you?'

'Not in the sense of ghoulies and ghosties and long-legged beasties, no, but the Caydens who owned the house originally were an odd bunch, to put it mildly. You know Arthur manages his Aunt Catherine's estate? Well, part of her land runs alongside the Birchen Bower land and, according to Arthur, every single Cayden was off their rocker in one way or another. For instance, old Mr Cayden, the one who died a few years ago, was a total recluse and his father, Josiah Cayden, sounds as if he was totally off his chump.'

'How d'you mean?'

'Have you heard of the legend of the Peruvian Princess?'

'Vaguely,' said Ashley. 'She was captured by the first Cayden in the Spanish Main or something, wasn't she?'

'Something like that,' agreed Jack. 'It's in the guide books. Anyway Grandpa Cayden, the Victorian one, apparently had an absolute thing about her and the legend. There's a chapel in the grounds where this princess is buried, and she's meant to haunt it in the form of a jaguar.'

'Go on,' said Ashley with a laugh.

'I know,' said Jack, stubbing out his cigarette. 'I didn't say I believed it, I'm just repeating the legend. However, it inspired Grandpa Cayden with a fascination for Peru and the Amazon. He went to South America and made quite a name for himself as an explorer and a big-game hunter. He corresponded with Alfred Wallace, Richard Spruce and, I think, Darwin himself, amongst other worthies. Arthur told me all about it.'

'That doesn't sound as if he was too barmy,' commented Ashley.

'No, that's all hunky-dory, as far as it goes. And, if he'd stayed in the Amazon, I don't suppose anyone would have a word to say against him. However, the trouble started when he got home.'

'What happened?'

'It was to do with the estate. There's a fair old bit of land attached to Birchen Bower, around three hundred acres or so. It used to support a tenant farmer and a good few farm labourers, but Grandpa Cayden evicted them all.'

'He did what?' said Ashley in surprise.

'He evicted them,' repeated Jack. 'He threw out the farmer and his family, together with everyone who'd worked on the farm.'

'But why?' asked Ashley. 'What had they done wrong?'

'Absolutely nothing,' said Jack, picking up his beer. 'By all accounts the farm had been perfectly decently run and the farmer and his family were well respected in the village. As you can imagine, it caused a lot of ill-feeling and old Cayden was more or less shunned by the county in consequence.'

'I imagine he was,' said Ashley. 'Good grief, I can only guess at the storm that would cause. You can't just turf people out of their homes for no reason.'

'Unfortunately, you can and he did. It was an absolute scandal. Old Grandpa Cayden became the most unpopular man for miles around. It's no wonder that his son became a complete recluse when he inherited the estate. No one wanted anything to do with the Cayden family.'

'But why did he do it?' asked Ashley once again. 'Did he want to put one of his cronies in there?'

Jack shook his head. 'No, it was nothing like that. Josiah Cayden – I told you he was pretty eccentric – didn't want a farm there at all. What he wanted was to recreate a piece of the Amazon in his own grounds.'

'He wanted to do *what*?'

'Recreate the Amazon,' repeated Jack. 'It sounds barmy, I know, but it was his land and no one could stop him, no matter how loopy it was or how unfair to his tenant. He forbade anyone to cut down or coppice the trees or do anything at all with them. He wanted the land to go completely back to the wild. To add to the fun, he imported a whole load of jungle animals, such as monkeys and snakes and what-have-you, including a few jaguars.'

Ashley's eyes widened incredulously. 'A *few*? What did he do with them?'

'He let them loose in the grounds.'

'Good God! He must've been mad.'

'It's certainly not normal, is it? He was a big-game hunter, as I said, and used to go hunting in his own woods. Apparently he shot a couple of the jaguars and gave them as an offering to this princess.'

'An offering? How the dickens did that work?'

'Don't ask me to explain it,' said Jack with a laugh. 'I tell you, the chap sounds doolally tap. It seems he thought the spirits of the jaguars would consort with the spirit of the princess and serve her in the afterlife, or something along those lines. By all accounts he believed in the legend's absolute truth. It was really a new religion he'd cooked up. He wrote a book about it, which he had privately printed. Arthur's Aunt Catherine's got a copy, which he got hold of for me.'

Ashley shook his head in bewilderment. 'He must've been as nutty as a fruit cake.'

'Absolutely. He sounds bonkers. I dipped into the book and it's weird. It's all about the law of the jungle mixed in with Inca myths or what he thinks are Inca myths. Grandpa Cayden camped out in the woods most of the time, which must've been a relief to his wife, but apparently the poor woman led a miserable existence, shut up in Birchen Bower. She hardly ever went out and there weren't any visitors to speak of.'

'I'm not surprised, with jaguars and monkeys and so on roaming the grounds. To say nothing of snakes.' He took a thoughtful sip of beer. 'He had children though, didn't he?'

'Yes, poor kids. His son was the chap who became a recluse and died a few years ago but there was a daughter as well. She managed to escape and, not surprisingly, didn't want anything to do with the estate.'

'And who can blame her?' said Ashley with feeling. 'What happened to Grandpa Cayden? I wouldn't be surprised to hear his wife had murdered him.'

'No, she didn't. She lived to quite a ripe old age but he came to a sticky end.'

'Serve him right. What happened? Tell me a jaguar got him in the end.'

'No, it didn't,' said Jack with a certain amount of regret. 'Some animals have no sense of the dramatic.' He rubbed the side of his nose and gave a wicked grin. 'No, it wasn't a jaguar, it was a crocodile. He was fairly chewed up and eventually died of blood poisoning. It's an unusual sort of death for Sussex.'

'You're telling me,' said Ashley with a laugh. 'Well, it sounds thoroughly deserved.' After a pause, he added, 'What happened to all those animals? I mean, I'm due to visit the house this afternoon. Don't tell me they're still there?'

'You'll be safe enough, Ashley. I imagine they've all died off years ago. Don't forget, this must be fifty or sixty years or so ago. However, no one goes near the woods, though, even now.'

'I'm not surprised,' said Ashley fervently, finishing his beer. 'I'm beginning to understand why everyone was so astonished that Birchen Bower was sold.' He stood up. 'Can I get you another?'

'With pleasure.'

Ashley picked up the pewter pots and departed to the bar. When he came back he leaned forward confidentially. 'Can you see the man who's just come in? Elderly bloke, about sixty, I'd say, with an old tweed jacket?'

'That whiskery chap? Yes.'

'That's Albert Burstock, who was caretaker at Birchen Bower.'

Jack looked at him with renewed interest. 'Was he, by Jove?'

'As a matter of fact, he still works there. He's a builder and a handyman, in a small way, and does odd jobs up at the house.' Ashley lowered his voice. 'He's known locally for being a bit light-fingered.'

'Really? He had a set of keys, I presume?'

Ashley nodded.

Jack picked up his beer but paused before drinking. 'I don't suppose he could've pinched the diamonds, could he?'

'I doubt it,' said Ashley. 'He'd have to know they were there, for a start.'

'Yes, that's true,' agreed Jack. 'On the other hand, if the trunks were delivered to the house and left unguarded, he might have decided to take a look and struck lucky.'

'He *might*,' said Ashley guardedly, 'but he'd have to break the locks and I can't see him doing that. He'd be one of the first people we'd suspect.'

'Were the locks broken?'

'No, they'd been unlocked when the Jagos found them,' said Ashley. 'And that, of course, presupposes a key.' He glanced quizzically at Jack. 'You don't honestly think there's any chance of him being guilty, do you?'

Jack looked at the stooped figure, leaning against the bar, and shook his head. 'No, not really. I was just trying to find an alternative suggestion for you, but I think Mr Burstock's out of it. If he didn't have a key he'd need a picklock and I think that's unlikely. Looking at him, I think diamonds are a bit out of his league.'

'It never crossed my mind, Haldean. I can see him poaching, yes, but diamonds? No.'

'And it doesn't explain where the Martins got to,' said Jack.

'No, it doesn't. Having said that, Burstock made a bad impression on me. The Jagos have kept him on, but I don't know if I would. He struck me as shifty.'

'He probably resented being interviewed.'

'True, but all I wanted to know was if he'd seen anything out of the way.'

'He could've seen a murder,' said Jack wickedly.

Ashley gave a snort of laughter. 'Drop it, will you? He never saw any such thing. He'd be scared stiff if he had. I'd have cottoned on fast enough if he was trying to cover up anything of that sort.'

'I wouldn't mind a word with him, though,' said Jack thought-fully. He looked at his half-full tankard. 'I don't want any more beer at the moment, but what about a spot of lunch? I can't imagine there's a wide cuisine but they probably run to pork pies. D'you fancy a pie?'

'Yes, that and a spot of cheese would go down nicely.' Ashley laughed as Jack stood up. 'If you get anywhere with Albert Burstock, I'll pay for the pie.'

'You're on.'

The plump, comfortable-looking barmaid smiled as Jack approached. 'Two slices of pie, sir? Certainly. And with a couple of pickled eggs, and some bread and cheese. I'll bring it over when I've served Mr Burstock.'

Jack raised his eyebrows in well-simulated surprise. 'Is this Mr Burstock?' He turned to the man beside him. 'Perhaps you'd let me buy you a drink. I was hoping for a word with you.'

Albert Burstock looked at him suspiciously. 'Are you in the police?' he said after an awkward silence. 'I seed you sitting with that policeman.'

'Mr Ashley, you mean?' Burstock nodded guardedly. 'No, I'm not in the police. Mr Ashley just happens to be an old friend of mine.'

'He arsked me a lot of tom-fool questions, so he did,' said Burstock resentfully. 'Where I've been and what I seed and all I've done is what I was paid to do. Damn nosy parker, interfering with honest folk.'

'Now, now, Mr Burstock,' said the barmaid. 'You can't blame a man for doing his job.' She looked at Jack, her eyes gleaming with excitement. 'There were diamonds stolen from the big house! Diamonds worth thousands of pounds! Ooo, I screamed, I did, when I heard tell.'

'Women!' commented Burstock dismissively.

'And Mr Burstock here knows all about it!'

'I don't know nothing,' said Burstock brusquely.

'But you did see something, didn't you?' the barmaid persisted.

Albert Burstock glared at her sullenly. 'I saw nothing.' He hesitated, looking away, and Jack suddenly knew what Ashley had meant when he'd described Burstock as shifty. 'I seed those trunks in the hall and that was that.'

'Ooo, Mr Burstock, you said you took on ever so when you found the house unlocked and thought there were burglars about, you did indeed.'

'I never took on,' grunted Burstock. 'Catch me.'

'And you hunted all over the house.'

'What if I did?' said Burstock impatiently. 'The house was unlocked and that wasn't right, I knew. Yes, I had a good look round, being as how that's what I was paid to do.'

'Burglars,' intoned the barmaid, breathlessly.

Burstock sighed testily. 'There weren't no burglars, woman.'

'But you thought there might be, and you went looking! I'd have hid, so I would. You wouldn't catch me looking for burglars.' She gazed at him in admiration. 'I think it was ever so brave, and you with a bad heart, too.'

'What do you know about my heart, woman?' demanded Burstock.

'You've told me so yourself, Mr Burstock, and I do thinks you were ever so brave.'

'Yes, well,' muttered Burstock, mollified. 'It wouldn't do for us all to be screaming and fainting and carrying on. When someone pays me to do a job, I do it,' he added with an air of righteous virtue.

Jack looked at him curiously. For an old man like Burstock to go hunting suspected burglars *was* brave. It showed more courage than he would've given him credit for. Either that, or a complete lack of imagination. 'I suppose you thought it could be kids trespassing,' he suggested.

'Kids!' snorted Burstock, obviously unwilling to relinquish his role as hero. 'You don't know much about Birchen Bower if you think kids would go there, mister. Folks keep clear of Birchen Bower, and that includes kids.'

'They do!' agreed the barmaid. She lowered her voice. 'It's *haunted*!'

Jack could've kissed her. That was exactly the territory he wanted to explore. At a guess, Burstock, grumpy at being questioned by the police, wouldn't say anything about the diamonds, even if he had anything to say. Get him onto the subject of hauntings and he might be a bit more forthcoming.

'I've heard there's stories about the place,' he said. 'Here, let me buy you that drink, Mr Burstock. And one for yourself?' he added with a smile at his ally, the barmaid, 'Miss . . .?'

'I'm Miss Todd. Ruby Todd,' she said, taking three pennies from his change and putting them into a glass. 'Thank you very much, sir. Are you interested in the diamonds?' She looked at him wistfully. 'Like you might be a Private Eye?' she added, giving the words the full benefit of their capital letters. 'Like in the pictures?'

'No, nothing like that,' said Jack with a laugh. 'No, but I am interested in old houses and legends. It's astonishing how many stories of hauntings build up around old houses.'

'There's a deal of tales about Birchen Bower,' put in Miss Todd.

'Exactly,' agreed Jack. 'That's why I wanted to talk to you, Mr Burstock. As caretaker of Birchen Bower, you're the best person I can think of to ask. Have you ever had an experience you couldn't explain, perhaps? A ghostly experience, I mean?' He put on a knowingly superior air.

Burstock stared for a long moment.

Jack sighed inwardly. Perhaps nettling the chap might get a result. 'Hardly any of these so-called sightings stand up to investigation, of course.'

'I bet you have seen things, Mr Burstock,' said Miss Todd eagerly.

Burstock slowly nodded. 'You wouldn't be so quick to dismiss hauntings if you'd been to Birchen Bower, young man.'

'It *is* haunted, isn't it?' said Miss Todd with a pleasurable shudder. 'I mean, there's the princess – everyone knows she haunts the woods. She turns into a wild thing, like a big cat such as a lion or a tiger might be, doesn't she, Mr Burstock?'

Albert Burstock gave a short laugh. 'I've never seen nothing like that. Them's stories, my girl.'

'But it is haunted,' persisted Miss Todd. She turned to Jack, round-eyed. 'The Caydens who used to own Birchen Bower were terrible people. Pirates and such like they'd been, and they'd lay traps and shoot anyone who came on their land. Old Mr Cayden, the last of them, he lived there all alone in that crumbling ruin, with only the one servant, and folks do say as he still walks.'

For some reason, this seemed to amuse Albert Burstock. 'Old Cayden walks? Yes, I'd say so.'

'Have you seen him?' asked Jack. 'Have you seen a ghost?'

Burstock gave a slow, sly grin. 'A ghost? Yes, you could say I *have* seen a ghost.'

Miss Todd gave a little scream, which seemed to gratify Mr Burstock.

'You be right to be scared, my girl. There's things in those woods that shouldn't be there. Don't you go poking about, young man,' he added, turning to Jack. 'You leave things as they are and no harm'll come to you. Ghosts,' he said reflectively. 'There's more truth in that than you'd give credit for.' He nodded towards Ashley. 'But you'll want to be getting back to your pal. You can tell him I know nothing about diamonds, no matter how many times he asks me.'

'I'll bring your food over, sir,' said Miss Todd, glancing up the bar at a couple of waiting customers. 'I'll just serve these gentlemen first.'

'Well?' demanded Ashley when Jack got back to their table. 'Do I owe you a pork pie or not? You seemed to be chatting away for a fair old time.'

Jack wrinkled his nose. 'I didn't find anything much out, though. Lunch is on me, worse luck. Mr Burstock obviously relishes being a bit of a hero for hunting down imaginary burglars in Birchen Bower and played up to that, but I've got the impression he's not telling us everything.'

'That's exactly what I thought, Haldean,' agreed Ashley.

'Could he have seen the Martins?' suggested Jack.

Ashley looked at him alertly. 'And they warned him to keep quiet, you mean? Yes, that'd account for it.'

Jack pulled a face. 'Yes, but on the other hand, surely he'd *expect* to see the Martins. That's where they were meant to be after all. What would it matter if he did see them? It was only after they vanished that anyone knew there was anything wrong.'

He broke off and smiled as Ruby Todd arrived with the food. 'There's probably nothing to it,' he said after a few mouthfuls of pie. 'I imagine it's just his manner. He struck me as a cantankerous old beggar who doesn't like the police.'

'Poachers often don't,' said Ashley, with a sigh. 'I must say,' he added, spearing a pickled onion, 'that after hearing about jaguars and crocodiles and what-have-you, I'm a bit leery about visiting Birchen Bower this afternoon.'

'You'll be all right,' said Jack reassuringly. 'After all, if our pal Burstock has been making regular trips up there without being chewed by something, I can't see there's anything to worry about. Why are you going?'

'That's a good question,' said Ashley morosely. 'Officially, of course, I'm going to interview Mr and Mrs Jago to see if they can give me any sort of clue that will help recover their diamonds. Really, of course, it's to reassure them that they're not being ignored and prevent them making too much of a fuss.'

'That's very cynical of you,' said Jack.

'It's true, though.' He sighed. 'As I said before, it's one of those thankless cases and I'm blessed if I know what action to take. We've contacted all the likely jewellers with a description of the stones and circulated a description of the Martins, but I can't see it getting us anywhere unless we're very lucky.'

He picked up a slice of pork pie. 'You say the Jagos are coming to dinner at the Stantons' tomorrow?' Jack nodded. 'Well, keep your ears open. If the Jagos say anything worth hearing, let me know. I could really do with some sort of clue.'

THREE

'How long,' said Betty, as she looked at her dress in the mirror, 'will it be before someone mentions the diamonds?' She frowned thoughtfully. 'Is the neckline on this dress suitable, Jack? And I did wonder if my hemline was a bit short. I know it's mainly friends but there's some county types at dinner and I don't want to give the wrong impression.'

'The neckline,' he said, dropping a kiss on her bare shoulder, 'is absolutely fine. Stylish yet restrained. The dress is beautiful, your hair is perfect, I love your perfume—'

'It's the one you gave me,' she put in.

'And all in all you look a real corker.' And she really did. Betty, with her rich brown hair, blue eyes and freckles – he thought they were adorable – was just the tops, but it was her smile that always did it for him. 'Now, if you'll just let me use the mirror . . .'

Betty stood aside as Jack, frowning with concentration, tied his white tie. 'What about the diamonds?' she repeated. 'Do you think the Jagos will find it an awkward topic? I wonder if we should have a word with Arthur and Isabelle and declare the subject out of bounds?'

'No, don't do that. I promised Ashley I'd keep my ears open and see if I could pick up any leads. He's stuck, poor man, and I'm not surprised.'

He smiled at her reflection in the mirror. 'C'mon, Betty. You've got to allow the locals some fun. Everyone was buzzing with the news that Birchen Bower had been sold and the robbery has added a whole new level of excitement.'

He extended his arm. 'Ready?'

She put her hand through the crook of his elbow. 'Ready.'

A buzz of conversation came up the stairs as they left the bedroom. 'Five minutes,' he muttered as they turned the corner of the corridor onto the stairs.

Isabelle, looking stunning in a grass-coloured, crêpe-de-Chine dress that really set off her chestnut hair and green eyes, was waiting for them in the hall. Her neckline, Betty was pleased to see, was as low as hers and her skirt as short.

She looked up at them cheerfully as they came down the stairs. 'Hello! You're in good time.'

'How's Alice?' asked Betty.

'Fast asleep. I looked into the nursery before I came down.'

She led the way to the drawing room. 'The Dysons have arrived so we're just waiting for Mr and Mrs Jago.' Betty was pleased. She liked the Dysons, the vicar and his wife. It was thanks to Mr Dyson turning a liturgical blind eye to the fact that Jack was a Catholic that had allowed him to become Alice's godfather. 'I thought it would be nice,' continued Isabelle, 'for the Jagos to meet some of their neighbours.'

'That's very thoughtful of you,' said Betty, then looked at Jack with a puzzled frown. 'Five minutes?'

Jack grinned. 'Until the diamonds are mentioned.'

There were about a dozen people in the room, mainly old friends.

Arthur, chatting to Colonel Mottram by the fireplace, looked up as they came into the room with a welcoming smile. 'There you are, Jack.'

Colonel Mottram, one of the county types Betty had had in mind, beamed at her appreciatively. Obviously the dress passed muster. In fact, she thought as she gauged the warmth of his smile, it did a bit more than simply pass muster.

'Let me get you a drink,' said Arthur. He signalled to Mabel, the maid, who brought over a tray of drinks. 'Sherry or Madeira?'

'Sherry for me,' said Betty.

'That's sherry for both of us,' said Jack, taking the glasses from the tray. 'Thanks, Mabel.'

He turned to the colonel, a spare, grizzled man of about fifty with an exuberant military moustache. 'It's good to see you again, Colonel. And Mrs Mottram, of course,' he added, nodding in her direction. 'I believe you know my wife?'

'Indeed I do,' said the colonel heartily. 'Delighted to meet you again, Mrs Haldean. By Jove, Haldean,' he added, 'I bet you were rubbing your hands together when you heard the news, what?'

'News?'

The colonel lent forward confidentially. 'About the robbery at Birchen Bower, man!' he said in a penetrating whisper. 'Gad! Thousands of pounds' worth of diamonds gone, just like that!' He snapped his fingers together to indicate speed.

'One minute forty-three seconds,' said Jack in an undertone.

Betty gave a squeak of a suppressed giggle, causing the colonel to blink at her in surprise. 'Hiccups,' she explained mendaciously.

'By George,' continued the colonel, 'I was just saying to Stanton a few moments ago that if you had a go at cracking the case, Haldean, you'd soon lay your hands on the Martins, I'll be bound.'

'That's very flattering of you, sir,' said Jack with a laugh. 'However, I think I'll leave this one to the police.'

The colonel gave a snort that made the ends of his moustache vibrate. 'The police!'

'They've got a far better chance of apprehending the Martins than anyone else. Certainly than I have.'

A hand touched his elbow. 'That sounds like modesty, Major.'

He looked round with a smile. It was Mr Dyson, the vicar.

'I gather you're talking about the robbery,' continued Mr Dyson. 'Hello, Mrs Haldean. It's nice to see you again. I believe you and my wife got together yesterday.'

'About the fete? Yes, we did. It was a very worthwhile session.'

'I'm glad to hear it. Haldean, you're not taking an interest in the robbery, are you?'

Jack shook his head. 'No, it's not my sort of thing. There's no puzzle, is there?'

'No, I suppose not,' agreed Mr Dyson. 'I must say, it seemed an open-and-shut case to me.' He raised his voice slightly. 'Phyllis! Come and join us!'

Mrs Dyson came across the room, sherry in hand. 'Hello, Major! Betty, my dear, what a lovely dress!'

'And you look charming, Mrs Dyson,' said the colonel with a gallant bow.

'Why, thank you. I thought the Jagos were meant to be coming this evening,' she added, looking round the room.

'So they are,' said Jack. 'I bumped into Mr Jago yesterday. He seems a decent enough chap.'

'So he does,' agreed Mr Dyson. 'I called at the house. I was over in Croxton Abbas and thought I'd call in and introduce myself.'

'And you wanted to see the house, Freddy,' said Mrs Dyson.

Mr Dyson gave a slightly embarrassed laugh. 'Well, that too, I suppose.'

'I'm not surprised,' said the colonel. 'There's so many stories about Birchen Bower that I dare say none of us could resist the opportunity to see it for ourselves. So Jago's a decent chap, eh?'

'I must say I took to him,' agreed Mr Dyson. 'He was with the Canadians at Arras.'

Colonel Mottram looked impressed. 'Was he, by George? They put in some first-rate fighting.'

'It's a pity about the robbery,' said Arthur. 'I hope it hasn't put them off England. It was a relief to hear that Birchen Bower had been sold at last. I hoped that someone would finally take a firm hand and knock the place into shape. It's a positive wilderness.'

'Is it really as bad as all that, Arthur?' asked Betty.

'Awful,' he said firmly. He ran a hand through his hair, his hazel eyes clouding in concern. 'God knows what's in those woods. There's no end of stories.' He leaned forward confidentially. 'Every so often, dogs and even ponies go missing.'

'What's the idea?' asked Jack with a grin. 'That they got eaten by a jaguar?'

'Don't be too cynical,' said Arthur seriously. 'There's something in those woods that shouldn't be there.' He broke off. 'Better leave it there. The Jagos have just come in.'

*   *   *

At dinner Jack sat between Mrs Dyson and Mrs Rosalind Jago.

She was a striking-looking woman, he thought. How old? About thirty perhaps, fair-haired, blue eyes and high cheekbones. Even before she spoke, he thought he'd have guessed her origins. She had that polished, nearly enamelled look of the wealthy American woman. With her perfectly fitting, highly fashionable clothes, flawless skin and a necklace of pearls, it was almost as if she carried her own personal spotlight with her.

So why didn't he find her attractive? Unlike most Americans he'd met, she wasn't outgoing or particularly friendly, but silent and obviously bored.

On his other side, Mrs Dyson was talking animatedly to Betty and Isabelle about the forthcoming fete. Dr Jerry Lucas, a cheery soul about Jack's own age, was discussing new thoughts in psychology with Arthur and Mr Dyson was explaining the church, or rather the lack of it, in Croxton Abbas to Mr Jago.

'You see, my dear chap,' said Mr Dyson, 'Croxton Abbas is more a hamlet than a village. Pretty little spot but not big enough to support its own clergy. It's part of my parish.'

Mrs Jago rolled her eyes. She clearly wasn't interested in churches or fetes or, indeed, any local chit-chat.

'How are you finding life in England?' asked Mrs Dyson politely to Mrs Jago as the soup was served. She'd caught the look as well.

'A lot more difficult than I'd anticipated,' said Rosalind, brightening.

She was obviously far more interested in her own concerns than those of her neighbours, thought Jack, then mentally ticked himself off for cynicism.

'Tom is pleased with the house,' she continued. 'He tells me the structure is fine but it needs so much *work*. Some of the rooms were thick with dust. I don't think it's been cleaned for years. And,' she added, a petulant note in her voice, 'I don't know what's wrong with the help in this neck of the woods, but I couldn't get anyone local to take it on.'

Mrs Dyson nodded intelligently. She knew all about the efforts to rid Birchen Bower of years of accumulated dirt. Her Mrs Royston, who obliged, as she put it, at the vicarage, had told her all about what sounded like a small army being drafted in from London, no less, to tackle the job. 'They wanted,' Mrs Royston had said, 'us local ladies to do it, but you wouldn't catch me going up to Birchen Bower, nor anyone else either, I'll be bound.'

'And,' continued Rosalind, 'would you believe it, there was no electricity!'

'Shocking,' muttered Jack.

Rosalind Jago turned to him. 'I'll say it was shocking!' She'd obviously completely missed the sarcasm, which, considering the glare he'd got from Betty, was probably just as well.

'No electricity and no telephone,' continued Rosalind. 'What's more there was no plumbing! Can you believe it? I said to Tom, what have you brought me to? It might be a mansion, but we might as well be living in a shack in the sticks. Anyway, he had to pay big bucks to get a generator installed double quick so that when we do get the help, we could have a heap of modern labour-saving devices. The agency insisted on it. They said the women wouldn't work without them.'

Mrs Dyson, to whom labour-saving devices were a thing of daydreams, allowed herself to nod sympathetically.

'It's not only the house,' continued Rosalind. 'I suppose you've heard all about the robbery? Gee, if I could get my hands on the Martins! Tom bought me a new necklace, which is only fair, but I've still been robbed! Robbed by people Tom trusted.'

Mrs Dyson who, in Jack's opinion, was rapidly qualifying for sainthood, showed absolutely no signs of envy. Instead she said, with every appearance of enthusiasm, 'A new necklace! How lovely.'

'I hope it's going to be. The jewellers still have it. We bought the diamonds from De Beers. Tom likes to choose the individual stones himself and have them made up into a setting we both like.'

'That sounds like a very good way of doing it,' said Mrs Dyson, sincerely. Jack could virtually see her halo.

'It's the only way, but we shouldn't have to do it. What's more . . .'

As she talked, Jack suspected she was enjoying the chance to get an accumulated raft of complaints off her chest. She was obviously relishing the opportunity to talk. So much so that he felt a small pang of guilt at his earlier cynicism. Diamond necklaces were all very well, but you couldn't talk to them. It sounded as if she'd been quite lonely. Did the poor woman know anyone locally? As a matter of course, he'd expect neighbours to make the socially obligatory call to leave visiting cards. Arthur and Isabelle had called, naturally enough, and so had Mr Dyson, but had anyone else?

He suspected the reputation of Birchen Bower had put off those who would normally expect to call on a new neighbour. This dinner party would help, of course. In fact, that was the main reason why Isabelle had arranged it, he thought, with a rush of appreciation for her kindness.

'What really gets my goat is that Tom pulled Derek Martin out of the gutter,' Rosalind continued. She would have said more but her husband interrupted her.

'Now, Rosie,' said Tom Jago from across the table. 'I don't think we should bore everyone with our concerns.'

'Not at all, my dear chap,' said Colonel Mottram. 'To find you've been robbed must've been most distressing.' He frowned. 'The gutter? I thought this chap, Derek Martin, came from Croxton Abbas. That's not a gutter, dash it. Decent little place.'

'His mother lives in Croxton Abbas, Colonel, but she only came here a few years ago,' put in Mr Dyson. 'I don't think Derek Martin has ever been to Croxton Abbas.'

'He certainly paid at least one visit, what?' said Colonel Mottram with a laugh.

'And was a jolly sight richer as a result,' murmured Jerry Lucas. He cocked an inquisitive eyebrow at Tom Jago. 'Would you mind telling us about the robbery? We all feel very sympathetic but all we know is the bare fact that a valuable necklace was stolen.'

'Where does the gutter come into it?' asked Betty, puzzled. 'I don't understand.'

'Do tell us about Derek Martin, Mr Jago,' said Mrs Dyson. 'I know his mother, of course. She's one of our parishioners, but I've never met him.'

'Tom did everything for Derek Martin,' said Rosalind bitterly. 'He saved his life. Literally, I mean.'

'Rosie . . .' began her husband, but was cut off by the buzz of comments around him.

'By George, that sounds a story worth hearing,' said Colonel Mottram. 'Saved his life, eh? What happened? Was it during the war?'

Tom Jago gave a wry smile. 'You're right, sir. It was in the war.'

'Do you want to tell us about it?' asked Arthur.

Tom Jago gave a deprecating shrug. 'If you're sure you want to hear an old war story, then OK. I first came across Derek Martin in France. Although we didn't know it then, the war was coming to an end. It was after the Battle of Arras and the Germans had retreated to the Hindenburg Line.'

He looked around the table. 'I don't know if any of you gentlemen were there?'

'I was,' said Jack.

'Then you remember what it was like, Major,' said Jago.

'Tell us, Jack,' said Betty softly.

Jack shrugged. 'If I must. It's hard to describe the state the country was in. The Jerries left a swathe of devastation behind them. They mined the roads, destroyed the railway tracks, poisoned wells and cut down fruit trees – anything that could be of any use, they wrecked.'

'I remember your letters home, Jack,' said Isabelle amidst the mutter of condemnation around the table. 'It sounded appalling.'

'It was,' he agreed. 'The villages were the worst. I mainly saw it from the air, of course, but the destruction turned my stomach.'

Tom Jago nodded. 'It certainly did. The villages were mainly piles of rubble but every so often you'd see something that brought it home that these were once people's homes, such as a broken piano stool or a little girl's doll.'

'It was vile,' said Arthur with feeling. 'Completely vile.'

'You're right, Captain Stanton,' said Tom Jago. 'Well, I forget the name of what had been the village we were in. It could've been Etreillers, perhaps?' He shook his head. 'That doesn't really matter. The village was devastated. We were looking for billets and one house – only one! – still had walls and a fair bit of roof. Together with the company doctor, I went into what had been the kitchen. We were wary of an ambush, so I had my pistol at the ready. The place had obviously been deserted in a hurry. German equipment was thrown in a corner, chairs were pushed back, there was unfinished food on the plates, thick with dust, and half-drunk glasses of beer stood on the table. There was also, hanging on the wall, a Prussian Guardsman's helmet.'

Jerry Lucas winced. He knew what was coming. Jack drew his breath in and exchanged a knowing glance with Arthur.

'That doesn't sound good,' said Jack.

'That's what I thought, Major,' agreed Tom. 'We were just weighing up the idea of using the place as a mess room, when two Englishmen, a lieutenant and a corporal, came in through the broken piece of wall where the back door had been. They didn't look happy to see us. "I reckon you've claimed this place," said the lieutenant.' He looked round the table. 'You'll have guessed that was Derek Martin. "Well, you were here first," he said, "so I suppose we'll just have to keep on looking." Then he saw the helmet and said, "My word, that's worth having!"'

Jack gave an involuntary grimace. Tom Jago saw his expression and gave a grim smile. 'You've got it, Major. Before I could stop him, Martin reached out to take it down from the wall. The table was between us. I did the only thing possible. As I said, I had my gun in my hand. I yelled at him to leave the helmet alone and fired.'

'But why?' asked Mrs Dyson in bewilderment.

'To save the idiot's life, I imagine,' said Jerry. 'Everyone knew enough to be wary. The helmet was booby-trapped, wasn't it?'

There was a murmur of comprehension from around the table.

'Dead right,' agreed Tom Jago. 'If he'd touched that helmet, we'd have all been blown sky-high. I didn't mean to hit him, but the bullet winged his arm. He was absolutely furious, of course. He went for his pistol, but his corporal, an older guy who had a bit of sense, knocked the gun out of his hand and told him, in no uncertain terms, how I'd just saved his life and everybody else's into the bargain. Well, once we'd all calmed down, I'm bound to say he apologised handsomely. The poor guy – he was only a kid – hadn't been in France long, unlike the rest of us, and wasn't up to the Huns' stunts.'

He looked round the table. 'That was the first time I met Derek Martin.'

'By Gad, what a story,' said Colonel Mottram, with a short laugh. 'This chap, Martin, must've been properly grateful to you. I know I would be.'

'Absolutely,' echoed Mr Dyson.

And they would be grateful, thought Jack. They were both straight-forward and sincere men, with the gift of honest gratitude to anyone who did them a good turn.

But Derek Martin? He was inexperienced, true, but even though he was still wet behind the ears, *everybody* knew to look out for booby-traps. He must've heard the stories. He'd just endangered everyone's life by his desire for a war souvenir. Not only that, but in addition to having his arm injured, he'd been made to look an idiot in front of his corporal.

That corporal, Jack was willing to bet, had been given the task of nurse-maiding the young lieutenant, to make sure he didn't make more of a fool of himself than could be helped. The tale of how he'd nearly killed them all would be known by every member of the company within hours. That must have rankled. No, the colonel and Mr Dyson might expect Martin to be grateful but burning resentment was at least a possible reaction.

'What happened next, Mr Jago?' Jack asked. 'Presumably you met Martin again.'

Rosalind Jago snorted bitterly. 'Yes, we did, worse luck for us. It was on Broadway. You felt sorry for him, Tom.'

'So I did,' said Tom. 'You can't blame me for that, Rosie. I don't know if any of you know New York?'

Nobody did.

'Broadway is in New York, is it?' asked Mrs Dyson.

Tom nodded. 'It certainly is, ma'am. I've heard it said that to a man who couldn't read, it must look like heaven.'

Mrs Dyson looked puzzled. 'Churches? Statues?' she suggested.

Tom Jago laughed heartily and even Rosalind smiled. 'Nothing like that,' he said. 'There's so much light it's as if night's been turned into day. It's a wonderful sight. Blazing lights and streams of cars.'

'Theatres,' said Rosalind with feeling. 'Wrigley's, the Strand, Ziegfeld Follies. We were going to Ziegfelds when you saw him. We got out of the Duesenberg and there he was. I thought he was some panhandler, but he called your name and you stopped to talk to him.'

'I couldn't place him at first,' continued Tom. 'We were with a couple of friends, Arnie and Wilma Bruce, and they and Rosie obviously thought he was some sort of tramp.'

'He was jealous of us,' said Rosalind. 'I could see that.'

'Well, you were wearing mink, darling, and it turned out he hadn't eaten that day.' He paused. 'As I looked at him, I suddenly remembered the young lieutenant in that ruined house in France and it all came back to me.'

He paused and looked round the table. 'I don't know if I can explain properly how it made me feel but, more than anything, I wanted to talk to him.'

'You sent me off with Arnie and Wilma,' put in Rosalind, who obviously hadn't forgotten her resentment.

'Sure I did,' agreed Tom. 'Did I mention it was January? It was a freezing night and you were better off in the theatre, out of the cold. And . . .'

He clasped his hands together. 'And I wanted to talk about the war. You all, in England – you've all experienced the war, women as well as men. It touched you all. It sounds crazy, but some of the best moments of my life were in the war.'

Jack looked up sharply. This was genuine experience talking. This was something so many found true, but it was never said.

Mrs Dyson was shocked. 'Surely not! You couldn't possibly want those dreadful times back again.'

Tom shook his head. 'Of course not, ma'am. And don't get me wrong. I had my fill of being frozen to the bone, wet to the skin, eyes full of mud and that foul smell of decay that we could never shake off in the trenches. Sure, that was all real, but the good times . . . They were very good.'

His voice grew wistful. 'An evening, say, and there were many, when we'd found a billet in a French farmhouse. A table with candles stuck in empty bottles, glimmering through the tobacco smoke. We've eaten and it was a decent meal. There's a bottle of whisky on the table. Outside, low down on the horizon, there's a faint flickering like summer lightening, where the guns are muttering. The guns we left that day.'

'The first night out of the line,' said Arthur softly. 'That first night was always good.'

Tom Jago turned to him eagerly. 'That's it! You remember. The war was only a couple of miles away but I've never felt so contented as I did on those nights.' He twisted his hands together, obviously searching for the right words. 'It was peaceful,' he said, with surprise in his voice. 'Peaceful. And I've never known such friendship as those evenings out of the line.'

He shrugged. 'That's what I wanted to talk about. Old times. To us Canadians the war meant a lot, but to New Yorkers like my pal Arnie . . . Well, it might never have happened. Besides that,' he added, looking mildly embarrassed, 'it was obvious that the poor guy was down on his luck.'

'So you ended up buying him dinner,' said Rosalind in a resigned way.

Tom nodded. 'Yes. What else could I do?' He grinned. 'We had our talk. He'd seen some pretty tense action after that day we'd first met. When it was all over, he couldn't settle.'

Jack flinched. 'Couldn't settle' was a hell of an understatement. His world had ended. Everything he'd ever known stopped. It was as brutal as a brick thrown at a gramophone record. He looked up and saw Isabelle looking at him. She knew. She'd been there. Betty gave a little gasp of sympathy and he consciously pulled himself together. This wasn't about him.

'That was fairly common,' he said, and felt a surge of relief that his voice hadn't betrayed him. This really wasn't about him. Derek Martin. He forced himself to think about Derek Martin. 'Is that why he went to America? He couldn't settle?'

Jago had obviously noticed nothing. Good.

'You've got it, Major. He'd had a job, a well-paid job, as an insurance adjuster, until he was asked to falsify a claim. He wouldn't do it and that was that. I must admit, I felt sorry for him. As we came out of the restaurant, I wondered what I could do for him. I didn't want to give him money. That's not my way and besides, the guy had his pride. I could see that. No, I wanted to find him a job. You won't know this, but in Times Square there was a huge neon sign. It said "It's June in Miami". Believe you me, in the bitter cold of a New York January, that sign made an impression. Anyway, to cut a long story short, he became my secretary for my business in Florida. He was used to handling money and I have to say I always found him scrupulously honest.'

'Doesn't that make the robbery a bit of a puzzle?' asked Mr Dyson. 'Here's a chap who has every reason to be grateful to you and yet turns out to be a wrong 'un. I suppose he just gave into sudden temptation.'

'Either that or his wife put him up to it,' said Rosalind.

Tom Jago shrugged. 'I guess it could be. He was crazy about his wife.'

'It's unusual to have a married secretary,' said Colonel Mottram with a touch of reproof. 'I've never come across the notion.' He gave a short bark of a laugh. 'Marriage clearly didn't do the fella any good, eh, what?'

'Perhaps we're a bit more liberal in the States,' replied Tom with a smile. 'He wasn't married when I ran across him in New York. He met Jean Rashford in Florida. He asked me if they could get married and I couldn't see why not.' He looked across at his wife. 'You got on with her, didn't you, Rosie?'

'So so,' she replied dryly. 'It would've been difficult to do anything else as you insisted on treating Derek as one of us.'

'I liked the guy!' he said sharply, then softened the sharpness with a smile. 'Even now, it's hard to believe he could've taken your diamonds.'

'I wish you would talk to his mother,' said Mrs Dyson. 'By all accounts Mrs Martin has taken things very badly. If you really don't believe that Derek Martin is guilty of theft, I'm sure it would ease her mind.'

'I'd be happy to talk to her if she'll talk to me,' said Tom. 'The last time we met her she was pretty riled up but if you think it'll do any good, I'll be happy to try.'

'Why don't you call to see her, Frederick?' asked Mrs Dyson to her husband. 'You could act as an intermediary.' She smiled at Tom Jago. 'It sounds as if you bear Derek Martin no ill-feeling.'

'I guess I don't . . .' began Tom, when he was interrupted by Colonel Mottram.

'With all respect, dear lady, I don't think that's such a good idea. Surely such a meeting would only give his mother a false hope of her son's innocence.'

'He might be innocent,' said Tom.

'Tom!' said his wife in exasperation. 'He's a crook. Accept it.'

'It can be very difficult to accept one has been taken in,' said Mr Dyson with an apologetic cough. 'I think your desire to think the best of Derek Martin does you great credit, but facts are facts.' He glanced across to his wife. 'You remember Frank Cox, my dear?'

'Indeed I do,' she said with some warmth. 'He was our sidesman and seemed such a pious man.'

'I thought of him as a pillar of the church,' said her husband wryly.

'What happened?' asked Rosalind Jago.

'You may well ask,' said Mrs Dyson. 'It turned out that not only had he regularly filched money from the collection but was keeping an irregular establishment in Brighton. It was an appalling scandal.'

'It's always the Holy Joes you have to look out for,' said Colonel Mottram with a laugh. 'Begging your pardon, vicar. You're quite right though. It can be deuced hard to credit you've been taken in. I remember a bearer I had in Darjeeling . . .'

And the conversation drifted onto well-worn paths.

Jack yawned as Betty wriggled down under the eiderdown. 'It's good to get to bed,' he said. 'Shall I turn the light off or are you going to read?'

'I've finished my book,' said Betty. Although she was tired she wasn't actually very sleepy. 'Let's just snuggle up for a few moments.'

'I'm all for that!' he said with an enthusiasm that made her giggle. He switched off the light and she felt his arms encircle her in the darkness.

'What d'you think of the Jagos?' she asked.

He gave a snort of laughter. 'Why on earth should I be thinking about the Jagos?' he murmured. 'I was thinking of something else.'

'You always are, my darling. But what do you think of the Jagos, Jack?'

He sighed, sat up, and turned the light back on. 'You want to talk about the Jagos. Go on,' he said patiently.

'Don't pretend you're not as interested as I am. That house of theirs, Birchen Bower, sounds very peculiar. Mrs Jago doesn't like it much.'

'Did you like her?'

Betty frowned. 'I'm not sure. To be honest, I didn't know what to make of her. She didn't say much in the drawing room after dinner. Isabelle did her best, but she was uphill work.'

'That's probably because she's not happy about the move,' said Jack.

'No, she isn't,' said Betty with feeling. 'According to her, they may as well be living in a cabin in the woods, the forest has encroached so much. She's all for going back to America.'

'So I gathered over dinner. Mr Jago, on the other hand, was waxing lyrical about Birchen Bower over the port and cigars. I think he rather fancies himself as lord of the manor. He's clearing the trees around the house and having the gardens landscaped. Arthur tried to get him to agree to cut down the trees on the estate and restore the farm that used to be there, but it turns out he's got a bit of a thing about the wilderness. He says it reminds him of Canada.'

'He's probably just saying that,' said Betty. 'It sounds as if he'd need very deep pockets to clear the entire estate.'

'He's got those, lucky beggar. It's not money that's stopping him.'

Betty digested this. 'Are they very rich, then?' She couldn't help the note of respect that crept into her voice.

'He's rolling in it. If he's not a millionaire, it sounds as if he's the next thing to it.' He looked down at her affectionately and hugged her closer. 'You shouldn't be so impressed.'

'Well, I am. I can't help it. I can't say I've ever met a millionaire, but from what you read in books and magazines, it sounds as if they should be immensely fat with about three chins who

are absolutely horrible to everyone and always end up getting
murdered.'

'The only millionaire I've ever met was as thin as a rail and
loved cats, but American millionaires are very handy targets in
a detective story,' said Jack. 'I've written a few myself. No one
minds very much when they get bumped off and the fact they're
so disgustingly rich gives a slew of motives to play with.'

'I hope no one bumps off Mr Jago,' said Betty with a
laugh. 'I liked him. I liked what he said at dinner about the war
and I liked what he did for that man, Derek Martin, even if it
did turn out badly in the end. Still,' she added doubtfully, 'if
the Jagos really are that rich I don't suppose the theft of the
necklace means that much to them.'

'Mrs Jago seemed pretty bitter about it. I think you're quite
right about Mr Jago's feelings, though. It's not so much the
money as knowing he was wrong about Martin. We got chapter
and verse over the port. He made no bones about saying that
it was partly because of Martin that he's as well-off as he is.'

'How's that?' asked Betty, puzzled. 'I mean, he was just
Mr Jago's secretary, wasn't he?'

'Secretary, yes, but also his land agent. Do you remember
the Florida land boom?'

'I've never heard of it,' said Betty.

'I'm not surprised. There was hardly anything about it in the
papers over here, but according to Mr Jago, it was virtually a
licence to print money. It's all gone to pot now. People have
lost fortunes. On the other hand, quite a lot of people made
fortunes and Mr Jago was one of the lucky ones.'

'How?'

'You remember that neon sign he saw in New York?'

'The one that said "It's June in Miami"?'

'That's the one. Apparently that more or less kick-started the
whole boom. Jago was interested before then, but seeing that
sign with Martin standing beside him, gave him the idea of
sending Martin to Florida to act as his agent and buy land. He
gave him a couple of hundred dollars to begin with.'

'That was very trusting of him.'

'That's more or less what we said,' said Jack with a grin.
'However, a couple of hundred dollars was neither here or there

to Jago and it turned out to be the best investment of his life. Florida was in the grip of a building boom and he was in at the start. Whole cities seemed to spring up like mushrooms and land was going for crazy prices. Anyone who bought at the start made a mint. Derek Martin turned that initial two hundred dollars into over two thousand within a fortnight, and that was just the beginning.'

'Good grief,' said Betty. 'And Derek Martin just divvied it up to Mr Jago?'

'Yep. And continued to be completely honest in all his dealings. There was a piece of scrubland in somewhere called Pinellas that Martin bought on Jago's behalf for two thousand dollars. A few months later Martin sold it for three hundred thousand dollars. He sounds to have been a real expert in judging what would turn a very handsome profit.'

'Three *hundred* thousand dollars!' Betty was silent for a few moments. 'How much is that in English money?'

'Crikey, darling, is this the time to ask me to do maths? I suppose it must be . . .' He thought for a couple of moments. 'It must be about seventy odd thousand pounds at a guess.'

'And two thousand dollars is . . .' Betty paused, trying to work it out.

'Around five hundred quid or thereabouts.'

'But that's incredible! That's an enormous profit! Jack, Derek Martin *must've* been an honest man. Unless Mr Jago kept very close tabs on him.'

'It sounds as if Jago came to trust him completely. According to him, Martin could've walked away with a good few thousand dollars any time after the first couple of months. A few figures falsified on the sales documents and Jago – this is Jago's own account mind – wouldn't even know he'd been robbed.'

'Perhaps he didn't,' said Betty doubtfully. 'Know he'd been robbed, I mean.'

'Perhaps,' agreed Jack. 'However, you're a decent enough judge of character, Betty. D'you think Jago's the sort of chap who'd let himself be taken in?'

Betty frowned. 'I wouldn't have said so. It's difficult though, Jack. Unless you know someone really well, it's hard to say what they'll do.'

'True enough,' he said with a yawn. 'Jago trusted him though. Which makes the whole thing a real puzzle.'

'Unless . . .' she began and then broke off. 'Jack, this is a horrible thought, but what if Derek Martin *was* honest? What could've happened to him? His wife vanished as well. Maybe she knows the answer.'

Jack hesitated. 'I'm sure if we could find her she'd have something to tell us.'

She drew her breath in. 'Is he dead?'

Jack said nothing.

She gazed at him, then shuddered. 'You guessed as much already, didn't you?' she said quietly.

He looked at her stricken face and hugged her. 'And maybe this is just a story we're telling ourselves. Come on, sweetheart. Time to go to sleep.'

FOUR

Three months later and there was still no news of either the Martins or the diamonds. They had, more or less, been forgotten.

The Jagos, on the other hand, were still news. Birchen Bower now had a telephone installed, and that, plus the electric generator and the plumbing – *Three bathrooms! Would you believe it, dear!* as Mrs Dyson remarked to Isabelle – had fuelled village gossip for weeks. What the Jagos hadn't done, as Isabelle commented in various letters to Jack and Betty, much to Arthur's annoyance, was clear the wilderness that constituted the estate.

There was a letter from Isabelle waiting for Betty as she sat down to breakfast.

'Anything interesting?' asked Jack as he sipped his coffee. 'Is Arthur still riled up about the Jagos?'

'I imagine so,' said Betty absently, reading the letter. 'She doesn't say . . .' She smiled. 'Alice has got a new tooth . . . Arthur's got a new hobby. He's renovating an old boat that belongs to the estate. Apparently he's becoming an enthusiastic yachtsman.'

'That sounds fun,' said Jack, reaching for the marmalade. 'With any luck, he'll take us out.'

Betty wrinkled her nose. 'I don't know anything about boats . . . Good grief!'

'What?'

'You know the field where the Croxton Abbas fete is held?'

'The one on the cliff? Yes. What about it?'

'There's been a landslip!'

'Was anyone hurt?'

'No . . .' Betty read on. 'No. Nothing and no one was injured, thank goodness, not even sheep, but it sounds pretty bad.' She read on quickly. 'Isabelle says the committee didn't know what to do, as there really isn't another suitable venue in Croxton Abbas, so the first thought was to transfer the fete lock stock and barrel to Croxton Ferriers, when Mr Jago stepped in. He's offered to have the fete at Birchen Bower.'

'Blimey,' commented her husband. 'He's really trying to be the Merry Old English squire, isn't he? How did that suggestion go down?'

Betty giggled. 'Like a brick zeppelin, to use one of your expressions, but he's charmed them into it. Mr Jago took them on a tour of the gardens which apparently have been de-treed, if that's a word, and then Rosalind Jago had them all in the house for a bun fight afterwards.'

'Is she any happier with life?'

'Resigned, by the sound of it. Apparently Mr Jago has always dreamed of owning an English country house and she's indulging him.'

'I told you,' said Jack. 'The Merry Squire.'

'It sounds like it,' said Betty, reading on. 'Mr Jago showed them the library. He was very excited about a collection of old papers giving the history of the estate. The Caydens seem to have been a peculiar lot.'

'I'll say,' agreed Jack. 'Pirates, smugglers, an Inca princess and then this bloke who turned the place into a wilderness.'

'There's a book as well. It must be the same one you read, Jack, the one by Josiah Cayden, who ruined the estate.'

'And is one of the weirdest books I've ever read. So the fete's at Birchen Bower, is it?'

Betty skimmed to the end of the letter and nodded. 'Yes. What's more, they're going to open up the old chapel – the Jaguar Princess chapel. I wouldn't mind seeing that.' She put down the letter. 'I'm quite pleased, really. Birchen Bower sounds so odd, it'll be good to have a chance to look round. As Isabelle says, let's just hope we get the weather.'

Jack, stripped to his shirtsleeves, looked at the mass of canvas on the ground, spread out like a collapsed balloon. 'This is the last one, isn't it, Dusty?' he asked.

Sam Miller, Arthur's gardener and odd-job man, who was inevitably called Dusty, nodded, rubbing his sweating face with a handkerchief that seemed, to Jack's way of thinking, about as large as a bath towel.

'That's right, Major. Once we get this tent up, we've finished. Until,' he added with a grin, 'it's time to take them all down again.'

'Sufficient unto the day are the troubles thereof, as the vicar would say,' said Jack, hunting for the doorway into the tent. 'We don't have to worry about that until tomorrow.'

He found the entrance and, wearing the heavy canvas like an inconvenient royal robe, wriggled himself into the middle. 'OK, Dusty, let me have the poles,' he called.

Miller passed in the centre pole, section by section. Jack fitted them together and the tent, mushroom-like, wavered unsteadily into the air.

Although it was hot inside the tent, the dim light, filtered through the canvas, was pleasantly soothing after the blazing sunshine outside. Isabelle had certainly got her wish about the weather, he thought. What she and the rest of the committee hadn't bargained for was the complete lack of help that Tom Jago could provide.

True, he'd employed a firm of landscape gardeners to clear the woods around the house and carve out a path through the trees to the chapel, but they had done their job and gone back to Lewes.

That meant the ladies of the committee had had to call on every available man they could find to actually put up the tents. The swings, roundabouts, helter-skelter and rifle range weren't a problem – they were hired from Thos. Makeshaft and Sons, who had come to all the local fetes for years – but some serious co-operation from the local male population was needed for everything else.

Jack emerged from the tent and, together with Miller, started to hammer the tent pegs and guy ropes in place. He stood up as Isabelle approached.

'Well done,' she said approvingly as Miller adjusted the last rope. 'We'll have this tent for the home-made jams and pickles. I must say the way everyone's pitched in and helped has been marvellous. I really am grateful to you, Jack and to you, of course, Dusty.'

'That's all right, ma'am,' said Miller. He stood up and massaged the small of his back in relief. 'It fair beats me, though,' he said, surveying the ground where it swept down to the dark mass of woods, 'that someone can have all this land and only one man to look after it.'

He sniffed disapprovingly. 'Albert Burstock,' he added with deep contempt. Jack guessed it was only Isabelle's presence that stopped him from spitting in disgust. 'I wouldn't pay him in washers. Where's he been, I'd like to know, leaving the rest of us to do all the work?'

'He's in the chapel,' said Isabelle, carefully avoiding the criticism of the Jagos' approach to estate management. 'It needed sweeping and cleaning before the visitors arrive this afternoon. Mr Jago has asked him to stay in the chapel this afternoon and take the admission money.'

Miller's eyebrows shot up. 'That's very trusting of him,' he said dryly. Jack smothered a grin. Obviously Albert Burstock's reputation wasn't lost on Dusty.

'We thought tuppence for admission was about the right sort of price,' continued Isabelle, again steering clear of criticism. 'And children free, of course. Jack, will you man the rifle range this afternoon?'

'I'd rather be in the beer tent,' he muttered, adding hastily as he saw her expression, 'only joking. Yes, of course I will. What's Arthur doing this afternoon?'

He picked up his jacket and together they strolled over to where Winnie, the nursemaid, was standing by the pram.

'He's acting as a general relief when anyone needs a break. Betty's looking after the hoopla. Mrs Dyson's sending over all the benches and tables we'll need and the men bringing them will set them out.' She lowered her voice. 'What did surprise me is that Rosalind Jago's offered to help out in the tea tent.'

Jack raised his eyebrows. 'Gosh. That's a bit unexpected, isn't it?'

'It is, really.' Isabelle bit her lip. 'I hope we don't have any trouble this afternoon. Mrs Martin's more or less bound to turn up for a cup of tea and she and Rosalind Jago can't stand each other. You remember the Jagos came to dinner a couple of months ago?' Jack nodded. 'Well, Mr Jago took up the idea that he should try and be reconciled with Mrs Martin – he still believes Derek Martin is innocent – and he held out an olive branch, so to speak. Mrs Jago resents it. She's got no doubts about the Martins' guilt.'

'To be fair, no one but Jago has, by the sound of it.'

Isabelle quickened her step as a wail sounded. 'Oh dear, there's Alice. I'll have to see to her. You and Betty can pop off back to the house now, Jack. There's a cold lunch ready.'

'I certainly want a wash and change,' said Jack. 'Can I give you a lift?'

She shook her head. 'I need to stay on to supervise. You'd better go, Jack. Don't forget. Be back for one o'clock. The gates open at half past.'

By half past three the fete was in full swing and, as it seemed to Jack, busily handing out air guns and taking in the sixpences on the rifle range, a roaring success.

For Isabelle's sake he was relieved. As she had told them, the prospect of holding the fete at Birchen Bower had been met with grudging approval from the committee and some downright opposition in the village. It was, grumbled the wiseacres in the Cat and Fiddle, asking for trouble to go fooling about round Birchen Bower. Besides that, it was a tidy step up from the village.

Tom Jago, who obviously wanted to make the absolute most of the occasion, had made it his business to call into the pub, where, with the help of a few rounds of beer, got the company to agree – at least while he was standing the drinks – that there was nothing in Birchen Bower woods but trees.

When it also became known that he'd hired a charabanc to run the villagers to Birchen Bower for the modest sum of a penny a ride (children free) the inhabitants of Croxton Abbas had forgotten their objections and taken full advantage of it.

The park, which for so many years had housed the last reclusive and silent Cayden, was thronged with what seemed like the entire population of Croxton Abbas, armed with balloons, paper bags, squeakers, ice creams and huge pink drifts of candy floss on sticks.

Tom Jago on the coconut shy was inviting people to 'Roll Up! Roll Up!' in a stentorian Canadian bellow. And that really was some voice he had, thought Jack, as he caught snatches of the words between the crack of the air guns, the wheeze of the steam organ of the roundabouts, the shrieks from the chair-swings and a deafening blast from the steam engine powering the swing boats.

A small procession of people were leaving the fete and following the path into the woods where a newly painted sign pointed to the chapel. And really, thought Jack, it would be worth visiting the place just for some peace and quiet.

'Six shots for sixpence!' he shouted, adding his own voice to the din. 'Six shots . . . Oh, hello, Betty.'

Betty, flushed, smiling, and with a new crop of freckles, beamed up at him. 'Arthur's coming to take over your stall for an hour, Jack. Sue Castradon's standing in for me on the hoopla so we can go for a cup of tea.'

'Tea?' questioned Jack. 'Not beer?'

'Tea,' said Betty firmly, as Arthur arrived. 'There's a reason why. There's a surprise. You'll find out soon enough.'

'Off to the tea tent?' Arthur asked with a laugh, ducking under the canvas sheet and into the stall. 'Isabelle kept me on the straight and narrow too.' He picked up an air rifle and squinted along the length of the barrel disapprovingly. 'How does anyone hit anything with one of these? It's like a banana.'

'I hit every target when I had a go,' said Jack.

'A likely tale! Bet you can't do it now. I'll take you on.'

'Right-oh,' began Jack when Betty interrupted.

'Tea! You can fool about with air guns later.'

Jack exchanged resigned looks with Arthur and, coming out of the stall, took Betty's arm as they negotiated their way between the stalls and the guy ropes.

Tom Jago waved a cheery hand as they paused at the coconut shy. 'How's it going, Major?' he called, lessening the volume a few notches down from his parade-ground bellow.

'Fine!' yelled Jack and would've said more, when Tom Jago turned his attention back to business.

'Come on, madam!' he shouted to a passing prospective customer. 'Roll, bowl or pitch! Ladies halfway and all bad nuts returned!'

Giggling, the woman stepped up to the stall, handed over her threepence and, with instructions from Tom Jago, was able to knock a coconut clear of its cup.

'He's got the argot down to a fine art,' said Betty admiringly. 'You'd think he'd been running a coconut shy all his life.'

'He ran over to the fair in Gifford St Mary to study the technique,' said Jack. 'He really wants the fete to be a success.'

'It's working,' said Betty happily. 'I honestly think this is one of the best fetes I've ever been to,' she added as they walked into the tea tent. 'There's so much to do!'

Jack, who'd been expecting the tea tent to be like a miniature inferno after standing all day in the baking sun, was astonished to be met with a blast of cool air.

'It's a steam fan,' said Betty with a laugh as she saw his expression. 'It's like a heater but in reverse. Mr Jago got it from America. This is the surprise I was talking about. Apparently virtually all cinemas in America have them. Isn't it wonderful?'

'It certainly is,' he agreed fervently. 'In some respects America is streets ahead.'

The tea tent was thronged with customers drawn in by the cool air and tea. Behind the counter, Isabelle, Mrs Dyson, two ladies he didn't know and Rosalind Jago were busily dispensing tea, cake and sandwiches.

'It seems strange to see Mrs Jago serving teas,' he said in a low voice. 'She doesn't seem the type, somehow.'

'Isabelle said that she came along to the committee meetings after it was decided to hold the fete here,' said Betty. 'It's because of her that we've got the steam fan. She was horrified we'd never heard of such a thing, so Mr Jago ordered one.'

Jack raised his eyebrows. 'How much is this all costing? The point of the fete is to make money for the Red Cross. I can't imagine a steam fan comes cheaply.'

'The Jagos are paying for it,' said Betty with a shrug, inching forward in the queue. 'Oh, crikey!' She nudged Jack in the ribs. 'Just look at Mrs Jago's expression,' she said in a low voice.

Jack did. Rosalind Jago was glaring at the woman in front of her as if she had just caught a whiff of a rank smell. 'It's Mrs Martin,' she said in an undertone. 'Isabelle was worried about them meeting up.'

'They can't start a row in here,' said Jack, hoping, for Isabelle's sake, that was true.

'I hope you're right . . .' she said uneasily. She broke off and stared at the entrance. 'Whatever's the matter with Mrs Mottram?'

Mrs Mottram, white-faced and trembling, with her husband's arm supportively around her, staggered into the tent and collapsed onto a chair.

Jack and Betty hurried through the crowd towards them. 'What is it, sir?' asked Jack. 'Has Mrs Mottram been taken ill? Shall I get a doctor?'

Mrs Mottram gulped and shook her head. 'No, no, I'm not ill,' she managed. 'It was just such an awful shock.'

'Awful,' echoed the colonel. 'Unbelievable.' He dropped a hand onto her shoulder. 'Still, you're safe now, dear.'

Mrs Mottram gave a long, juddering breath, shook herself, then looked up at Betty. 'Perhaps a cup of tea . . .?'

'Of course.' Betty wriggled her way through the circle of concerned spectators and returned a few minutes later, cup of tea in hand, followed by Rosalind Jago and Isabelle. 'Here you are, Mrs Mottram. I've put plenty of sugar in it. That's the best thing for a nasty shock.'

Mrs Mottram took the tea eagerly and drained the cup. 'That's much better,' she said with a sigh, the colour returning to her face.

'But what happened?' asked Isabelle in concern.

Mrs Mottram started to speak, then stammered to a halt. 'Tell them, Clarence,' she pleaded. 'I can't.'

Colonel Mottram straightened himself up. 'We heard a noise,' he said, looking at Rosalind Jago. 'We were on the path through the woods to visit the chapel when we heard a rustle in the trees. A rustle as if a large animal was there.'

'And the noise it made!' interjected Mrs Mottram.

'Yes, the noise,' repeated the colonel grimly. 'It was a cat.'

Rosalind Jago shook her head in irritation. 'A cat? That's nothing to be scared of.'

'A large cat,' said the colonel with heavy emphasis. 'It growled.'

'It snarled,' put in Mrs Mottram. 'The most terrible snarl.'

'Nonsense,' said Mrs Jago crisply. 'You must have imagined it. It must've been the wind in the trees or something of that nature.'

The colonel squared his shoulders aggressively. 'Madam, I am not a fanciful man. I know what we heard and it was not the wind in the trees. Moreover, I have experience in these matters. I know the sound of a big cat. I have hunted tigers in India.'

'A tiger?' repeated Jack incredulously. 'There can't possibly be a tiger in the woods.'

'Perhaps not,' agreed the colonel. 'However, it was certainly a big cat.'

'A jaguar,' breathed Betty then stopped in embarrassment as everyone looked at her. 'The Jaguar Princess. That's the legend,' she said defensively. 'I know it's only a legend.'

The colonel rounded on Mrs Jago. 'Is it or is it not a fact that a previous owner of this estate imported a whole menagerie of South American animals?' Rosalind Jago nodded. 'Including,' continued the colonel, 'jaguars?'

'Yes, but that was years ago,' she protested. 'They must be dead by now. You must've been mistaken.'

Jack had a sudden vivid memory of Arthur's serious face before the dinner party a couple of months ago. *There's something in those woods that shouldn't be there.* 'Perhaps we should go and have a look,' he suggested.

'I want to be armed before I venture into those woods again,' said the colonel. 'Have you got a gun, Major Haldean?'

'A gun? Not unless you count the pop guns on the rifle range. Of course not.'

'Mrs Jago?'

'Tom's got guns in the house,' she said impatiently, 'but you can't expect me to hand them to you. The idea's ridiculous.'

She looked up gratefully as her husband came into the tent. 'Tom! Colonel Mottram's got some loco story about a jaguar, of all things, in the woods.'

Tom Jago gazed at Colonel Mottram, then shook his head incredulously.

'I suggest,' said the colonel tightly, 'that you arm yourself, Mr Jago, and go and look. I'll come with you. I know what I heard. I heard a big cat in the woods and so did m'wife.'

Tom Jago stared at the colonel as if trying to make sense of his words. 'What did you say? A big cat?'

'Yes, sir,' said the colonel.

Tom Jago turned to his wife. 'Rosie, what's all this about?'

She started to explain but before she could finish, Tom cut her off impatiently. 'I don't believe a word of it.' He glanced at the colonel. 'I've walked through those woods dozens of times. There's nothing there.'

The colonel bristled with anger. 'Are you doubting my word, sir?'

Tom put up his hand pacifically. 'No, not really. I guess you heard something, but it was probably a cow that had strayed or a sheep or something.'

'A sheep?' barked the colonel. 'A cow? Let me tell you, sir . . .'

'Look, I've got to go to the chapel,' said Tom. 'A whole bunch of folks turned up at the coconut shy, complaining they'd walked to the chapel and it was locked. It shouldn't be. I've got a man there to show people around but where he's got to, I don't know. I had to get that guy of yours, Mrs Stanton, Dusty Miller, to take over the stall so I could go and take a look.'

'Could he have taken a break and be in the beer tent?' suggested Jack.

'I checked,' said Tom. 'If he had been, I'd have had a few things to say, but he wasn't there. I only came in here on the off-chance he was here.'

'Who is it?' asked Isabelle. 'Albert Burstock?'

Tom Jago nodded. 'Yep, that's right. These people apparently waited for some time outside the chapel, but there was no sign of him.'

'He's been attacked by the jaguar!' said Mrs Mottram shrilly.

Tom sighed. 'Mrs Mottram, there isn't a jaguar. I don't know what you saw but whatever it was, it wasn't that. I'm sorry you've had a fright, but perhaps the best thing to do is to go home and lie down quietly. I'm going to the chapel to check out what Burstock's up to. And give him a piece of my mind.'

'Take a gun,' said the colonel. 'I'll come with you. In fact, sir, I insist.'

Tom rolled his eyes, then shrugged. 'Just as you like.' He glanced at Jack. 'Do you want to come, Major?'

'Yes, of course.'

Jack saw Betty's startled glance. Taking her arm, he drew her to one side. 'It'll be fine. I can't believe there's anything there,' he said in a low voice.

Betty took a deep breath. 'In that case,' she said, 'I'm coming with you.'

'Darling, no!'

'So you do think there's something there,' she said accusingly.

Jack cast a look at Mrs Mottram, still visibly shaken with fright. 'Well, yes. Or no. Or not really. Blimey, Betty, I don't know. Shouldn't you stay and see Mrs Mottram's all right?' he added persuasively.

'She's got a flock of people around her, including Isabelle. She'll be fine. Please, Jack. It's horrible just having to wait. I'd much rather be with you.'

He looked at her mulish expression and capitulated. He knew that look. 'Oh, all right.' He turned to Tom Jago and raised his voice. 'If the chapel's locked, is there another key? There's not much point going if all we're going to do is look at a locked door.'

'There isn't a spare key. It's an ancient building. Burstock's got the only key. However, I imagine he'll be back by the time we arrive,' said Tom.

'We need to arm ourselves,' insisted the Colonel.

Tom clicked his tongue. 'If you insist. I've got guns up at the house.'

'Have you anything that'd suit Betty?' asked Jack. 'She wants to come along.'

'I guess I can find something,' said Tom with a lift of his eyebrows.

Colonel Mottram pulled at the ends of his moustache. 'I really cannot advise it, Mrs Haldean. You are familiar with guns, I take it?'

'Say yes,' muttered Jack.

'Of course,' said Betty mendaciously.

The Colonel was still unhappy. 'Even so, you may be in grave danger.'

'There's nothing there,' insisted Tom, clearly nettled by the Colonel's attitude. 'Come along if you want to, Mrs Haldean. The more the merrier.'

FIVE

About a quarter of an hour later, a shotgun broken open over his arm, Jack followed Colonel Mottram into the woods, with Tom Jago bringing up the rear. Betty was beside him, armed with a .410 shotgun. It wouldn't be effective against anything much larger than a rabbit, but at least it wouldn't dislocate her shoulder as a twelve-bore might.

Although he'd heard about the Birchen Bower woods, Jack wasn't prepared for the extraordinary feeling of otherness the woods gave him.

Almost immediately, the raucous noise of the fete was cut off, becoming a dim, fading background as they went further along the path. A few yards in and the only sound was the wind rustling in the trees. There weren't even, he thought with a little prickle of unease, any birds singing. It was easily one of the quietest places he'd ever been, but it was the closed-in quiet of a great cathedral, not the quiet of the open air.

It was dark under the trees, with only the occasional shaft

of sunlight showing up the knotted, straggling roots that snaked across the path. It was hard to account for his feeling of unease. True, he didn't know what had caused Mrs Mottram to be so upset and Colonel Mottram's conviction there was a wild animal in the woods was hardly reassuring, but that wasn't all of it.

Betty shuddered. 'It's creepy, isn't it,' she said, slipping her hand into his. 'It should be a nice walk and it isn't.'

It really should have been a pleasant walk. They were on the coast, after all, and every so often a break in the trees showed a glimpse of a brilliant blue sea, but he couldn't enjoy it.

It would be very easy, he thought, to get the jumps in a place like this.

'If this was my land,' said the colonel pointedly, after catching his foot on a tree root, 'I'd have it cleared and put to good use. As I understand it, there used to be a thriving farm on this estate.'

'I like it,' said Tom pacifically. 'There's plenty of farms in England but there's not many woods you can lose yourself in. Besides that, this is how this land should be.'

'Nonsense,' retorted the colonel.

'No, you're wrong,' said Tom without heat. 'I've read up the history of this place.' He nodded his head to include Jack in the conversation. 'I'm right, aren't I, Major? In Anglo-Saxon times all this land was forest.'

'So I've heard,' agreed Jack. 'But these aren't Anglo-Saxon times.'

'It's like stepping back in time,' said Tom dreamily. 'The forest was so dense that it was a haven for rebels after the Norman Conquest. The guys who wrote the *Doomsday Book* couldn't get into these woods. There were wolves, wild boars and even bears.'

He grinned down at Betty. 'Don't worry, Mrs Haldean. The wolves have all gone. But I like these woods. They remind me of Canada.'

'Canada be damned,' muttered the colonel. 'It certainly wasn't a Canadian animal I heard. It was a big cat.' He stopped and examined the path. 'It must've been roundabout here we heard it.'

'Did you see anything?' asked Jack.

'No, unfortunately.' He regarded the thick undergrowth of

bushes, brambles, ferns and cow parsley with disfavour. 'You can see for yourself how an animal could conceal itself in that.' He peered at the ground. 'Yes, here we are. I remember that clump of nettles against that rotting tree trunk. I was hoping to find spoor. Pug marks would give us an idea of what we're up against.'

'Pug marks?' questioned Tom.

'Footprints,' snapped the colonel testily. 'Footprints of the animal we're looking for.'

Over the colonel's stooped back, Tom exchanged a long-suffering look with Jack and Betty, shaking his head in disbelief. 'There's nothing here,' he mouthed.

And it did seem incredible but Jack knew Colonel Mottram. He didn't suffer from an over-active imagination and something had certainly scared Mrs Mottram badly. He wished Betty had stayed in the tea tent. What had seemed so incredible as to be verging on ludicrous back in the crowds and bright sunlight seemed only too possible out here.

It was a matter of record that there had been savage animals in these woods, but that was years ago. Was it really possible they had survived?

Betty had immediately thought of the Jaguar Princess which took the Mottrams' experience into another realm altogether. Again, that idea, which seemed so ridiculous in the homely setting of the tea tent, didn't seem nearly so unbelievable under the brooding canopy of the trees.

It was with a real jolt of relief that he heard voices coming towards them.

A party of four, two men and two women, rounded the path. Although he didn't know the men, he recognised the two girls. Pam and Linda Norris, who worked behind the counter in their father's tobacconist in Croxton Ferriers.

'Hello, Mr Haldean, Mrs Haldean,' said Linda. 'Are you going to the chapel?'

'That's right,' said Jack, tipping his hat to them.

'I wouldn't bother,' said one of the men, a burly type in a striped shirt. 'Save yourself a walk. It's all locked up.'

'Disgraceful, I calls it,' said Pam. 'I didn't want to go and look at an old chapel anyway, not with the fete being so good, only Wilf and George insisted.' She tossed her head. 'Fancy walking all that way and finding it locked! If I knew who was in charge, I'd give them a piece of my mind and no mistake.'

'Well, I guess that's me, miss,' said Tom easily. 'I own this place.'

'Ooo!' said Pam, shocked. And then, in complete contradiction of her earlier statement, added, 'I'm sorry, I'm sure, but it is annoying.'

'It sure is,' agreed Tom. 'I'm paying a guy good money to look after the chapel and show visitors round.'

He felt in his pocket and drew out his wallet. 'Here,' he said taking out a visiting card. He scribbled a note on the back. 'Show this when you get back to the fete and you can have a free ride on anything you like. Or a free tea, if you'd rather. That's to make up for your disappointment.'

'Well, ta very much,' said Pam, taking the card. 'Do you really own everything? You talk just like someone off the pictures, not like a toff.' She looked at him with round eyes. 'Are you American?'

Obviously to be an American was the height of glamour.

'I'm Canadian, actually,' said Tom with a grin.

'That's very decent of you, sir,' said Wilf grumpily, as Pam put the card safely away in her bag. He was clearly irritated by how impressed Pam and Linda were. Then, in an effort to make up for his mood, eyed up the guns and added, 'Off for a spot of shooting?'

'Perhaps,' said Colonel Mottram grimly. 'Have you heard anything?'

'What sort of thing?' asked George warily.

'Noises,' said Betty. She nodded at the colonel. 'Colonel Mottram and his wife heard a very odd noise and thought there might be some sort of stray animal about.'

'Ooo!' said Pam once more. 'No, we've not heard nothing. Everyone's heard tales, though, haven't they?' she added.

'Is it ghosts?' asked Linda with a nervous giggle. 'My mum, she said as how this place was haunted. I only came for a dare and 'cos George insisted. Everyone knows it's haunted.'

'Don't be soft, Linda,' said George. 'You don't chase ghosts with guns.'

'There aren't any ghosts . . .' began Tom when one of the ghastliest sounds Jack had ever heard ripped through the air. It started as a growl, rising in volume, laced with menace, and ended in a ferocious snarl.

A few things happened at once.

Betty yelped and seized hold of Jack. Jack, with a protective arm around Betty, froze. Tom swore, Linda and Pam screamed and grabbed hold of George and Wilf in sheer terror. They yelled in shock and Colonel Mottram snapped his shotgun together and fired off a blast into the undergrowth.

'Now do you believe me?' he roared.

'It's ghosts!' shouted the two girls. 'Ghosts!' With a scream of terror, they ran off down the path, the two men close behind.

'Hey!' yelled Tom. 'Stop!'

Predictably, they ignored him.

'Damn it!' he exclaimed, kicking the ground in anger. 'They'll burst back into the fete and we'll have the whole village round our ears, panicking.' He rounded on Colonel Mottram. 'What the devil d'you mean, firing that gun? We had enough noise with those silly girls screaming without you adding to it.'

'I intended to hit the animal which was skulking in the bushes, sir,' said the colonel with icy dignity. He lofted the gun again. 'What's more, I'm damn well going to do it!'

Tom caught hold of the muzzle of his gun, forcing it down. 'Stop!' he shouted. The colonel tried to pull the gun out of his grasp but Tom held firm. 'Stop!' he repeated. 'It's crazy firing at something you can't see.'

The colonel drew himself up to his full height and was about to protest when Jack clapped a hand on his arm. 'Colonel, no! Mr Jago's right.' He held up his hand for silence. 'Listen!'

Nothing. No snarls, no growls, no rustling in the undergrowth, just the wind in the trees.

Jack breathed a deep sigh of relief. 'Well, whatever it was, I don't think you've wounded it, otherwise we'd surely hear something.'

'Jack, what was it?' asked Betty, her voice shaky.

'God knows.' He took a cigarette from his case, passed one to Betty and lit them both, swallowing hard to steady his nerves.

'Whatever it is, thank God it's gone.' That was, without exception, one of the most hair-raising sounds he'd ever heard.

He looked at the colonel. 'I think you must've scared it off. With the noise we all made, an elephant could've escaped without us hearing it.'

'Let's go after it. Are you with me, Major?'

Betty grabbed his arm compulsively. 'Don't worry,' he reassured her. 'I'm not going anywhere.'

'I expected better from you, Major,' said the colonel. 'I intend to go.'

'No, sir, you mustn't! Look at the terrain. Anything could be lurking in those bushes. We can come back later with dogs. We have to have some means of tracking it, whatever it was.'

Tom was clearly shaken. 'Whatever it was?' he repeated. 'I've never heard a sound like it. What the hell d'you think it was?'

'A big cat,' said the colonel. 'I told you so. A big cat.'

Tom rubbed his forehead. 'It can't be,' he muttered. He shook himself. 'Let's get to the chapel. If Burstock heard a noise like that, he might have locked himself in.'

'And I wouldn't blame him,' said Jack. He put his hand on the colonel's arm once more. 'Come on, sir. I really don't think we can do anything here.'

The colonel paused for a moment, then reluctantly broke his gun open. 'Very well, Major. In this instance, I'll be guided by you. Besides,' he added, 'there's Mrs Haldean to think of. Dogs, you say? Good idea.'

It took them another few minutes to come out into the clearing where the chapel stood. The sunlight was brilliant after the gloom of the forest.

The chapel itself was pleasant enough but hardly worth making an effort to come out of the way to see, especially as it was locked. Jack could understand why Pam and Linda Norris had been unimpressed.

It was a small rectangular building, built with the traditional Sussex materials of flint and mellow red bricks, with a bell tower at the far end. The wall facing them had two tall plain windows and a flat-arched doorway. The door, a massive affair of ancient oak and studded with nails, was firmly shut.

Tom tried the handle. As the Norris sisters had told them, it was locked. 'Burstock!' called Tom. 'It's us! Let us in.'

There was no answer. 'Damn the man,' muttered Tom. 'What now?'

The colonel snorted in irritation. 'I'll shoot the lock off!'

Tom was shocked. 'No, sirree! That door's hundreds of years old. I'm not having my property damaged.'

'We need to get in,' said the colonel, grasping his shotgun in a meaningful way. 'Unless you can come up with another solution, I insist we force an entrance.'

'You fire that gun and—' began Tom.

'Maybe there's an open window,' said Jack quickly, anxious to stop what looked like developing into a full-blown row.

The colonel subsided and Tom looked mollified.

'Well done,' whispered Betty.

The two windows at the front were shut. Jack led the way round the side of the building where, to his relief, there were two long, narrow windows. The nearest one was swung open on a pivot halfway up. Jack knew the type. They were opened by a cord from inside and looked easy to get through.

'Burstock!' Tom shouted again.

No answer.

The windowsill was about seven feet from the ground. 'Give me a leg-up, Jago,' said Jack, putting down his shotgun.

Tom obligingly made a stirrup with his hands and Jack, holding onto the windowsill, heaved himself up, so he was sitting astride the frame.

The chapel had plain whitewashed walls, box pews of dark oak and, set on a raised dais at the far end, a pulpit and a plain wooden altar with the door of the belfry behind it.

To one side of the altar, at the front of the chapel, was an elaborately carved box tomb. Above an inscription was carved a leaping jaguar. That, presumably, was the tomb of the Jaguar Princess. All these details he took in at a glance.

What the chapel didn't have was Albert Burstock.

'Well?' called Tom impatiently from below.

'No sign of him that I can see,' said Jack. 'Give me half a jiffy. I'll get into the chapel and have a look round.'

'Open the door if you can,' said Tom.

'Right-oh.' Jack swung his other leg over the sill and, holding onto the stone window frame, dropped lightly to the tiled floor.

The first thing he noticed was the smell. It was a smell that whisked him back to the war, but mingled in with it was something odd. Old socks? With an irritated shake of his head, he dismissed it. 'Burstock?' he called, more in hope than expectation. As expected, all was quiet.

'Haldean!' called Jago from outside. 'Open the door!'

He wanted to explore but an impatient shout from Colonel Mottram made him hesitate. With a shrug, he walked down the centre aisle to the massive door. A key of monumental proportions was in the lock. No wonder there wasn't a spare.

Fortunately the lock had obviously been oiled recently, because, despite its size, the key turned easily enough.

Betty came in first, with Tom Jago and Colonel Mottram following on impatiently behind. The sunlight streamed in as the door swung open, bringing out the rich colours of the oak pews. 'How did you open the door, Major?' demanded the colonel.

'With the key.'

The colonel frowned at the key in the door. 'But how the devil – the dickens, I mean,' he corrected himself, 'begging your pardon, Mrs Haldean – can there be a key in the door? Are you sure the door was locked?'

'Certain,' said Jack.

Tom frowned in incomprehension. 'But that's crazy. If Burstock locked himself in, he's here.' He stepped into the middle of the aisle, threw back his head and bellowed, 'Burstock!'

'If he didn't hear that, the man's deaf,' said the colonel.

Or worse, Jack commented to himself uneasily. 'Is there another way out of the chapel, Jago?'

'You can see for yourself there isn't.'

Jack felt his stomach clench. At a pinch, he supposed Albert Burstock could have climbed out of the window, but there didn't seem to be any very good reason why he should. Besides that, he remembered from his meeting in the Cat and Fiddle that Burstock was a short bloke, only five foot four or five or so. He'd have needed a chair to stand on to get out of the window and there was no chair or anything else under the window.

So that meant . . . He looked at the other two men. They clearly hadn't got it yet. What's more, Betty hadn't twigged it either.

'Betty, darling,' he said softly. 'I think you'd better wait outside.'

She looked startled. 'But what if that . . . that thing comes back? The thing which made the noise?'

Yes, what if? So that was out of the question. But . . . he felt an odd reluctance to spell out what was so obvious to him. Burstock couldn't have got out of the chapel, therefore he must still be here.

'Could you just sit in one of the pews?' he suggested. 'I'm not sure what we might find.'

'I'll be fine, Jack,' she said. 'I'm sure we're perfectly safe in here.'

Colonel Mottram frowned at him. 'What the devil – dickens – is bothering you, Major?' he demanded.

Jack hesitated. 'Let's just say I think we'd better have a very careful look round.'

'Well, I can certainly do that,' said Betty. She was obviously trying to conquer her nerves after the shock of that appalling noise. Before Jack could say anything more, she set off towards the altar, climbed the steps – and screamed.

'Betty!' yelled Jack. He raced up the aisle towards her, catching her as she staggered away. She buried her face into his shoulder, sobbing with fright.

She had found Albert Burstock.

'What the hell!' shouted Tom, clearly startled. With Colonel Mottram behind, he strode past them and up the steps.

With a hand to his mouth, he drew back.

It was no wonder Betty had screamed.

Jack had more or less been expecting that Burstock would be either unconscious or dead, but what he wasn't expecting was the truly horrific injuries he had suffered.

One side of his head was a bloody mess and his shirt, ripped open, exposed blood and white bone.

'Good God,' muttered the colonel beside him. 'Good God, I knew it.' He rounded on Tom. 'I damn well knew there was an animal in these woods!'

Tom shakily came down the steps, collapsed into a pew and buried his head in his hands.

When he looked up, his first words were to Betty. 'I'm so sorry you had to see that, Mrs Haldean.'

She gulped and, her voice breaking, managed to say, 'It . . . it is Mr Burstock, is it?'

Tom nodded. 'Sure is. He's pretty messed up but I'd recognise him and that tweed jacket of his anywhere.'

She gave a little cry of sympathy. 'Poor man!'

Poor man, indeed, commented Jack to himself. He gave her a hug. 'Will you be all right for a moment? I really should take a closer look.'

She clung to him for a moment, then let go.

'Well done,' he said softly.

Jack stood up and, taking a deep breath, braced himself to climb the steps and go behind the altar. With some reluctance, he knelt down beside the body, forcing himself to touch the out-flung arm.

The body wasn't cold yet but it was a warm day. Gritting his teeth, he moved Burstock's arm. It moved easily, so the poor bloke hadn't been dead long enough to stiffen up. He glanced at his watch, making a mental note of the time. Just gone twenty past four. Probably the only way to fix the time of death was to find the last visitors Burstock had shown into the chapel but there could only be an hour or so in it at the most.

One last thing. Putting his hand gently under the man's chin, he turned Burstock's head so that the wounded side of his face was against the stone floor of the apse.

It was Burstock all right.

Picking himself up, he turned to the colonel, who, grasping the altar for support, was looking on with horror.

'I knew it,' the colonel muttered to himself. 'I knew what I'd heard in the woods. By Gad, sir, I knew it.'

'So you did,' agreed Jack. He rocked back on his heels. 'We have to let the police know. If you and Mr Jago could go and get some help, Betty and I will stay here . . .'

'Hello!' called a new voice from the doorway. 'What's been going on, gents? We had two girls turn up at the fete, yelling and crying and a-carrying on, and they and the two lads they were with said they heard dreadful noises in the woods.'

Tom blinked at the newcomer, rubbing his eyes. 'It's . . . It's Constable Catton, isn't it?'

'That's right, sir,' said Constable Catton, taking off his hat and coming into the chapel. 'I'm not wearing m'uniform as it's m'day off. Phew! What's that smell? It's like old socks.'

'Or nail varnish,' said Betty. 'I noticed it, too.'

Constable Catton gave a little start. He hadn't noticed Betty in the pew. 'Hello, miss. Yes, it might be nail varnish. I expects one of the ladies dropped a bottle. Yes, me and the wife, we were enjoying our day at the fete but when those two Norris girls came a-yelling and a-carrying on about hearing noises, I thought I'd better come and see what's what.'

'Did you hear any noises?' asked Colonel Mottram, his voice strained.

'No, sir, I can't say as I did. In view of what the girls said, though, I asked a couple of lads to guard the path, to stop anyone else coming along, while I came to see what was what.'

He looked curiously at the three men. 'Excuse me, gents, but you all look right put-about. Is everything all right?'

'No, constable, it is not all right,' said Colonel Mottram. 'I regret to say that . . . Well, dash it, you'd better come and see for yourself.'

'Burstock's dead,' said Jack quickly. He didn't want Constable Catton seeing the truly shocking state of the dead man unprepared. 'It's a pretty nasty sight.'

Ernest Catton's eyes bulged. 'Burstock? Albert Burstock, you mean? Where is he?'

'Behind the altar,' said Tom in a strained voice.

Constable Catton came up the aisle, looking at them doubtfully, as if he didn't quite believe what he'd been told.

He stepped up on the dais and looked behind the altar. With a retching noise, he turned away and plumped down heavily on the steps. 'Good God,' he repeated over and over again. 'My good God, I never thought to see a thing like that.'

He buried his head in his hands and breathed deeply. 'Who did it?' he said at last. 'The man must've been a lunatic.'

'No man did this,' said the colonel. 'In my opinion he was attacked by a big cat.'

Catton looked at him blankly. 'A big cat?'

'Yes, damnit, man, a big cat. Knowing the history of the estate, I imagine it's a jaguar.'

'A jaguar?' repeated Constable Catton. He turned and stared at the box tomb. 'It came out of there, didn't it?' he said, his voice rising. 'We've always known this place was haunted. It's the Jaguar Princess. She came out of the tomb and killed Burstock.'

The colonel sighed testily. 'Nonsense, man. I tell you there's a cat, probably a jaguar – a real live jaguar – at loose. We all heard it and I can tell you that Burstock's injuries were caused by a big cat. I've had enough experience to know what I'm talking about.'

Constable Catton, his face the colour of putty, shook his head. 'That's as may be, sir, but we all know about the Jaguar Princess. Ask anyone and they'll tell you about the sheep found slaughtered in the fields roundabout. There's been horses, too, and the occasional dog. Been going on for years, that has.'

'This is the first time a person's been killed though, is it?' asked Jack.

Constable Catton considered the question. 'As far as I know, yes.' He shifted uneasily, looking round the chapel. 'She's growing in power.' His voice went up a pitch. 'There's evil here. I can feel it.'

He pointed a shaky finger at the tomb. 'Read what's written there if you don't believe me. Just read it!'

Jack stooped down beside the tomb. '"Anna-Maria Cayden",' he read. '"1597 to 1638. Princess of Savages, wife of William Cayden, Gentleman. My soul is among lions, even the sons of men, whose teeth are spears and arrows. Psalm 57.4." Good grief!'

'See?' said Constable Catton with a degree of triumph.

'For heaven's sake, man, get a grip,' barked the colonel. 'We aren't talking about ghosts, we're talking about a savage animal.'

'If you say so,' said the constable truculently. 'But where is it?'

'It's in the woods,' said Tom. 'We heard it on the way here.' He shuddered. 'I guess it must've escaped out of the window.' He glanced up at the colonel. 'Could a jaguar do that, Colonel?'

'Very easily, I'd say. But what puzzles me is, why was the door locked?'

'That's easy enough to understand,' said Jack. 'Say Burstock heard the creature growling as we supposed earlier. Naturally enough, his first action would be to lock the door and then . . .' He shrugged. 'Well, Colonel, you've told us the animal could get out of the window. It could just as easily come in that way.'

Betty clapped her hand to her mouth. 'Jack, that's terrible!'

'So the guy found himself locked in with a jaguar?' asked Tom, his voice unsteady. 'And it's still around?'

'Calm yourself, man,' said the colonel crisply. 'You've got a gun, haven't you? It's just a pity poor Burstock wasn't armed.'

He shifted restlessly, clearly anxious to be doing something. 'Major, come with me, will you? I want to have a look outside. We might be able to find some trace of the creature. Mr Jago, if you stay here with Mrs Haldean for the time being, that would be as well, I think.'

Tom nodded dumbly, obviously glad of the excuse not to move.

'This needs reporting,' said Constable Catton, who was evidently still trying to come to terms with what he had seen. 'I'd better get back to the station.'

'Not without us,' said Jack quickly. 'We'll all go together. Why don't you wait here for a few minutes? We won't be long.'

It was good to be out in the open air.

'That,' said Jack, lighting a much needed cigarette and drawing on it deeply, 'is an absolutely rotten thing to have happened.'

'Terrible,' agreed the colonel. 'However, I'm glad your nerves are holding up, Major,' he added approvingly. 'We'd better see if we can find any spoor.'

He put his back to the chapel wall under the window and walked forward slowly, peering at the ground. 'Jago took it on the chin. I'm surprised he was so affected, granted he went through the war.'

'Maybe that's why he was so affected,' said Jack, joining him in his search. 'Lots of men who were brave enough to begin with ended the war with their nerve gone.'

The colonel looked doubtful. 'I daresay you're right. However,

I mustn't impugn the chap's courage, eh, what? The Canadians did themselves proud in the war.'

'So they did,' agreed Jack absently. 'I've a question for you, Colonel. I suggested inside the chapel that the jaguar or whatever it was could have jumped through the window. Would it, though?'

Colonel Mottram considered the matter carefully. 'I'll be absolutely honest, Major,' he said at last. 'I know nothing about jaguars. I've never been in South America in my life. However, I do know something of tigers and leopards. I've never been after a man-eater myself – Gad, no – but you can't live in India for as long as I have without hearing stories.'

They reached the edge of the clearing. The woods were dark and deep, thick with undergrowth. Jack didn't have the slightest intention of battling his way through the trees.

The colonel, obviously torn, hesitated, then drew back. 'Dash it, I want to carry on searching but perhaps we'd better not.'

'Let's get back to the chapel,' said Jack.

Regretfully, the colonel turned away from the woods. 'It's probably the wisest course in the circumstances. I wouldn't care to say as much in front of your wife – bad form to worry a lady, eh? – but I think we're all in danger. There was one instance I can swear to of a leopard attacking a door of a hut for hours while the villagers huddled inside, scared out of their wits. There's plenty of other stories of leopards breaking their way into houses. That's always at night, of course. A leopard who's a man-eater will only attack at night, whereas a tiger who's become a man-eater loses all fear of human beings and will attack during the day as readily as at night. Dashed dangerous creatures.'

'After seeing that poor beggar Burstock, I couldn't agree more.' Jack drew a deep breath. 'Are all big cats man-eaters?'

'Well, humans, unless they're armed, make pretty easy pickings. There are some who say a tiger or leopard will only become a man-eater if they're injured in some way and are unable to hunt their ordinary prey, but as I said, they're all dashed dangerous creatures. One thing I do know about man-eaters is that they always return to their kill.'

Jack felt as if ice water had just trickled down his spine.

'Come on, sir. I want to get Betty away from here as quickly as I can.'

The colonel cast another longing look at the woods. 'Yes, perhaps it would be as well.'

He gave an impatient sigh. 'Jago's nerves are shot and Constable Catton has his duty to do, but what d'you think of the notion of you and me staying behind on guard? We're both armed and if the creature does return, we can deal with it once and for all. I'd like to have a crack at it.'

'No, sir,' said Jack firmly. He had never been big-game hunting and he didn't want to start by keeping vigil in a supposedly haunted chapel over a rapidly cooling and mutilated corpse. 'We're going to shut the window and lock the door so that even if the animal does return, it won't be able to get at the body.'

'Eh, what? Leave the body in situ until we can come back better prepared, you mean?'

Jack rubbed his nose. 'Not exactly. Leave the body, certainly, but until it can be properly removed.' He saw the colonel's expression. 'Come on, sir. I don't know if Burstock had any family or not, but we can't leave him out as a sort of bait. It's not decent.'

The colonel gave a deep sigh that made the ends of his moustache curl up. 'I suppose you're right. Ah well, there's nothing for it. Let's get back to the chapel.'

It was a nerve-racking walk along the dark path back to the fete, made worse by Colonel Mottram's insistence on snapping his shotgun together and stopping, gun raised, every time there was a rustle in the trees.

After this had been repeated four or five times, Tom Jago's patience gave way. 'For Pete's sake, Colonel, stop waving that dammed gun about!' He turned to Jack. 'Haldean, you remember the first time I met you? You were with a policeman, a superintendent, I think you call him.'

'Superintendent Ashley? Yes, he's a friend of mine.'

'He's the one we want. He came to see Rosie and me up at the house. He didn't have any luck finding Rosie's diamonds but he struck me as a capable sort of guy, all the same. We've had a telephone installed. Can you call him?'

SIX

'Attacked by a *jaguar*?' said Ashley incredulously. 'You're having me on.'

'I only wish I was,' said Jack into the telephone. 'Poor old Burstock has been shockingly mauled. He looks a real mess, poor beggar.'

There was a deep sigh from the other end of the line. 'Look, is there anyone still in this chapel?'

'No, we all left in fairly short order. I couldn't wait to get out of the place.'

'Were you rattled, Jack?' asked Ashley in surprise. 'That's not like you.'

'You weren't there,' said Jack with feeling. 'After hearing that noise in the woods and seeing what'd happened to Burstock, yes, I was rattled and I don't mind admitting it.'

'Well, I suppose I'd better come and take a look for myself. I'll meet you at Birchen Bower House as soon as I can.'

'Thanks. And Ashley – can you arrange for someone to come and take the body away? Colonel Mottram wanted to leave the poor chap there. He told me that man-eaters always return to their kill. He had the goofy idea that we should wait for the ghastly thing to come back to see if we could pot it, but I nixed that. I was dammed if we were going to use that poor beggar Burstock as bait.'

There was a shocked silence on the other end of the phone. 'That's a revolting idea,' said Ashley eventually. 'He's a bit of a fire-eater, this colonel of yours, is he?'

'You can't doubt his courage, that's for sure. His common sense perhaps, but not his courage.'

'All right. Leave it with me.'

Jack came down the steps of Birchen Bower House and, leaning against the gatepost, lit a weary cigarette. Footsteps made him turn round. It was Arthur.

'Cigarette?' said Jack, offering him his case.

'I'll say,' said Arthur with feeling. 'Thanks.'

'So you managed to escape as well?' asked Jack with a faint smile.

'Not half.' Arthur drew on his cigarette gratefully. 'Isabelle looked daggers at me and I didn't think Betty was too thrilled with you, but honestly, Jack, I couldn't stand much more of Rosalind Jago.'

'Absolutely. She was a bit hard to take, wasn't she?'

Rosalind Jago had veered from frank and scathing disbelief to what was, in Jack's opinion, nearly hysteria. When the Norris girls, together with Wilf Mapperton and George Rodden had turned up with their tale of a shrieking ghost in the woods, people had started to trickle away.

Rosalind Jago had dismissed their story as complete nonsense and stayed in the tea tent. Then, when the shaken Constable Catton, unwisely in Jack's opinion, announced that Albert Burstock had been mauled to death in the chapel, something like panic had ensued.

Rosalind, still wrapped in disbelief in the tea tent, snorted that it was all completely ridiculous, that it was a deliberate plot to undermine her, her husband, and the success of the fete and was probably a vicious rumour started by Someone She Could Name.

Once her husband, Jack, Betty and Colonel Mottram had managed to convince her it wasn't a rumour but the unvarnished truth, that Albert Burstock really had been mauled to death, she had fled into the house, sobbing, and demanding to be taken back to Florida.

Colonel Mottram, impatient with this display of emotion, escorted the still stricken Mrs Mottram home, and vowed to return, ready for the fray and to give that police chappie the benefit of his experience when the feller turned up.

The only good thing, in Jack's opinion – he was hunting around for anything that could be described as good – was that, as Betty said, they didn't have to worry about inquisitive crowds. The fete was deserted.

The two men had finished their cigarettes when Isabelle and Betty came down the steps from the house.

Jack looked enquiringly at his wife. 'Has Mrs Jago calmed down yet?'

'Mr Jago's administering brandy and sympathy,' said Betty wryly. 'You shouldn't have pushed off like that, Jack.'

'And neither should you, Arthur,' added Isabelle.

'Sorry, but I just couldn't take much more,' said Arthur. 'To listen to her, it was as if that poor bloke wanted to get killed, just to put her out.'

'She's as self-centred as a gyroscope,' chipped in Jack. There was a snort of laughter from Isabelle and the atmosphere lightened perceptibly. 'It was when she started fretting about not being able to get any men to dismantle the fete, that I had to skedaddle.'

'Well, I was able to reassure her that'll be taken care of,' said Isabelle. 'I told her our men will lend a hand in the morning, Arthur.'

'Well, of course they will, but it's a bit heartless, isn't it, to be fretting about dismantling the fete?'

'She's still trying to deny it happened. And really, it seems too incredible for words.' Isabelle shook herself impatiently. 'It can't have been a jaguar! That just beggars belief!'

'There's something in those woods,' said Arthur quietly. 'As to what it is . . .' He put his hands wide. 'I just don't know.'

He looked up as a van and two cars, one driven by Ashley and the other by Colonel Mottram, crunched up the drive. 'Hello! Here's the colonel back. Ashley's got Jerry Lucas and another bloke with him.'

Jack brightened. 'Jerry? Ashley must've roped him in as the doctor. I imagine the stretcher-bearers are in the van.'

As Arthur introduced the colonel to Ashley, Jack went over to the car. 'Good to see you again, Jerry.'

'And you,' said Jerry, getting his bag out of the car. 'Yes, Ashley asked me to lend a hand. We're taking the body back to my house as I've got somewhere to park it until the inquest, at least. I presume there is going to be an inquest.'

'Without a doubt, I'd say. Colonel Mottram is certain Burstock was killed by a big cat.'

Jerry looked at Jack in bewilderment. 'So I've been told but

I don't believe it. He was one of my patients. I treated him for angina. There must be another cause, surely.'

'Well, he certainly didn't die of a heart attack,' said Jack grimly. 'It's a rotten sight, Jerry.' He nodded to the third man in the car, who, from the equipment he had with him, was evidently the photographer.

The photographer, a plump, middle-aged man, recoiled in alarm. 'You say it's a nasty piece of work?'

Jack nodded.

The photographer drew his breath in unhappily. 'I suppose I'd better go through with it. I can't say I've ever done any police work. My name's Newton, by the way. Percy Newton. Mr Ashley telephoned me, but I didn't know what I was letting myself in for, and that's a fact.'

Colonel Mottram had heard them. 'You'd better brace yourself, man. It's certainly a big cat attack,' he said in a voice that forbad any argument. 'What's more, m'wife and I heard it in the woods. Unmistakable!'

He gave a little bow in Isabelle's direction. 'You're not coming to the chapel, are you, dear lady?'

Isabelle hesitated, looked at Arthur, and then shook her head. 'No, I don't want to.'

Ashley nodded in approval. 'I don't want anyone who hasn't a reason to be there. That's you, Haldean, Dr Lucas and Mr Newton, of course, and you, Colonel, and . . .' He looked around. 'Where's Mr Jago?'

'In the house, looking after his wife,' said Arthur. He pulled a huge key out of his pocket and handed it to Ashley. 'He told me to give you this. He doesn't want to leave Mrs Jago.'

'Well, I suppose we can manage without him,' said Ashley. 'You can show us the way to the chapel, Haldean.'

'We might as well go home,' said Arthur. 'Betty, are you coming with us?'

She shook her head with a mulish expression. 'I want to go to the chapel.'

'Mrs Haldean . . .' began Ashley.

'I found the body,' she said with determination. 'I should be there.' She turned to her husband. 'Please, Jack. I was scared. I didn't like being scared. And you know how it is.

The only way to stop being scared is to face the thing that scared you.'

He looked at her earnest face and decided it really would be worse for her to stay behind.

'All right,' he agreed reluctantly. 'If you must.' He looked at Isabelle and Arthur. 'See you later.'

'It looks a bit sad like this,' said Ashley, leading the way out of the house and down the drive to the gardens. He looked round the field with its empty tents and marquees, their flags and banners fluttering forlornly in the breeze. 'It's a bit rough on that poor chap, Jago, and his wife. I can see they put a lot of effort into making the fete a success.'

He regarded the woods dubiously, then squared his shoulders. 'Well, I suppose we'd better get on with it.' He nodded to the two stretcher-bearers. 'All set? Come on then. Let's go.'

It was a fairly nervous group who plunged into the woods once more along the winding path to the chapel, led by Colonel Mottram, still armed with a shotgun. He was relating hunting stories with great gusto and was obviously itching to have the chance to shoot a jaguar.

After a diet of Colonel Mottram's stories, it wasn't only Jack who was relieved when they reached the chapel unscathed. Mr Newton was sweating visibly. That wasn't, Jack guessed, so much because he was laden with camera, tripod and flash-gun but had much more to do with his state of nerves.

'Hello,' said Ashley, as they crowded in. 'What's this?' There was a chair and a small table by the door, with a bowl containing a small heap of pennies mixed with the occasional sixpence.

'It must be the admission money,' said Jack. 'That was Burstock's job. It was tuppence each, children free.'

Ashley nodded approvingly. 'If we count the money, that should give us an idea of how many people visited the chapel. What time did you meet those two Norris girls and their young men, Haldean?'

'It must've been about ten past four or so.'

'And they found the chapel locked.' Ashley did a rapid calculation in his head. 'Having just walked that path, I reckon they must've been here roundabout four o'clock. That means, if your idea is right and Burstock locked himself in because he heard this creature, he must've been killed shortly before.'

'His body was still warm when I found him,' said Jack. 'I think that means he must've been killed in the previous hour. Not much longer than that, I'd say.'

'That's probably a good guess, Haldean.'

'Don't forget my wife and I heard the creature,' said Colonel Mottram. 'That was about half past three or thereabouts.'

Ashley looked at him thoughtfully. 'I wonder why it didn't attack you, sir?'

'I made as much noise as I could. That probably put the animal off. As I see it, it had been disturbed by the comings and goings to the chapel and was prowling about, looking for prey. It wouldn't tackle us, but decided to try its luck at the chapel instead.'

'You might be right, sir,' said Ashley. He turned to the photographer. 'It's over to you, now, Mr Newton. If you come with me, I'll show you what pictures we need.'

Faced with the mutilated remains behind the altar, Mr Newton was nearly sick. It was Betty who saved the day.

'Poor man,' she said, slipping past the men and kneeling down beside Burstock. She rested a hand on his tweed jacket and glanced up at the photographer. 'I felt like you when I first saw him,' she said. 'I could only see how horrible it all was, but now? I can see *him*, not the horrors.'

That, thought Jack, was pretty astonishing. He'd seen enough ghastliness in the war to be fairly hardened to such sights, but Betty, without his experience, had seized on the essential humanity of the poor bloke.

Mr Newton gulped, muttered something under his breath about not being shown up by a slip of a girl and, under Ashley's guidance, set up his tripod and camera.

'Well done,' Jack murmured to her as she drew back. 'You said just the right thing there. I thought our Mr Newton was going to have forty fits.'

'I had to say something, Jack,' she said quietly, as the flash-gun went off. 'After all, Mr Ashley wants the job done.'

She shivered and looked round. 'I know this is a chapel,' she

said, 'but it doesn't feel very religious, so to speak. I can usually
feel an atmosphere in churches, but there's none here.'

'Well, it hasn't been used for goodness knows how long.
Over a hundred years or so at least. I know it's been cleaned
and the locks on the doors and windows must've been
oiled and so on, but there hasn't been a service here for donkey's
years.'

'The window cords must've been replaced,' said Betty.
'They'd have rotted away in all that time. What's the door
behind the altar?'

'The belfry, I think.' Jack walked across the sanctuary and
opened the door. 'Yes, that's right.' He turned as the flash-gun
went off once more.

'That's fine, Mr Newton,' said Ashley. 'You can pack up and
go now, if you like.'

'Not ruddy likely,' said the photographer, emerging from
under his black cloth. 'I'm not going through those woods alone,
thank you very much.'

'Just as you like, sir,' said Ashley. He turned to see Jack
climbing the ladder in the belfry. 'Haldean, what are you doing?'

'I thought I'd take a dekko to see if it's all as it should be,'
said Jack, pushing at the trapdoor above his head. The door
creaked open and thudded back against the wall.

'Anything there?' called Ashley.

Jack came down the ladder. 'Nothing, except a lot of dust.
It must be years since anyone's been up there.'

'It was as well to check, though,' said Ashley approvingly.
He turned to Jerry Lucas. 'Dr Lucas? I'd be obliged if you
could examine the remains. Over to you, sir.'

'Keep the belfry door open, Jack,' said Jerry, as he knelt
beside Burstock. 'We need as much light as we can get.' He
heaved a deep sigh. 'Poor devil. To see him like this . . .'

He let the sentence trail away unfinished, then, with professional calm, examined the body. First of all he looked carefully
at the massive wound to the head, then lifted the ripped shirt
away from Burstock's chest.

'I'd say the cause of death is this attack to his chest,' he said
thoughtfully. 'I'll do the post-mortem, but there's no doubting
what this poor chap died of. The damage to the skull is more

striking, but it's the chest wound that's bled more. The ribs are broken and the heart and lungs have been damaged.'

'He must've faced the creature head-on,' said the colonel. 'Dashed plucky of him. I take it you can confirm it was an attack by a big cat, Doctor?'

Jerry Lucas rocked back on his heels. 'That's more than I can say. During the war I saw injuries worse than this, but they were caused by high explosive. I've never seen the victim of a big cat attack. However . . .' He indicated the ripped shirt and the deep wounds on the chest. 'I must say these look like claw marks. The injury to the head could easily be caused by a savage bite.'

He glanced up at Colonel Mottram. 'Is this the sort of injury you'd expect to find, sir?'

'Not exactly,' said the colonel dubiously. 'In my experience, which I have to admit is limited, tigers and leopards go for the neck rather than the head. The animal could've missed, of course, or jaguars might be a different kettle of fish altogether.'

Jerry stood up and, looking down at the body, shuddered. 'It was all over pretty quickly, I'd say. Most of the damage was inflicted after death.'

'How can you be so calm?' demanded Mr Newton. 'I'll have nightmares for weeks! If I'd known where we were going to end up, I'd never have come. A police job is one thing. I didn't expect it to be pleasant but to come here . . .!'

He glanced round the chapel and shuddered. 'Don't you know the reputation this place has? No one ever comes into these woods.'

He turned and pointed to the box tomb. 'And that's why. Everyone around here knows about *her*.'

'Her?' questioned Ashley.

'The princess,' said Mr Newton crossly. 'You must've heard the rumours.'

'It's just a tale,' said Jerry uneasily. 'A local legend.'

'Look at that tomb and tell me it's a tale,' said Mr Newton. 'Everyone knows it's not an ordinary tomb.'

The tomb was an ordinary box tomb in shape but was anything but ordinary in its inscription and decoration. '"My soul is among lions",' muttered Ashley to himself. 'It seems wrong to use scripture like that.'

Mr Newton clearly felt vindicated. 'You've got the writing and you've got the picture. What more d'you want?'

The carving really was remarkable. The unknown mason had managed to catch the sinuous lines of a leaping jaguar, but what really stood out were the outstretched claws and the four dagger-like teeth in the snarling mouth.

Jack glanced from Burstock's body to the carving and winced. If those teeth closed on you, you wouldn't have a chance.

Ashley frowned at the carving. 'I've never seen a jaguar in real life, you know. Lions at the circus, yes, but nothing like that.'

'I think it's dashed good,' said Colonel Mottram. 'Extraordinary. Very lifelike. It beats me where someone in 1600 and odd could have seen a jaguar.'

'It was probably carved by a London mason,' said Jack. He knew he was trying not to think of the mutilated body by the altar. 'There was a menagerie of exotic animals in the Tower of London from medieval times. They had big cats.'

'That's right,' agreed Jerry. 'I remember reading about it. The inscription's a bit much, isn't it?'

'I think it's creepy,' said Betty. 'Is it really a psalm, Jack?'

'I'm blowed if I know.'

'It's a warning, that's what it is,' said Mr Newton. 'She was kidnapped years ago by the first Cayden. None of the Caydens were anything to write home about, pirates and smugglers and so on, but he was one of the worst. Treated her something awful, he did, but she had her revenge. She was a witch or something like it, and could turn herself into a savage beast.'

He pointed at the leaping jaguar on the tomb. 'That beast there. That's her. She died, swearing she'd come back and not twelve months later, William Cayden's corpse was found, mauled by a beast. Everyone knew it was her.'

Ashley snorted in disgust. 'Come on, man!'

'Folks round here *know*, I tell you,' said Percy Newton stubbornly.

Ashley sighed impatiently. 'Mr Newton, I grant you, all this may be of interest to a collector of fairy tales, but this is a police matter. I haven't got the time or inclination to go hunting down ghosts.'

'Quite right,' chipped in Jerry Lucas. 'I obviously don't believe these rumours, but having said that, Mr Newton's quite right. These woods have got a bad reputation and the tale of the Jaguar Princess is very well known. Not just locally either. Over the years we've had a few . . .' He broke off. 'What do you call a ghost-hunter who's a respectable man? It's still a lot of tosh but they dress it up as a science.'

'A psychical researcher?' ventured Jack.

'That's the one. Not that any of them got very far. Old Cayden was a complete recluse and wouldn't let anyone onto his property. It didn't stop articles and so on being written, though. It's more or less what Mr Newton has told us but dressed up in fancy language.'

'Maybe you should get one of those fine gentlemen down here,' said Mr Newton, obviously nettled by Jerry Lucas's and Ashley's scepticism. 'Maybe if a psy . . . psy . . . what you said . . . told you different, you'd believe them.'

'Maybe,' said Ashley impatiently. 'Somehow I doubt it, though.'

'Oh!' said Betty suddenly. Everyone turned to look at her. 'What you said just rang a bell,' she explained, blushing slightly. 'Jack, do you remember when we were invited to an At Home by Sylvia Usborne? And you said to go if that was my idea of fun, but you wouldn't touch it with a bargepole, because Sylvia always had some ghastly would-be panjandrum she was bear-leading that she wanted us all to lionise?'

'It sounds like a trip to the zoo,' said Jack with a grin. 'Yes, I remember. What of it?'

'Well, the panjandrum in question was Simon Lefevre. He's a psychical researcher and very well-known. He's written stacks of books and articles and so on, and investigated ever so many haunted houses.' She frowned. 'I'm not sure if I cared for him much but he does know his stuff. He hinted he could do real magic. Pentacles and poltergeists and so on.'

'He sounds a complete charlatan,' said Ashley with a snort.

Betty shook her head. 'No, he's not.'

'I don't think we'll be troubling him,' said Ashley firmly. 'I'm not hunting ghosts.' He turned to Jerry Lucas. 'Is around three o'clock about right for the time of death, Doctor?'

'I'll be able to tell you in a couple of minutes,' he said. He lifted the ripped shirt from the dead man's torso, and slipped a thermometer under Burstock's arm.

'One thing that does surprise me,' he commented, rocking back on his heels, 'is that he doesn't seem to have been . . . er . . . eaten.'

'Thank heavens for that,' said Ashley. 'Is that usual, do you happen to know, Colonel?'

'Oh yes. Tigers will sometimes kill without consuming their prey on the spot. But as I said before, tigers and leopards always return to their kill.'

There was a distressed, strangled cheep from Mr Newton.

'And, of course,' continued the colonel, 'the animal could've been disturbed by those trippers we met – the Norris girls, I think you said they were called?'

'You mean it leapt out the window while they were knocking and shouting at the door?' asked Ashley. He drew his breath in. 'It sounds as if they had a narrow escape.'

'I think they weren't the only ones,' said Jack, remembering that hideous snarl they'd heard. He glanced at his watch. 'It's getting late. Have you finished, Jerry?'

'Give me a few more moments,' said Jerry, looking at the second hand of his watch. 'That should do it,' he added after a short pause. He drew out the thermometer and looked at it, his lips moving in silent calculation. 'Three o'clock, you say? Yes, that's about right, give or take half an hour or so on either side.' He straightened up. 'I've done all I can here.'

Ashley nodded. 'Thank you, Doctor.' He turned to the stretcher-bearers. 'All right, men, you can take him away now.'

'I'm glad we're going,' said Jack as the men lifted Albert Burstock onto the canvas stretcher. 'It's dark enough in the woods at the best of times and I certainly don't want us to be making our way back in the twilight.'

'Too right,' muttered Mr Newton. He turned away, wincing, as the stretcher was brought down the steps. 'I'd have never have come if I'd known I'd have to face *that*.'

SEVEN

'Would you like some more beer, Ashley?' asked Arthur, reaching for the bottles beside him.

'I don't mind if I do,' said Ashley, appreciatively. Arthur's beer was the home-brewed, supplied by Jno. Brandreth of the Red Lion and that, together with the pleasure of relaxing in the sunshine on the terrace with agreeable company after the hubbub of the past couple of hours, was a welcome relief.

It was Monday afternoon, two days after the discovery of Albert Burstock's body in the chapel. Jack and Betty were, of course, staying with Arthur and Isabelle, and Arthur had invited Ashley and Jerry Lucas back for beer and sandwiches after the inquest.

Baby Alice was sleeping quietly in her pram close by, oblivious to all upsets and sudden deaths and, as Ashley lit his pipe and blew out a relieved mouthful of smoke, he couldn't help envy her tranquillity. Because, as he admitted to himself, he didn't have a clue what to do next. And the inquest hadn't been much help.

'My word,' he said. 'I'm not sorry that's over. It was a dickens of a crush.' The inquest had been held in the Red Lion. Although it was a fairly large pub, there wasn't nearly enough room inside for all the local attendees supplemented, as they were, by a sizable contingent from Fleet Street. 'You gave your evidence very well, Mrs Haldean,' he said approvingly. 'The coroner was very complimentary.'

'There wasn't anything to it, really,' said Betty with a smile, reaching for a ham sandwich. 'I dread to think what the papers are going to make of it all, though.'

'The papers,' said Jack, popping the cork out of a beer bottle, 'are having a field day. I was collared by my old pal, Ernie Stanhope of *The Messenger*, and what with Inca princesses, jaguars, a grisly legend and a gruesome death, he's in seventh heaven.'

'It's a bit callous,' said Jerry disapprovingly. 'I felt sorry for the chaps on the jury. They looked really shaken after they'd seen the body and I don't blame them.'

'From what you've said, it sounds horrible,' said Isabelle. 'Mind you, it was funny when the jury tried to give their original verdicts.'

Jack grinned. That had been funny. The foreman, Wigston, the local butcher, a large red-faced man, had, after some deliberations, handed the coroner a note.

The coroner had stared at the note in disbelief, then briskly informed the jury that these were properly constituted legal proceedings, not a society for the promulgation of fairy tales and he couldn't accept the verdict.

That verdict was, as Ashley had told them, that Anna-Maria Cayden, deceased, was responsible for the death of Albert Burstock.

Jerry Lucas had been recalled and, in answer to a question from the foreman, restated that although he couldn't say for certain that Albert Burstock *had* been killed by a jaguar, he couldn't say he *hadn't*.

The second verdict, that Burstock had been killed by a jaguar, the coroner also refused to accept. Grumpily, under the coroner's instruction, the jury then returned an open verdict, which was, as Jack said, about the only one possible.

'I don't know what all that malarkey this morning was meant to achieve,' said Arthur. 'I can't see we're any the wiser.'

'It's just procedure, Captain Stanton,' said Ashley. 'Inquests are occasionally very useful but not this time.'

'I don't know what to think,' said Jerry Lucas. 'Burstock was savagely attacked but by what, I can't guess. I know there's been rumours about Birchen Bower going back to the year dot, but I can't ever remember anything like this.'

'There's something in those woods, though,' said Arthur. 'I must admit, I've never come across anything myself, but there's a history of dead and mutilated animals being found around Birchen Bower woods.'

'That's interesting, Captain,' allowed Ashley. 'But animals aren't people. Besides that, I imagine the tales have lost nothing in the telling. If there is any truth in the stories, you'll find it's a savage dog or some such, you mark my words.'

'Like *The Hound of the Baskervilles*?' asked Jack.

'Nothing like the hound of the blessed Baskervilles,' said Ashley with a laugh. 'That's all storybook stuff.'

'Actually . . .' said Isabelle, and broke off thoughtfully.

Arthur looked at her curiously. 'What have you got in mind?'

Isabelle clicked her tongue. 'Well, it's just that in the book, there's a legend, isn't there, about a monstrous hound that haunted the Baskerville family. Didn't the villain use the legend to cover up the fact that he was a murderer?'

'There was a real hound, though,' said Jack. 'That's the plot twist. Everyone was working on the assumption it was a ghostly hound – a hell-hound, I presume – when it was actually a real dog. With a fairly rocky temper.'

'But the hound had been used,' said Ashley thoughtfully. 'It's some time since I've read it, but, as I recall it, the hound was used as a murder weapon.' He took a long drink of beer. 'I wonder if we've got the same situation here?'

Jerry Lucas stared at him incredulously. 'You mean someone's got a pet jaguar? And he's using it to murder people?'

'Put like that it sounds loopy,' agreed Jack. 'Besides, I don't know if you can actually tame a jaguar.'

'A pet jaguar does sound a bit far-fetched,' agreed Ashley. 'It's just that . . .' He shook himself in irritation. 'The whole thing's far-fetched. If Burstock had been shot or stabbed, I'd know what to do about it, but it seems to beggar belief that there's a jaguar on the loose.'

'Jack and I heard something in the woods,' said Betty. She glanced up at her husband. 'That noise was one of the scariest things I've ever heard.'

'It certainly was,' agreed Jack. 'And Colonel Mottram had no doubt it was made by a big cat. But what if it wasn't? I don't know what could make a sound like that, but I suppose it's possible there could be some machine or something that could produce that noise.'

'But why, Jack? Why would anyone do that?' asked Betty.

He shrugged. 'Well, it certainly scared us. Quite honestly, my inclination was to get away from there as soon as possible. That'd certainly be the case if we were just ordinary sightseers who wanted to visit the chapel. Those Norris girls and their boyfriends had the sense to do just that. And, granted that is the natural reaction, it'd give any killer extra time.'

'You didn't turn back, though,' said Ashley. 'You went on to the chapel.'

'Yes. And having heard that noise, I was prepared for what we found.'

'Were you?' asked Isabelle in surprise.

Jack shrugged. 'I'll be honest.' He squeezed Betty's shoulder affectionately. 'I don't think anything could prepare anyone for what poor Betty found, but I was expecting something nasty.'

'Haldean,' said Ashley. 'Tell me. Is this a ghastly accident or is it murder? Or, to put it another way, am I looking for an animal or am I looking for a human being?'

Jack rubbed his face with his hands. 'I honestly don't know. If we say we're looking for an animal, I suppose the only course of action is to get hold of someone who knows about jaguars or whatever and hunt for the wretched thing. If we say it's a murder, though – well, who would want to murder Burstock?'

Ashley pulled thoughtfully on his pipe. 'When I interviewed him after the diamond robbery, I thought he had something up his sleeve. It could be just his manner but I was certain he was concealing something.' He nodded to Jack. 'So did you.'

'When did you come across Burstock, Jack?' asked Arthur in surprise.

'Ashley and I went for a drink in the Cat and Fiddle in Croxton Abbas a couple of months ago. It was after the diamond robbery at Birchen Bower. Burstock came into the pub and I had a chat with him. I thought he might know something about the diamonds.'

'What? That he stole them, you mean?' asked Isabelle.

Jack shook his head. 'No. Although he had a reputation for being a bit light-fingered, both Ashley and I thought the diamonds were very much out of his league. He did seem smug, though.'

'Perhaps he knew something about Derek and Jean Martin?' suggested Betty.

'Yes, but what?' asked Jerry. 'What was there to know? Unless, perhaps, he saw them take the diamonds and hide them somewhere.'

'I doubt it,' said Jack.

Betty sat up straight. 'Why, Jack? Surely that's it! That must've been what he was covering up. He saw the Martins take the diamonds and they bribed him to keep quiet!'

'Blackmail, you mean?'

'That's not a bad idea, Mrs Haldean,' said Ashley. 'He wouldn't see it as blackmail, of course, just a chance to make a bit on the side by not helping the police. He wasn't the kind to go out of his way to help the police, that's for sure.'

Jack pulled a face. 'Really? He'd have to be awfully sure of his ground to try a bit of blackmail, whatever he chose to call it. After all, the Martins were supposed to be there. The trunks were unlocked and it can only be the Martins who unlocked them. Fair enough. That's probably what they were meant to do.'

'You're right there,' put in Ashley. 'Mr and Mrs Jago said as much when I interviewed them at the time. The Martins should have unpacked the trunks and put the house in order.'

'So I doubt very much, granted they had the house to themselves, they'd choose the one hour or so when the odd-job man was about to embark on their life of crime. Even if Burstock saw them with the diamonds actually in their hands, he wouldn't know – he *couldn't* know – they'd stolen them until they'd actually done a bunk.'

'I thought we were onto something there,' said Betty in a disappointed voice. She wriggled impatiently, then her eyes brightened. 'I say! We know the Martins stole the diamonds. What if they hid them in the chapel? They could've come back from wherever they've got to, but the chapel's locked and Mr Jago has the only key. He said as much. So they have to wait until the chapel's open . . .'

'And persuade their pet jaguar to drop in to take pot luck with Albert Burstock?' Jack finished with a grin.

'Steady on, Jack,' said Arthur with a frown. 'The poor blighter's dead. You shouldn't joke about it.'

Jack shrugged apologetically. 'I know I shouldn't, Arthur. I wasn't, really, but why should the Martins, with a whole fortnight at their disposal to make a getaway, hide the diamonds anywhere? And then, on the day of the fete, with sightseers coming and going, lurk around in the shrubbery outside, with or without a jaguar? After all, before the Jagos arrived, no one knew the diamonds had been stolen. It's a perfect theft. And really, although of course I'm sorry the poor devil's dead, he was a cantankerous old beggar.'

'That probably accounts for his attitude towards you, Ashley,' said Jerry. 'If he was one of the awkward squad, I mean.'

'I imagine you're right,' said Ashley unhappily. 'Much as I'd like to think he was holding something back, he could be guilty of nothing more than having an unfortunate attitude. Forget the diamonds, Mrs Haldean. It's the afternoon of the fete that's the real worry.' He shook his head impatiently. 'I'm blessed if I know where to begin, but I'll certainly hear about it from the chief if I don't do *anything*.'

'You certainly will,' muttered Jack. He and General Flint, the chief constable, had cordially disliked each other from the first time they'd met. Although he couldn't care less what Flint thought of him, he did feel a twinge of guilt about how it affected Ashley. Flint not only disliked him, he disliked the way Ashley let him poke his nose in, as he'd heard the general express it.

'What if you do treat it as murder?' he suggested. 'Forget for the moment how Burstock was killed and just concentrate on who would want him dead.'

'All right.' Ashley drew on his pipe for a few moments. 'That's no use, either. He wasn't popular, but you don't get murdered for being unpopular. I thought we might be getting somewhere with the talk of blackmail, but I don't see who he could've been blackmailing.'

'The Jagos,' said Betty.

Jerry Lucas laughed. 'Why the Jagos? It was their fete that was ruined.'

'I don't think we should accuse anyone without proof,' said Arthur seriously.

Jack gave him an affectionate punch on the arm. 'Relax. We're just throwing ideas about. Come on, Betty, why the Jagos?' he said with a grin.

'It's their chapel and, come to that, Burstock was their odd-job man.' She gave a defiant toss of her head. 'You're always looking for connections, Jack. You know you are.'

'Yes, but they have to fit together the right way, sweetheart. I imagine a whole raft of people have worked for the Jagos at some time or other. They must have some servants up at the house. With a place that size they can't be rattling round inside it by themselves. I'd say an indoor servant was a much better candidate to be a blackmailer than an odd-job man.'

'We don't know anyone's blackmailing anybody,' said Arthur, obviously unhappy at the way the conversation was going. 'It's all guesswork and, although I find Mrs Jago a bit hard to take, they are our neighbours, after all.'

'Neighbours or not, Captain,' Ashley said, 'the death did occur on the Jagos' property, just as Mrs Haldean said.' He took another draught of beer and shook his head. 'I suppose I'd better start by interviewing them.'

He saw the expression on Arthur's face and smiled. 'I don't think for a minute they're guilty of anything, but I have to start somewhere.'

'Well, Tom Jago certainly isn't guilty of anything,' said Jack. 'I was manning the air-rifle stall. Jago had the coconut shy across from me, bellowing his head off all afternoon.'

'Are you sure he was there all afternoon, Haldean?'

Jack nodded. 'Certain. Betty, you came to take me away to the tea tent at about half three or so, and he was in full voice then.'

'Did someone take over the stall from you?' asked Ashley.

'Yes,' said Arthur. 'I did.'

'And that was at half three, you say?' Ashley pursed his lips. 'Actually, Burstock could've still been alive then.'

'That's right,' put in Jerry. 'He could.'

'Not that that gets us anywhere,' said Ashley. 'If you, Haldean, saw him up to half three and you, Captain, saw him afterwards, then he's in the clear.'

'He's in the clear anyway,' said Jack, lighting a cigarette. 'After I'd handed over the air-rifle stall to Arthur, Betty and I went into the tea tent.'

'I know,' said Isabelle. 'Although we were kept busy, thanks to the steam fan it was probably the best place to be.'

Ashley ignored the steam fan. 'Who was with you, Mrs Stanton? Serving tea, I mean.'

Isabelle considered for a moment. 'Mrs Dyson – she's a

mainstay of the committee – Mrs Jago – she wasn't much use – and a Mrs Curtis and a Mrs Buchanan from Croxton Abbas. I didn't actually see you and Betty come in, Jack, but you were certainly there when poor Mrs Mottram and the colonel came into the tent.'

'Yes, we were. Tom Jago turned up very shortly afterwards.'

Jack glanced at Ashley. 'That's why I said Jago was in the clear. Apparently some grumpy would-be customers had turned up at the coconut shy, complaining that the chapel was locked. Jago went looking for Burstock. He'd checked the beer tent and then came into the tea tent where the Mottrams were pouring out the story of the awful noise they'd heard. The thing is, having trudged to and from that ghastly chapel twice, I can swear to it that Mr Jago wouldn't have had anything like enough time to get there and back in the time after Betty and I had left him. Loads of other people must've seen him before he came into the tea tent.'

'That's worth knowing,' said Ashley. 'Thanks, Haldean. Mrs Stanton, can you remember who was in the tea tent when Colonel and Mrs Mottram turned up?'

'Well, the ladies I've mentioned, of course,' said Isabelle thoughtfully. 'Who else? We were there all afternoon. It was very busy. It's going to be difficult to think of who was where.' She looked at Betty with a smile. 'However, as Mrs Jago was beside me in the tea tent all afternoon, you really can absolve her of anything to do with blackmail or murder or anything else.'

Jerry Lucas was shocked. 'Steady on! I know Mrs Jago can be a bit hard to take but surely neither she or any other woman would commit a crime like that.'

Betty and Isabelle exchanged glances. 'It's nice of you to think like that, Jerry,' said Isabelle. 'But Albert Burstock was only a small man, you know.'

'Even so . . .' said Jerry. 'You can't possibly think a woman is responsible.'

'Well, Mrs Jago certainly wasn't,' said Isabelle decisively. 'She was an absolute wash-out but she was certainly there. When Mrs Martin came in for a cup of tea, Mrs Jago was very cutting about her. Although I felt very sorry for poor Mrs Mottram, it's just as well the Mottrams came in when they did.

If they hadn't, there's every chance Mrs Martin would have overheard something of what Mrs Jago was saying and I'm sure they'd have had a blazing row.'

'What have the two ladies got against each other?' asked Ashley curiously.

'Derek Martin,' said Jack succinctly. 'Mrs Martin is convinced, in the face of all the facts, that her boy Derek is as pure as the driven snow.'

'Well, she is his mother,' said Betty. 'You'd expect her to be biased.'

'And Mrs Jago is biased too,' put in Jack. 'As she's the one that had her diamonds pinched, I can see her point of view.'

Isabelle shook her head. 'That's perfectly true, but from what I've heard, there's more to it than that.' She looked at Ashley. 'You spoke to Mr Jago after the diamonds went missing, didn't you?'

'I did. He was hugely reluctant to believe that Derek Martin had stolen them. Apparently Martin had been scrupulously honest in all his dealings with Jago.' He cocked an amused eyebrow at Jack. 'Which, I must say, led to some speculations that I don't for a minute believe.'

'What are those?' demanded Arthur.

Jack laughed. 'I was just throwing a few ideas around.' He rubbed the side of his nose. 'I suggested that, as Derek Martin seemed to be the absolute elephant's eyebrows, maybe his wife had bumped him off and disappeared with the loot.'

'Good God, Jack!' said Arthur. 'Robbery's one thing, but murder! Whatever made you think that?'

Jack put his hands wide. 'Nothing, apart from the fact that a previously honest man seems to have taken to crime. It is odd, you must admit.'

'It is odd,' admitted Arthur after a few minutes' thought. 'But there isn't any evidence to suppose such a thing.'

'None whatsoever,' agreed Jack cheerfully.

'The thing is,' said Isabelle, 'that because Mr Jago does think Derek Martin's an honest man, he made a point of calling on Mrs Martin and telling her so. Mrs Jago told us all about it at the fete.'

'I hope he didn't throw in any speculations about murder,' said Arthur.

'No, of course he didn't,' she said impatiently. 'I can't imagine the idea's crossed his mind. He hasn't got Jack's lurid imagination. He was trying to mend fences, not knock them down. Mrs Jago resents it. She told us that she thought that Tom was being perfectly stupid about the whole business.' She frowned. 'She's not a very forgiving type.'

'She strikes me as a bit of a snob,' said Betty. 'She probably thinks Mrs Martin is beneath her notice. And Mr Jago's.'

'As a matter of fact, she does. I've heard her say as much.'

'Well, there's one good thing at any rate,' said Arthur. 'I'm blowed if I know what the Mottrams saw or heard, but at least it stopped what sounds like a first-class row breaking out in the tea tent. That would've been very awkward for you and everyone else, darling.'

'What the Mottrams heard . . .' repeated Ashley. 'Haldean – Mrs Haldean – you heard it too. Could it really have been a big cat?'

Jack shrugged. 'So Colonel Mottram said. He admitted he knew nothing about jaguars, but he's hunted tigers and leopards in his time. I couldn't have told you what the dickens it was, apart from appalling, but he was absolutely certain.'

'It was an awful noise,' said Betty, shuddering. 'Mr Ashley, granted that murder seems to be so . . . well, so *unlikely*, don't you more or less have to presume that it is a jaguar?'

'I suppose I'd better,' he said ruefully. 'The trouble is, it seems so incredible. But yes, Mrs Haldean, you're right. I suppose I'd better presume we're looking for an animal.' He shook his head. 'I think I'm going to give Inspector Rackham a ring, Haldean.'

'Give Bill a ring? This isn't a matter for Scotland Yard, is it?'

'No. Unfortunately. I may say this is one case I wouldn't mind handing over to the Yard. No, I can't ask him to get involved, but I'm going to ask him if he can lay his hands on an expert in big-game hunting.'

'I'll speak to him first, if you like,' offered Jack.

Ashley looked at him gratefully. 'Would you?'

'I think I'd better. The thing is, Ashley, you're just radiating scepticism about the whole idea of a jaguar on the loose. I think you'll have a job convincing Bill Rackham that you really want a big-game hunter.'

'I think I'd have to wait until he stopped laughing his head off. You heard it, though. He can't argue with that. Ask him if he can find someone who knows about jaguars. Everyone seems convinced that's what the wretched thing is.'

'That's because of the legend,' said Betty.

'Well, I'm not asking anyone to investigate legends, that's for sure. It's bad enough chasing ruddy jaguars without chasing fairy tales as well.'

'That would be a stretch even for Scotland Yard,' said Jack with a grin. 'Cheer up. Ashley. You can always keep the alternative in mind.'

'What? That we've got a very human agent behind all this? Don't worry,' he said grimly, 'I will.'

EIGHT

Bill Rackham's reaction was, predictably, one of complete incredulity. And yes, thought Jack, holding the telephone away from his ear as he waited for Bill's laughter to subside, Ashley had gauged Bill's response correctly.

'You can't be serious,' Bill managed to say at last. 'A *jaguar*? It has to be a set-up, Jack.'

'That's what Ashley thinks too, but he has to act as if there really is a jaguar in the woods. You can read all about it in tomorrow's newspapers. We had the inquest this morning. They returned an open verdict but the press had a field day.'

'Do you believe it, Jack?' asked Bill, the laughter fading from his voice.

'I don't know what to believe,' said Jack impatiently.

'And this jaguar idea is because of that nutty Victorian bloke you told me about? The one who did his best to turn his land into the Amazon?'

'That's right. He certainly imported jaguars and a whole zoo-load of other creatures.'

'Talk about there's one born every minute. Your jaguar – if there is one – must be a bit long in the tooth by now.'

'I presume there were at least two of them and they've bred.'

'That's possible, I suppose,' Bill said cautiously. 'Blimey, Jack, I can hardly credit I just said that.'

'So will you find someone who knows how to look for a jaguar?'

'All right,' said Bill indulgently. 'Tell Ashley I'll dig up your expert.'

Bill was as good as his word. The following morning Ashley telephoned Jack. 'Rackham's got hold of a big-cat man for me.'

'Oh, really? Who is he? Some sort of hunter?' asked Jack, imagining a younger, leaner, more hard-bitten version of Colonel Mottram.

'As a matter of fact, no. He's attached to Regent's Park Zoo. He's a man called Dane, Sir Havelock Dane. He does hunting expeditions for them apparently, or used to at least. He's got a string of qualifications and is the best man the zoo have got on South American cats. He's due to arrive on the two thirty-six this afternoon at Croxton Ferriers.'

Ashley paused. 'The thing is, Haldean, I wondered if you could meet me and Sir Havelock at the station and come to Birchen Bower with us.'

Jack mentally postponed the picnic planned for that afternoon. 'Yes, of course I will. Are you really sure you want me hanging around, though?'

'I'm absolutely certain of it,' said Ashley fervently. 'Apart from anything else, you're a material witness to finding Burstock's body. Add to that . . .' He broke off.

'Add to that I think there might actually be a jaguar to find?'

'Got it in one,' said Ashley in relief. 'You know how I feel about it, Haldean, but I'd rather Sir Havelock didn't get the impression I've dragged him down from London to chase a will-o'-the-wisp.'

'Okey doke. I'll meet you at the station. Two thirty-six it is.'

'Can you be there a bit earlier? I've had some news about Derek Martin. I don't want to say more on the telephone, but I'll bring you up to date this afternoon.'

* * *

'So what's this news about Derek Martin?' asked Jack, leading the way to the bench under the welcome shade of the canopy outside the ladies' waiting room.

It was, he thought, a good place to hold a private conversation. A quick glance through the clear glass on top of the frosted window assured him the waiting room was empty and the only other person on the platform, a peaked-cap porter, was dozing idly in the sun beside an array of milk churns and wicker baskets containing, from the gentle clucking within, hens.

Ashley glanced around, reassuring himself that they were, indeed, alone. Taking out his cigarette case, he offered it to Jack, and lighting a cigarette, sat back. 'You might well ask. You know you had the idea Martin could've been bumped off?'

'You haven't found a body, have you?' asked Jack sharply. The match he was holding burnt out.

'No,' said Ashley, pushing his hat back. 'But the reason you floated the idea about murder was that you couldn't see why a completely honest and trustworthy man should suddenly take to crime.'

'That's right.'

'Well, the news is, is that he wasn't honest and trustworthy.'

'Wasn't he, by Jove?' said Jack, striking another match and lighting his cigarette. 'That changes things. What did he do? And how did you find out?'

'We were notified by the American police. You know about Prohibition, don't you?'

Jack admitted to being aware of Prohibition.

'Well, as far as I can make out, all it's really done is spawn a whole host of criminal gangs trading illegal alcohol.'

'I've had a couple of pals who've been to the States tell me that it's pretty vile stuff, too. Bathtub gin and so on.'

Ashley blew out a dissatisfied mouthful of smoke. 'Homemade spirits? I'll say. Damn dangerous, too. And as for crooks getting involved, any fool could've told them that was a likely result. Anyway, in Florida, where the Martins lived, the gangs are called rum runners. Apparently they don't make the stuff, which is something, but smuggle it over from the Caribbean.'

'Of course!' said Jack. 'Avast me hearties! Fifteen men on a dead man's chest. Yo ho ho and a bottle of rum.'

Ashley looked at him blankly.

'You know,' said Jack with a grin. 'Pirates and so on. Rum,' he added, seeing Ashley hadn't caught on. 'They make rum in the Caribbean,' he explained patiently. 'I think it's made out of sugar cane. Anyway, they make rum.'

'And that made you think of pirates?'

'Well, rum always does make me think of pirates unless it's in a daiquiri or something.'

'In a what?'

'A daiquiri. It's a rum cocktail. Betty and I had a couple at the Savoy last week.'

'How the other half live, eh?' said Ashley with a laugh. 'I think I'll stick to whisky. Although, as a matter of fact, you're not so far off the mark with your talk of pirates. Anyway, after the diamond robbery, I made a request to the American police for any information they had about Derek and Jean Martin. At the time they had nothing on file but three weeks ago a Kevin Costello was arrested in Chicago for various crimes, including running a protection racket, bootlegging, and a whole host of violent offences. He sounds a nasty piece of work, but the point is that he made a bargain with the police and squealed.'

'He became an informer?'

'That's right. And what he said, in addition to doing the dirt on his fellow crooks, was that he'd been part of a rum-running gang in Florida, led by none other than our Derek Martin.'

'Wow!' Jack paused. 'Is that such a big deal though? I mean, I know it's a crime under American law but, apart from dodging the tax, it isn't really criminal by our standards.'

'Perhaps not,' agreed Ashley. 'What is criminal, by anyone's standards, is that when the gang was cornered, thanks to an informer called Hanson, Derek Martin immediately cottoned on who'd shopped them to the coastguard. He shot Hanson, killed him and threw the body overboard.'

Jack stared at him. 'And this is the bloke who Tom Jago thinks is scrupulously honest?'

'That's the one.'

Jack whistled. 'That isn't scrupulously honest. In fact, that's not nice at all.'

'No, you could say that. It didn't end there. Apparently the gang was split up into at least two factions, Martin on one side, and a Vern Stoker on the other. According to Costello, who was one of the Stoker faction, there'd been bad blood between the two men for some time. Costello stated that Martin had cheated Stoker and his pals out of a good few thousand dollars.'

Jack raised his eyebrows. 'That'd do it, every time. Cause bad blood, I mean. How come this chap, Hanson, brought in the coastguard?'

'According to Kevin Costello, Hanson had shopped them to the coastguard so they could get Martin.' Ashley shrugged. 'I must say I don't think much of the way they do things over there. The coastguard had promised Hanson, Stoker and his crew that they'd be let off scot-free as long as they could lay their hands on Martin and his gang.'

'Half a gang being better than nothing, I suppose.'

'I suppose so, too. And . . .' Ashley hesitated. 'I can imagine that money might have changed hands as well. You do hear about the American authorities being open to bribes.'

'Yes. I've heard there's a fair amount of corruption. So what happened next?'

'What happened next was a humdinger of a fight, which ended in Martin shooting another one of the gang and two coastguard officers. They all died. Stoker's crowd and the coastguard also had guns. Altogether there were seven deaths from the gun fight.'

Jack drew his breath in. 'That's a pretty high total. Was Martin arrested?'

'No. He escaped, leaving some very unhappy men behind. Apparently he got away with a good few thousand dollars and no one saw hair nor hide of him until he turned up here.'

'Blimey.' Jack smoked for a few minutes in silence. 'Martin might've been leading a double life, I suppose,' he said doubtfully. 'After all, having a totally respectable life to cover up dodgy goings-on isn't unknown.' He stubbed out his cigarette. 'How come all this has only come to light now? After all, the diamond robbery was months ago. The American police must've had your request on file for ages.'

'Martin was operating under a false name. It was only when Kevin Costello squealed that the truth came out.'

'I see. Well, it gives our Mr Martin another very good reason to lie low, to say nothing of having a few thousand pounds' worth of diamonds rattling round in his pocket.'

'I'll say. Apparently the Stoker faction have threatened to kill him. I daresay they mean business.'

'I take it you're going to ask Mr Jago about this?'

'Too right, but I don't want to bring it up while we've got Sir Havelock on our hands.'

'He's quite a big shot, isn't he?'

'So I understand.' Ashley sighed. 'Thank goodness we were able to keep the fact that we'd called in Sir Havelock quiet, otherwise we'd have a pack of reporters round our necks.' He tutted irritably. 'I wish we could keep things out of the newspapers.'

'A story like this?' said Jack with a laugh. 'Not a chance. And when the papers find out that Derek Martin, the diamond thief, is also wanted for murder, they'll have something else to write about.'

'I'd like to keep it quiet for as long as I can though. You won't mention it to Sir Havelock, will you?'

'Trust me. I am as the sealed tomb.' He glanced at his watch as the railway lines in front of him thrummed and, in the distance, came the chug of an engine and a blast on the hooter. 'And here's his train now.'

Jack took to Sir Havelock at first sight. He was a wiry, intelligent-looking man in his vigorous early sixties, wearing a Norfolk jacket, plus fours, sturdy shoes and carrying a gun case. Sir Havelock, he was willing to bet, was a lot hardier than he appeared at first sight.

He also took to Sir Havelock's dog, a good-natured springer spaniel called Robin. Robin, Sir Havelock explained, had been his companion on a good few hunting trips, had an infallible sense of smell where big cats were concerned and rock-solid nerves.

'Mr Jago said he'd be happy to see us,' said Ashley, as Jack drew the Spyker to a halt on the drive beside the steps leading up to the front door. 'Hello, here he is now.'

The door opened and Tom Jago walked down the steps towards them. 'I saw you drive up,' he explained. He nodded a greeting to Ashley and Jack and held out his hand to Sir Havelock. 'So you're the guy who's going to find our jaguar for us?'

He stepped back with a friendly, if quizzical, expression. 'We had big cats in Florida, you know. Pumas and mountain lions and so on. Even a few panthers or jaguars, so I heard. You'll excuse me, sir, if I say you don't look like the sort of guys I knew who went hunting out there. They were . . . well, tough.' He smiled. 'And you're kinda dressed fancy, too.'

Jack glanced at Sir Havelock to see his reaction to this less than enthusiastic reception. Sir Havelock, he was pleased to see, wasn't offended by Jago's remarks. If anything, he seemed amused. 'If what you're really asking me, young man, is if I have much practical experience, I can answer most certainly, yes I have.'

'Don't get me wrong,' began Jago hurriedly. 'It's just that after seeing what happened to Burstock . . .'

'You wondered if I was up to the job, eh?' finished Sir Havelock. His smile broadened. 'You seem to have some doubts on the subject, Mr Jago. I know you rang the zoo to enquire into my antecedents. I would've thought they would have reassured you.'

Ashley was shocked. 'Sir Havelock's a very experienced man, Mr Jago. It's very good of him to come and help us.'

Tom Jago ran an awkward hand through his hair. 'Yeah, I'm not disputing that, but the zoo people said you were a top brain on the subject of big cats with a string of qualifications. I guess I was hoping for a practical sportsman. Have you done much shooting, sir?'

'I have done a great deal of shooting, Mr Jago,' said Sir Havelock firmly. 'In latter years the only animals I have killed have been either man-eaters or inveterate cattle-stealers. I have also been responsible for supplying – that is capturing – quite a few of the big cats now in the Regent's Park Zoo.'

Jago's face cleared. 'If you say so, sir.' He turned to Ashley and Jack with a deprecating grin. 'You'll have to excuse me. I keep on tripping up between the differences between here and home.'

He glanced down at the gun case Sir Havelock was carrying. 'I see you're armed. What've you got?'

He gave a whistle of approval as Sir Havelock unstrapped the case and drew out a .275 rifle. 'Now that's some gun.' At Sir Havelock's unspoken invitation, he took the rifle and ran his hand lovingly over the stock and barrel. 'You say you've killed man-eaters?'

'With that gun, yes. I never shoot unless it's absolutely necessary, but this will stop most things.'

'I bet,' said Jago with respect. 'Mr Ashley, Major Haldean, you're not armed. D'you want to borrow a couple of guns?'

'I'd rather I was the only one armed,' said Sir Havelock swiftly. 'Too many guns increase the danger rather than lessen it.'

'Fair enough, sir,' agreed Ashley. 'I've never really handled guns, anyway. I'd rather leave it to the experts.'

'How are you planning to go about looking for the jaguar or whatever it is?' asked Tom Jago.

Ashley cleared his throat. 'As I said on the telephone, Mr Jago, I thought we'd start at the chapel. After that, it's up to Sir Havelock to decide.'

'Is there any fresh water on the estate, Mr Jago?' asked Sir Havelock. 'A stream or a river, perhaps? Any animal needs water. It's a good place to look.'

'Sure,' said Jago. 'As a matter of fact, we've got a lake. It's fed by . . . well, I don't know if you'd call it a river or just a broad stream.'

'How do I get to it? Starting from the chapel?'

Tom Jago frowned in concentration. 'Come out of the chapel and scout around until you find a path. That leads down to the lake. You might find it overgrown but it's not as bad as it was.' He grinned. 'I had some men clear it. I fancied building a boathouse by the lake but I haven't done anything so far.'

Sir Havelock nodded. 'That's an obvious place to start. Thank you, sir.'

'Are you coming to the chapel with us, Jago?' asked Jack.

Jago shook his head. 'I'm going to decline, if you don't mind, Major.' He hesitated, obviously a little embarrassed. 'The fact is that place spooks me.' He looked at Sir Havelock. 'D'you know, if you do find a jaguar, I'll be relieved. Mighty relieved.'

'Why, sir, what d'you mean?' asked Sir Havelock, surprised.

Jago scuffed his shoe in the gravel. 'It's the legend,' he

explained reluctantly. 'Yeah, I know it sounds crazy to talk about this sort of stuff in broad daylight, but the legend of the Jaguar Princess is believed by nearly everyone in this neck of the woods and I have to say it explains a good deal. The more I think about what happened to Burstock, the less I can make it add up.' He looked at them in puzzled incomprehension. 'It hardly seems real and yet it *was* real.' He half-smiled. 'I can see you don't agree, Mr Ashley.'

'I can't say I believe in legends, sir,' said Ashley stolidly.

Jago nodded. 'Have it your own way. I guess you've got common sense on your side.' He pulled the key to the chapel out of his pocket and handed it to Ashley. 'Good luck. I'll be interested to hear what you think after you've had a look around.'

Ashley tactfully waited until they were out of earshot before voicing his opinion. 'If you ask me, he's got a bee in his bonnet about that legend,' he said as they walked along the path to the chapel, Robin at their heels. 'It's complete nonsense.'

'It doesn't do to be too dismissive, Superintendent,' said Sir Havelock. 'I've been to many places in this world, and I've seen and experienced a few things I can't explain by any rational means.'

Ashley's expression was a masterclass in polite incredulity, thought Jack, repressing the urge to laugh.

Sir Havelock had seen Ashley's expression too. 'Don't be too sceptical. It's astonishing how legends seem to abound around big cats. I was born in India, in Garhwal, and there's not a soul there who doesn't believe that any particularly dangerous tiger or leopard is really an evil spirit, a *shaitan.* Africa has its own mythologies and as for South America – well, there's no end of stories surrounding jaguars.'

'Such as?' asked Jack.

'Jaguars were frequently worshiped as gods. I was intrigued when the zoo referred your request to me and made a point of looking up what I could find about the Jaguar Princess.' His eyes lit up with enthusiasm. 'It's an excellent story, isn't it? An Inca princess, captured from the Spanish by a man who can only be described as a pirate.'

He frowned. 'I understand that she became, nominally at least, a member of the established church, but I strongly suspect she kept up her own worship of her jaguar gods, which probably accounts for the substance of the legend.'

'What, that she haunts the place?' asked Ashley, interested despite himself.

'Yes, indeed. And I may say that such stories of transformations of humans into jaguars are commonplace among the natives of the jungle regions of South America.' He smiled briefly. 'It's an odd story to find in Sussex, though.'

'Birchen Bower is a pretty odd place altogether,' began Ashley, when he stopped. The dog came to an abrupt halt and gave a low growl. 'Damn me, what's the dog scented?'

'A jaguar?' asked Jack softly.

Sir Havelock shook his head. 'No.' He paused, a worried look on his face. 'That's not how he reacts when there's a big cat about.' He bent down and patted the spaniel. 'What is it, Robin?'

The dog gave a little whine, and shivered, looking at his master for instruction.

'Come on, boy,' said Sir Havelock.

Robin didn't move. The path was cut through a thick mass of scrubby undergrowth, dark beneath the overhanging canopy of broad-leaved trees. In the stillness Jack could hear the gurgle of water. The river must be somewhere close by.

Sir Havelock patted the dog again. 'We can't go in there, boy.'

The dog whimpered unhappily, his body rigid, looking into the tangle of bramble, ivy and bushes.

'Robin!' commanded Sir Havelock and set off down the path. With another whine, the dog reluctantly followed.

'What do you think it might be, sir?' asked Jack.

Sir Havelock sucked his cheeks in. 'Hard to say. It's probably nothing more than a rabbit or some such.'

Jack gave him a sharp glance. There was an odd, brittle note in Sir Havelock's voice. He hadn't liked this dark, overgrown path through the woods the first time he'd walked along it and the dog's odd behaviour didn't help endear it to him. There was something in the woods and he didn't believe it was a rabbit. What's more, he didn't think Sir Havelock believed it either.

It was quite a relief when they came out of the tree-shrouded darkness and into the clearing around the chapel. Ashley unlocked the door and led the way in.

'So this is where it happened,' said Sir Havelock.

'Yes, sir,' said Ashley.

He pointed to the window, the one Jack had climbed through. 'The idea is that Burstock locked himself in here after having heard the jaguar' – Jack could hear him trying very hard to keep the scepticism out of his voice – 'outside. And then the jaguar jumped through the window and attacked him.' He rubbed his chin thoughtfully. 'I ask you, sir, is that possible?'

Sir Havelock eyed up the window. 'Yes,' he said after a few moments' thought. 'It's possible but unlikely, I'd say. Jaguars can hunt during the day but prefer to hunt under cover of darkness. They eat virtually anything but unless this man – Burstock, did you say he was called? – provoked the creature in some way, I'm surprised that the jaguar had him marked down as prey.'

'Could the jaguar have smelt him, perhaps, and marked him down that way?' asked Jack.

Sir Havelock shook his head doubtfully. 'It's possible, I suppose, but none of the big cats have a particularly acute sense of smell. They hunt by sight. A jaguar has excellent vision, particularly in low light. Not that that's a factor here . . .' He broke off, evidently puzzled. 'I'd like to see the body.'

'We had to move the body, of course,' said Ashley. 'The undertakers have it now, but I've got photographs though, if you'd like to see them.'

He opened the briefcase he was carrying and, taking out a manila envelope, handed it to Sir Havelock.

Sitting down in a pew, Sir Havelock drew his breath in as he looked at the photographs. 'These are nasty,' he remarked. 'Very nasty indeed.'

'Do you think those wounds were caused by a jaguar?' asked Jack.

Ashley gave a sceptical grunt.

'Oh, yes, these are typical wounds from a jaguar kill,' Sir Havelock said thoughtfully. 'They have the most powerful bite of any of the big cats. One can even bite through a caiman's hide. They typically attack with a bite to the skull and I can see this is what happened to this poor chap.'

Ashley stared at him. 'So you'd say that's definitely a jaguar attack?' he asked incredulously.

'Looking at these wounds, yes. No doubt about it.'

'Well, you should know,' said Ashley, clearly taken aback.

Sir Havelock pulled a pipe from his pocket then, glancing up at the altar, put it back. 'I'd better not smoke in here,' he muttered. 'The question is, where did the animal come from?'

'It couldn't be left over from Victorian times, could it?' suggested Ashley. 'This chap, Cayden, who chucked out his tenants and did his best to turn this place into a jungle lived about fifty or sixty years ago.'

'You can discount that possibility,' said Sir Havelock with a smile. 'Although, in captivity, a jaguar can live for thirty years or so, in the wild, as far as we know, they only last about fifteen at the most.'

'I did wonder,' said Jack, 'granted the peculiar history of the estate, if there could be a breeding pair left over from old Cayden's time.'

Sir Havelock's smile broadened. 'That's quite impossible, Major Haldean. Jaguars are solitary animals. Once a mother has had her cubs, she will attack any other jaguar that comes close. That includes the father of the cubs.'

'We keep on talking about jaguars,' said Ashley. 'Isn't there another creature that would fit the bill? I took my kids to the zoo last year and I know we saw other big cats. Lions, tigers, a puma or a panther, say? Could it even be a savage dog?'

Sir Havelock tapped the photograph. 'It's certainly not a dog. These wounds are typical of a jaguar attack. Each species of cat has its own method of killing.' He looked at the photographs again, clearly puzzled. 'And, just out of interest, a panther is a melanistic jaguar,' he added absently.

'It's a what?' asked Ashley.

'It's a black jaguar,' explained Sir Havelock. 'The two are identical apart from the colouring.' He scratched his chin. 'The thing is, gentlemen, that a jaguar typically has an enormous range. A female's range is slightly smaller but a male can have a range of up to two hundred and seventy-five square miles.'

'Crikey,' muttered Jack. 'You'd only need a few to cover all of England.'

He looked at Sir Havelock's puzzled face. 'Hang on. This isn't adding up, is it?'

Sir Havelock nodded.

'You see,' continued Jack, 'according to my pal, Arthur, Birchen Bower has had a history going back years of sheep, cattle and dogs coming to grief here. Arthur was very certain that there's some sort of dangerous creature around. But if a jaguar only lives fifteen years or so and needs hundreds of miles to roam around in, it's surely a very odd creature that apparently enjoys an unnaturally ripe old age and confines itself to these woods.'

'You're quite right, Major,' agreed Sir Havelock. He cocked an eye at the box tomb which stood to one side of the altar. Jack followed his gaze.

'I'm not chasing legends,' said Ashley firmly.

'No?' Sir Havelock frowned. 'In that case, all I can suggest is that the stories surrounding Birchen Bower woods have lost nothing in the telling—'

'That's what I said, Haldean,' put in Ashley.

'And that as we know we are dealing with a jaguar,' Sir Havelock said, tapping the photographs once more, 'we're looking for an animal that has recently escaped from a zoo or a private collection.'

'A private collection?' repeated Ashley. 'You mean, people really do have these things as pets?'

'I'd hesitate to call them pets, Superintendent. I must say, although lions and tigers frequently appear in circuses, no one, as far as I am aware, has ever tamed a jaguar. Dear me, no. However, although the number has declined since the war, there are still many shops in London where you can buy a jaguar or, indeed, any other animal that takes your fancy. I have only ever hunted to capture animals for the zoo, but the capture of wild animals for sale is a thriving trade.'

'We live and learn, Ashley,' commented Jack.

Ashley shook his head, digesting what he had just heard. 'An escaped jaguar. My word. It beggars belief.' He looked at Sir Havelock in bewilderment. 'How do we go about looking for it?'

Sir Havelock boxed the photographs together and, putting

them back in their envelope, gave them to Ashley and stood up. 'I propose to have a hunt around the woods.' He leaned down and patted the dog. 'Robin here is the best companion any man could wish for and jaguars leave very distinctive marks. They mark a boundary by either leaving their waste or clawing the trees,' he explained in answer to Ashley and Jack's questioning looks.

'Do you want us to accompany you, sir?' asked Ashley.

Sir Havelock shook his head. 'I'd far rather be alone. For one thing, I know exactly what I'm looking for and for another, three of us will make much more noise than one.' He smiled. 'If there is a jaguar in the woods, it'll be resting on a tree branch. I can trust myself, with Robin here, not to disturb it. They can move as noiselessly as a shadow. If the three of us went after it? Well, gentlemen, I'd rather not have a jaguar drop on us from above.'

'Certainly not,' agreed Ashley fervently. 'We'll see you up at the house, sir. And thank you, once again, for the help you've given us.'

NINE

'I'll be honest, Haldean, I just don't know what to make of all this,' said Ashley as they walked back up the path. He shuddered. 'I can see why this place gives Mr Jago the creeps.'

'I think it's only the chapel which gives him the heebie-jeebies,' Jack pointed out.

'Well, I don't mind the chapel so much as these damn woods. I don't like them anyway and the idea that a blooming jaguar might decide to drop down on us at any moment just about puts the tin lid on it.'

'So you think there might be a jaguar after all?'

'What else can I think, after listening to Sir Havelock? He knows his stuff all right, there's no doubt about that, and he was certain that it was a jaguar that killed Burstock. It fairly took my breath away when he said as much. Mind you, I did like his explanation of how such a creature comes to be here. It's one thing getting tied up with legends and stories about idiots who want to live in the ruddy Amazon, it's quite another to think that someone's bought the wretched animal and it's escaped.'

'You're fairly hot under the collar about all of this, aren't you?' said Jack with a grin.

'I should damn well say I am. It shouldn't be allowed. If a man absolutely has to buy a savage animal, it ought to be kept well and truly behind bars, not allowed to roam free. And,' he added, stumbling as he caught his foot on an exposed tree root, 'I *don't* like these blasted woods!'

'Bear up!' said Jack, catching hold of Ashley's arm to steady him. 'Sir Havelock's explanation has a lot going for it, I must say, but what about all the reports of mutilated animals? Dogs and sheep and so on?'

'That just has to be rubbish, Haldean.' He sighed. 'I don't know if I'll get anywhere, but you must've seen the newspapers this morning. Inca princesses and pirates! It's all nonsense.'

'Be fair,' said Jack tolerantly. 'You can't expect them to ignore a juicy tale like this.'

'Well, I'm glad someone's happy about it,' grumbled Ashley. 'Throw you in as the one who found Burstock's body and they must've thought it was Christmas.'

Jack winced. His part in discovering what the papers described as the 'mutilated remains' had, indeed, been extensively discussed.

'Anyway,' continued Ashley, 'the press does have its uses. Sir Havelock Dane's a well-known man. If he would tell the press we're looking for an escaped jaguar, it'd get a lot of attention, that's for sure. That way we might be able to track down where it came from.'

'Would he tell them?' asked Jack doubtfully. 'He didn't seem the sort of chap who goes out of his way to court publicity.'

'Well, if he won't mention it, I will. Or,' he added with a smile, his habitual good humour returning, 'you can. You have a way with the gentlemen of Fleet Street.'

Jack groaned.

'Come on,' said Ashley. 'Apart from anything else, it'll sell a few more books for you.'

'I suppose so,' said Jack unenthusiastically. 'I don't really like the limelight, you know.'

'Don't give me that,' said Ashley with a laugh, then drew his breath in unhappily. 'I can't say I'm looking forward to this interview with Mr Jago. He liked Derek Martin. I don't know if he'll believe it.'

Tom Jago, predictably, didn't believe it. Sitting in the large square hall, which also did duty as a drawing room, he faced Ashley and Jack. Flushing angrily, he raised his hand for silence as Ashley tried to speak.

'Hold it right there, Superintendent. I'm not going to listen to another word of this nonsense.'

'I told you what the American police said . . .'

'And I'm telling you it's nothing but bull.' He shook himself angrily then reached out and pulled the bell rope. 'Ask Mrs Jago to join us,' he snapped at the maid who appeared in answer to the summons. He glared at Ashley and Jack. 'If I do have to listen to a load of total baloney, I want my wife here. I'm damned if I'm repeating it to her.'

It was a few minutes before Rosalind Jago came down the stairs into the hall. 'What is it, Tom?' she asked, then stopped with a polite smile as Ashley and Jack got to their feet. 'Don't tell me you've found something in the chapel?' She glanced around the hall. 'Where's the other guy? Sir whatever he's called?'

'He's still in the woods,' grunted Tom from the sofa. 'These two jokers . . .'

'Tom!' she exclaimed, shocked.

He rubbed his face with his hands. 'OK.' He glanced at his two guests. 'I'm sorry. I shouldn't have said that, but to have you come in and spout a load of complete garbage about Derek . . .'

'What about Derek?' said Rosalind, her voice sharp. She walked across the hall to sit down beside her husband. 'Please take a seat, gentlemen. Now, Tom, stop acting like a bear with a sore head and tell me what this is all about.'

He gave a dangerous sigh. 'I'll leave that to the

superintendent. Apparently he has all the facts at his fingertips.'

She looked at them inquisitively.

'The fact is, Mrs Jago,' said Ashley, 'that despite Derek Martin's honesty in dealing with your husband's affairs, we have a report from the American police that he was very far from being an upright citizen.' He ignored Jago's angry grunt of disapproval.

Rosalind Jago sat forward alertly. 'I told you there were rumours, Tom. You'd never hear a word against him, but don't you remember Barbara and Doug Milward and the O'Ryans saying he wasn't to be trusted?'

'And a few others,' he bit back. 'They were jealous of him, Rosie. And of us. I was glad to be out of that crowd.'

'At least we had a crowd, even if they were jealous.' She looked at Ashley. 'What did he do?'

'He engaged in an activity called rum-running.'

Her face fell. 'Is that all? Yes, I know it's technically a crime,' she added, cutting across Ashley's attempt to explain further. 'But everyone we knew in Florida was in on the game. Even the cops joined in.'

'What? As smugglers?' asked Ashley, startled.

'Oh yeah. The runners slip them sweetners and they turn a blind eye. It's a stupid law, anyway. There's a whole load of cops very much better off for helping the rum runners. They're the smart ones. Why shouldn't they take a cut? Everyone else does.'

Ashley's expression left Jack in no doubt what he thought of policemen who took bribes.

'I thought it was something serious,' she said, obviously disappointed.

Tom scowled angrily. 'Just wait until you hear what other story's been cooked up against Martin.'

'I don't think you can say it's been cooked up, sir,' said Ashley heavily.

'What? You'll take the word of a small-time crook against Derek Martin?' said Jago derisively. 'He's squealed to save his own neck. You said that Martin was operating under a false name. It could've been anybody on that boat but you've chosen to believe this guy – Costello, you say? – and damn Derek Martin as a result.'

'Tom! What boat? What's happened?' demanded Rosalind.

'They say,' said Tom Jago, his voice bitter, 'that Derek . . .' He paused, then spat the words out. 'That Derek got into a fight on the boat.'

'So what?' Rosalind was clearly still disappointed. 'A fight's nothing.'

'A guy called Hanson shopped them to the coastguard and the coastguard jumped them.' Jago stopped angrily, unable to go on.

'According to the American police,' said Ashley firmly, 'Derek Martin shot and killed Hanson.'

Rosalind Jago stared at him. 'He killed a guy?'

'Not just one. He shot and killed another member of the gang and two coastguard officers.'

'No,' whispered Rosalind. 'I . . . I don't know if I believe that.' She turned to her husband. 'I thought he was rooking you, Tom. I thought you were far too trusting but I never thought he was violent.'

Jago reached out and squeezed his wife's hand. 'Thanks, Rosie.' He turned to Ashley and Jack. 'It's as I said. This guy Costello made up a stack of lies to get himself a better deal from the cops. It's as simple as that.'

'There is the coincidence of dates, sir,' said Ashley. 'It was only a fortnight after the shootings that the Martins left for England.'

'So? They did what we'd asked them to do. That is, come over here.'

'Nevertheless . . .'

'Nevertheless this guy Costello must've known Martin and his wife had left for England. He's a handy guy to pin something on.'

'What about the diamonds?' said Jack, speaking for the first time. 'If Martin took them, he's not honest.'

Jago rubbed a hand through his hair, then lit a cigarette. 'I just don't know,' he said wearily. 'Martin may have been involved in rum-running in some way. Believe you me, that's no sort of crime. Not a real crime. That I could believe. But I'm certain he didn't kill anyone or steal Rosie's diamonds.'

He looked at them helplessly. 'All I can say is that I knew the guy.'

'You certainly thought you did,' said Rosalind. She looked up as a ring sounded at the doorbell.

'The maid'll get it,' said Tom. 'Look, gentlemen, it's probably Sir Havelock. Don't let's talk about this with him around. I don't want to argue and I don't want to explain. But I'll tell you this, Mr Ashley. You've got it wrong about Martin.'

He stood up, bracing himself, as Sir Havelock was shown into the room, Robin at his heels. 'Well, sir,' he said with an attempt at a smile. 'Please, won't you sit down? Did you find our jaguar?'

Sir Havelock settled himself on the sofa. He looked very grave. 'Not exactly, Mr Jago. However' – he reached down and patted the dog – 'thanks to Robin here, I found where the jaguar had been.'

There was a collective intake of breath from everyone else in the room. 'You said you were going to look for scratch marks or droppings,' said Jack. 'Did you find them?'

Sir Havelock shook his head. 'No, Major. I'm very much afraid to say that I – or rather Robin – found a dead body.'

Rosalind Jago started to her feet. 'No! No, you can't have done!' Then her shoulders relaxed and she gave a little high-pitched laugh. 'You mean an animal, don't you? For a moment I thought you meant you'd found a man. Silly of me.'

'Mrs Jago,' said Sir Havelock, 'I'm afraid that's exactly what I do mean.'

She stood rigidly still, then started to shake. 'No,' she said softly. 'No, it's not true. I won't have it. It can't be true.'

'Rosie!' Tom Jago stood up and put an arm round his wife's waist, pulling her to him.

'Tell them it's not true, Tom. It can't be true.'

Jago looked at Sir Havelock who nodded his head.

'We've got to believe it, Rosie,' he said gently.

'This horrible place!' she broke out. 'Why did we come here? It's that woman's fault. It has to be that horrible woman's fault.'

Ashley and Jack frowned a question at each other. 'Horrible woman?' repeated Jack.

'*His* mother. Derek Martin's mother. We'd never have come

here if she hadn't told her darling Derek all about it. Now he's
gone and she doesn't want us. She doesn't want *me*.'

'Rosie . . .' began her husband helplessly.

'She hates us, Tom. You know that, for all you've tried. She
hates *me*.'

'No, she doesn't.'

'She does! I don't believe there's a jaguar,' she said, her
voice rising hysterically. 'There can't be. *She's* doing it. She
killed the other guy and now she's killed again and it's all a
plot to get us out of here because she hates us.' She paused,
gulping for breath. 'Why can't you see it?'

She buried her face in Jago's chest, her body shaking.

'I think you'd better come upstairs, Rosie,' said Jago, his
voice firm. 'Come on. Come with me.'

Ashley stood up. 'Shall I send for a doctor, sir?'

Jago, his wife clutching at his shoulders, looked totally
distracted. 'Yes. Yes, I think you'd better. She needs him, that's
for sure. The telephone's in the entrance hall. Come on, Rosie.
The doctor'll be here soon and he'll give you something to help
calm you down.'

His arm firmly round her, he led her to the stairs. Halfway
up, he paused and turned to them. 'Look, gentlemen – and I'm
sorry for how I spoke earlier, Mr Ashley – don't go without
me, will you?'

'I could do with inspecting the body right away, sir.'

Jago sighed as Rosalind gave a little cry. 'Rosie, please!
Superintendent, I insist on coming with you. This is my property,
after all.'

Ashley's mouth narrowed in annoyance but he nodded
agreement. 'Just as you say, sir. We'll wait.'

'Thanks. Help yourself to cigarettes, by the way. They're
in the box on the table.'

'It was her, Tom,' they heard Rosalind say from the top of
the stairs. 'I know it was her!'

Ashley raised his eyebrows expressively but said nothing.
When all was quiet upstairs, the three men in the room gave a
collective sigh of relief.

'Is it really another jaguar attack, Sir Havelock?' asked
Jack.

'Yes . . .' He paused reflectively then added, 'there's no doubt a jaguar was involved.'

Ashley blew his breath out in a deep sigh. 'I'd better ring for the doctor. I hope I can get hold of Lucas. As he saw Burstock, I won't have to explain matters in detail over the telephone.'

'You'd better tell him there's a hysterical woman to be dealt with as well,' said Jack.

'Don't worry, Haldean. I will.'

With Ashley out of the room, Jack didn't want to ask for more details of what Sir Havelock had found. He wouldn't want to go through things twice. He glanced at the man. He'd taken a pipe from his pocket and was placidly stuffing tobacco into the bowl.

It must've been a gruesome discovery. Having seen Burstock, he was fairly sure it would be gruesome. Sir Havelock seemed unperturbed. He must be hardened to some pretty appalling sights.

Through the open doorway into the hall, he could hear the murmur of Ashley's voice. He seemed to be taking some time. It was a relief when he heard the jangle of the telephone being replaced and Ashley came back into the room.

'I rang Lewes,' he said. 'This is far beyond the local chap. I want some more men here and a rather more hardened photographer than we had last time.'

'Did you get through to Jerry Lucas?' asked Jack.

'Yes, I'm glad to say,' he said. 'Fortunately, he's fairly quick on the uptake so I didn't have to spell things out on the phone. The last thing I want is for the girl in the exchange to hear what's happened. She'd never keep something like this to herself. Once this gets out, we'll have every newspaper man in Fleet Street round our ears again.'

He hitched up the knees of his trousers and sat down. 'Now, Sir Havelock, will you tell us what you found?'

'Hadn't I better wait for Mr Jago?'

'At a guess he'll be some time dealing with his wife,' said Ashley. 'I'd rather have the details now.'

'Just as you like, Superintendent. I set off from the chapel hoping, as you know, to find traces of the jaguar, although I wasn't at all sanguine about my prospects. As I explained earlier, a jaguar has a very wide range.'

'You were looking for the lake, weren't you?' said Jack.

Sir Havelock nodded. 'That's right, Major. I found the path that Mr Jago mentioned and that did, indeed, lead down to the lake. Rather to my disappointment, although there were various tracks of birds and small animals, there were no pug marks. However, I decided to try my luck along the riverbank.'

He paused. 'Do you remember stopping on our walk to the chapel? Robin had obviously scented something.'

'Yes,' said Ashley. 'You said it was probably a rabbit.'

Jack remembered just how much he'd disbelieved in that rabbit.

Sir Havelock gave a deprecating smile. 'I'm afraid I was paltering with the truth there, Superintendent. If I'd told you what I really believed, there was every chance of you wanting to investigate there and then. That, I thought, would be a mistake. There was no way through those bushes unless we had machetes and not only did I want to get to the chapel, I wanted to be able to take a look by myself later on.'

'Why didn't you want me to investigate, sir?' asked Ashley in a very stiff voice. He was clearly not very happy about having been fobbed off with an untruth, however innocent.

Sir Havelock raised his eyebrows in surprise. 'What? Have the three of us crash through that undergrowth when there might be a jaguar in the trees?'

Ashley opened his mouth to argue, then stopped. 'That is a point, sir,' he conceded.

'What did you believe was there?' asked Jack.

Sir Havelock pulled at his pipe. 'From the way Robin reacted, I was pretty certain it would be carrion, Major.'

'*Carrion?*' Jack felt revolted.

'I didn't realise it would be human.'

'Oh, my good God,' said Ashley softly. 'Carrion.' He gulped. 'Had it been . . . er . . . eaten?'

'It's hard to say. There are certainly some injuries that, as far as I can tell without a more rigorous examination, indicate that a jaguar had indeed found the body. Jaguars, I may say, do eat carrion, so I imagine the answer to your question is yes.'

'But has this body been eaten?' persisted Ashley.

'It's hard to say,' said Sir Havelock, between puffs of smoke. 'The body's obviously been there for some considerable time. Most of the flesh has gone, but the injuries to the skull are quite distinctive.'

'Hold on,' said Jack sharply. 'You're talking about the body as carrion. Does that mean that the man was killed before the jaguar found it?'

'I believe so. Although the skull has been damaged, it lacked the force of a jaguar attack. There's some crushed undergrowth around. In my estimation, the kill was made elsewhere and the jaguar dragged the body to where I found it. Which was, as you have probably realised, the other side of the undergrowth from where Robin scented it on the path.'

Ashley swallowed hard. 'Killed beforehand?' He looked at Jack. 'I wonder if you've been right all along?'

Sir Havelock looked a question, but Ashley shook his head. 'It's merely a possibility that the major and I discussed earlier. I'd rather not say any more at the moment, sir.'

'Just as you like,' said Sir Havelock, puffing placidly at his pipe. He had the gift, Jack realised, of complete stillness. For some reason he was reminded of snipers during the war. A hunter was a sort of sniper, he supposed, able to keep alert, keep quiet and keep still.

'Nice house, this,' he said after about ten minutes silence. 'It's the sort of place I've always fancied.'

'The estate's a wilderness, though,' said Jack, glad to have a neutral topic to discuss.

Sir Havelock blew out a thoughtful mouthful of smoke. 'I wouldn't want the estate. Too much land for me, but the house? Perfect.'

The conversation, if you could call it that, lapsed once more. It was about half an hour and a couple of cigarettes later that Tom Jago came down the stairs. 'Did you get hold of the doctor?' he asked Ashley.

'Yes, sir. Dr Lucas. He's on his way.'

'I wish he'd hurry up,' he muttered. 'Rosie's a lot quieter

now.' He raised his eyebrows expressively. 'As you saw, she was pretty upset.' He bit his lip. 'I want to see this body. Who the hell is it?'

Ashley and Jack exchanged glances. Was it Derek Martin? Jack felt chilled at the memory of how he'd light-heartedly floated the idea that lunchtime weeks ago in the Cat and Fiddle. He really had just been playing about with ideas. He'd laughed about it and now? He couldn't help feeling a twist of guilt.

'We can't possibly say at this stage,' said Ashley cautiously.

'No, of course you can't.' He shook his head irritably. 'It wasn't a real question. I can't believe it's happened again. Where is it?'

'It's on the riverbank between the chapel and the house,' said Sir Havelock.

'It can't be!' exclaimed Jago. 'I walked along there a couple of days ago. I'd have seen it.'

'I think the jaguar dragged the body from where it originally was,' said Sir Havelock. 'That, I may say, is very common behaviour. A jaguar can carry its prey for quite some distance.'

'Don't say *prey*,' begged Jago. 'It's a horrible word.'

It's better than *carrion* thought Jack. He looked up as the doorbell rang.

Jago gave a sigh of relief. 'At last!'

Jerry Lucas was shown into the room. 'Hello, Jack!' he said in surprise. 'I didn't realise you'd be in on this. Mr Ashley, I'd better see Mrs Jago first, but hopefully I won't be long.'

He was as good as his word. It was only ten minutes or so before the doctor and Tom Jago came downstairs.

'She will be all right, Doctor?' asked Jago anxiously.

'Nothing to worry about,' said Jerry reassuringly. 'She was virtually asleep when we left the room.' He looked quizzically at Jack. 'Has there really been another jaguar attack? I can hardly believe it. There must be some mistake, surely.'

'There's no doubt about it,' said Sir Havelock.

Jerry Lucas looked at him. 'You seem very certain, sir. You are?'

'I'm sorry, Jerry, I should've introduced you,' said Jack. 'This is Sir Havelock Dane. He's London Zoo's big cat expert.'

Jerry Lucas's eyes widened. 'Good Lord! Are you, by Jove! I suppose you must know all about jaguars and so on.'

'I know more than most,' agreed Sir Havelock. 'I can understand your scepticism, Doctor, but there really is no doubt in my mind that the body I found had been attacked by a jaguar.'

'If you say so,' muttered Jerry.

'Can we get going, gentlemen,' said Jago. 'Please?'

'Certainly, sir,' said Ashley. 'I'm expecting some men along from Lewes. They'll be a while yet, but it'd be as well if you warned your servants to expect them.'

'Sure thing,' said Jago and rang the bell.

'What this estate needs,' said Ashley savagely to Jack as a bramble caught at his sleeve, 'is some proper maintenance.'

'So I've heard you mention before. You could perhaps err on the side of tact and not say it quite so loudly with Jago in earshot.'

'He didn't hear me,' muttered Ashley. Tom Jago was a few yards in front, intent on a conversation with Jerry Lucas. 'I do want to ask him something, though. Mr Jago!' he called.

Jago stopped and turned round. 'Yes? What is it?' Although polite, he was clearly still put out by Ashley's accusation of Derek Martin.

'Why is your wife so convinced that Mrs Martin, Derek Martin's mother, is behind these killings?'

Jago sighed and, after searching his pockets, pulled out his case and lit a cigarette. 'I don't think she is really, Superintendent, but you know what women are like. The best of them simply won't listen to reason once they've got their knife into someone. She's convinced the Martins stole her diamonds and told Mrs Martin so.'

He shrugged and glanced at Jack. 'As you know, Major, I've tried to mend fences with Mrs Martin. Despite everything' – he gave Ashley a very unfriendly look – 'I still maintain that Derek is innocent. Rum-running's one thing. Theft and murder is quite another.' He pulled at his cigarette. 'Rosie resents it.' His mouth narrowed. 'It seems ridiculous but it's almost as if she's jealous.'

'That's a very poor reason to accuse someone of murder, sir.'

'Don't I know it,' said Jago with a rueful laugh. 'I wish I

could get it through to her.' His voice took on a note of warning. 'However, I would ask you gentlemen to remember this is my wife we're talking about.'

'Just as you say, sir,' said Ashley stolidly.

They walked on in silence but as soon as Tom Jago's back was turned, Ashley exchanged a very expressive look with Jack. 'Idiotic woman,' he muttered.

And, thought Jack, slinging out accusations of murder was idiotic, not to put it any stronger than that. However, he did have some sympathy for Rosalind Jago. She was a creature of the city and bright lights and her husband had asked a dickens of a lot by asking her to bury herself away on a neglected country estate.

He looked at Sir Havelock. 'Have we much further to go, sir?'

'We're virtually there,' said Sir Havelock. The dog gave a little whine. 'Good boy, Robin. You can smell it, can't you?'

With a twist of his stomach, Jack realised that the dog could smell it but he could *hear* it. Over the gurgle of the river came the angry buzzing of flies.

And now they could see it. Ashley made a choking noise as he looked at the body half-hidden by the bushes. It was a grim sight, but Jack had seen sights at least as bad in France. So had Jerry Lucas. He reminded himself that Ashley may be the older man, but he hadn't had their experience.

The man had evidently been dead for some considerable time. He was face down, his arms flung out. The back of his skull was crushed and fragments of bone lay scattered about. His shirt was in tattered fragments where his back had been ripped into, exposing the white bone of ribs. Worst of all, though, were the flies moving slowly over what remained of the flesh.

'What can you tell us, Doctor?' asked Ashley.

'Nothing much,' said Jerry. He waved away a fly, his face contorting in distaste. 'I can't examine him here. I'll need to carry out a post-mortem before I can tell you anything definite.' He glanced up at Sir Havelock. 'Would you say these injuries are typical of an attack by a jaguar?'

'Certainly,' agreed Sir Havelock. 'With one obvious reservation. You'll agree, Doctor, that he was killed before the jaguar got him?'

Tom Jago spoke, his voice a croak. 'How the hell can you tell that?'

'None of these injuries have bled,' said Jerry. 'Which means they were inflicted after death.'

Ashley looked at him sharply. 'So if he didn't die from these injuries, are you saying he was killed? Murdered, I mean?'

'I suppose he could've died by accident,' said Jerry. 'He could've fallen over and hit the back of his head. That's impossible to tell, with the skull in the state it is.'

Tom Jago glared at Ashley. 'Of course he wasn't murdered. I don't believe in an accident, either. Look at the state of him! Do you really need to find another reason to explain how he died?'

'Unfortunately, sir, yes we do,' said Ashley. 'The doctor and Sir Havelock are perfectly correct. There's been very little bleeding. You can see that for yourself. Look at his clothes.'

'His *clothes*!' yelped Tom Jago in a strangulated voice. 'Oh my God, his clothes!'

'What about his clothes?' asked Ashley sharply.

Jago put a hand to his mouth. Reluctantly he moved closer to the corpse then, bracing himself, knelt down beside the body. With an impatient hand he waved away the cloud of flies then tentatively rolled the body over.

Ashley started forward. 'You shouldn't do that,' he began, then stopped. He shrugged and looked at Jack. 'I don't suppose it matters. Not if a ruddy jaguar's been carting it about.'

The face, or what was left of it, was unrecognisable. Jago looked down at it and shuddered. Then, obviously bracing himself, he hesitatingly reached out and pulled back the ripped jacket so he could see the inside breast pocket. 'I thought I recognised these clothes,' he said, his voice cracking. 'The label. Can you read the label?'

Jack stepped forward and, taking a deep breath, knelt down beside the body. 'It's discoloured,' he said after a few moments, 'but that must be the maker's name. Something son and Flynn.'

Jago swallowed. 'Jackson and Flynn. I know them. Martin used them. They're pretty fancy tailors.'

'I can make out part of an address and . . .' Jack stopped. 'I'm sorry, Jago,' he said heavily. 'You know what's there.'

'Haldean?' asked Ashley. 'Haldean, what is it?'

Jack stood up and squared his shoulders. 'It's Derek Martin. The jacket was made for him. His name's on the label.'

Jago stood up and backed away from the corpse. 'No.' He gave Ashley an imploring look. 'It can't be him.'

Ashley's voice was gruff with clumsy sympathy. 'I'm sorry, sir, but that's what it looks like.'

'But it's only his jacket!' broke out Jago. 'Anyone could've taken his jacket. He could've given it to someone. To anyone.'

'Is there any way you could identify him?' asked Jack. 'Did he ever visit a dentist, say?'

Jago shook his head. 'No. Not as far as I know.'

'He was in the army, wasn't he?' said Jerry. Jago nodded. 'There'll be his army medical records. They might help.'

'They might,' agreed Ashley dubiously. 'It'll be difficult though, with the remains in this condition.'

'Don't call them *remains*,' bit out Jago. 'He was a man.'

'Is there anything you can think of that can help us?' asked Jack. 'Did he have a tattoo, say?'

'No,' began Jago, then looked up. 'Yes! He did. I don't know what it was. It was on his upper arm.' He looked down at the body again and winced. 'I suppose that's gone.'

'Maybe not,' said Jerry. 'If it's his upper arm, that's protected by his shirt and his jacket. I'll make a point of looking for any traces I can find. Did he ever break a bone, say? That might help us identify him.'

Jago didn't answer.

'Did he ever break a bone?' prompted Jerry, his voice sympathetic.

Jago looked up. 'What?' He paused. Jack could see him thinking. 'Hold on. Yes. He broke a couple of ribs. He was on a sail boat and fell against the bulwark. He had to take it easy for a time.'

Jerry nodded in satisfaction. 'That should settle matters, especially if I find that tattoo.' He looked down at the body and sighed. 'I'm glad we've got something to go on, at any rate. If you have him brought to the surgery, I'll tackle the post-mortem there. And now,' he added in disgust, waving away the flies in front of his face, 'for pity's sake let's get out of here.'

'Just a moment,' said Jack. 'Sir Havelock, did you find any tracks?'

'No. However, you can see for yourself, Major, how the body is lying, half in and half out of the bushes. Unless the jaguar came onto the path, I wouldn't expect to find any marks.'

'There is a footprint, though,' said Ashley. 'A man's footprint.' He pointed to where the edge of the path was muddy from the river.

Tom Jago shook himself, obviously making a conscious effort to pull himself together. He walked to where Ashley was pointing and pressed his foot into the mud. 'It's mine,' he said, bending down to look at it. 'I was wearing these shoes when I walked along here the other day.' He straightened up. 'Come on. Let's do what the doctor said and leave. I hope to God it's not poor Derek.'

TEN

I t was a relief to get back to Isabelle and Arthur's. Jack parked the car in the old stable block and, following the sound of voices, walked round the side of the house and looked onto the terrace.

For a moment he stood in the shadows, looking at Betty, Arthur and Isabelle. Arthur had Baby Alice on his knee, bouncing her up and down. Alice's delighted chuckles were echoed by the two girls. Arthur looked at them with a grin. 'Any offers to hold her? This is getting exhausting.'

Betty reached forward, arms outstretched. 'Let me have her.'

Jack's heart gave a twist as he saw Betty take Alice, kiss the top of her downy head, and hug her close. He suddenly wanted to retreat, to escape into the house or even drive away – anything but spoil this simple happiness with the story of the ghastliness of the body in the bushes.

Still, it had to be done. Bracing himself, he walked forward.

Betty glanced up, smiling, then her face changed. Pushing her chair back, she handed the baby to Isabelle and, getting up, took his hands in hers. 'Jack, what on earth's the matter? You look worried to death.'

He sank into a chair and tried to smile. 'It's been a rough afternoon. Is that lemonade in the jug? Can I have some?'

'Yes, of course,' said Arthur. He poured out a glass. 'Is lemonade OK? You look as if you could do with something stronger.'

'No, this is fine, thanks,' said Jack, taking a long drink.

'What's happened?' asked Isabelle in concern. 'Did you meet Sir Havelock whatshisname?'

'Yes, Ashley and I met him. He's a sound chap and obviously knows his stuff.' He paused. 'The thing is, Sir Havelock found another body,' he said quietly.

They stared at him in horror. '*Another* body,' said Betty at last. 'What, like Burstock, you mean?'

He nodded. 'This poor devil had obviously been dead some time. Days, maybe weeks, I mean. It was pretty beastly. Thank God you weren't there.'

Arthur winced. 'I can guess what he looked like. Who is it? Could you tell?'

'Not from looking, no. Not only had he been dead for some time, Sir Havelock reckoned that he'd been attacked after he'd died. However, I'm very much afraid it's Derek Martin.'

Betty stared at him. 'Derek Martin! But Jack, you guessed as much. Ages ago, I mean.'

He nodded. 'So I did,' he said bitterly.

Isabelle gazed at him in astonishment. 'You never said anything to us.'

'It was more or less a joke, rather than a serious suggestion,' he said wearily. 'I was throwing a few ideas around with Ashley about what could've happened to the Martins. It was fun to see him go off the deep end when I suggested that the honest-as-the-day-is-long Derek Martin had been murdered by his wife. The thing is, I was wrong about him being honest.'

There was another stunned silence. 'You'd better tell us everything, old man,' said Arthur eventually.

They wanted the details. He didn't really want to go through the story but, oddly enough, it helped.

'That's just horrible,' said Betty after he'd finished. 'But Jack,

how can you be sure it's Derek Martin? Surely you have to
have more to go on than the jacket he was wearing?'

'That's what Tom Jago said. What will settle the matter is
that Martin broke a couple of ribs in a sailing accident. Poor
old Ashley has to break the news to Mrs Martin, so he'll probably ask for confirmation of that, and anything else that'll help
to confirm his identity. If Jerry finds the bones have been broken,
that should do it. Tom Jago doesn't want it to be Martin but
I'm blowed if I know who else it could be.'

Betty shuddered. 'This is all to do with the diamonds, isn't
it?' she said, then paused. 'But Jack, it doesn't make sense. It
did when you thought Derek Martin was honest, but if he was
a smuggler and killed those men on the boat, he's not so honest
after all. He could've easily stolen the diamonds. You thought
his wife might have killed him, but why? Why should she if
they were in it together?'

'Greed?' suggested Jack. 'A whole necklace is better than
half. Besides that, I was struck by something Jago said. The
whole story of the fight with the coastguard rests on the word
of a thug and a gangster. Jago thinks that's a pack of lies and
he might be right. So we're back to an honest man with a pretty
dodgy wife.'

Betty looked up at him in distress. 'If his wife killed him, I
don't think greed's enough. I think she must've hated him.'

Jack reached out and squeezed her hand. 'Buck up, sweetheart,' he said. 'Don't dwell on it.'

'I'm right though, aren't I?'

'As always,' he said as lightly as he could manage. 'It's the
first rule of domestic content.'

'Jack,' said Arthur soberly. 'You say Sir Havelock's certain
about the jaguar?'

Jack nodded. 'Yes. He's convinced poor old Burstock was
killed by a jaguar – Ashley showed him the photographs – and
although this second poor devil was probably killed by other
means, he was certain that a jaguar had been at the body.
Apparently they do eat . . . eat dead things.' He was damned
if he was going to say 'carrion'.

Arthur heaved a deep sigh. 'I knew it. There's something in
those ruddy woods and there has been for years. It all goes

back to what that loony beggar Cayden let rip on his estate. He had jaguars, didn't he? It's obvious. They must've bred.'

'But that's a puzzle, Arthur,' said Jack, leaning forward and lighting a cigarette. 'Sir Havelock was certain that can't be the answer. At the most a jaguar lives for about fifteen years in the wild. They're completely solitary. Apparently once a female's had cubs, she won't even let the father near them.'

'Nevertheless . . .' began Arthur.

'Add to that, they have a range – a solitary range – of about two hundred and fifty square miles.'

Arthur's eyebrows shot up. 'Good God! Two hundred and fifty square *miles*?'

'It's an enormous area, isn't it? I don't know how big Birchen Bower woods are but they're titchy in comparison.'

Arthur thought for a moment. 'They're about three hundred acres, I'd say. Dash it, Jack, that's not even half a square mile.'

Jack shrugged and held his hands wide. 'I know. So although Sir Havelock was convinced we were looking at jaguar attacks, he flatly refused to believe the creature confined itself to the woods.'

Betty swallowed hard. 'It's at loose in the countryside?'

'But Jack,' said Isabelle. 'You say it's impossible that it's descended from the animals old Cayden, the nutty one, had. I suppose we've got to believe that. So where did it come from?'

'Well, Sir Havelock's explanation is that we're looking for an animal that's escaped from a private collection. He told us there're plenty of shops in London where you can go and buy virtually any animal that takes your fancy. Apparently capturing wild animals for sale is a thriving trade.'

'You do see photos of film stars and so on with all sorts of animals,' said Betty doubtfully. 'Snakes, monkeys, even tigers and so on. And there's always circuses, I suppose. At least that explanation makes some sort of sense.'

Arthur looked worried. 'But it doesn't. Jack, I've told you before there's a long history of animals – sheep, cows, what have you – being found dead and mutilated around Birchen Bower woods.'

Jack looked at his friend squarely. 'Do you know that? Know

it from your own experience, I mean, or is this just a long-standing rumour?'

Arthur bit his lip thoughtfully. 'There haven't been any attacks recently, I must say.'

'Surely those are just rumours,' said Betty. 'It's not surprising when you think of the legend of the Inca Princess.'

Arthur shook his head. 'No, it's not just rumour. There's more to it than that.'

'When was the last attack?' asked Jack.

Arthur put his hand to his chin. 'I'd say it must be four or five years ago now,' he said eventually. 'Before my time. Last year I decided to pasture sheep in Knep End, the field adjacent to the woods. It's excellent grazing, but the older men weren't happy. Lutton, the shepherd, told me he'd lost his favourite dog there and some livestock. The poor bloke was obviously upset. I don't blame him. Rotten thing, to see animals torn up.'

Having just seen a torn-up human, Jack agreed whole-heartedly. He looked at Arthur thoughtfully. 'I don't suppose you've got any photographs, have you?'

'Good God, no. Why on earth would you want a photograph of that?'

Jack shrugged. 'If there were photographs, I could've shown them to Sir Havelock Dane. His opinion would be worth getting.'

'All the farm hands are convinced it's the Jaguar Princess, of course,' put in Isabelle. 'It's funny, though. You'd expect a tale like that to grow in the telling but it doesn't. I remember how reluctant Lutton was to say what was actually bothering him about pasturing the sheep in Knep End. All the men are like that.'

'I read a book about folklore and legends,' said Betty. 'You remember I said I'd met the author at a party, Jack?'

'Simon Lefevre?'

'That's the one. He said that it was often difficult to get at the actual story behind the legend. People thought it was unlucky. It'd sort of call the spirit up if it was talked about.'

Isabelle nodded. 'I'd say that's certainly the case here, wouldn't you, Arthur?'

'It took me a while to get the truth out of Lutton, that's for sure.'

Jack leaned back in his chair, running his finger thoughtfully round the rim of his glass. 'When you say there's a long history of these attacks, Arthur, how long?'

'Crikey, I couldn't say for sure. Back to the last century at least – maybe longer than that.'

'I suppose it could've been a local lunatic,' said Isabelle thoughtfully. 'Someone with a grudge against local farmers or the Caydens in particular?'

'You're maybe right,' agreed Jack. 'The thing is, with the legend of the Inca Princess so well established, people are more or less bound to think of that as an explanation.'

Arthur nodded. 'Perhaps.' He shrugged impatiently. 'Ugh! It's lousy to think about.' He paused for a few moments, then shook himself. 'Come on, everyone. It sounds heartless to say let's forget about it, but I think we need something to cheer us up after poor old Burstock and this latest poor devil.' He looked at Isabelle with the beginnings of a smile. 'I've got an idea.'

'I know!' said Isabelle impulsively. 'It's glorious weather. Let's take the boat out and escape for the day.' She looked at her husband with bright eyes. 'That's what you were going to say, isn't it?'

Arthur laughed. 'Mind reader! Yes, I was, if you must know.'

'You mentioned the boat in a letter ages ago,' said Betty.

'Arthur's become quite a yachtsman,' said Isabelle with a touch of wifely pride.

'Well, I don't know about that,' said Arthur modestly. 'I've stuck to the coast so far but the boat's a little beauty. She was built by Hillyards,' he added, as if that explained everything.

Betty gave a snort of laughter. 'That doesn't mean a thing to me.'

'It didn't mean a thing to me until a few months ago,' said Isabelle with a grin. 'However, Arthur tells me Hillyards are just about the best boat-builders there are. You'll love it, Betty. We can take a picnic and make a day of it. If you bring your bathing things, we can bathe off the boat.'

'If we take the dingy we can land on a beach,' said Arthur. 'There's all sorts of little coves and beaches along the coast you can only get to by sea.'

'That sounds lovely,' said Betty. 'Let's do it.'

The conversation turned to boats, sailing and places to picnic. Jack joined in enthusiastically, grateful to think of something else than that hideous sight by the river. And all the time, he couldn't rid himself of a niggling feeling that he'd missed something important.

Edward Ashley paused outside the garden gate of the trim, square-built house with its manicured lawn, regimented flower beds, squared-off privet hedges and sighed. Breaking the bad news to relatives was a job he absolutely loathed but it had to be faced.

Bracing himself, he walked up the path and rang the bell. It was answered by the maid, a round-faced, comfortable-looking, country girl. The girl's eyes widened as he handed her his card. 'This is an official visit, I'm afraid,' he said. 'If your mistress is in, I do need to see her.'

'The mistress is at home, sir,' she said breathlessly, obviously agog with curiosity. 'If you'll come in and wait, I'll tell her you're here.'

She hung up his coat and hat and, leaving him in the hall, went into a room off to one side. Ashley could hear the low murmur of voices.

The entrance hall was as orthodox, neat and uninspiring as the front garden. It was papered in dark Lincrusta which was, as Ashley knew, excellent for not showing the dirt but always made him feel mildly depressed. Above the dado rail hung various prints of pictures he'd seen many times before. All Edwardian favourites whose preferred subject seemed to be droopy females painted in various shades of brown.

If Mrs Enid Martin's choice of decoration was a reflection of Mrs Martin's personality, he judged her to be old-fashioned, conventional and painfully respectable. However, even though she probably wasn't someone he could ever warm too, he had to break some rotten news.

Dr Lucas had found traces of the tattoo and, what seemed to clinch the matter, confirmed the man had broken two ribs in the past. What he had also found – Ashley had seen them for himself – were slashes on the ribs that could have only been caused by a knife. The man had been stabbed. Murdered.

He remembered that lunchtime in the Cat and Fiddle with Haldean a couple of months ago when Haldean, a wicked gleam in his eye, had suggested Derek Martin had been murdered. He had, he'd said, just been throwing ideas around, chiefly for the pleasure of seeing Ashley's reaction or . . . had it really been nothing more than a joke?

Because Haldean had suggested that Derek Martin had been murdered by his wife in order to steal the diamonds. And in the pocket of Derek Martin's jacket, where they'd slipped through a hole in the lining, Dr Lucas had found two diamonds. That suggested a quarrel over the loot. Exactly what Haldean had guessed.

The door from the sitting room into the hall opened and the maid dropped a small curtsey. 'Will you come in please, sir?'

Mrs Martin was sitting bolt upright in a stiff-backed chair, his card on a salver beside her. 'Thank you, Clara, that will be all,' she said in dismissal to the maid. 'Superintendent, please take a seat.'

'Thank you for seeing me, ma'am,' said Ashley. She said nothing. Feeling slightly awkward, Ashley plunged on. 'It concerns your son, Derek.' She raised her eyebrows inquisitively but still said nothing. 'Before I say anything else, can I ask if your son ever broke a couple of ribs?'

That did get a response. Evidently surprised, she drew back in her chair. 'Has he ever broken his ribs?' She thought for a moment. 'Why, yes. It was while he was in Florida. There was an accident on a boat. He mentioned it in a letter, but that was quite some time ago. I'm glad to say he made a complete recovery. Why?'

That settled it, thought Ashley gloomily. Not that he doubted Tom Jago, but it was as well to get what confirmation he could. Here goes. 'I'm sorry to say, ma'am, I've got some very bad news.'

He spared her the more gruesome details but as he related the bare facts he was puzzled by her response. She certainly listened – listened intently – but as he came to an end, he cleared his throat and added, 'I would like to offer my sympathies.'

'Your sympathies, Superintendent, are not required.'

'I beg your pardon?' said Ashley, taken aback.

'You seem to be under the delusion that my son is dead. What's more,' she added, with a disdainful expression, 'killed by an act of violence. That is not so.'

'But . . .' began Ashley.

'Whoever this unfortunate man is, it is not Derek. Doubtless it was some associate of the Jagos, a couple of whom I do not approve. It would not surprise me in the least that any associate of theirs was *murdered*.' She pronounced the word with a sniff.

'But . . .'

'My son and I are very close.'

'He's been in America for the last few years,' broke in Ashley. It hadn't been what he'd intended to say but he couldn't help it.

She closed her eyes wearily. 'So close, in fact, that I would know instantly if anything had befallen him. I am speaking of a spiritual connection.' Snapping her eyes open she glared at him. 'One which I do not expect you to comprehend.'

'You haven't heard from him, have you? A letter, perhaps?' That would explain her complete certainty.

She hesitated. 'It pains me to say so, but I have not. Derek was never a frequent correspondent. Granted the disgraceful story the Jagos have put out, he perhaps thinks it best not to communicate with me.'

Or he's dead, Ashley commented to himself. He swallowed manfully. 'I'm sorry ma'am, but I really think you should face the truth. His name was on his jacket.'

'His jacket? Really, Superintendent, what sort of proof is that? Doubtless Derek left his jacket at Birchen Bower and it was picked up by this other unfortunate soul.'

'Yes, but his ribs . . .'

'Other men can break their ribs. I tell you, if anything had happened to Derek, I would know. Now, Superintendent, if you have nothing more to say, I would ask that you leave.' She reached for the bell beside her.

'Very well, ma'am,' said Ashley stiffly as Clara came into the room in answer to the bell. Dr Jerry Lucas was, he knew, keen on psychology. At a guess he'd say that Mrs Martin's attitude was a way of coping with grief, but Ashley hadn't sensed any grief; just flat denial.

He sighed once more. She may deny it but Ashley had no doubts. Derek Martin had been murdered, just as Haldean, joke or not, had suggested months ago.

Steve Marston, idly reading the evening edition of the *Standard* in the bar of Clement's Hotel, could sense the interest of the woman sitting alone at the table in the corner. She took out a tiny mirror from her handbag, ostensibly to check her lipstick, glanced in his direction, and let her eyes meet his.

Grinning, Steve let his gaze fall and, picking up his newspaper and whisky, stood up and walked to her table. 'D'you mind if I join you?'

'Sure! I'd be glad of the company. I'm waiting for a friend but he hasn't showed up.'

The friend he thought, was fictitious but that was, all things considered, a good thing. Was the accent – a honey-coated American accent – fictitious as well? 'Are you from the States?'

Her eyes widened in a smile. There was a definite invitation in the smile. 'Well, yeah, I am. Ain't you the bright boy?' There was no sarcasm, only admiration in her voice and Steve couldn't help but preen himself.

The accent was real, he decided. Unlike her hair colour, but what the hell. She was a peroxide blonde, attractive, generously proportioned and interested. 'Can I get you a drink?'

'Why, thanks. I'll have a highball.' He turned to the waiter and snapped his fingers. As he gave the order for drinks, she wriggled a bit closer. 'It's real nice of you . . .' The light had caught the folded newspaper on the table. She stopped and swallowed.

Steve glanced down. The front page of the *Standard* featured a lurid account of the 'gruesome discovery' at Birchen Bower.

'Things like that scare me,' she breathed, looking up at him with big eyes. 'Unless I was with someone to look after me, that is.'

That was a cue if ever he'd heard one. 'I'd do that.'

She looked delighted. 'I guess you would, too. My name's Cindy. Cin for short.' She giggled. 'I guess it's more appropriate.'

*   *   *

Steve blinked himself into drowsy wakefulness, some instinct warning him to keep quiet.

In the shadowy light cast by the street light outside Clement's Hotel, he could see the woman he had met in the hotel bar that evening. *Cindy. Call me Cin.*

She was fully dressed, which certainly hadn't been the case earlier. He raised his head. She was very quietly going through the things on the dressing table. He heard her give a little grunt of satisfaction and heard the crackle of paper. His wallet!

He slipped out of bed. Cindy, intent on his wallet, didn't hear him until he was a few steps behind her. She dropped the banknotes and whirled, a silver pistol in her hand.

As he made a leap for the gun, she fired, the shot like a thunderclap in the silent room.

The bullet went wide and then he was on her. He wrenched the gun out of her hand, wrestled her down onto the bed, and stood panting, the gun pointed at her.

To his surprise, she laughed. 'What you gonna do now, big boy?'

'See you nailed for this.'

Her grin widened. 'Hadn't you better put some pants on first? And what you gonna say to your wife? You know, the one who doesn't appreciate you?'

'I . . .'

What he was going to say was drowned in a series of shouts and running footsteps along the corridor, followed by a pounding at the door. 'Oi! You in there! Open up!'

'Stay there!' he snarled at Cindy. 'All right!' he yelled in answer to the knocking. Swearing, he picked up his trousers from the floor and hitched them up while she looked on, highly amused.

Striding to the door, he flung it open. A burly porter, followed by two other men, crowded into the room. They stopped short when they saw the gun in his hand.

'It's her's . . .' he started to explain.

'Give me that,' said the porter, cutting in.

Steve put the gun into the outstretched hand. The porter, gun in one hand, dropped the other hand onto his shoulder. 'You're going straight to the police, mate.'

'She's the one who fired the damn thing!' Steve protested,

but they were three to one. Reluctantly, he allowed himself to be ushered downstairs. His only satisfaction was that Cindy, voicing a loud string of complaints, was forced to come too.

Detective Chief Inspector William Rackham concealed his distaste as he looked at the woman on the other side of the desk.

Her lavishly powdered cheeks and vivid scarlet lipstick may, for all he knew, have looked all right in artificial light but in the sunshine flooding the room it merely looked artificial. Hard as nails in his opinion, for all the aura of cheap glamour she exuded.

'Well?' she demanded, blowing out a cloud of cigarette smoke. 'What's happened to the boyfriend? Steve?'

'He was released without charge this morning,' said Bill stiffly.

She snorted in disgust. 'And you think that's fair? I thought you guys on this side were fair. Do me a favour, why don't you?'

'You attempted to rob him and fired a gun when he tried to stop you.'

'So what?' She blew out another cloud of smoke. 'Some ginks believe they get it for free. Like it's their beautiful blue eyes that I'm sweet on or sumfin.' Her expression hardened. 'Everyone pays. Now, that's fair. You think he's one of the good guys?'

Bill shook his head. 'I think he's stupid but he's done nothing against the law.' He pulled a file on the desk towards him and tapped it with his forefinger. 'Now you, on the other hand, Miss Lyne, seem to have been quite busy since you graced these shores. Your fingerprints have been found at no less than seven hotels where a robbery took place.'

'Yeah, yeah, yeah. You've got a lot of dumb-bells in this town. As I say, everyone pays.' She flicked the stub of her cigarette onto the floor and ground it out. 'I can tell you, this dame you're so interested in . . .'

'Jean Martin,' put in Bill.

'Yep, Jean Martin, now what game's she on? Sumfin good, I'd say.'

'You stated to my sergeant that you'd seen Jean Martin last week,' said Bill, which was, indeed, the reason why he was conducting this interview.

'Yeah.' She looked at him shrewdly. 'You doing a deal?'

Bill shook his head.

'You'd better. Because I can tell you that what I read in the papers was just bullshit. A hundred per cent hogwash.' She raised an inquisitive eyebrow. 'Interested now?'

Bill leaned back in his chair. 'Go on,' he said cautiously. 'We'll see what happens *if* your information's good. There's no free pass on offer, but if you're co-operative, it won't do you any harm.'

She lit another cigarette and looked at him thoughtfully. 'OK. If that's the best deal, I'll buy it. Derek Martin's dead, right? And it said in the paper that the police are looking for Jean Martin in . . . in . . .' She paused, trying to recall the unfamiliar phrase.

'In connection with their enquiries?' prompted Bill.

Cindy Lyne nodded. 'S'right. That means you think she bumped him off?'

Bill hesitated. Yes, of course that's what the phrase meant but it went against the grain to acknowledge it. 'Go on,' he said cautiously.

She blew out a long mouthful of smoke. 'I saw Jean Martin last week.'

Bill sat up alertly. 'Did you, by Jove?'

'Yep. She didn't see me. She was coming out of one of those fancy stores in Knightsbridge.'

'Did you speak to her?'

'Nah. There's reasons.' She shrugged. 'Besides, she was always far too good for the rest of us in the gang.'

'Gang? What gang?'

'The rum-running gang, of course. What other gang would I mean? The rest of us girls, well, we handed out a bit more than sweetners to the cops, if you get what I mean.' She flashed him a very meaningful smile. 'I like red-headed boys. Like you.'

Bill drew back. 'If you try to offer me any form of induce-ment – *any* form, Miss Lyne – this interview will be terminated immediately.'

She opened her eyes wide. 'Are you guys for real?'

'Just go back to talking about Jean Martin,' he said evenly.

She gave a petulant wriggle of her shoulders. 'Suit yourself. OK. Jean wasn't one of the girls. Not in that way, I mean. She was just a real goody two shoes and thought herself better 'n the rest of us. Her guy, Derek, he was the boss. No one messed around with his girl.'

'She was his wife.'

She shrugged. 'Whatever.' She knocked the ash off her cigarette. 'She was just crazy about him. He was a real tough guy only . . .' She frowned in concentration.

'Only what?'

'He didn't act tough,' she said after a few moment's thought. 'But his temper – it used to kinda come outa nowhere. I guess it might be the accent that fooled us – you Britishers all talk like you've got too many teeth or sumfin – but we were all a bit scared of him. Even Vern knew enough to be careful and he could be real dumb at times.'

Bill glanced at the file. 'Is that Vernon or Vern Stoker?'

'Sure. That's the boy. Him and me . . . Well, we had a good thing going, you know?'

For the first time, Bill saw a flicker of genuine emotion under the carapace of cynicism. To his surprise, he felt a stab of sympathy for her. They'd *had* a good thing going, he noted.

'So what happened?' he asked. 'To you and Vern Stoker, I mean?'

'You know about the fight on the boat? With the coastguard?' Bill nodded. 'Well, Vern was real mad. Martin had whipsawed the boys and Vern knew it.'

'Whipsawed?'

'Cheated,' she translated. 'Yep. Vern wanted to get even. Vern knew that Jago, the fancy dude Martin worked for, was sending him and Jean to England, but that didn't stop Vern. If Martin was going to England, Vern was going right after him. And,' she added with a cynical smile, 'after the run-in with the coastguard it was probably healthier for Vern to disappear as well.'

'So the two of you came to England?'

'You've got it. Vern hired a guy, a 'tec to find out where Jago was and he came up with the name of this place that's in the papers.'

'Birchen Bower?'

'That's the one.'

'So what happened?'

For the second time Bill caught a genuine emotion. 'He went to find Martin,' she said with a catch in her voice. 'I guess he met him, too.'

Bill looked at her sharply. 'Are you suggesting that Vern Stoker killed Derek Martin?'

'Well, sure as hell Jean Martin didn't kill him. I knew her, remember? What I'm telling you is, there's no way, no how, that Jean would've bumped off Martin. She was crazy about the guy. He was stuck on her, too.'

Bill looked up alertly. The second victim at Birchen Bower had, he knew, been identified as Derek Martin but if Vern Stoker was on the scene as well . . .

Two men, literally daggers drawn, and one man killed. The question was, which man was it? 'Had Vern Stoker ever broken a couple of ribs?'

Cindy Lyne raised her pencilled eyebrows. 'What sort of question is that? I was his girl, not his nurse.'

'So had he?'

She shrugged. 'He might've done. Likely so. Why not? He was a real tough guy and liked a fight.' She smiled slowly. 'Once he lost it, I'd back him against anyone, even Martin.'

Bill leaned forward. 'You do realise, Miss Lyne, that you've just accused Vern Stoker of murder?'

She shook her head, unimpressed. 'Nah.'

'Derek Martin was stabbed.'

'And you think Martin wouldn't pull a knife? It's a fight, yeah? That ain't murder. That's just two guys in the gang. Back home, the cops wouldn't take no notice.'

'This isn't America,' said Bill evenly.

She blew out another mouthful of smoke. 'Tell me sumfin I don't know, why don't you?'

'Have you heard from Vern Stoker? Has he written, perhaps?'

She gave a crack of laughter, genuinely amused. 'Vern *write*? Gee, he ain't no scholar. Besides, where would he write me?'

And that was true enough, commented Bill to himself.

'Look, mister,' she continued. 'Vern's no college boy, but he's smart enough to lie low. He'll show up again when the heat's off, but in the meantime . . .'

She looked at him with a return of the cynical smile. 'That's why I'm playing the hotel game with guys who think they can get it for free.'

Jack put down the telephone and went back into the drawing room.

'Well?' demanded Betty with breathless interest. 'What did Bill have to say?'

Jack looked at his wife and Isabelle and laughed. 'Blimey! You look as if you could model for a painting called *Expectation* or something.'

Standing by the sideboard, Arthur grinned and reached for the whisky. 'Here, drink that,' he said, putting the glass into Jack's hand. 'These two have been beside themselves to hear what Bill said.'

Jack added a splash of soda, settled into an armchair and lit a cigarette. 'The headline news is that the police have arrested Vern Stoker's girlfriend.'

'Who's . . .' began Arthur, then stopped. 'Hang on. He was part of the rum-running gang, wasn't he?'

'That's right. And according to Bill, the girlfriend, one Miss Cindy Lyne, is a real piece of work. However, she did come up with an interesting piece of evidence.'

As succinctly as he could, he ran through the gist of his telephone call.

'Jean Martin's in London?' repeated Isabelle blankly.

'But surely that means she's innocent,' said Betty with a frown. 'If she really had killed her husband, surely she'd try and get as far away as possible. This Cindy Lyne doesn't sound like the most reliable witness but I can't see why she'd make up a story like that.'

Arthur pursed his lips. 'She might, if she was trying to do a deal with the police.'

Isabelle shook her head. 'Not that story, Arthur. She might say she'd seen Derek Martin, perhaps, but why invent something that drops her boyfriend right in it? If she really was his girl-friend, that is.'

'Bill seemed convinced she was genuine on that point,' said Jack, circling his whisky round in its glass.

'She doesn't sound much of a girlfriend,' said Arthur, unimpressed. 'Not if she's happy to call Stoker a killer.'

Jack shrugged. 'That didn't seem to bother her. In fact, if anything, she admired him for it. As far as she was concerned, it was two gangsters slugging it out, which seemed pretty commonplace to her.'

'Does Ashley know about this?' asked Arthur.

Jack nodded. 'Yes, of course. Bill spoke to Ashley before he called me. Ashley doesn't want Vern Stoker's name to come out at this stage, so he's going to ask for the inquest to be adjourned.'

'That's probably just as well,' said Arthur. 'No point warning the blighter he's wanted by the police.'

'Yes, but . . .' began Isabelle with a frown. 'Hang on. It couldn't be the other way round, I suppose? What if it was Vern Stoker who was killed and Derek Martin's the killer?'

'That can't be it,' said Betty. 'If the Martins really are a devoted couple they'd be together, and why on earth should they be together in London? They'd escape as soon as they could. Besides that, don't we know it's Martin who was killed? His jacket's neither here or there, I suppose, but we do know he had two broken ribs.'

Isabelle frowned in concentration. 'I know his mother is convinced he's alive, but that's just wishful thinking. Jack, what d'you think?'

Jack clicked his tongue. 'I agree about the wishful thinking. You're right, too, Betty. If Martin was alive, he'd hardly be wandering round London.'

'M'yes,' agreed Arthur. He picked up his pipe and, reaming it out, stuffed tobacco into the bowl. 'Do the dates tie up? For Stoker and Miss Lyne to be in England at the same time as the Martins, I mean?'

'Yes, they do. Stoker knew he was wanted by the American police and, according to Miss Lyne, was desperate to get even with Martin, so the pair of them did a runner and arrived in Southampton a couple of days after the Martins.' He shrugged impatiently. 'What does puzzle me is why the Martins were still at Birchen Bower. I'd have expected them to take the diamonds and leave right away.'

'Maybe they were planning their escape,' said Betty. 'And why should they rush? After all, they couldn't know Stoker was after them.'

'No, that's true.'

'It has to be Martin who was killed,' said Arthur. 'There were two diamonds in his pocket. I can't see why Stoker would have any diamonds on him.'

'Unless Martin was trying to buy him off,' said Isabelle thoughtfully. She shook her head. 'No, that won't work. If Stoker's got the diamonds, Jean Martin would hardly be shopping in Harrods or wherever. What does strike me as peculiar is how long it took for the body to be found. I know Sir Havelock Thingy said a jaguar had carried it about, but that sounds too ridiculous for words. I just can't believe it.'

'You might, if you'd heard the sound we heard,' said Betty. 'Actually . . .' She paused, evidently slightly nervous. 'Arthur, you know you've talked about attacks on animals?'

Arthur looked at her inquisitively. 'Yes. Go on.'

'Well, they do chime in with the legend,' she said in a rush. 'And I was very struck by Sir Havelock's account of how a jaguar would behave, how it needs so much territory and so on.'

'Don't tell me you believe in the legend,' said Isabelle. 'That's ridiculous.'

Betty turned a troubled face to hers. 'Is it? I don't want to believe it, of course I don't, but if the thing in the woods doesn't act like a real jaguar would, then maybe it's not a real jaguar but the princess.' She looked at her husband. 'You've got to admit it's a theory.'

Jack laughed. 'It's a theory all right. A mental theory but a theory.'

'Is it? Really that mental, Jack?'

Jack started to speak, then hesitated. 'All right. What's on your mind?' He smiled encouragingly. 'I can tell you've got an idea.'

'It was meeting Simon Lefevre that's really made me think of this,' she admitted. 'You know, the psychical researcher. He's uncovered loads of frauds but also plenty of things he can't explain.' She gave an impish grin. 'I don't know if you'll like him but I'm sure he'd come down if I asked him. He took quite a shine to me.'

'Did he, by Jove!' said Jack indignantly. 'The cheeky beggar.'

'Oh, don't worry,' said Betty dismissively. 'He was very

polite but I could tell, you know? Anyway, as we've had an expert in real jaguars, what about an expert in unreal ones, so to speak? The Jagos would have to agree, of course, but I think it's worth doing. If they write to him and I drop him a line as well, the Birchen Bower legend is so well known I'm sure Mr Lefevre would be happy to investigate it.' She looked appealingly at her husband. 'Jack? What d'you think?'

Jack drummed his fingers on the arm of his chair, then laughed. 'All right. As long as he confines himself to investigating imaginary jaguars, why not? There's one thing, though. If your precious Simon Lefevre does come, I want to be in on it.'

'Jack!' said Isabelle, shocked. 'You can't believe the legend. It's all nonsense. It has to be.'

Jack picked up his whisky. 'Is it?'

'Of course it is,' said Isabelle crossly.

'Well, I think it's a damn good idea, Betty,' he said, raising his glass to her. He smiled slowly, his eyes bright. 'Because don't you see, Belle, if there is any sort of rannygazoo going on, I want to know.'

ELEVEN

The following morning, Jack and Betty called on Tom and Rosalind Jago. As the maid showed them into the drawing room, Tom Jago rose to greet them with a wry expression.

'Come on in, Major. Mrs Haldean, good to see you again. I don't suppose you've found yet another body, have you?'

'Tom!' said his wife, shocked. 'You mustn't joke about such things.'

He rubbed his face with his hands. 'No, I guess I shouldn't.' He gestured to a chair and looked wearily at Jack. 'It's strange to think that this time last week all that was on my mind was the fete.'

'It's been a long week,' agreed Jack, sitting down. 'Last Saturday I was putting up tents with Dusty Miller.'

'And since then . . .' Jago shrugged expressively. He cocked his head to one side, looking at Jack. 'You'll excuse me asking, Major, but is this just a social call? I guess Rosie and I have got kinda twitchy. I feel as if there should be something we should do, but I'm damned if I can think what.'

'As a matter of fact, that's what we've come about,' said Jack. He looked at Betty. 'This is your idea. Over to you.'

Gathering her thoughts, Betty plunged into an account of her meeting with Simon Lefevre, only to be stopped short by Tom Jago.

'Hold on! The guy wrote me soon after we moved in. He wanted to look into the legend. At the time we were fixing the house so visitors were out of the question.'

'And he was a complete stranger,' added Rosalind. 'For all we knew, he was some sort of con man. You say he's on the level, Mrs Haldean?'

'He's a well-known man with a good few books to his credit. He does quite a bit of public speaking, too.'

Rosalind looked at her husband. 'Well, Tom, what d'you think?'

He got up and paced slowly round the room, stopping to lean his hands on the back of the sofa where she was sitting.

'Let's do it,' he said eventually. He raised his head and looked at Jack and Betty. 'You may think I'm crazy but the more I find out about the legend, the less sceptical I am. There's a heap of old papers in the library which give the history of the Caydens. They were real tough guys.'

'I know they had a reputation as smugglers,' said Jack. 'Not that that's unusual on this coast but they seemed to run the whole show for miles around.'

Jago nodded. 'Yep. They were the big cheeses, sure enough. Successful, too. If anyone else tried to muscle in, they didn't last long. The thing is, in the papers I'm talking about, there's references to "unleashing the jaguar".'

'Are there?' said Jack, startled.

'Yep. And that's followed by accounts of men found as we found Burstock and . . .' His voice wavered. '. . . And Derek.'

He was silent for a few moments, then shrugged. 'The thing is, in Florida I'd have laughed at the idea of a legend coming to life. But now? I d'know. I wouldn't mind this Lefevre guy taking a look at those papers and the chapel. There's Josiah Cayden's book too. I'll write him today. It'll be interesting to see what he thinks.' He very nearly smiled. 'Lefevre might find an answer, even if it's one that your pal, Ashley, won't accept.'

'Shall I write to him as well?' asked Betty.

'Sure. And, as you've met the guy, you'd be very welcome to come to dinner.' This time he did smile. 'Let's call it a date.'

Simon Lefevre replied to Betty in a letter dripping with enthusiasm. Three days later, dinner at the Jagos well underway, Jack had a chance to sum up Simon Lefevre for himself.

Betty had warned him he probably wouldn't take to Simon Lefevre but that was an understatement. The man made his hackles rise.

He must be, thought Jack, nudging fifty, a sleek beggar with an old-fashioned manner, a gold-rimmed monocle and a suspiciously black imperial beard. He bowed over Betty's hand, murmuring 'dear lady' in an Edwardian way. From the way his eyes widened when he was introduced to Rosalind Jago, he clearly very much appreciated her, too.

A ladies' man, decided Jack. He wouldn't like Betty to be alone with him. An Edwardian ladies' man, with what, Jack was prepared to bet, was a carefully cultivated and slightly sinister air of mystery which led to brief speculations on how exotic his private life was.

If it was as exotic as his taste in literature, then it didn't bear investigation. Mr Lefevre had arrived that morning, paid a short visit to the chapel, then spent the rest of the day in the library, wallowing in the Cayden family papers. He was bowled over by finding Josiah Cayden's *The Dark Heart*.

He had the book on the dinner table beside him and constantly ran nervous, fluttering fingers over the cover.

'This book,' said Simon Lefevre, his eyes alight, 'is the most wonderful find. I knew it existed but even the British Museum doesn't possess a copy.' He caressed the cover of the book lovingly. '*The Dark Heart*. Have you any idea how rare this volume is?'

Tom Jago shook his head with a smile. 'I can't say I do, no.

I turned it up in the library, quite by chance.' He looked across the room to Jack. 'You've read it, haven't you?'

'That's right,' agreed Jack then, seeing an explanation was called for, added, 'my friend's aunt has a copy.'

Lefevre drew his breath in with a greedy hiss. 'Two copies! I wouldn't be surprised if they were the only copies extant. That's utterly remarkable.'

The most remarkable thing about it, thought Jack, was that if Arthur's Aunt Catherine had the slightest idea what the book contained, she wouldn't have it in the house.

Lefevre fixed Jack with a penetrating stare. 'Have you read it?'

'Yes,' said Jack then, forcing himself to be polite, added, 'I found it . . . interesting.'

Lefevre shot him an appraising glance then, with a dismissive smile, turned away. Jack knew he'd been summed up and found wanting.

He took a conscious grip on himself. After all, Betty was doing her bit, the dinner was excellent and the conversation good. Rosalind was more relaxed than Jack had ever seen her and Jago was a very good host.

As much as he disliked Lefevre, he wanted to be included in any scheme the man cooked up to look into the legend. He had to play up to him. 'There are some fascinating theories advanced in the book,' he said. 'I'd value your opinion on them, sir.'

Lefevre steepled his fingers together. 'The ideas are, as you say, fascinating. The only way to evaluate the truth is to carry out a proper experiment. A psychic experiment.'

'Are you going to take another look at the tomb in the chapel, Mr Lefevre?' asked Rosalind. Her voice, when she wasn't bored to death or having forty fits, was actually very attractive, thought Jack.

'With your permission, dear lady, I would very much appreciate the opportunity to do so. I wanted to include the stories surrounding Anna-Maria Cayden, in my latest book, *Folklore and Legends*.'

He ran his fingers over *The Dark Heart* once more. 'However, without this most valuable resource, I was unable to find anything more than the unsubstantiated rumours mentioned in Lamont's *Rambles in Sussex and Hampshire Byways*.'

'You can look all you like and welcome, Mr Lefevre,' said Tom Jago. 'I'll give you any help I can. As you know, we've had two deaths.'

'Yes, an account was in the newspapers,' said Lefevre. 'Both bodies had been mauled, hadn't they? As if by a jaguar,' he added with satisfaction.

Tom Jago winced. 'So our expert, Sir Havelock Dane, said.'

'What have the police had to say?'

Jago snorted in disgust. 'The police? The famous British police that we hear so much about? They haven't a clue.' He glanced at Jack. 'Unless you know anything, Haldean?'

No one, thought Betty, could've doubted the innocence of Jack's expression. 'If they do, they haven't told me,' he said with a smile.

'Derek Martin's mother refuses to believe he's dead,' said Rosalind with an ironic twist in her voice. 'Tom offered to pay for the funeral but she wasn't grateful.'

'Well, I guess she doesn't think she's anything to be grateful for.'

Rosalind was gearing up for a reply when Betty intervened. She knew quite enough about Rosalind Jago's opinion of Enid Martin not to want it aired at the dinner table.

'I'm interested in the book, Mr Lefevre,' she said, looking at the copy of *The Dark Heart* beside Lefevre. She gave a wide-eyed, innocent smile. 'What's it about?'

Jack suppressed a grin. Betty knew exactly what it was about, because he'd told her, with derogatory comments. *Josiah Cayden's attempt to invent a new religion. It's loony.*

Simon Lefevre virtually purred. 'It's hard to sum up in a few words, dear lady. In essence, of course, it's a way to achieve what all men want. Power. Power,' he repeated, evidently savouring the word.

Rosalind Jago looked blank. 'Power? What sort of power?'

'Psychic power. Spiritual power. Using things of the spirit to control men's minds.' He turned to Jack. He'd obviously sensed his antagonism. 'Or don't you agree?'

'Absolutely I agree,' said Jack with total honesty, adding, in the privacy of his own thoughts, the rider that although he agreed with Lefevre's opinion of the book's contents, he loathed them.

He gave a smile which everyone, apart from Betty, read as eager enthusiasm. 'I was fascinated by the historical basis for his theories. It's all based on Inca beliefs, or his reading of them, at least.'

Mr Lefevre screwed his monocle into his eye, looking on Jack with approval. 'Exactly, Major.'

'I don't know anything about Incas,' said Rosalind. 'Are they some sort of South American Indians?'

'The Incas,' said Simon Lefevre, with a faint note of reproof, 'had the largest empire in South America. From their capital, Cusco, in Peru, they ruled over nearly a million square miles.'

'Gosh,' said Betty, impressed. 'So what happened to them?'

Lefevre heaved a deep sigh. 'The Spanish, dear lady. The Spanish and Christianity. However . . .' He caressed the cover of *The Dark Heart* once more. 'I'm glad to say Josiah Cayden appreciated their ideas. They were polytheistic, of course.'

'They were what?' asked Rosalind Jago.

'They believed in many gods,' explained Lefevre. 'The king, the Sapa Inca, as he was called, was believed to be divine.'

'Like the Romans,' said Betty intelligently. 'Their emperor was meant to be a god, wasn't he?'

'Exactly, dear lady,' replied Lefevre. 'However, unlike the Romans, they practised human sacrifice.'

Betty winced. 'That's pretty nasty.'

'Yes, but understandable, wouldn't you say? It's surprisingly common in ancient civilisations. It's a way of marking their most significant occasions, such as the death of the Sapa Inca.' His eyes gleamed with a fervour that made Betty feel uncomfortable. 'After all,' he continued, 'what could be more fitting to mark the passing of a great king and a god by sending him into the afterlife with servants to do his bidding?'

'How different from the funeral of our own dear Queen,' muttered Jack, unable to help himself. Betty gave a snort of laughter.

Simon Lefevre looked put out. 'I hope, Major Haldean, you are going to treat any investigation in a truly objective spirit.'

Jack looked suitably abashed. Betty turned away, desperate

not to catch his eye and disgrace herself with another giggle. She knew that expression only too well.

Lefevre tapped the book. 'Josiah Cayden appreciated the rare chance given to him by his ancestors to revive Inca practices. He honoured the memory of Anna-Maria Cayden and was convinced of her continued existence as the Jaguar Princess. He gives specific instructions on how to summon up the princess. "Unleash the jaguar", as the fascinating family papers put it.'

Tom Jago looked alarmed. 'Say, Lefevre, isn't that dangerous?'

Lefevre smiled indulgently. 'Do not concern yourself, Mr Jago. I have means of arranging protection.'

His tone altered, slipping into his public speaker mode. 'Cayden gives the specific times when we may hope for success. It all depends on the phases of the moon. These instructions I intend to follow to the letter by the tomb of the princess. "My soul is among lions, even the sons of men, whose teeth are spears and arrows",' he quoted in satisfaction, rubbing his hands together. 'The Inca believed that the dead could take physical form and counsel the living on specific days of the year. I have checked the phases of the moon and the day after tomorrow is, I am glad to say, the perfect time for my experiment. That will give me enough time to make thorough preparations.'

'This experiment,' said Jack in a suitably hesitant voice. 'Could I be in on it? I really want to know if there's any substance in Josiah Cayden's remarkable ideas.'

'Permission, my dear sir, rests with our host and hostess,' said Lefevre, turning to Tom Jago.

Jago shrugged. 'You're welcome, Haldean. The more the merrier, I guess. Obviously I'm going to be there. It's my property, after all.' He looked at Jack with a frown. 'You're gonna treat this seriously though, aren't you?'

'I'll treat the occasion with the seriousness it deserves,' said Jack solemnly. He saw Betty's eyes sparkle as Lefevre nodded gravely, completely missing the double meaning.

Tom Jago didn't though, judging from his expression. 'I think you need to approach the experiment, to call it that, with an open mind.'

'But I will,' protested Jack. 'Sir Havelock Dane suggested we were dealing with a jaguar that's escaped from a private collection, but there has to be more to it than that. After all, not only does the legend go back hundreds of years, but there's the odd series of attacks on animals I told you about. All that needs explaining.'

'So you do believe in a supernatural explanation, Major?' asked Lefevre, in a much friendlier voice.

Jack hesitated. 'I believe it could be supernatural, yes.' He saw Betty look at him quizzically but continued. 'There's problems with a completely natural explanation. Sir Havelock pointed those out and he really knows what he's talking about. So,' he added with a shrug, 'I'm willing to be convinced.'

'Now that,' said Lefevre approvingly, 'is a proper state of mind in which to approach the unknown.' His monocle glittered as he gave a little sigh of relish. 'It is, I may say, a truly scientific attitude. The spirits, who exist on a different plane to us earthly mortals, are sensitive to negative thoughts. I know of many cases where phenomena, phenomena that has been attested to by unimpeachable witnesses, be decried as false, simply because no manifestation took place in the presence of a sceptic.'

'You mean, if you don't believe you'll see anything, you won't see anything?' asked Rosalind.

Simon Lefevre beamed at her. 'That's exactly right, Mrs Jago. Very well put. And, of course, even in the purely earthly sphere, a failure to appear means precisely nothing.'

Jack looked at him, apparently much struck. 'You mean that just because a number sixteen bus, say, doesn't turn up, that doesn't mean that there's no such thing as a number sixteen bus?'

'Exactly right, Major,' said Lefevre fervently. He looked around the room. 'As I said, the evening of the day after tomorrow seems the perfect time and we will, of course, be in the chapel, which is the focus of the phenomenon. I take it that we three men will all be present. Do you ladies intend to join us?'

'Not me,' said Rosalind with a shudder. 'Count me out.'

'I . . .' began Betty then stopped as Jack gave an almost imperceptible shake of his head. 'I don't think I will either.' She looked at her husband. 'You don't mind, do you, darling?'

'I'd much rather you didn't. If there's any danger, I don't want you involved.'

'Is there any danger, Lefevre?' asked Tom Jago sharply.

'To us?' Lefevre shook his head positively. 'Not if you follow my guidance. I propose to enclose us inside a pentacle.'

'A what?' asked Jago.

'It's a five-pointed star, drawn on the ground, with a candle in the points of the star. There is, of course, more to it than that, but the pentacle is a sovereign defence against any manifestation I have ever investigated. However, it's vital that we all keep within the defensive ring.'

Betty glanced at Jack. Although she wouldn't have expected him to openly ridicule the idea that a chalk star, even with candles, could be any sort of defence, she did expect a raised eyebrow.

Instead he hunched forward with rapt attention. 'I've heard of such things before,' he said in all seriousness. He looked at Tom Jago. 'I can see we're going to be in safe hands.'

'It's always as well to have an expert along,' said Jago.

Jack laughed and took a sip of wine. 'Rather like tomorrow, eh, Betty? We're going sailing,' he added in explanation to the polite puzzled looks from Tom and Rosalind Jago. 'Arthur Stanton's renovated a boat and becoming quite an expert sailor.'

'Has he?' said Jago with interest. 'I've done a bit of sailing myself. What sort of boat is it?'

'It's a small yacht.'

'What size is it?'

'Size? It's about twenty-odd feet long I'd say.'

'That's pretty useful,' said Jago, knowledgably. He sat forward thoughtfully. 'Stanton wouldn't mind if I looked him up, would he? After all, we are neighbours. I've thought about buying a boat myself. I'd appreciate his advice.'

'I'm sure he'll be happy to give it,' said Jack with a grin. He turned politely to Simon Lefevre. 'Have you done any sailing, Mr Lefevre?'

'None at all,' said Lefevre, in what was obviously meant to be the last word on the subject. However, the conversation, spurred on by Jago, turned to boats and the coast, much to Simon Lefevre's evident chagrin. He gave a bored sigh and picking up *The Dark Heart*, retreated into the book for the rest of the evening.

*   *   *

'Jack,' said Betty in the car on the way home. 'Why don't you want me to come to the chapel on this ghost-hunting trip?'

'You are quick on the uptake, Betty,' he said approvingly. 'I saw you twig it right away.'

'You don't really expect the Jaguar Princess to leap out of her tomb and start savaging everyone, do you?'

He laughed. 'Certainly not. Especially with a pentacle to protect us. With candles.'

'Now I know you're pulling my leg. So why don't you want me along?'

'It's not that I don't want you along. I want you, without drawing any attention to the fact, to keep an eye on Rosalind Jago. It'll be entirely natural for you to come with me up to the house and even more natural for you to wait for our experiment, as the learned Mr Lefevre calls it, to finish.'

'I see . . .' began Betty then stopped. 'No, I don't know if I do. When I suggested the Jagos had seen off that poor man, Burstock, you said I was talking through the back of my neck.'

'I didn't put it quite like that, darling. And they absolutely couldn't have bumped off old Burstock.'

'So why do you want me to keep tabs on Rosalind Jago?'

Jack hit the steering wheel in frustration. 'Because we've got two deaths to account for and I'm damned if I know what's going on. It is, as you pointed out, on the Jagos' property but are they involved? Bill Rackham's certain the murderer is this bloke, Stoker, and he's probably right, as far as Derek Martin's concerned. There doesn't seem much mystery about that, but Burstock's another matter entirely. If anything happens in the chapel on Wednesday night I want to make sure Mrs Jago isn't responsible. If Jago's beside me in that wretched pentacle or whatever it's called, that's him ruled out, too.'

'And where does that leave us?'

Jack's lips tightened. 'Just at the moment,' he confessed, 'without a clue.'

'So could it be something supernatural, Jack?' Betty ventured cautiously. 'I couldn't work out if you were serious or not earlier on. You know, when Mr Lefevre praised your scientific attitude.'

'Scientific attitude, indeed!' said Jack with a dismissive laugh.

'That's one thing your Mr Lefevre certainly hasn't got. He's a crank, pure and simple. And a creep. You really ought to be more careful who you pick up at parties.' He said nothing for a few moments, then shrugged. 'The thing is, darling, that I have experienced things I can't explain. It's never been anything much, but it's certainly happened. Feelings, atmospheres, sometimes even more than that.'

'I think most people have had that sort of experience, Jack,' she said thoughtfully. 'I know I have. Some people won't acknowledge it of course.'

'Yes, but this is in a different league altogether. Looked at objectively, it seems half-baked to suggest that a woman who died in the seventeenth century haunts the place in the form of a jaguar.'

'"Unleash the jaguar",' Betty quoted softly.

Jack winced. 'And then mutilated bodies turn up. I know.'

'Do you believe it, Jack?'

'I believe it's in the family papers, yes. If it's true or not is another matter.' He gave a worried sigh. 'I don't believe what's in that ghastly book of Josiah Cayden's or Lefevre's paraphernalia of pentacles and candles and so on. That just seems like nonsense, and I'm fairly sure it is. So really?' He shrugged. 'I just don't know what to make of it.'

Betty was silent for a few moments. 'I was trying to be open-minded, Jack. I really was and, having met Mr Lefevre, it seemed too good an opportunity to pass up. I agree he's a crank – and a creep – but he is an expert on this sort of thing.'

'An expert in nonsense is still nonsense.'

She looked at him acutely. 'But you're worried, aren't you? You're worried there really might be some truth in the legend.'

'Having seen the state our two corpses were in, of course I'm worried. Anyone would be. And,' he added hesitantly, 'I am a Catholic. My conscience is twinging. I shouldn't be lending myself to this sort of malarkey at all.'

'Come on, sweetheart. No one's asking you to attend a séance and you're certainly not doing it for fun. This is different. And,' she added, 'the church does have a rite of exorcism for evil spirits. That must mean something.'

He didn't answer but she could see her last remark had gone

home. She reached out and, putting her hand on his knee, gave it an affectionate squeeze. 'You'll find an answer, Jack. I know you will.'

It was delightful out on the water. Jack felt his spirits lift as the *Moonstone*, with Arthur at the wheel, creamed through the waves.

He could hear Betty and Isabelle in the cabin, Betty exclaiming with delight at the neatness of the fittings, from the tiny galley and the roomy cupboards to the comfortable benches. Betty was thoroughly enjoying herself and as for himself . . .

Everything, from the creak of canvas in the rush of wind, the diamond droplets of spray, the rich varnished oak, the red of the sails and, most of all, the deep blue of the sea under a cloud-flecked sky made his dark imaginings of the night before seem like the dried-up fragments of a nightmare. He wanted to fix the colours in his mind. He wanted to paint it. He hadn't painted for ages but this was a moment worth capturing.

'She's a beautiful boat, Arthur,' said Jack, raising his voice to carry against the wind.

'She's not bad, is she?' said Arthur. The words were casual but Jack could see the pride in his eyes. 'I thought we'd take her out to sea for a while, put her through her paces, then drop back to near the coast to find a cove where we can drop anchor.'

'I'm looking forward to a swim, I must say.'

'And the picnic afterwards. There's a cold chicken, ham sandwiches, cheese, hard-boiled eggs and a couple of bottles of Bollinger. And cake, of course.'

Jack grinned appreciatively. 'It doesn't sound as if we're going to starve.'

'Absolutely not.' Arthur frowned at the rigging. 'Close to shore, I'll have to tinker about with the sails.'

'I'll take your word for it, Cap'n,' said Jack with a grin. 'Just tell me which rope to pull and I'll pull it.'

'You really ought to take a proper interest in the technical side,' said Arthur, laughing. 'Talking of taking an interest, I ran into Jago in the harbour this morning. Apparently he's thinking of buying a boat.'

He frowned as he gave the wheel a couple of turns. 'I just

hope he stays at Birchen Bower. He really needs to do something about the estate.'

'Is he thinking of leaving?' asked Jack, puzzled. 'He didn't say anything last night.'

'His wife has got the wind-up about the place,' said Arthur. 'She's all for selling up. She wants to live in London or Paris. Anywhere but here.'

'I can't say I blame her but the chances of finding anyone else willing to take on Birchen Bower are nil, I'd say.'

'So would I. They'll probably end up taking a flat in town and coming down for the odd weekend. Which means,' he added gloomily, 'that the estate will probably remain a blinkin' wilderness.'

After an hour or so on the open water, Arthur turned the prow for shore and nosed his way along the coast.

'What about here?' he asked as they rounded a spur of thickly-wooded cliffs and came into a cove.

Isabelle frowned. 'I'm sure we can find somewhere nicer,' she said. 'That cliff cuts all the sunlight off from the beach . . . Oh!'

As she spoke, a shaft of sunlight cut across the beach, making a brilliant golden pathway on the sand.

'What caused that?' asked Arthur.

'There must be a split in the rocks,' said Betty.

Jack snapped his fingers. 'That's it! It's more than a split, though. Look, there's a rock tower close to the cliff. It's only because the sun's at this angle we can see it.'

Isabelle picked up Arthur's field glasses and focused them on the tower. 'You're right. I say! There's a cave behind the tower.'

She handed the glasses to Jack.

'So there is,' he said. 'It must be completely hidden most of the time.' He glanced up at the sky. 'A few minutes more and it'll all be in shadow again. We talked about smugglers yesterday. That'd be a great smuggler's hide-out.'

Arthur gave a little start of surprise. 'A smuggler's hideout? I wonder if it is?'

Isabelle laughed. 'Not in this day and age, Arthur.'

'No, but years ago, I mean. I think we're pretty close to

home.' He gestured to the cliffs. Look, beyond the trees. I'm
sure that's Knep End.'

'Knep End?' asked Betty.

'One of our fields,' explained Arthur. 'I've never seen it from
the sea before. Those must be Birchen Bower woods above the
cliffs.'

'And the Caydens were smugglers,' said Jack, his eyes alight.
'I wonder if it was their hideout? I wouldn't mind having a
look.'

Betty shuddered. 'Can we go somewhere else?' she asked
impulsively. 'There's bound to be nicer beaches and we're back
at Birchen Bower tomorrow night.'

Jack squeezed her hand. 'All right,' he agreed. Despite
the sea air and the sunshine, he felt his spirits dampened.
Smugglers belonged to the exciting – and safe – world of long-
ago adventures but tomorrow night . . .

That was an entirely different matter.

TWELVE

As they picked their way along the path to the chapel,
Jack was glad to feel the weight of Arthur's old service
Webley in his pocket. Tom Jago was armed with a
shotgun but Simon Lefevre had recoiled at the thought of
carrying a gun.

'I have never,' he said severely, 'gone armed to any investigation. I wish I could've prevailed on you gentlemen to do
likewise. If the manifestation is a trick – which, in view of what
Josiah Cayden wrote, I do not for a moment believe – then my
predicament, if I shot the trickster, would be awkward in the
extreme.'

Perhaps not as awkward a predicament as the trickster's,
thought Jack, wryly. Lefevre really was a pompous beggar and
no mistake.

'If a manifestation is genuine,' continued Lefevre, 'then a
mere firearm will be useless. No, gentlemen,' he added, tapping

his large Gladstone bag, 'this contains everything we need for our defence.'

He had also frowned at the hip flask Tom Jago had slipped into his pocket to 'while the night away', and the powerful electric torch he insisted on bringing. 'If you think it absolutely necessary,' he said in a world-weary way. 'However, on no account must it be utilised inside the chapel. Natural light, such as a candle, is acceptable but I have found that electric light has a deleterious effect on the spirits.'

Jack, on the other hand, felt his spirits much relieved as the torchlight picked out the overhanging bushes and stones in the path in sharp-edged relief. This path was bad enough in full daylight and the idea of blundering their way along, helped only by a candle in a lantern, was just not on.

'How's your nerve holding up, Major?' asked Jago in a low voice.

'Not bad so far,' said Jack, the memory of that savage snarl he and Betty had heard vivid in his memory. That had been in these woods. 'I'll be glad when it's over though.'

'Me too. I don't know what to expect but I'll be glad when we're inside. This guy seems to think it all happens in the chapel, but we know different. Derek wasn't in the chapel.' He gave a sigh of relief. 'Here we are.'

They stepped out into the clearing where the chapel stood, bathed in moonlight. Jago felt in his pocket and produced the ancient key.

'Switch the torch off,' said Lefevre. 'Remember what I said about electric light.'

Jago sighed and, snapping off the torch, put it in his pocket, and unlocked the door.

They left the door open. There was enough moonlight to make out the pews and the altar, but it was still a relief when Lefevre struck a match and lit a candle. 'Let's look at the tomb,' he said, his voice quivering with excitement. 'These conditions are perfect, exactly as Josiah Cayden's book describes.'

It may have been the flickering candlelight or it may have been sheer imagination, but the figure of the leaping jaguar seemed more *alive* than Jack remembered. If he let himself, he could imagine that figure moving . . .

He took a firm grip on his nerves and ran a hand over the stone carving on the box tomb. Stone. Solid. Immovable. Stone.

Beside him, Tom Jago made an unhappy noise in his throat. 'Rosie wants to leave this place,' he said quietly. 'I guess I'm coming round to that idea.' He looked around and shivered. 'I wanted a country estate. I seem to have landed us in some sort of Gothic novel.'

'You mustn't let your imagination run away with you,' said Lefevre severely. 'And, once the pentacle is completed, gentlemen, on no account must you leave it.'

He held the candle high and, looking round, walked to the altar, standing in the space between the altar steps and the first line of pews, frowning in dissatisfaction. 'I hoped there would be room enough here, but there isn't enough space to make a large enough pentacle.'

He climbed the steps up to the altar, holding the candle aloft. The belfry door stood open, the belfry dimly lit by the faint light from the windows.

'What about the belfry?' asked Jago. 'Is there enough room in there?'

Lefevre led the way into the belfry. 'Ah!' he said in gratifica-tion. 'This is perfect. The altar cuts off a view of the right-hand side of the chapel, but the tomb is clearly visible.'

Taking a stick of white chalk from his bag, he bent down and drew a large five-pointed star on the stone flags. 'I'll complete the pentacle once we are safely inside.' In the point of each star he placed a large pillar candle. Standing up, he looked at his work with satisfaction. 'Mr Jago? Major Haldean? If you could join me inside the pentacle, I can proceed with the rest of the preparations.'

Jack and Tom Jago exchanged wary glances, then, rather unwillingly, joined Lefevre.

'What happens now?' asked Jago. 'Do we just wait and see what happens?'

'By no means,' said Lefevre earnestly. 'Josiah Cayden left detailed instructions for the procedure of calling up the Jaguar Princess.' He gave a wintery smile. 'You need not be alarmed, gentlemen. If we stay inside the pentacle, we will be perfectly safe.'

Jack frowned. 'Hang on. You're talking about calling up the Jaguar Princess. I don't know about Derek Martin, but I can't see poor old Burstock calling up any sort of spirit. I doubt he was that sort of man and, for another thing, he surely wouldn't know how.'

Lefevre screwed his monocle firmly into his eye. 'You are making a very elementary mistake, Major. Simply because there is a ritual for calling up the princess, that doesn't mean that the princess is bound by the ritual. I imagine the spirit can appear at any time if she so desires.'

Tom Jago looked thoughtful. 'I guess that answers a question I had. You were keen that we should do this at the first full moon, but Burstock wasn't killed at night. It was late afternoon when we found him.'

Lefevre looked rather pleased. 'That is a perfect demonstration of what I inferred. As I said, Mr Jago, the spirit will, Cayden assures us, appear in answer to the ritual, but is obviously free to manifest itself at other times. Noon, you may be interested to learn, is often associated with psychic appearances.'

'OK,' said Jago. 'I guess you must be right. So what's this ritual then?'

'As you would expect from any ritual stemming from Inca traditions, the ritual requires a blood sacrifice.'

Jack drew his breath in warily. 'Blood?'

'Yes, indeed.' Lefevre brightened with academic fervour. 'Cayden's favoured sacrifice was, of course, a jaguar. He would kill the animal beforehand and place its body on the tomb. Although he had, of course, shot the creature, he would slit the animal's throat once it was in situ, ensuring that enough blood dripped onto the tomb to be efficacious.'

Jack knew that. He'd read that passage in the book as well, but to hear it calmly detailed by a man who evidently didn't think it was sheer madness but a perfectly rational way to proceed, was chilling.

'Now,' continued Lefevre, 'although I can't, of course, run to a jaguar, I did think this would be an adequate substitute.' He delved into the bag and brought out first a clasp knife, then a small cage containing a white dove.

The dove, which had evidently been bounced about in

Lefevre's bag, gave an indignant squawk and ruffled its feathers defensively.

Jack swallowed hard. 'Do you intend to kill it?'

'Why yes, of course, Major,' said Lefevre in surprise. 'The book is quite clear. We need blood.'

'No!' Jack's stomach twisted in revulsion. 'No, you're not. I don't care what that lunatic, Cayden, wrote.'

Lefevre, cage in hand, looked astonished. 'What possible objection could you have? The ritual is quite clear. It's only a bird. I bought it specifically for this purpose.'

'Damnit, no!'

Lefevre put down the cage and ran a hand through his hair in perplexity. 'You're not a vegetarian by any chance, Major?'

'Of course I'm not.'

'Then I fail to see any logic in your objection. I presume you've been invited to shooting parties in your time? I imagine you've shot many a bird before now.'

'I've shot *men* before now,' said Jack, his voice icy. 'That was in the war and, believe you me, it's not something you forget easily. What I've never done is killed anything without a good and proper reason. What's written in that blasted book isn't any sort of reason.'

Tom Jago moved uneasily. 'If it's part of the ritual, Major, we'd better let it go ahead.'

'No!' Jack, eyes gleaming, took a step forward to Lefevre. Betty, with her mention of exorcism, had reassured him to some extent, but this? It was like dark magic. Damnit, it *was* dark magic. He felt his skin crawl. Every instinct he had told him this was just wrong. 'Give me the knife.'

Taken aback, Lefevre dropped the knife into Jack's hand.

Jack strode out of the pentacle to the tomb. Opening the clasp knife, he held up his hand and ran the top of his ring finger across the blade. He held up his hand so the others could see. 'Look! Blood.' He pressed his finger onto the top of the tomb.

'Nothing's happened,' said Jago in a disappointed voice.

'Did you really expect it?' said Jack, trying to keep the anger out of his voice. 'It's just arrant nonsense . . .'

He broke off, coughing. A smell, a rich, unpleasant, fetid smell, filled his nostrils.

Jago stood frozen, then gave a little whimper of fear. 'It's the jungle!' His voice was a croak. 'It smells like the mangrove swamps! It's the jungle, I tell you!'

'Get back in the pentacle, Major!' commanded Lefevre, his voice urgent.

What Jack wanted to do was run. He glanced longingly at the open door with the moonlight streaming through it. He wanted to get away, get out into the open air, leave this ghastly chapel and all this idiocy behind but he'd committed himself to seeing it through. Telling himself he was a complete fool for going along with it, he walked back into the pentacle.

Lefevre gave a sigh of relief, then, chalk in hand, drew a circle round the outer points of the star. Striking a match, he lit all five candles.

'What do we do now?' asked Jago. He wrinkled his nose in disgust. 'That smell!' He pulled his handkerchief out of his pocket and held it to his mouth and nose.

'We wait,' said Lefevre in deep satisfaction. 'My word, Major, you couldn't ask for a clearer demonstration.'

'I suppose I couldn't,' said Jack dryly. The truth was, he was rattled. He'd been looking directly at Lefevre and Jago when the reek of the jungle had filled the chapel and he could swear they hadn't moved.

He pulled his cigarette case out of his pocket but Lefevre put a hand on his arm. 'No light must come from inside the pentacle,' he warned. 'You mustn't light a cigarette.'

Tom Jago sighed unhappily. 'No smoking? That's tough but I suppose if you say so. That smell's really getting to me.' He broke off, staring at the tomb. 'Did that picture – the picture on the tomb – did it move?'

Jack looked hard at the figure of the leaping jaguar. 'It's just the candlelight flickering.'

Jago rubbed his hand over his face and sat heavily on the floor. 'The trouble is, after a time you don't know what's real and what isn't.'

Jack joined Jago, sitting on the stone floor. No one said anything for what seemed an endless time. The cold of the stone struck up through his body and he shivered. What the hell was he doing, sitting on the floor in an old chapel, with the moonlight on the empty pews and the candlelight showing the dim bulk of the altar? Waiting, he told himself. Waiting to see what had savagely attacked Burstock. It *couldn't* be supernatural, could it? And all the while, that foul, rotting, jungle smell filled the air, sapping his confidence that this simply couldn't be real. As for the tomb . . . It was just the candlelight flickering, wasn't it?

Jago couldn't seem to wrench his gaze away from the tomb. 'Why jaguars for Pete's sake?' he said breaking the silence. 'What is it with jaguars?' His voice sounded strained and unnatural.

'All the South American civilisations worshipped the jaguar,' said Lefevre with the air of a lecturer. 'Josiah Cayden codified various disparate beliefs, melding them into a coherent whole. The result is one of the most remarkable books I've ever had the pleasure to read.'

And that, thought Jack, told him all he needed to know about Simon Lefevre.

'The Mayans, for instance, considered the jaguar to be the ruler of the underworld, a symbol of darkness and the night sun.'

'The night sun?' queried Jago. 'What's that?'

'It's where the sun goes to at night. It's carried through the underworld on the shoulders of its lord. Cayden has no doubt that the lord is a jaguar, citing the belief that, in the last days, the supreme god will send his jaguars to devour mankind.' Lefevre sounded pleased, if anything, at the prospect. '"Unleash the jaguar", as the Cayden family papers so happily put it, Mr Jago.'

'Marvellous,' murmured Jack, his hand to his mouth. The smell was really oppressive.

'The Aztecs, Mayans and the Inca built temples to the jaguar,' continued Lefevre. 'It's obvious why. The jaguar embodies power, ferociousness and bravery. One who is truly possessed of the spirit of a jaguar can aggressively face any fear or enemy. Because of his acute eyesight, he can see in the dark, both physically and metaphysically.'

'You've lost me there,' said Jago. 'I'm a practical man, Lefevre. What's meta whatever it was you said?'

'It's the philosophy of the first principles, principles that deal with the essence of abstract ideas.'

Jack could see Jago was still struggling with the notion.

'Ideas such as being and identity,' he said. 'That's in the book. Cayden thought he'd been imbued with an extra power that common mortals didn't possess, a power that enabled him to virtually read their minds.'

'Exactly, Major,' said Lefevre. 'The jaguar can see the dark places of the human heart. Cayden expounds at length upon the subject. The jaguar has the gift of knowledge of things to come. One of the jaguar's chief abilities is to warn of disaster.'

'I imagine a disaster would follow pretty closely on meeting any jaguar,' said Jack. It was a pretty lame joke but the truth was, he was trying to get a grip on his nerves. In the uncertain light, with that smell of rotting vegetation that seemed to stick to his hands, face and clothes, he needed some humour. Even if it was, he told himself with a shiver, graveyard humour.

Lefevre didn't like it. 'Major Haldean!' he said reprovingly. 'I have had reason before to upbraid you for unseemly levity. May I remind you that we are . . .' He broke off with a gasp. 'Something touched me!'

'What?' asked Jack, starting to his feet.

Lefevre was clearly shaken. 'I don't know. Something touched my face! Don't you see?' His voice cracked. 'We're inside the pentacle. *Nothing* should be able to touch us!'

Jago stood up, shotgun in hand. 'If someone's fooling around . . .' He broke off with a little yelp, clutching at his face. 'It's the jungle!' He saw Jack and Lefevre's puzzled faces. 'Have you never been in the jungle? There's webs, creepers, foul things.' He raised the shotgun.

'Don't shoot!' said Lefevre urgently. 'There mustn't be any light.'

Jago lowered the gun, panting slightly. 'I like to see what I'm shooting at,' he said, clearly ashamed of his nerves, then, with a startled cry, staggered back.

Jack rammed a hand against his back, just in time to stop him falling out of the pentacle. 'What the devil is it, Jago?'

Jago put a hand to his hair, then stared at his open palm in the light of the candles. 'Cobwebs,' he said shakily. 'Look!'

Jack took the grey mass from Jago's hand. It was certainly a spider's web. 'It . . . It could've fallen from the roof,' he said uncertainly. 'It could be natural.'

'Natural be damned,' snarled Jago. 'I tell you, it's the jungle!' He hefted the shotgun again.

'Don't shoot!' cried Lefevre in an agony of apprehension. He seized hold of the muzzle of the gun. 'You'll put us all in danger.'

Jago looked at him for a long moment, his mouth working in anger, then reluctantly lowered the gun. 'All right. But . . .' He shuddered. 'I can't bear spiders.'

He took a deep breath, broke open the shotgun, and sat down again. 'I'd trade the mangrove swamps for this any time,' he said eventually. 'Sure, there's alligators and jaguars too, for that matter, but at least you can see them. This is crazy. This princess – are you saying she actually became a jaguar?'

Lefevre, breathing rapidly, stood poised and watchful. After a minute or so, he relaxed and swallowed hard. 'It shouldn't be able to penetrate the pentacle,' he muttered. He looked down at Jago. 'What was that you said, Mr Jago?'

'I said, did the princess become a jaguar?'

'Assuredly, yes.'

'Come on,' said Jack. 'That has to be nonsense.'

'Nonsense you say, Major?' He adopted his public speaking manner once more. 'Some of the greatest civilisations the world has ever seen – South American civilisations – taught of the power of letting the spirit of the jaguar enter into your consciousness or soul.'

His manner, thought Jack, was probably his way of dealing with what had obviously been a moment of near panic. By making it academic, Lefevre took himself into familiar mental territory. It placed a barrier between himself and the consequences of that ghastly ritual.

'The Ancient Greeks and Romans too,' continued Lefevre, 'knew of the power of the great cats. Bacchus, for example, whom the Greeks knew as Dionysus, was nursed by panthers.'

Tom Jago was staring blankly at the tomb, the shotgun cradled on his knee. Jack was sure he hadn't taken in a word.

'I am sure you have seen,' said Lefevre, 'ancient images of Bacchus riding a chariot pulled by panthers. Those panthers were, of course, melanistic leopards. Although we usually think of Bacchus as the god of wine and excess, a more accurate reading is to link him with the gratification of desire.'

And I bet you see those desires as pretty dark, thought Jack savagely. And approve of them.

'It is fascinating to see how ancient civilisations, untouched by what we think of as progressive thought, saw the jaguar as a symbol of raw, untrammelled power.'

Tom Jago was still staring at the tomb. 'I'm sure that damn thing's moving,' he said hoarsely.

Lefevre winced but ignored him. 'Both the Aztecs and the Mayans taught of the power of becoming half-human, half-jaguar. This, I postulate, is the state that Anna-Maria Cayden entered into. That, and the ancient teaching, is something Cayden records and celebrates in his book.'

'Quiet, damn you!' said Jago suddenly. 'Listen!' He put his head to one side, straining to hear.

There was no sound, apart from Jago's rapid breathing. 'I must've imagined it,' he said shakily. He put his hand to his forehead. 'With that evil smell and whatever it was that touched me, it's too easy to imagine . . .'

He stopped abruptly. They all heard it. A series of soft thuds. Then silence.

Jack dug his nails into the palms of his hands. That sounded like footsteps. The sort of footsteps a big cat would make? He forced himself to control his breathing but he knew his heart was beating faster. The silence lengthened.

Lefevre gave a shuddering gasp. 'Footsteps,' he remarked, 'are a common psychic phenomenon. There is nothing to be alarmed about.'

Jago made a sound that was probably meant as a laugh. 'Are you kidding?' He swallowed hard. 'That damn thing's coming nearer.' He turned to Jack. 'What d'you say? Let's get out of here, shall we?'

'You mustn't leave the pentacle,' said Lefevre, his voice rising. He clapped a hand on Jago's shoulder. 'If you do, we're all in danger.'

Jago shrugged him off defiantly. 'I guess I'll go wherever I damn well please.'

'But think, man!' pleaded Lefevre. 'You came here to see if

there was any truth in the legend. We're close to the truth now! Besides that, think of what we can learn. By a stupendous chance we're in touch with the very essence of the Incas.' His monocle gleamed in the candlelight. 'Just think! We can capture some of that power for ourselves. They taught that one who lets the jaguar in can face down all his merely cultural inhibitions. He can be truly himself. All men have forbidden desires that mere convention stops them from acting upon. We all do. Cayden called upon the jaguar and it set him free to stop dreaming, to be strong, to act on his hidden desires.'

Jack stared at him. 'You think that's a good thing? To give in to every urge, to use other people, just to satisfy some hideous desire?'

Lefevre drew himself up. 'We know, thanks to Freud, how dangerous repressions can be. The Ancients knew that too.'

'Will you shut up!' snarled Jago. His voice trembled. 'I can hear those damned footsteps.'

The soft thuds sounded again. Jack shut his eyes, willing himself to keep his nerve. It was unbelievably eerie, to be trapped inside this chalk star, while those soft footfalls came nearer and nearer.

He was furious with himself, ashamed of the way his courage seemed to be draining away. The footsteps stopped, leaving a horrible, desolate silence. What the hell was the matter with him? Why was he so – better put a name to it – frightened? Because, said the inner voice, the detached onlooker, the observer that was always with him, when you've been in danger before, you could act. There was literally nothing he could do but sit and wait. He couldn't act. He could only wait.

He shut his eyes and dug deep. He seemed to virtually *see* a light inside his head. He knew it was nothing but a mental trick, but the light was his courage – and the light was dimming.

No! Almost without thinking, he soundlessly said a prayer, the same prayer he'd said so many times when he'd been up against it in the war. He concentrated hard. The light had to be brighter. He could make it brighter. I'm going to count to three, he told himself. And despite the smell of rotting vegetation, despite the soft footfalls, that light will be bright and I'll open my eyes and I'll *see* what's coming closer. One, two, three . . .

He opened his eyes and sat up with a jerk. Nothing had changed. And then the light from the candle in front of him went out with a hiss.

Lefevre – he was sure it was Lefevre – made a choking noise. Tom Jago smothered a cry. His voice cracked. 'It's coming.'

One by one, the candles in the points of the pentacle went out. The tomb, which had seemed huge in the wavering candle-light was plunged into darkness. There was a grating noise as if one stone had rubbed against another, then, from out of the darkness, came a low, menacing growl.

'Run!' yelled Jago. 'Run!' He turned and struck Lefevre on the shoulder. 'Come on!' He hurled himself out of the pentacle, down through the chapel and out through the open door.

Lefevre seemed paralysed. As much as he disliked the man, Jack simply couldn't abandon him. He pulled at his arm but Lefevre wouldn't move. Desperate, Jack flung back his hand and walloped him across the face.

He couldn't see but could feel the shudder that ran through Lefevre's body. He pulled at the man's arm again. 'Come on!'

Lefevre moved like a drunken man. With Jack supporting him, he stumbled down the aisle.

Another growl ripped into the darkness.

Lefevre whimpered and would have collapsed if Jack hadn't been holding him up. Bracing himself, Jack heaved Lefevre bodily to the door and out into the open air.

Tom Jago, his face deathly pale in the moonlight, was in the clearing. 'What's . . . what's up with him?' he managed.

'He's fainted,' said Jack tightly. 'You'll have to help me with him.' Jago didn't move. Lefevre was a dead weight. Jack lowered him to the ground and turning, deliberately faced the black emptiness of the open door. Think of the light, he told himself. Come on light, *burn*!

With what scraps of courage remained, he darted to the chapel door and seizing the handle, pulled it shut. He knew they'd found the mutilated body outside. He knew he'd heard that sound in the woods. He knew that the thing inside the chapel could escape but it still felt better with the massive door between him and it.

Jago still hadn't moved. 'Help me with him!' called Jack.

'I . . . I can't,' mumbled Jago. He had his torch in his hand. 'You see?' A brilliant beam of light shot out. 'That's here, but if I come closer . . .' He stepped forward and the light abruptly went out. He gave a little gasp and retreated. The light shot out once more. 'It's there,' he said, his voice quavering. 'It's where you are. Where he is.'

Jack took a deep breath and, taking Lefevre under the shoulders, pulled him to where Jago was standing.

'Come on, Major,' said Jago anxiously. 'We've got to get out of here.' He looked at the unconscious Lefevre. 'You'll have to leave him. We can't carry him.'

Jack jerked his head up in shock. 'We can't just leave him.'

Jago swallowed. 'We need to get out of here. Come *on*,' he added urgently. 'D'you think he'd care about you?'

'Probably not. Does that matter?' Jack went down on one knee beside Lefevre and shook him. 'Jago, give me your hip flask.'

Jago took the flask from his pocket, stepped forward, hesitated, then stepping back, threw the flask to where Jack was kneeling. He backed away. 'I'm getting out of here.'

'Stop!' Jack's voice was savage. 'If you take the torch, I'll never get him back.'

Jago paused irresolutely as Jack, with one arm under Lefevre's shoulders, sat him up and put the flask to his lips. To his huge relief, Lefevre spluttered and flickered his eyes open.

'Take it easy,' Jack warned. Despite himself, he couldn't help giving an anxious glance at the chapel door. 'If I help, can you stand?'

Lefevre blinked uncomprehendingly but allowed himself to be helped to his feet. With an arm over Jack's shoulder, he stumbled out of the clearing and onto the path, Jago leading the way with the torch.

It was with a feeling of real relief Jack felt Lefevre's steps grow stronger to the point where he could walk unaided and a feeling of near bliss when they came out onto the lawn across from the house.

As they got into the hall, he glanced at the grandfather clock. They'd been gone less than two hours. Betty came into the hall, Rosalind Jago behind her. 'Is everything all right?' began

Rosalind and stopped as she saw her husband's face. 'Tom! What's happened?'

For a moment he buried his head in his hands, then looked up. 'Plenty. We all need a drink.' He shuddered. 'Plenty.'

Betty's urgent voice came out of the darkness. 'Jack! Jack, wake up! You're dreaming.'

He didn't hear her. All he heard was the jaguar, all he saw was the jaguar, a monstrous snarling face so close that the stinking, fetid breath swamped his senses. He lashed out and Betty yelped in pain.

That did wake him. He started upright in bed and the jaguar vanished. 'Betty!'

'You . . . you hit me,' she said, rubbing her ribs, her voice a cross between reproach and amusement.

He wasn't remotely amused. He held her close to him, his body trembling. 'I'm so sorry,' he said at last. 'Did I hurt you?'

'Not much.' She smoothed his hair and kissed him, then drew back, startled. His face was wet with tears. 'Jack?'

He rubbed his hand across his face. 'It was coming for you,' he said shakily. 'In the dream, I mean. I tried to protect you but I couldn't.' She could hear his ragged breathing in the darkness, then he drew a deep breath. 'The dream seemed very real. And . . . And I was frightened last night, darling. Scared stiff.'

'You still helped Mr Lefevre, Jack. Horrible man.'

He was silent for a long time. When he spoke again, his voice was nearly back to normal. 'Well, you know. Couldn't leave him.' His voice grew stronger. 'Even if he is an absolute wart. But I'll tell you this much. I *really* think you ought to be more careful who you pick up at parties.'

She giggled, as much in relief as anything. Jack sounded himself again. 'I didn't take to him much but I have to admit I was flattered. After all, he is quite a famous author.'

'I'm the only author you need.' The smile in his voice was evident. 'Here. Let me prove it.' He kissed her tenderly, then they snuggled back in each other's arms.

'I was scared,' he said flatly after a few moments. 'I didn't like it.'

'It sounded terrifying.'

'I've been scared before.' Betty said nothing. His voice was pensive, analytical almost, and she didn't want to interrupt his chain of thought. 'Last night was different though. Previously, when I've had the wind-up, there's always been an actual cause. You know, a physical threat, such as that ghastly time I was trapped under a burning log or have some idiot wave a gun at me. But last night? What actually happened?'

'Quite a lot, by the sound of it.'

'Really? I couldn't let that pompous ass, Lefevre, kill that wretched bird, so I cut my finger – it still stings – planted it on the tomb, and almost immediately there was a foul smell. Then the pair of them started yelping something had touched them and that was followed by a whole succession of noises.'

'The candles went out,' Betty reminded him.

'Yes . . . But what actually *happened*? Nothing. The only actual harm I came to, I inflicted on myself. The noises were beastly but I could almost wish I'd toughed it out.'

Betty shivered. 'I'm glad you didn't. Jack, there's something in that chapel. Something – well I don't know what to call it, but evil seems the best word. I felt it before, when we found poor Mr Burstock.'

'You're sensitive to atmospheres,' said Jack thoughtfully. 'Even though you are one of the most sensible people I know. You're right. There's something in that chapel. I'm going to root it out, Betty.' His voice was determined. 'I'm not going to be beaten by an old legend.'

'You're going to fight?'

'Damn right.'

'Then I'm fighting with you.' Jack was silent. 'Don't stop me, Jack. You weren't the only one who was scared last night. I want to face down the demons too.'

There was a long pause. 'My dearest Betty, my darling girl, you're an absolute star.' He kissed her once more and yawned. 'If I start dreaming again, kick me out of bed. I'll go and sleep on the sofa.'

The yawn was catching. 'No you don't. There isn't room on the sofa for two. Where you go, I go.' She held him close and added, in a whisper, 'Sleep well.'

THIRTEEN

'You're very quiet, Jack,' said Isabelle, as she poured him out a second cup of tea at breakfast the next morning. 'I'm not surprised,' said Arthur, looking up from his bacon and eggs. He gave his friend a sympathetic glance. 'What you've told us sounds enough to knock the stuffing out of anyone. Are you going to tell Ashley?'

'Yes . . .' said Jack, drawing out the word. 'Eventually. After I've been back to the chapel.'

Arthur paused with a piece of bacon halfway to his mouth. 'You're going *back*?'

'We both are,' said Betty, finishing her slice of toast. She gave her husband a determined look. 'That's what we decided last night.'

Arthur swapped an expressive look with Isabelle. 'It's probably,' he said unexpectedly, 'the best thing you could do.'

Although he was determined to be strictly rational, Jack had to brace himself as he approached the chapel door. He looked down at Betty and smiled. 'Ready?'

She squeezed his hand. 'Ready.'

Tom Jago clearly thought they were insane to want to go to the chapel and flatly refused to accompany them. Privately Jack was pleased about that. He'd far rather he and Betty had the place to themselves. Jago had been so jumpy last night that he was almost bound to let his nerves get the better of him once more.

Simon Lefevre had gone. Now the crisis was over, he had regained his former rather condescending swagger. He'd told Tom and Rosalind Jago that they ought to be honoured to have what was undoubtedly an authentic (*absolutely astounding!*) psychic phenomenon on their property. He had been very put out when Tom Jago had refused him permission to write up the night's experiences.

'We're thinking of selling up,' Jago explained. 'I don't think anyone could blame us for that, especially after last night. I don't want some guy telling the world that Birchen Bower is a home for spooks and God knows what else. We'd have every ghost-hunting freak in the country descend on us. Add to that, we've got two dead bodies to account for and that isn't going to help any. No, sir. I guess you and Mrs Haldean can go and poke around if you must, but count me out. You can lock up and bring back the key, though.' He smiled thinly. 'I don't think I'll be using it again, but I'd better have the key back, all the same. I left it on the altar.'

Jack cautiously pushed the door of the chapel open. He was trying very hard to fight down the memory of his nightmare. In the dream he'd swung the door open and then, with a hideous snarl – the same snarl that they'd heard not a fortnight ago in the woods – a monstrous creature, far larger than a real jaguar, had attacked Betty.

She seemed to know what he was thinking. With a reassuring squeeze of his hand, she smiled up at him. 'This isn't your dream.'

'Of course it's not,' he said as briskly as he could. The sunlight helped. The dream had been in darkness. But Albert Burstock had been mauled to death in the chapel, he added to himself. There'd been sunshine then. Even so, he let the sunlight flood through the open door before stepping inside.

Nothing. He breathed an unconscious sigh of relief.

Betty wrinkled her nose. 'What's that horrible smell?'

'It was here last night. It's a lot fainter now but it reeked last night.'

Betty walked up the aisle. 'It all looks so normal,' she said. She paused. 'There's no *atmosphere*,' she said in surprise. 'It feels normal as well as looking normal.'

She paused by the box tomb, wincing as she saw the smear of dried blood. 'So everything kicked off once there was blood on the tomb?'

'That's right.'

She turned to face him. 'Jack, what are we dealing with here? Is it supernatural?'

He ran his hands through his hair. 'Honestly? I just don't

know. Ashley's clinging to the idea that there's an escaped jaguar on the loose but that doesn't explain last night. He's had no luck, by the way, in tracing anyone who's lost a jaguar, so to speak.'

'They might not be too happy to own up, even if they had,' said Betty thoughtfully. 'I mean, it's not like losing a handkerchief or a bunch of keys, is it?'

'Hardly,' agreed Jack with a laugh.

'So was it supernatural?'

'I just don't know. It certainly felt supernatural but look at this place.' He indicated the chapel with a wave of his arm. 'An old empty chapel with that tomb and all the locals muttering about the legend . . .'

'It was Arthur who told us about the mutilated animals,' she reminded him.

'So it was, and he's not prone to flights of fancy. Well, add all that up and it's virtually begging to be haunted.' He clicked his tongue impatiently. 'But I hate that explanation. Albert Burstock's dead, Derek Martin's dead, and Sir Havelock is certain both of them were mauled by a jaguar. If I say it's the ghost of this ruddy princess who's turned herself into a jaguar then I won't trust myself to think straight ever again.'

'But Martin was murdered though. By a human being, I mean. He was only attacked by the jaguar afterwards.'

'That's true enough.' He bit his lip in frustration. 'Nothing adds up.'

'It could be a lunatic,' Betty suggested. 'I've read that someone who's really a lunatic has enormous strength.'

'Yes, but it doesn't give them enormous teeth, does it? Or claws, come to that. Sir Havelock was certain we were looking at the real deal. And then there's last night.' He shivered. He couldn't help it.

'Jack,' said Betty after a pause. 'Are you quite sure that neither Mr Lefevre or Mr Jago arranged things? I must say I can't see why Mr Jago would, but Mr Lefevre might. It'd be good for his reputation as a ghost-hunter to have an experience like last night to crow about. I can imagine him really believing in the princess but thinking he had to help matters along.'

'He helped them along to some purpose, then. Don't forget,

he fainted with fright. That was absolutely genuine. He was terrified.'

'So he's out of it,' said Betty thoughtfully.

'So's Jago. He didn't move. And with you keeping tabs on Rosalind Jago, she can't have had a hand in it either.'

Betty sighed impatiently. 'Mrs Jago didn't leave the house. We were together all evening. You weren't actually gone all that long. We had a couple of drinks and she told me all about life in Florida and New York and so on. She doesn't like it here much. I can't say I blame her.'

'You're sure you were with her all the time?'

'Certain. She never left the room. But Jack, I really am suspicious of Mr Lefevre. I think he could easily be a fraud. Just think. A stage magician can perform all sorts of tricks that you'd swear were impossible but that's all they are – tricks.'

'A stage magician has assistants. Lefevre certainly wasn't getting any assistance from Jago or me.' He shrugged helplessly. 'He didn't move out of the pentacle, Betty. I was the only one who did, when I did my stunt by the tomb.'

'Where's the pentacle?' asked Betty, looking round.

'It's in the belfry. That was the only space big enough for Lefevre to draw the wretched thing.' He jerked his head up suddenly in remembrance. 'Oh no! That poor bird must still be in its cage. We'll have to let it out.'

They climbed the steps to the altar. As Tom Jago had said, the key was on the altar. Jack slipped it into his pocket and followed Betty up the steps.

The belfry door stood open, as it had been left last night. Betty went into the belfry first. 'I'm glad you managed to stop Mr Lefevre killing the poor thing,' she began, then stopped. She put her hand to her mouth with a little cry.

The cage was to one side of the pentacle, but the dove was a crumpled feathery heap at the bottom of the cage.

'It's dead,' she said blankly. 'Don't say it died from lack of water or something.'

Jack knelt down beside the cage, feeling oddly moved. The cage was still fastened. He unclipped the door and took out the dove. It was rigid in his hand, as he had expected. After all, rigor mortis affected birds as well as men. He gently rubbed the bones in its neck and felt them grate under his fingers. With rigor broken, the bird's head drooped sadly.

Jack looked up at Betty. 'Its neck's been broken.' She looked horrified. With a mounting surge of anger that he could hardly explain, he swallowed hard. 'Its neck's broken.' Forcing himself to move calmly, he put the little body back in the cage and stood up, wiping his hands together.

With an effort, he kept his voice level. 'Someone – not something but some*one* – has come in, opened the cage, took the bird out and wrung its neck. Then they put it back in the cage for us to find.'

Betty, hand clasped to her mouth, stared at the dove. 'But why, Jack? Why would anyone do that?'

'To make sure we're frightened stupid. To scare us off. To convince us death is in the air and this place is haunted. And it's not working. I'm damned if I'm going to let it work.'

Betty's lip was trembling. 'I'm scared,' she whispered.

He was with her in two strides. His arm around her, he caught hold of her hand and willed strength into her. 'Don't be scared. Someone's playing games, Betty. Someone wants us to be scared.'

She looked up, seeking reassurance. 'How can you be so sure?'

For an answer, he turned her round to face the box tomb. 'Think of the legend of the Jaguar Princess. It's centred round the tomb. In that foul book there's a blood ritual that supposedly conjures up the jaguar. Lefevre followed the ritual and what *should've* happened, was that the princess appeared as a jaguar. And, right at the end, that's exactly what seemed to be happening.'

Betty shuddered. 'It must've been so scary, Jack.'

'It certainly was. Lefevre was terrified. It wasn't an act. He was so shocked, he fainted.'

'But why?' asked Betty with a frown. 'After all, he *expected* the ritual to work.'

'Because he relied on the pentacle to keep us safe,' said Jack, kicking at the chalk star dismissively. 'That illusion was shattered fairly early on. But don't you see, Betty? If the jaguar had appeared, it wouldn't have hands, it'd have claws. You need hands, hands with fingers on them, to open that poor bird's cage.'

'I don't know much about it,' said Betty, 'but in stories about werewolves, aren't they part human, part wolf? Wouldn't they have fingers?' She tossed her head impatiently. 'I know it sounds like absolute nonsense. I can hardly credit I'm saying it, but maybe the Jaguar Princess is the same. A sort of were-jaguar, I suppose.'

Jack shook his head. 'No. As far as stories about werewolves go, it depends on what story you're reading whether they become part wolf, part human, or all wolf. But look at this legend and look at what we know. The animals Arthur told us about were killed and mutilated by something with teeth and claws, not hands.'

'What about the noise we heard in the woods?' persisted Betty.

'What about them? They didn't come from a human throat. I must admit, I've never actually heard a jaguar, but it sounded like a pretty ferocious wild beast to me. We're back to a jaguar again. Sir Havelock Dane was certain that a jaguar killed Burstock and mutilated Martin. This isn't a creature that's part human, part jaguar, it's a jaguar. And that's according to the legend and what evidence we have as to what the damn thing's actually done.'

Betty looked worried. 'I don't understand, Jack. Are you saying the legend's true? That the princess actually becomes a jaguar?'

'No, my darling. I'm not saying anything of the sort.'

She looked understandably relieved, then clutched at his arm in alarm. 'There's a real jaguar, you mean? Superintendent Ashley's right and there's an actual jaguar on the loose?'

He rubbed his chin with his hand. 'As far as that goes, I think the jury's out on that score. I certainly don't want to contradict someone of Sir Havelock Dane's standing. However, what I *do* know is that no jaguar, real or legendary, opened that bird's cage and snapped the poor creature's neck. That needs human hands and a pretty twisted human mind to go with it.'

Betty was silent for a few moments. 'So what do we do

now?' she asked in a small voice. 'I think what you've just said is nearly as frightening as believing in the legend.'

'No, it's not.' Jack took her arm and led them to a pew, consciously choosing a seat where they couldn't see that pathetic little white body in its cage. He took out his cigarette case and offered it to her.

She reached out, then stopped. 'Should we smoke? In here, I mean?'

'It's a long time since anyone used this place as a chapel. I don't think you'll offend anybody's sensibilities.'

She took a cigarette and relaxed thankfully. 'So what are we up against, Jack?'

He liked the 'we' in that sentence. 'A real person who's using the legend to scare the living daylights out of anybody who's fool enough to believe in it.'

Betty's eyes widened. 'But that's what we said before! You remember, after the inquest. You mentioned *The Hound of the Baskervilles* and Isabelle said in that story the villain used the legend to cover up a murder.'

Jack smoked thoughtfully for a few moments. 'Let's leave murder out of it for the time being and stick to last night. After all, no one actually saw what happened to Burstock or Martin, but I was a witness last night. What happened to that poor little dove proves what I saw wasn't supernatural but a set-up. And that,' he added, with a reassuring grin, 'is a weight off my mind, I can tell you.'

Betty gave a puzzled frown. 'Who could have known you were going to be here last night?'

He blew out a long mouthful of smoke. 'A whole raft of people. After Burstock's death, everyone roundabout was chatting fit to bust about the Jaguar Princess. Then Martin's body was found, which didn't exactly abate anyone's interest. Havelock Dane's visit added a bit more fuel to the fire and Simon Lefevre's a well-known bloke. When we had dinner with the Jagos the proposed investigation was talked about very freely.'

'You're right,' agreed Betty. 'The servants were in and out of the room all evening.'

'Add to that, Lefevre was staying at the house. From my

brief acquaintance with that gentleman, I imagine he talked about it endlessly.'

'Yes. The servants were bound to know and,' she added, 'I bet they talked about it in the village.'

'I bet they did. It would be a real hot topic. For all I know, Tom Jago could've easily mentioned it when he was out and about, as could Rosalind Jago. It wasn't a secret. If you were planning some monkey tricks, you'd make it your business to find out exactly what the plans were. It might even have been nothing more than a huge practical joke.'

'A joke?' repeated Betty incredulously.

'I didn't say it was very funny, but I can see how it would strike a certain sort.'

'But the dove – why kill the poor creature? That's no sort of a joke.'

Jack nodded. 'You're right. Killing the dove takes it onto another level.' He stubbed out his cigarette and lit another one with nervous fingers. 'It was so unnecessary!'

'It can't have been a joke,' said Betty quietly. 'I'm sure I'm right. A practical joker wants to see the reaction to the joke, to call it that.' She looked around. 'There's no one here but us.'

Jack rolled his cigarette between his fingers. 'You're right. Last night was a deliberate attempt to scare us stupid.'

'But who would do such a thing, Jack?'

'That's a damn good question. I haven't got an answer. Perhaps if we try and think of why rather than who, we might get somewhere. What reason would anyone have for scaring us stupid?'

'In scaring you and Mr Lefevre stupid or just Mr Jago?' asked Betty acutely. 'I can't help feeling this all centres on him. After all, both you and Mr Lefevre are visitors. Mr Lefevre's gone and you're going to leave of your own volition soon enough. But Mr Jago – he lives here. Who wants him gone?'

Jack sat back. 'Rosalind Jago is convinced Derek Martin's mother wants them gone,' he said thoughtfully. 'It goes back to Rosalind Jago accusing the Martins of stealing her diamonds. And as,' he added, 'Derek Martin had two diamonds in his pocket, I think Rosalind Jago is absolutely right.'

'Absolutely.' She frowned. 'But back to last night. Could

Mrs Martin really be responsible? Leaving aside the *how* she could've done it, d'you think she really *would've* done it? It seems an awfully elaborate way to go about getting rid of a neighbour you don't like.'

'There, my darling, you're getting into the realms of human nature and what any one person would or wouldn't do. But I agree, it seems a fantastically elaborate way to get rid of your neighbours, especially when there's no reason for them to meet up.'

'I thought Mr Jago called to see her. He must've done if he offered to pay for Derek Martin's funeral. Rosalind Jago said that Mrs Martin wasn't grateful.'

'You're right,' said Jack. 'As a matter of fact, Tom Jago's been to some lengths to extend the olive branch.'

'Which Rosalind Jago bitterly resents.'

'Well, she has no doubts about who swiped her diamonds. As we know, Tom Jago thought Derek Martin was the bee's knees.'

'And Mrs Martin might resent that, too,' added Betty. 'If she's a very possessive woman, she would begrudge anyone coming close to her blue-eyed boy. If that's the case, I can feel quite sorry for Mr Jago, with his wife on one side and Mrs Martin on the other.' She sighed in exasperation. 'Look, you think last night was a set-up. Can we find any evidence?'

'Spoken like a true detective. C'mon. Let's go and look.' He stubbed out his cigarette and stood up.

He led the way in the belfry and stood once more in the chalk outline of the pentacle. Seeing Betty's expression, he picked up the dead dove in its cage and put it out of sight, on the other side of the altar.

'Thanks,' she said softly. 'I feel I can think straight now. So then, you're certain that no one moved out of this chalked circle.'

'Ker-rect.'

'And the first spooky thing that happened was the jungle smell?' She wrinkled her nose. 'It must've been disgusting. I can still get a whiff of it now.'

'Also ker-rect. Actually . . .' Jack stood rigidly still, then relaxed. 'Shorn of its supernatural suggestions, what did we have? A foul smell. And how can a foul smell be artificially produced?'

Betty's eyes widened. 'Jack! It's a stink bomb! It has to be a stink bomb!'

'Ten out of ten!' he said enthusiastically. 'That's exactly what I was thinking. Damnit, I remember getting six of the best for loosing one off at school.'

'If it smelt anything like this, that sounds richly deserved. What goes into a stink bomb, Jack?'

'Blimey, now you're asking. I know I made one in a chemistry lesson, but that was years ago.' He thought for a few moments. 'You can use ammonium hydrosulfide but that doesn't seem right, somehow.'

'What does ammonium thingy smell of?'

He scratched his head. 'Rotten eggs. I'm sure it's rotten eggs.'

'Ugh! That's horrible.'

'So it is,' he said with a grin. He took another sniff of the air. 'And it's not right, either. It's . . . it's . . .' He snapped his fingers together. 'I know! Ethanethiol! That's what earned me six juicy ones. And, as you say, richly deserved.'

'And ethan-whatitsface smells of . . .?'

'Cooked cabbage.'

She smiled at him in delight. '*That's* what I can smell! Jack, we've cracked it. Someone let off a stink bomb last night. Are you sure it wasn't Mr Lefevre?' she asked suspiciously.

'As certain as I can be. The same goes for Tom Jago. I was looking directly at them. I was pretty wound-up, but I'm sure they didn't move. Lefevre yelled at me to get back in the pentacle and so I did. He completed the circle and lit the candles and there we were, supposedly safe.'

'Only you weren't, were you?'

Jack shook his head. 'No, we weren't. That's when Lefevre started to get really jumpy. All of a sudden, he leapt six feet, yelping something had touched him. Tom Jago stood up, waving that shotgun of his around, shouting out that something had touched him too.'

'What sort of thing?'

'Jago went off on a rant about creepers in the jungle. Lefevre had forty fits because nothing should've been able to cross the pentacle but, as we know, we're not dealing with anything supernatural. Then – this was really startling – Jago yelled his head off and pulled a mass of spider's web out of his hair.'

'That's horrible,' said Betty. 'Or . . . Was it really spider's web, Jack?'

'Oh yes. I took it out of his hand. It was real, all right. Jago was pretty rattled by it.'

'I'm not surprised,' she said with a shudder. 'Anyone would be.'

Jack, eyes bright, looked at Betty, head cocked inquisitively to one side. 'Remember this is a set-up. How d'you think it was done?'

'It can't be anything too obvious,' she said thoughtfully. 'You said the spider's web is real, so that explains itself, but the creepers can't be creepers.'

'No, they can't. I'd have seen them and I saw nothing.'

She frowned. 'That means it must've been a thread. A sewing thread?'

'Or a fishing line. That'd be my choice. They're virtually invisible, especially in that light.'

'Jack! I bet that's it! But where did it come from?'

'There's only one place it could've come from.' He stood and pointed upwards. 'And that's the roof.'

She gazed upwards. 'You mean someone was above you the whole time?'

He nodded. 'That's exactly what I mean. Come on. Let's go and find out.'

'They're not still there?' she asked anxiously, following him into the belfry.

Jack laughed. 'Juggins! Of course not. But if someone was fooling around up there, they might have left some sort of traces behind.'

'Footprints or cigar ash, you mean?'

He laughed once more. 'Only if we're very lucky, but let's take a gander, all the same.'

The belfry was a square room about twelve feet or so across, constructed, like the rest of the chapel, of flint and mellow red bricks. After the gloom of the chapel, it was a much brighter space, lit as it was on three sides by lancet windows. Dusty oak panelling clad the walls to head height.

The chapel proper had exposed oak roof beams but, here in

the belfry, about twenty feet or so above them, the roof was of solid oak, supported by massive oak beams running across the width of the roof. A bell-rope hung down, looped into a metal ring in the wall. Beside it was a broad-stepped ladder, secured to the wall.

Jack looked up to where the ladder ended in a trapdoor. 'The only way is up,' he said, giving the ladder a shake. He turned to Betty. He knew she wasn't keen on heights. 'You wait here.'

'Not a chance,' she said robustly. 'I go where you go, remember?'

'Thanks,' he said softly. 'However, I don't think this is a case of ladies first. Let me get the trapdoor open before you come up.'

He swarmed up the ladder. The trapdoor opened at a push and rested against the wall. Jack clambered through the trapdoor, then stopped, shining his torch around the room.

He had hoped for footprints but the central part of the room looked as if it had been swept clean. When he'd been up here previously, after they'd found Burstock, the floor had been thick with dust. 'Up you come,' he called, stooping down to give Betty a hand into the room.

Up here, although the light was dim, the air was fresh, blown through the unglazed, louvred windows. It was a relief to get away from that faint but persistent smell of cooked cabbage. The bell, a dark circle of bronze, hung above them, on its wheel inside the bell-cage. The bell-rope hung down, disappearing through a hole in the middle of the floor.

'That trapdoor opened very easily,' said Betty.

'So it did.' He knelt and ran his finger along the hinges. 'It's been oiled,' he said, wiping his fingers on his handkerchief.

'That sounds as if it should be significant,' she said.

'It could be,' he said absently, gazing down the hole left by the raised trapdoor.

'What are you looking for, Jack?' asked Betty.

'We're not over the pentacle. If I'm right, whoever was fooling around up here would need to be more or less directly above us.'

He lay full-length on the floor, peering over the side of the hole. 'The pentacle's in the middle of the belfry, about six feet away.' He gestured vaguely with his hand. 'Over there.'

'Here, you mean?' said Betty brightly, stepping forward. 'By the bell-rope?'

He jerked his head up in alarm. 'Stop!'

Betty stopped. 'What is it?'

'Stand still!'

She did what he said, looking at him curiously. 'Whatever's the matter, Jack?'

He came towards her and took her hand, sighing in relief. 'Don't you see, darling? If someone was directly above us, there's a hole in the floor. There has to be a hole.'

Betty's eyes widened in horror. 'Oh, Jack,' was all she said but he felt her shudder.

He gave her hand a squeeze then, kneeling down, took out his torch and, lying it on the floor, shone the beam along the planks of the floor.

In the dusty light from the louvred windows, it would've been impossible to see, but the bright beam of torchlight picked out a raised edge of three of the planks lying side by side.

Jack stood up and, leaving the torch where it was, walked to the raised edge. Kneeling down once more, he put his hand on one of the planks. It rocked under the pressure.

'Look,' he said, pointing to where a long nail had been driven into the plank. 'There's one at each end of the three planks.'

'Is that to make a handle, Jack?'

'I imagine so. Have you got a handkerchief, Betty?'

'Yes, of course. Why?'

'Because I'd like to have a look underneath but if we disturb any fingerprints, Ashley will have my guts for garters.' He pulled his handkerchief out of his pocket and holding it between his fingers, took hold of the broad head of the nail. 'Now if you do the same at the other side . . . And up she comes.'

They lifted the plank up. It was about a yard long and a foot wide and rested in the middle, like a see-saw, on the massive roof beam underneath.

He swallowed hard, feeling a prickle of cold sweat on the back of his neck. If Betty had stood on the edge of the plank, it would've tipped up and she'd have plunged to the belfry floor, twenty feet below.

Beside him, Betty had evidently had the same thought. 'I nearly trod on that,' she said in a shaky voice.

'You didn't, thank God,' he said, rocking back on his heels. 'Let's see what's underneath.'

They lifted the three planks up and put them to one side. The pentacle was directly below them.

Jack's mouth twisted. 'I feel an absolute idiot,' he said ruefully. 'To think of the three of us, three grown men, huddled in that ruddy chalk star, scared witless, while someone up here was laughing themselves stupid to see how scared we were.'

'Anyone would've been scared, Jack,' Betty said firmly. 'You know that.' She paused. 'How come you didn't see them, though? You must've looked up.'

'In that light? Remember, all we had were candles. We could see the tomb, but the roof was as black as pitch. They might – in fact, they probably did – have a scarf around their face so there was no chance their skin would catch the light.'

Betty shivered. 'Can we go down?' she asked. 'I don't like it up here.'

'Give me a couple of minutes.'

He fetched the torch from where it lay and gave it to Betty. 'Just hold that,' he asked. 'I want to have a proper shufti at these planks.'

He sat back, looking closely at the plank in the light of the torch.

'It was originally nailed onto the roof beam,' he said. 'Look, you can see the holes where the nails went in.' With his fingers wrapped in his handkerchief, he delicately turned the plank lengthways, examining the edges. 'It's been sawn through at both ends. Now why would anyone go to that trouble? You could get exactly the same result – a hole in the roof – by taking up the entire plank rather than sawing bits off.'

Betty shone the torch along the floor. 'These planks are very long,' she said thoughtfully. 'We can probably see this better from below, but they more or less have to run from roof beam to roof beam. They'd be very awkward to move.'

Jack nodded. 'I bet you're right.' He looked up at her, frowning. 'That's an awful lot of effort for someone to go to. I wonder why they did it? You'd have to lever the whole plank up to saw a section off. Give me the torch a minute.'

He put the plank down and, taking the torch and still on his knees, ran his hand along the length of the plank away from the hole. 'Yes, I'm right,' he called. 'Someone's had a crowbar to these planks. Why not just leave them out instead of sawing bits off?' He rapped his knuckles on the wood. 'This is pretty solid stuff.'

'Perhaps they didn't want the gap to be noticed,' suggested Betty. 'After all, three whole planks would make a jolly big hole.'

Jack clicked his tongue. 'You'd only see it in daylight. When we arrived last night, the whole blinkin' floor could've been taken up and we wouldn't have been any the wiser. It doesn't make sense.'

He stood up and walked back towards Betty.

'Stop!' she said suddenly. 'What's that on the floor by your feet?' Her voice faltered. 'It's . . . It's not a maggot, is it?'

Jack glanced down. There was something small and white. He picked it up. 'Bear up,' he said with a grin. 'It's not a maggot, it's a grain of rice.'

'A grain of rice?' repeated Betty. 'What on earth is that doing there? I know people throw rice at weddings but they wouldn't throw it around up here.'

'And no one's been married here for donkey's years – if anyone ever was.'

'Jack, shine the torch around will you?' He obediently shone the torch around in a circle. 'There's more rice. You can see it in the torchlight.' She stooped down and picked up four grains. 'Why is there rice up here?'

Jack held out his hand and she dropped the grains of rice into it. 'That really is odd. Unless . . .'

He snapped his fingers together. 'I know! This explains the footsteps we heard! If you put rice in a cloth bag and thumped the floor with it, it'd make very stealthy sounding footsteps.'

'That would sound *really* creepy.'

Jack nodded. 'It did.' He shone the torch around, looking for more rice. A glint of gold in the corner of the room caught his eye. 'Hello! What's that?'

Betty walked across the floor, stooped down and picked it up. It was a large brass button with a distinctive raised pattern of an acorn emblazoned on an oak leaf. There was a dark thread still attached. Mindful of the caution Jack had shown about the possibility of fingerprints on the planks, she picked it up by the thread. 'This looks as if it was from a man's blazer.'

'It might,' agreed Jack, doubtfully. 'It's a bit big for a blazer, I'd say, but you might be right. I can see why it wound up here. The floor's a bit uneven. That's why it's rolled across the room.'

He frowned. 'I don't think we'll get anything useful in the way of fingerprints off it, but you never know.' Taking out his handkerchief, he wrapped it up and put it in his pocket.

'What else is there to explain?' asked Betty.

Jack frowned. 'There was a sound as if the tomb was opening.' Betty looked startled. Jack grinned. 'It was stone grating on stone. Which, I imagine, is exactly what it was. However, I can't explain the growling. There might be a jaguar on the loose but it's too much to expect it to growl on cue.'

'Could it be a record?' asked Betty. 'I suppose you can get records of animal noises. If someone had a wind-up gramophone they could just put the record on.'

Jack bit his lip. 'I suppose so,' he agreed doubtfully. 'The sound I heard doesn't seem quite right for a record somehow, but it could be the answer.'

Betty took the torch and peered at the floor. 'I was hoping to see a square shape in the dust,' she said. 'The sort of impression a gramophone would make but there's not really much dust to speak of.'

'No, there isn't. It's obviously been swept. The first thing I did was look for footprints, of course. There's enough dust at the sides of the room,' he added. 'And cobwebs. It's easy enough to see where the spider's web came from.' He grinned. 'Poor old Jago jumped six feet when that landed on him.'

'I'm not surprised,' said Betty. 'It must've felt disgusting.' She looked at the hole and frowned. 'Jack, as you say, all this must've taken a lot of effort but none of it would've worked if you'd had the pentacle somewhere else. Who decided where the pentacle should be?'

'That's a good question,' said Jack. 'It was Jago who suggested it, I think, but it was Lefevre who gave the deciding vote. I couldn't care less where the damn thing was.'

'But that doesn't make sense, Jack. We've proved – or, at

least, I think we've proved – that the tricks were worked from above.'

'Well, the rice is a dead giveaway and I don't suppose anyone would've sawn up these planks for fun.'

'No, they wouldn't. You're certain neither Mr Jago or Mr Lefevre weren't guilty of any deception?'

'They can't have been, Betty. I was standing next to them.'

'But how did the person who was doing all this know where the pentacle was going to be? It could've been anywhere in the chapel.'

Jack shook his head. 'Not really. It was a question of space. The only area with enough clear space for the pentacle is the belfry.'

'They'd have to know how big a pentacle is, surely?'

'Maybe there's directions in the sort of book your pal Lefevre writes,' said Jack with a shrug. 'If they knew as much as they obviously did, they'd also know there'd have to be enough space for the three of us to share it.'

'I suppose so,' said Betty in a dissatisfied voice, 'but it still seems very chancy. And,' she added, 'what about the key? Mr Jago told us there was only one key. Could he have set it up, Jack? I know he couldn't have carried out all the shenanigans last night, but could he be in league with someone?'

'I suppose he *could*, but why, for heaven's sake? What on earth would he get out of it? Although he wants to be a country squire, he's been so rattled by what's happened, he's thinking of selling up. He told me last night it was like living in a Gothic novel and we know what Rosalind Jago thinks about this place. She hates it.'

'Yes, she does,' agreed Betty. 'That's true, but what's your point, Jack?'

'The point is that if Jago wants to sell this place, last night won't have helped. Birchen Bower had enough of a bad name as it was. Although Jago refused Lefevre permission to write up an account of last night's goings-on, I bet Lefevre will talk about it and then some. Why the dickens should Jago act against his own interests by staging a fake haunting? It doesn't add up.'

'No, it doesn't, really,' said Betty, clearly unconvinced. 'But what about the key?'

'What about it? That lock is ancient. It'd be very easy to pick by anyone with a smidgen of knowledge. I could do it with a screwdriver.' Betty rolled her eyes heavenwards. 'All right, maybe two screwdrivers then,' said Jack. 'But I certainly could do it. Picking a lock's quite easy, once you know how.'

'I'll remind you of that next time you forget your key.'

'Never pick a lock that you want to use again,' said Jack with a smile. 'I was taught that was a golden rule. But the chapel lock would be awfully simple. Take my word for it.'

'I suppose so,' said Betty. 'So our Mr Whoever wouldn't have any problem getting in. What about the lights, Jack? From what you said, it was when the candles went out and the growling started that Mr Jago panicked.'

'Jago went off like a bullet from a gun,' said Jack. 'Lefevre, on the other hand, was paralysed with fear. I had to manhandle him out of the chapel and he fainted halfway to the door.'

'So how was that done? How were the candles put out?'

Jack stood, arms folded, silent for a few moments. Then he looked up, grinning broadly. 'Remember I heard a hiss.'

'A hiss?' repeated Betty puzzled. 'You don't mean a snake, do you?' She shook her head impatiently. 'No, of course you don't. That's silly.' She pushed her hair back from her eyes. 'What do you mean?'

For an answer, Jack lay down on the floor once more and with his finger and thumb at an angle, pointed an imaginary gun into the hole. 'Yep. That's a nice clear shot. And out go the candles.'

Betty's eyes widened. 'Jack! That's the easiest of the lot. A water pistol!'

Jack grinned up at her. 'It's so easy, it's sinful.'

'I'll say. It's like a magic trick, isn't it? It's all imagination and atmosphere. And preparation.' She paused. 'Do we tell the Jagos what we've found? It'd be a relief to him, I'm sure. After all, he was scared stiff last night.'

Jack rolled over, stood up, and dusted himself down. 'He certainly was, poor beggar.' His smile faded. 'And there we were, last night – there *I* was last night – scared witless by a stink bomb, a bag of rice and a ruddy water pistol.'

'Don't forget the growl you heard,' reminded Betty.

'No. And I won't forget the dove, either.' His face hardened. 'That's nasty. Perhaps I'm reading too much into it, but I honestly think the sort of person who would kill an innocent creature for effect is the sort of person who wouldn't baulk at murder.'

'Jack! You can't mean that,' protested Betty.

'Can't I?' He shrugged. 'Maybe you're right. And yes, I think we should tell the Jagos, but before we do, I want a word with Ashley.'

FOURTEEN

Jack and Betty managed to get away from Birchen Bower without seeing either Tom or Rosalind Jago. Jack handed over the key to the maid with a promise he'd call later.

Ashley had, of course, returned to Lewes but, as Jack said to him half an hour later on the telephone, 'I think you'd really better see Tom Jago again. I've got a nasty feeling that things are going to take a turn for the worse.'

'We've already got two deaths, Haldean,' complained Ashley. 'And one of those is murder for certain. How much worse could it be? All my enquiries seem to have come to a dead end. Obviously I want to take a look at the chapel but I've got an official dinner tonight. I won't be able to get to Croxton Abbas and back in time. You promised you'd see the Jagos today?'

'We more or less have to. It is their chapel, after all.'

'Fair enough. It's Friday tomorrow. I'll be able to come over to Croxton Abbas then. Let's say eleven o'clock. Does that suit you?'

'That'll be fine.'

'Good. I'll telephone Mr Jago and make an appointment. Ask him to stay out of the chapel and keep it locked till tomorrow. You can tell him it's a hoax – not that there was any doubt about that to my mind – but don't mention the button you found. Keep it safe and let me have it tomorrow.'

'OK. See you then.'

*   *   *

The Jagos were on the terrace, a coffee pot and biscuits on the table beside them. Tom Jago stood up as the maid showed them through the French windows.

'Well, hello! Take a seat, won't you? You'll have coffee? Good. You said on the phone you had something to tell me.' He handed them the coffee with a tired smile. 'If it's any more ghost-hunting, you can do it without me.'

Jack stirred his coffee. 'About last night. It wasn't real.'

Jago stared at him. 'Are you crazy? What d'you mean, it wasn't real? You were there, man. You know what we saw – what we heard! It was real, sure enough.'

Jack shook his head. 'No, it wasn't. We were tricked.'

Rosalind gave a little cry. 'Tricked? But who . . .?' She broke off helplessly.

'I'd think you'd better explain,' said Jago icily. 'I'm not used to being played for a fool.'

Jack, with comments from Betty, plunged into an explanation of what they'd discovered. He couldn't complain of a lack of attention. Tom and Rosalind listened with growing astonishment.

As Jack finished, Tom Jago stood up restlessly, shoulders squared and hands braced behind his head. 'I can hardly credit it, Major. You're absolutely certain that it was all a trick?'

'Absolutely.'

Jago took a deep breath. 'When I find out who did it, my God, they're going to pay.' He broke off and glanced at Jack. 'The growling we heard. You've explained everything else but you haven't explained the growling.'

'I thought it might be a record,' said Betty.

Jago snapped his fingers together. 'Why, yes!' He lit a cigarette and flicked the match away in disgust. 'You have to be right. To think I was taken in by a bunch of cheap tricks . . . Hang on!' He looked up, puzzled. 'My torch didn't work. You remember, Haldean? You'd got Lefevre out of the chapel and, when I tried to come near, my torch wouldn't work. It worked fine when I stepped away from the chapel.'

'Maybe it's just a loose battery, Tom,' said Rosalind.

'Perhaps,' said Jago dubiously. 'Yep. You're probably right,

Rosie.' He puffed his cheeks out in a long sigh. 'I was so jittery, I probably shook the battery loose myself. I can't get over being taken in like that!'

'It was very convincing,' said Jack. 'I fell for it.'

'And yet you worked out how it was done,' said Jago with an appraising look. 'That's pretty smart work,' he said slowly. He was silent for a few moments. 'I still can't take on board it's all tomfoolery.' He shook himself. 'I had a phone call from that police pal of yours. He wants to come over tomorrow. You in on that?'

Jack nodded.

'I'm coming too,' said Betty.

'Sure,' said Jago absently. 'However . . .' He paused, evidently putting thoughts together. 'Why's Ashley coming, Haldean? I'd like to get my hands on the guy responsible, but what's it got to do with the police?'

'There've been two deaths,' Jack reminded him.

'But no one was hurt last night,' said Jago. 'Deaths are one thing, but this joker didn't kill anyone. Hell, now we know the truth – if there really is nothing more to it – I'm inclined to think it was nothing more than a huge practical joke.'

'That's an idea we had,' said Betty.

'Well, I'm not laughing,' said Rosalind. 'Who's responsible, Tom?'

'Lefevre spent a lot of time alone in the chapel,' said Jago slowly. He bit his lip, frowning. 'Damnit, he could've arranged the whole thing. He'd have to have an assistant, of course, but he could've easily pulled the whole stunt off.'

'But why, Tom?' asked his wife.

'For publicity, of course. You heard him this morning, Rosie. He writes books about this stuff. He could fill a hall with a story like this and no mistake.'

'We did wonder,' said Jack, 'if it was an attempt to scare you away from the house. It seems a bit elaborate, I know, but it's a thought.'

Rosalind Jago stirred. 'Are you thinking of Mrs Martin, Major Haldean?'

'The idea did cross my mind, yes.'

Jago gave a derisive snort. 'What? You can't be serious.

I can't say she's a fan of ours, but she's an old lady. Can you really imagine her pulling off a stunt like this?'

'Is she that old?' questioned Jack. 'I'd say she's what? Fifty odd? And fairly active, I'd say.'

'Yes, but even so, the idea's ridiculous.' He buried his chin in his hand. 'Scare us off, you say?' He pulled a face. 'That can't be it. It has to be nothing but a bad joke. I can't believe Mrs Martin's responsible, but someone doesn't like us, that's for sure.'

'Tom,' said Rosalind anxiously. 'You'd promised we could leave. It was only this morning you agreed to leave. I don't want to stay.'

'No, I know that, but that's when I thought last night's stunt was real.' He chucked away his cigarette, frowning. 'I don't want anyone saying I'm a coward.'

'Tom . . .' said Rosalind with rising anxiety. 'What does it matter what anyone thinks? It's my opinion that matters.'

He looked at her, then gave a sudden short laugh. 'It sure is. OK, Rosie, where should we go? London?'

She gave a sigh of relief. 'Let's go soon. Now, even. We can stay in a hotel somewhere. Let's do it, Tom.'

'We've got to see this guy, Ashley, tomorrow.'

'After we've seen him, then.'

'OK.'

'There's one thing,' said Jack, as he and Betty got up to go. 'I locked the chapel but Ashley asked that nothing should be disturbed until tomorrow.'

'Don't worry about that,' said Tom. 'I know you think it's a set-up, but the place gives me the creeps.'

Tom Jago shifted on the uncomfortable horsehair sofa, looking across the room at the woman on the hard chair. It was later that afternoon. As always, when he was with Mrs Martin, he was uncomfortably aware of her intensity. It was almost as if she was *hungry*. He'd tried his best, but his best was never good enough.

To get away from that intense gaze, he glanced round the room. They were in the parlour, which had an unused quality about it. There was no friendly clutter, no rumpled cushions, no half-read books on the table. It was like an exhibition in a museum. The room, he thought, reflected Mrs Martin's personality. The old mahogany sideboard was polished to a sheen, as was the brass fender on the fireless grate. How long was it since a fire had burned there? The few pictures on the walls were gloomy oils, darkened with age. Everything was stiff, ordered and formal. Just like the woman herself.

And yet . . . Haldean had been quite right, he thought. Enid Martin was still an active woman, despite her age. How old was she? Fifty-three? Fifty-four? Despite her grey hair, she really wasn't all that old. Could anyone really suspect her of being the joker behind last night's affair? He knew what Rosie had said but surely the police couldn't credit it. Did Haldean? He couldn't, could he? After all, what possible motive could there be?

The door opened and Mrs Martin's maid, Clara, came in with a tea tray.

'Put it on the table, Clara,' said Mrs Martin.

'Yes, ma'am.' Clara put down the silver tray then stood, looking wide-eyed at Jago.

'What is it, girl?' asked Mrs Martin irritably. 'You've seen Mr Jago before.'

Clara gulped. 'It's just that it's all over the village, sir, that you and some other gentlemen saw the Jaguar Princess in the chapel last night and Cook and me, we were wondering if it was true.'

'We certainly had an experience,' said Jago dryly.

Clara's eyes bulged. 'So it is true then, sir?'

'We heard a jaguar growling and I smelt the jungle. There were other things too, such as some very creepy footsteps.' Clara clasped her hand to her mouth. 'There are some,' continued Jago, 'who say it was all a prank but I doubt if anyone in the village will believe that.'

Clara shook her head vigorously. 'Oh no, sir. It's been going on for far too long to be something made-up, like. We all know it's true.'

'Thank you, Clara,' said her mistress icily. 'You may go. And what,' she said, rounding on Jago, once Clara had left the room, 'do you mean by filling the girl's head up with nonsense?'

Jago shrugged. 'What if I'd said it was all a trick? Do you honestly think she'd have believed me?'

'Probably not,' said Mrs Martin after some thought.

Jago glanced at the door. It was ajar. 'And she's quite right, you know. The legend of the princess is centuries old. These are just the latest manifestations of it. Mr Lefevre – and you know what an authority he is – believes it implicitly.'

Mrs Martin raised her eyebrows but said nothing. She glanced at the door, then walked to the table and busied herself with pouring out the tea.

'Anyway, last's night's affair brought things to a head for Rosie,' said Jago, accepting a cup of tea. 'She's determined to leave.'

Mrs Martin gave a little gasp. 'Leave? What, sell the estate, you mean?'

'I can't imagine anyone would want to buy it. No,' he added ruefully. 'I think I'm saddled with it.'

'But . . .' Mrs Martin sank down in her chair. 'You can't leave. You've spent so much money on the place. Electricity, plumbing . . . It's been transformed.'

'The house, yes, but we've done very little with the grounds. I think I'll have a word with that guy, Arthur Stanton. He runs the place alongside ours. He might be interested in renting the woods. That'd be something.'

Mrs Martin ignored Arthur. 'Leave? You can't mean it.'

'After last night? I certainly do mean it. Rosie and I have attracted a bit too much attention for my liking. We need some time away to let everything quiet down. Later, perhaps, we may come back.'

'You won't,' said Mrs Martin bitterly. 'Your wife will see to that.'

Tom Jago frowned but said nothing. He finished his tea and stood up. 'Thanks for the tea.' He looked at Mrs Martin. 'I know you and Rosie haven't exactly hit it off. Well, I don't think you'll have to worry about that for much longer.'

Superintendent Edward Ashley couldn't refrain from tutting as he looked at the scuffed outlines of the pentacle on the belfry floor. 'I can't credit that you lent yourself to this tomfoolery, Haldean,' he remarked.

'Don't rub it in, Ashley. I was hardly the most enthusiastic participant you could ever hope to meet, but I did want to see what happened.'

'You weren't happy, Major. I can vouch for that,' agreed Tom Jago. 'Especially when Lefevre wanted to kill the dove.'

'Kill what dove, Tom?' asked Rosalind Jago. She had, with a certain unwillingness, accompanied Jack, Betty, Ashley and her husband. She didn't, she said, want to be left alone in the house – the servants didn't count apparently – but she obviously wasn't happy in the chapel.

'It was a dove he'd brought with him,' said Jago with a shrug. 'It was all part of the ritual in Cayden's book. I couldn't see what there was to get upset about. It was only a bird, after all.'

'The poor thing was killed,' said Betty with a shudder.

'It died,' corrected Jago. 'You can't know for certain how it died. It had no food or water in its cage, remember.'

Jack, who had told Ashley exactly how the dove had died, didn't contradict him. Instead he cocked an eyebrow at Jago. 'You still believe there's something supernatural going on, don't you, Jago?'

Jago looked rather shamefaced. 'I guess in my heart of hearts, I do, Major. In the cold light of day it might sound stupid, but this place is centuries old. And although I don't think I'm oversensitive, this place has an atmosphere.'

'I've felt that,' agreed Betty. 'Not a nice atmosphere, either.'

Ashley rolled his eyes. 'If you're all determined to give yourselves the creeps, there's not much I can say to convince you otherwise.' He glanced upwards. 'I suppose I'd better take a look up above.'

Rosalind clutched at Tom's arm. 'Don't you go, Tom. Don't leave me down here.' It obviously didn't occur to her that she should climb the ladder up to the bell loft.

'You'll be fine,' began Tom, then capitulated as he saw the look on his wife's face. 'OK. Have it your own way.'

'That's probably for the best, sir,' said Ashley. 'The fewer people up there, the less disturbance there'll be. If you'd like to stay with the ladies, Major Haldean and I will have a look round.'

With Jack leading the way, Ashley followed him up the ladder.

'That chap Jago's on edge about something,' he said in a low voice after he'd levered himself into the bell loft. 'So's his wife.'

'I don't think you can really blame them after everything that's happened,' agreed Jack. He flashed his torch across the floor. 'Careful where you step, Ashley. Those sawn planks make a real deathtrap.'

Ashley looked at the planks warily. 'I can see that.' He took out an insufflator from his pocket. 'Let's see if there's any fingerprints. I know you and Mrs Haldean handled these with kid gloves, metaphorically speaking. Let's hope someone else wasn't so careful.'

Squeezing the bulb of the insufflator, he dusted the planks and nails with a coating of fine grey powder. The surface remained blank.

'Someone's wiped it,' Ashley said in disgust. 'There's nothing there. But whoever did this put some real effort in.' He shook his head, puzzled. 'What gets me is *why*? I can understand someone wanting to have a laugh, perhaps make ghostly noises or jump out at you, say. I've asked around and it was fairly common knowledge in the village that the three of you were going to be here the other night. That's almost inviting a practical joker to take a hand.' He looked down at the planks again. 'But this? I hadn't appreciated how much work was involved.'

'That made me think a bit too,' agreed Jack. He clicked his tongue in irritation. 'I wish we'd found some prints. I can't help thinking that our unknown friend knows a damn sight more than they should about Burstock and Martin.'

Ashley looked at him sharply. 'You really think so?'

'Don't you?'

Ashley paused. 'Well, I must say I hadn't connected your escapades with anything else, but that was when I thought someone had been having a laugh at your expense. Now?' He nodded his head slowly. 'Yes, you may be right.'

He looked at Jack. 'Come on, Haldean. Haven't you got any ideas? We've got a diamond robbery and two deaths to account for, to say nothing of this supernatural stuff. None of it seems to add up.'

'I'm sorry, Ashley, I'm stumped. Like you, it's the motive which puzzles me.' He shone the torch around the room. 'You can see the grains of rice. That's easy enough to explain, like everything else, but it's the question *why*? Why would anyone go to all this trouble? And as for who, the only material evidence so far is the brass button Betty and I found.'

'Talking of which, let's have a look at it.'

Jack unwrapped the button and the insufflator came into play once more. A few smudges showed on the rim of the button, but Ashley shook his head. 'Nothing useful there, I'm afraid.' He frowned at the button. 'It's a bit big for a blazer, I'd say, but I'd hate to be definite about it.'

He took an envelope from his pocket and put the button inside. 'It'll be worth asking about. It might give us some sort of clue. By the way, what sort of buttons did Lefevre have on his jacket? Did he wear a blazer?'

Jack shook his head. 'No. He had a tweed jacket with leather buttons. You know the sort. But although he could've been responsible with the aid of an assistant, I'd swear he wasn't. He wasn't faking, Ashley. He was terrified.'

'It's all negatives,' said Ashley in disgust. 'Ah well, we've seen everything that is to be seen. Let's get back down the ladder. And,' he added bitterly, 'I bet that Mr Jago will swear that he never came near the place and the key's never been out of his possession.'

Ashley's prediction was absolutely correct.

'Of course I didn't visit the chapel, Superintendent,' said Jago. 'No one could've got at the key, either. You told me to leave it locked up and that's exactly what I did.' He paused, looking at him curiously. 'Is everything as you expected?'

'Exactly as Major Haldean described, sir,' said Ashley stolidly. 'I was just checking that it'd been undisturbed. I think you've been the victim of nothing more than an elaborate practical joke.'

Tom Jago's face cleared. 'Is that all it was?' He gave a snort of anger. 'Gee, if I could get my hands on them, I can tell you they'd be laughing on the other side of their face.'

'I can well understand you feel like that, sir.'

'Absolutely I do.' He looked round the chapel and shivered. 'A joke, eh? If you say so. Well, if you've finished here, we might as well get back to the house.'

They came out of the chapel, Jago locking the door behind them. 'Yes,' he said thoughtfully as they came into the clearing. 'I know you believe it's all phoney, Haldean, but I've still got the uneasy feeling that there's an actual presence at work here. An uncanny presence, I mean.'

Ashley drew his breath in significantly but said nothing.

Jago shook his head. 'You can be as sceptical as you like, Superintendent, but there's things gone on in and around these woods you can't explain.'

'The mutilated animals, you mean?' asked Jack.

'Yes, that's so. They've been going on for years.' Jago looked sharply at Ashley. 'Now, how d'you explain that?'

'I can't, sir,' said Ashley. 'That's the honest truth but those incidents are probably entirely unrelated.'

Rosalind tossed her head petulantly. 'Do stop talking about it, Tom,' she said sharply. 'It's enough to know we'll soon be away from this horrible place and . . .'

She broke off with a scream as a ghastly howl rang out, followed by a series of savage snarls. Rosalind clutched at her husband's arm. 'Tom! What is it?' She was terrified.

Jago couldn't speak. He looked utterly bewildered. With a quick movement, he pulled an automatic from his pocket. 'If I see it . . .' he began.

Ashley stared at the pistol. 'You've got a gun?'

'Too damn right I've got a gun,' snarled Jago. He spun round. 'Rosie, get out of here!' He turned to Jack. 'Haldean, get Rosie and your wife back to the house!'

'Yes . . .' began Jack but Rosalind interrupted him.

'No!' She was shaking with terror. 'Tom, come with me.'

He pulled her arm away from him. He wasn't rough but he was very firm. 'Rosie, listen! We need to find what made that noise. You'll stay with me, Superintendent?'

'Of course, sir,' said Ashley, white-faced. 'But shouldn't we all get back to the house? My God! I've never heard a noise like that.'

Jago thrust out his chin stubbornly. 'Let's track this thing down once and for all. Rosie! Please! Go back to the house!'

Betty, trembling with shock, put her hand on Rosalind's arm. 'Come on!' she pleaded.

'Come with me, Mrs Jago,' said Jack, holding out his hand. Jago gave her a little push. 'Go on!'

Reluctantly, Rosalind took Jack's hand.

'Hurry!' shouted Jago. 'Will you get out of here!'

Rosalind still seemed very reluctant to move. Jack tugged at her hand. 'Quickly, Mrs Jago!'

With a rush of relief, he saw Rosalind nod. She turned to him, real fear in her eyes. 'Come on!' he urged. 'It might be anywhere!'

With Betty on one side of him and Rosalind on the other, Jack hurried the two girls along the path as quickly as he could. It was a tight squeeze in some places but he didn't want to let go of either of them. He had a horrible suspicion that if he let Rosalind Jago go, she would crumple.

Cursing under his breath at the snaking tree roots and over-hanging branches, Jack could feel Rosalind trembling. Betty's breath was coming in short little gasps. 'Courage, sweetheart,' he muttered.

'Don't worry,' she was able to say. 'I won't let you down.'

He squeezed her hand in gratitude. They were parallel to the river now, he thought inconsequently, more or less at the same spot where they'd found Martin's body. Then, to his horror, he heard a crashing noise in the bushes.

Rosalind screamed.

'Rosie!' came Tom's voice from the distance. 'Rosie!'

With a feeling of utter disbelief, Jack saw a flash of some-thing orange and black in the bushes. He thrust the two women behind him and stood at a crouch, facing the bushes. 'Get back!' he yelled, knowing as he said it, it was a stupid thing to say. 'Get back!'

There was another crash, then another. It seemed to be moving away from them.

Betty gave a choked-off cry. Rosalind stood, frozen to the spot.

'Betty, help me with her!' shouted Jack.

Rosalind seemed paralysed with fear, then, as the noise came from the bushes again, her eyes rolled upwards and she slumped forward in a dead faint.

Jack caught her just in time to prevent her sprawling to the ground.

'She's out of it,' gasped Betty. 'Jack, what shall we do?'

There was another crash from the bushes. With a surge of relief, he realised it was definitely moving further away.

'If you take her legs, we'll carry her,' he said shortly. Damn the woman! Why couldn't she stay on her feet? With Betty leading, he picked up Rosalind's unconscious body. At least she was lighter than Lefevre.

How long was this bloody path? And what the hell was in the bushes? Could it really be a jaguar? *There's something in those woods that shouldn't be there.* Arthur had said that. Arthur, one of his oldest friends.

'Nearly there, Jack!' called Betty encouragingly. She really was a star. Thank God she hadn't fainted too. With two unconscious women to look after, he'd have been helpless, but Betty had real courage.

They came off the path and onto the lawn.

'Give me a couple of minutes, Jack,' begged Betty, lowering Rosalind to the grass. 'I need a breather.'

'All right.' He picked up a fallen branch and, facing down the path, hefted it, ready to strike. The branch was a rotten weapon, but it was all he had.

Fragments of thought blazed across his mind. *The most powerful bite of all the big cats. Burstock's chest ripped open. Carrion. Derek Martin was carrion. Havelock Dane says it's certainly a jaguar. The most powerful bite . . .*

'She's waking up, Jack,' said Betty.

Rosalind's eyes flickered open. She gave a terrified little whimper. 'Has it gone?' she croaked.

Jack stooped down and shook his head. 'Come on, Mrs Jago. We need to get into the house.'

'I . . . I can't move.'

He helped her to sit up, then whirled round towards the woods as two shots rang out. Rosalind clutched at him in terror. 'Tom! I want Tom!'

Incredibly, she caught onto his arm and scrambled to her feet. She staggered towards the path. Jack caught hold of her. 'No, Mrs Jago!'

'Tom!' she yelled. 'Tom!'

She was still struggling feebly when Tom Jago, Ashley behind him, emerged from the woods, his face grim. Ashley looked as shocked as Jack had ever seen him.

'I heard the shots, Ashley,' said Jack. 'Did you get it?'

'No, we didn't. We saw it, though. At least we saw something orange and black. Mr Jago took a couple of pot-shots, but it escaped.'

Jago, gun at the ready, put an arm round his wife. 'You're safe, Rosie. That's all that matters.'

She put her head in her hands and burst into racking sobs. 'I'll never be safe. Never.'

'Oh yes, you will,' he said grimly. 'I'll see to that.'

FIFTEEN

It was a very chastened group that got back to the house. Rosalind collapsed on the sofa, head in her hands. Tom Jago pressed a brandy into her hands. 'Here, Rosie,' he said, putting an encouraging arm round her. 'Drink this.'

She gulped down the brandy, then put the glass down on the table. 'I want to leave now, Tom,' she said, her voice shaking.

'We'll leave later this afternoon.'

Rosalind grasped his hand. 'Do you mean it, Tom?'

'I certainly do. We'll book into a hotel. I'll need to come back but you can stay there.' He turned to Ashley. 'Well, Superintendent? Do you still think it's nothing but a practical joke?'

'What happened in the woods just then wasn't a joke,' said Ashley soberly. He was obviously very shaken. He looked at Jack. 'Did you see anything, Haldean? I heard you shouting.'

'There was a crashing in the bushes and I saw something orange and black.'

'It was it, Tom,' said Rosalind, her voice rising. 'I know it was it. Did you see it?'

'I saw something, certainly. So did the superintendent.'

Ashley nodded. 'I couldn't tell you what it was, though. It was just a glimpse through the bushes, but it was certainly orange and black. I don't think you managed to hit it, sir.'

'I'm pretty certain I didn't, worse luck.' Jago's lips were thin with anger. 'My God, it's come to something when we're driven out of our own home.' He lit a cigarette with shaky hands, tossed the match into the empty fireplace, and flung himself into a chair.

'Superintendent, I know you're doing your best, but don't you think this is a case for Scotland Yard?'

Ashley pulled a face. 'It's not as simple as that, sir,' he began when he was interrupted by an impatient snort from Jago.

'Why not? I'll be frank. Surely you must see this has got beyond you.'

Ashley swallowed hard. 'I can understand how you feel, sir, but it's a question of procedure. For Scotland Yard to be involved, the chief constable has to request their help.'

'Well, get him to request it for Pete's sake!'

From Ashley's expression, Jack knew exactly what he was thinking. The chief constable, Major General Flint, was dead against calling in the Yard. Derek Martin might've been murdered by Stoker, an American – Jack thought that was easily the most probable explanation – but the crime had been committed in Sussex. To ask the Yard for help in a local crime was, in the general's eyes, a failure. Jack felt a stab of sympathy for Ashley. Major General Flint was not one to tolerate failure.

'I can ask him, certainly,' conceded Ashley with a wooden expression. 'That's not to say he'll agree.'

Tom Jago jutted out his chin angrily. Jack interposed.

'Perhaps I can suggest a compromise?'

Jago whirled round on him. 'What?'

'To call in the Yard officially will take time. As you're going up to London this afternoon, why not go there in person?'

'And get fobbed off with some nobody?'

Jack shook his head. 'No. I can give you an introduction to my old friend, Chief Inspector Rackham.'

Jago hesitated. 'Chief inspector, huh?' He chewed the title over for a few moments. 'He sounds important,' he admitted grudgingly. 'Would he see me?'

'If he's there, he certainly will. If you like, I can telephone him now and arrange an appointment.'

Jago relaxed. 'Say, if you would do that, Major, that'll be a real help.' He glanced at the clock. 'If you could make it for five o'clock, that'd give us enough time to get up to London and check into a hotel.' He paused. 'And thanks.'

'I saw your pal, Tom Jago, this afternoon, Jack,' said Bill Rackham that evening on the telephone. 'My word, he's an angry man. He's convinced poor old Ashley is nothing but a local hick, as he expressed it and he was a bit scathing about you, as well.'

'Me?' said Jack in surprise. 'What've I done?'

'It's what you haven't done that's getting to him,' said Bill with a laugh. 'He's been told you're a sort of Sherlock Holmes but you haven't caught his jaguar, or found out who was fooling around in the chapel. Or, come to that, found out who murdered Derek Martin.'

'But you've done that,' protested Jack. 'It more or less has to be Stoker.'

'That's what I said. I didn't mention Stoker's name, of course, but I told Jago we had a pretty good idea who the murderer was. I also told him that, although we're looking for the man, the chances are he's slipped away to the Continent. Anyway, I put him right about Ashley and about you too, into the bargain. As to what the Yard can do – well, I hope I managed to convince him that the answer is not much. I don't know what you're mixed up in down there, Jack, but it's one of the weirdest affairs I've ever come across. If you could find out who was responsible for scaring you all witless in the chapel, I reckon that'd be a massive step forward.'

'I couldn't agree more, but the only clue we've got to go on is a brass button.'

'A brass button?' asked Bill.

Jack told him about the button. 'Jago doesn't know about it, by the way. Ashley wanted to keep that to ourselves.'

'Quite right, too. I don't know if you want to see either Mr or Mrs Jago again?'

'Not particularly. Especially as he thinks I'm a complete wash-out.'

'Well, if you do, they're holed up in the Ritz. Nice for some, isn't it?'

Bill rang off with a laugh. Jack turned to go back into the sitting room, but before he could leave the hall, the phone rang again.

It was Tom Jago.

'Hello,' said Jack guardedly. He was annoyed with Jago's opinion of Ashley – and himself, he had to admit. Particularly as it was nothing but the truth. 'Did you want me, Jago?'

'No, I wanted Captain Stanton.'

'Hold on a moment. I'll get him for you.'

Arthur put down his whisky and soda as Jack put his head round the sitting-room door. 'Jago? For me? What on earth does he want?'

'You'd better find out,' said Isabelle practically, frowning over the little pink-and-white cardigan she was knitting. She looked at Jack reflectively. 'Do you like Mr Jago?'

Jack poured himself a whisky and took a cigarette from the box on the table. 'I did. And to be fair to the chap, he's had a rotten time of it, but he was sounding off about Ashley to Bill Rackham and that's not fair. He had a pop at me, too,' he added.

'At you?' Betty was indignant. 'What have you supposed to have done?'

'That's just it,' said Jack, lighting his cigarette. 'I haven't done anything, have I?'

'You worked out that it was a set-up in the chapel.'

'Yes, but that doesn't tell me who or why. As far as that goes, I'm still as much in the dark as ever. I might as well admit failure and go back up to London for all the good I'm doing.'

'Don't do that,' said Isabelle. 'You were going to stay for another week at least. I'm sure you'll find an answer, Jack. You always do.'

'I wish I shared your faith,' he said gloomily.

He looked up as Arthur came back into the room. 'What did Jago want?'

'He wanted to invite us to lunch,' said Arthur, strolling over to the sideboard.

'To lunch?' said Jack in surprise. 'That's a turn-up for the books. From what Bill said, I thought I was about as popular with Jago as fog at a football match.'

Arthur paused, his hand on the decanter. 'Er . . . Not you and Betty, old man. Just Isabelle and me.'

Isabelle put down her knitting. 'Just us, Arthur? Whatever for?'

'He wants to talk about the estate. Can I get you a sherry, Isabelle? Betty?'

'Mm, yes,' said Isabelle. 'What about the estate?'

'He's got an idea we might like to rent the land. Some of it, at least.' Arthur handed Betty and Isabelle their drinks then, whisky in hand, sat down and looked at Jack. 'Apart from anything else, I feel a bit rum about him not inviting you both. After all, he knows you're staying with us. It feels a bit off leaving you at a loose end.'

'That doesn't matter, Arthur,' said Jack easily. 'That's the least of your worries.'

'Why don't we run over to Stanmore Parry and visit your Aunt Alice and Uncle Philip?' suggested Betty. 'It's ages since we've seen them.'

'That's a good idea,' said Jack.

'It's a very good idea,' agreed Isabelle. 'My mother'll be pleased, you know that.' She turned to her husband. 'What did you tell Mr Jago?'

'I said I'd ring him back. The thing is, in normal circumstances, I'd be very interested indeed, but granted what happened today . . . I just don't know.'

He looked at Jack. 'He's suggested that we – Isabelle and I – should go to lunch on Monday, then have a tour of the estate.' He ran his finger round the top of his glass. 'Is it safe, Jack? I know you've proved that malarkey in the chapel was nothing but tricks, but what about today? It sounds as if something or someone was definitely out to cause harm.'

'It certainly felt like it,' said Jack dryly.

'But no one *was* harmed,' put in Betty. 'It was really frightening but nothing actually happened apart from the fact we all had a bad scare.'

'And Tom Jago wasted a lot of ammunition,' agreed Jack.

'So is it safe?' repeated Arthur.

Jack blew out a long mouthful of smoke. 'I'll be honest. I don't really know. These attacks seem to be directed at the

Jagos, in an attempt to get them to leave. OK, they've left. For the time being at any rate.'

Isabelle put down her glass with a clink. 'I want to go. I don't know what's going on, but I'd like to find out.'

'But if it's dangerous . . .' began her husband.

Isabelle shook her head vigorously. 'I can't see that it is. It's as Jack said. These attacks or happenings or whatever have to be directed against the Jagos. I think we'll be safe enough. Besides that, Arthur, if we do end up renting the land, you'll be able to clear the estate. You've been itching to do that ever since we moved in.'

'That's true enough,' agreed Arthur, 'but I still feel very iffy about the idea of wandering around those woods.'

'I've got an idea,' said Betty. 'Everyone in the village is buzzing about Birchen Bower. Let it be known that you're going to have a look round the estate with a view to renting it. If you and Jack drop into the Cat and Fiddle, Isabelle mentions it to your Mabel and if you, Arthur, tell Dusty Miller, I can virtually guarantee that everyone in Croxton Abbas will know where you're going and why.'

'That's true enough,' said Arthur with a grin.

'And that means if your visit's a success the Jagos will leave permanently. We've worked out that's what whoever's doing this wants. Make a big point of that.'

'Good idea, Betty,' said Isabelle enthusiastically. 'Come on, Arthur. Let's do it.'

Arthur said nothing for a few moments, then slowly nodded his head. 'All right. Lunch on Monday it is.'

Tom Jago led the way down the path to the chapel, a shotgun under his arm. 'So you want to see the chapel, Mrs Stanton?' he asked, with a wry twist to his voice.

'It's because I've heard so much about it,' said Isabelle defensively, then smiled. 'I must own up to my ordinary share of curiosity.'

Tom Jago nodded. 'I guess that's only natural but speaking for myself, I'd be happy if I never clapped eyes on the place again. Rosie feels the same. It was as much as I could do to get her to come back to the house.'

Arthur nodded. Although the soup had been excellent and the lamb cutlets had been perfectly cooked, lunch had not been a success. Rosalind Jago seemed nervy and conversation had been stilted. She obviously didn't like being back at Birchen Bower.

'Yep,' continued Jago. 'She made me promise we'd go back to London tonight.'

'Why did she come?' asked Isabelle. 'If you're going back tonight, I mean.'

'Clothes,' said Jago succinctly. 'Because we left at such short notice, there's a whole heap of clothes and stuff she didn't take. Sure, there's plenty of shops in London which won't be any the poorer for our stay, but Rosie wanted her own things.' He grinned. 'I did suggest that she gave me a list and I'd pick up whatever she wanted, but she didn't trust me.'

'Would you trust me, Isabelle?' asked Arthur with a smile.

'To pick out my clothes? Absolutely not.'

Jago grinned, then glanced at Arthur. 'So from what you've seen so far, would you be interested in renting the land?'

'Interested, certainly, but I'll be frank, Jago, not in its present state.'

'OK. I was more or less expecting that. So what d'you reckon I should do?'

'Clear the undergrowth in the first instance,' said Arthur. 'You've done a good job clearing the grounds around the house.'

'All right. How many men d'you think I'll need?'

'Six men should do it,' said Arthur. 'But I doubt if you'll get any locals willing to tackle it.'

'I can get men from an agency easily enough,' said Jago. 'That won't be a problem. I'm not surprised the locals won't do it. Gee, I wish I could work out what's going on with this place,' he added disconsolately.

'So does Jack,' said Isabelle.

Jago hesitated. 'Look, about your pal, Haldean. I know that policeman, Superintendent Ashley, values his opinion, but he's only a local guy after all and Haldean's what? A writer? Sure, he might *write* detective stories but this is for real. We've got two dead bodies to account for. I like the guy, but what can he know about serious crimes? This isn't Chicago, after all. I think it's beyond them.'

'I wouldn't discount Mr Ashley or old Jack,' said Arthur. 'He's sorted out some pretty knotty problems in his time.'

'I've heard something about a murder at a fairground, was it?'

'The Breedenbrook fete, yes. Jack got to the bottom of that.'

Jago grimaced. 'Fetes or fairs seem to be unlucky in this neck of the woods. OK, but anyone can get lucky once. What else has he done?'

Arthur shrugged. 'Well, amongst others there was the Hunt Coffee affair and the Otterbourne case, to say nothing of the dust-up at Lassiter Aircraft.'

Jago looked surprised. 'You don't say? Has he written about it? I guess he gives lectures and so on?'

Isabelle laughed. 'Lectures? Jack wouldn't give a lecture. You'll just have to take our word for it, Mr Jago.'

Jago looked at her appraisingly. 'I will. It sounds as if he's had more experience than I gave him credit for.'

'He knows what he's talking about, that's for sure,' said Arthur.

'I wish someone did,' grumbled Jago. 'Over in the States, we hear all the time about how wonderful the British police are, but even the guy I spoke to at Scotland Yard couldn't offer any real help. I wanted him to grill Lefevre. Rosie's convinced he was behind the supernatural stuff in the chapel. But no. "You'll have to leave it with us, Mr Jago", was all I got.'

They came out into the clearing round the chapel. 'Well, here you are, Mrs Stanton,' said Jago, taking the key from his pocket. 'You can look your fill and welcome.' He walked towards the door, then stopped. 'The door's open.'

Arthur and Isabelle stared. The massive door was swung back a few inches.

'There must be someone inside,' said Isabelle nervously.

All three stopped dead. 'We'd hear them, wouldn't we?' said Arthur. 'Listen.'

There was dead silence.

Jago's face was grim. He snapped his shotgun closed. 'If someone's fooling around in there, they'll be sorry.' He reached out to the handle, then changed his mind and, with a hefty kick, slammed open the door.

Isabelle looked inside and screamed.

SIXTEEN

About five feet into the chapel, sprawled half across the kneeler of the back pew, was a body. A mutilated body. That much Arthur saw straight away, then Isabelle was in his arms, sobbing. 'It's horrible,' she said over and over again. 'Horrible.'

Arthur held her close. He wanted to shield her, to stop her seeing the body but, like him, she couldn't tear her gaze away from that awful sight. Because it was, as he saw, with a twist of his stomach, truly awful. He seemed to see it in little flashes of sharp-focused details.

Grey hair, matted with blood, straggling over the face. White flecks in the hair. Bone? A tweed cloche hat that had rolled a little way from the body. A hand stretched out towards the hat, as if in a vain effort to reclaim it. A pale grey coat, ripped and dark with blood. Silk-stocking-covered legs stretched out at odd angles. Blue leather laced-up shoes.

'It's a woman,' he muttered incredulously.

Isabelle gave another convulsive sob and he held her closer.

Tom Jago stood, shotgun at the ready, frozen to the spot. 'Stanton,' he said, his voice cracking. 'Will you see who it is?'

Arthur stirred but Isabelle held him tight. 'No, Arthur,' she pleaded. 'No. What if . . . if *it's* still there?'

'I can't—' he began but Jago interrupted him.

'All right,' he said, his breath coming in little, uneven gasps. 'Stay with your wife. She needs you.'

Walking very gingerly, Jago took a few steps into the chapel.

'Careful!' called Arthur. 'It might still be there!'

Jago stopped dead, shotgun at the ready. The chapel was utterly silent. Arthur could see his shoulders relax. 'It's gone,' he said quietly. 'We're alone.'

Another couple of steps brought him to the body. He knelt down beside it and reached out as if to brush away the blood-matted hair, then stopped, obviously repelled. Instead, using the muzzle of the shotgun, he lifted some of the hair away from the face.

With a cry he scrambled to his feet and staggered back, hand to his mouth. Turning, he regained the open air and sank down against the chapel wall.

'Who is it?' asked Arthur, his voice shaky.

Jago couldn't speak for a few moments. 'Mrs Martin,' he managed to say at last.

'*Mrs Martin?*' repeated Arthur in shock.

Jago looked up. 'Did you know her?'

Arthur shook his head. 'No. But I know who she is. Derek Martin's mother.'

Jago nodded. 'First him, now her. She didn't like us. I tried . . .' He trailed off. 'None of that matters,' he added wearily. He lent his head back against the flint wall.

'Stanton,' he said eventually. 'Will you get the police?'

Isabelle tugged at his arm. 'Please, Arthur. Let's go.'

'All right.'

Jago closed his eyes briefly. 'Thanks. And Stanton – please be careful how you break it to Rosie.'

'We will,' promised Arthur.

Jack couldn't shake off his feeling of unease. He should be enjoying himself. After all, he was at Hesperus with Betty, Uncle Phil and Aunt Alice – baby Alice was named after her, of course – which should add up to a feeling of total contentment. It didn't.

'Jack,' said Aunt Alice, as she handed him his after-lunch coffee, 'what on earth is the matter? You're as twitchy as a cat on hot bricks.'

'I'm sorry,' he said with an apologetic smile. 'I just can't stop thinking about Isabelle and Arthur.'

'But surely they're safe enough,' said Betty. 'We worked it all out.'

'Yes, I know, but . . .' He broke off as Egerton, the butler, came into the room.

'What is it, Egerton?' asked Uncle Phil.

'A telephone call, sir,' replied the butler. He turned to Jack. 'Captain Stanton is waiting to speak to you.'

Jack felt as if the bottom had dropped out of his world. He raced into the hall and picked up the receiver. 'Arthur! Are you all right? How's Isabelle?'

'We're fine,' came the reassuring answer.

Jack felt his heart steady. 'Thank God for that. Has anything happened?'

There was a slight pause. 'Yes. Look, I don't want to say too much on the phone, but there's been another one. Like Burstock and Martin.'

Jack's skin crawled. 'Who?'

'Mrs Martin.'

'Mrs *Martin*?'

'We found her. In the chapel.'

'You poor beggars,' breathed Jack. 'Is Isabelle all right?'

'She's upset, of course.' Arthur paused once more and Jack could hear the emotion in his voice. 'It . . . It was pretty nasty. Ashley's here. He wants to see you.'

Jack took a deep breath. 'All right. Tell him we'll be there as soon as we can.'

It was about an hour and a half later when Jack and Betty got to Arthur and Isabelle's.

'It was absolutely horrible,' said Isabelle. She looked at Betty. 'You found Burstock, didn't you? And you went back. That was pretty brave of you. I'll never forget seeing the poor woman like that.'

'I'll never forget it, either,' agreed Betty, sitting down.

'I think we all need a drink,' said Arthur practically. 'The body's been moved to Jerry Lucas's, Jack. Ashley's there. He said he'd wait for you.'

Jack nodded. 'That's good of him. Obviously they'd have to move her, otherwise she'd be as stiff as a board.' He took the whisky and soda Arthur gave him and, lighting a cigarette, looked at his friend. 'I don't want to keep Ashley waiting but if you could tell me what happened . . .?'

Arthur, with interjections from Isabelle, told him.

'Is Jago still at Birchen Bower?' asked Jack.

Arthur nodded. 'He wanted to go back to London, but Ashley asked him to stick around. Mrs Jago's gone back though – the poor woman couldn't wait to get away. Jago took her to the station and saw her onto the train.'

'I can see she'd want to leave,' said Jack. He glanced at the grandfather clock. 'I'd better get off to Jerry's.'

'What about dinner?' asked Betty.

Jack dropped a kiss on her cheek. 'Don't wait for me. I'll have something when I get back.'

Jerry Lucas had evidently been on the lookout for Jack's arrival because he opened the door himself. 'Come on in, Jack,' he said, leading the way into the sitting room. 'Ashley's waiting for you.' He ran his hand through his hair. 'This is a devil of a business.'

Ashley, gloomily smoking a pipe, stood up as Jack came in. 'It's good of you to come, Haldean. I can't believe we've had another death.'

'From what Arthur and Isabelle told me, it sounds like a carbon copy of what happened to Albert Burstock.'

'More or less,' agreed Jerry, drawing up a chair. 'You can have a look for yourself, of course. She's in the room at the back of the house. I'll take you along in a few minutes. I'll do the post-mortem this evening but there's not much doubt what she died of. She's got a massive wound to the head. One half of her face is destroyed, poor woman, and there's various injuries to her body.'

Jack winced. 'Tell me what happened,' he said, sitting down. He lit a cigarette from the box Jerry offered him. 'I've spoken to Isabelle and Arthur, but I wouldn't mind going over it again. When was the body discovered?'

'About ten past two. As you know, the Stantons had lunch with the Jagos. Mrs Stanton wanted to see the chapel, so Mr Jago took them along. Mrs Jago stayed in the house.'

Jack looked at Jerry Lucas. 'You were able to estimate the time of death, I suppose?'

'That's right. Death must've occurred about two o'clock, give or take twenty minutes or so.'

'Two o'clock!' repeated Jack, startled. 'Blimey! That means the poor woman was killed just before Arthur and Isabelle found her.'

'I know,' agreed Ashley fervently.

'Are you sure about the time she was discovered?'

'As sure as we can be,' said Ashley. 'Mr Jago stayed in the chapel while the Stantons went back to the house to telephone for us. Captain Stanton had the sense to look at his watch, as did Mrs Stanton. They agree it must've been ten past two or so when they discovered the body.'

Jack raised his eyebrows. 'The killer must've been close by. It sounds as if they had a narrow escape.'

'Absolutely,' agreed Ashley. 'That's all to the good, of course, but I'm sorry they didn't catch a glimpse of who or what was the killer. Captain Stanton came back with me to the chapel. I wanted him to verify the body was as he'd found it. I wanted to make sure Mr Jago hadn't interfered with anything.'

Jack tapped the ash off his cigarette. 'And had he?'

Ashley shook his head. 'No. Apparently he did think about covering her up,' he continued, 'but couldn't find anything suitable. He had a good hunt round the chapel while he was alone – he was armed with a shotgun – but couldn't find anything out of place.'

He looked blankly at Jack. 'And neither could I. So here we are again. We have to get to the bottom of this, Haldean. This simply can't go on.'

'Dammed if I can think of a way to stop it,' muttered Jack. 'What on earth was Mrs Martin doing in the chapel?'

'I asked the Jagos that. They're as puzzled as we are. She certainly had no reason to be there. After Dr Lucas took charge of the body, I went to Mrs Martin's house and broke the news to her maid, a Miss Clara Langland. Naturally I asked her if she knew why her mistress should have gone to the chapel, but she didn't know a thing.'

'What's the maid like?'

'She seemed a capable girl. She was shocked, of course, but not heartbroken by her mistress's death. I did wonder if Mrs Martin would have confided in her friends or neighbours, but according to the maid, her mistress kept herself to herself. She'd pass the time of day with them, but there was no one she was close to. She didn't come from Croxton Abbas. Apparently she's originally a Londoner.'

'Did she have any family connection to the village?'

'Not that she ever mentioned. I've set Constable Catton onto making enquiries in the village, but from what the maid told me, I doubt we'll learn anything.'

'I wonder why she came to live in Croxton Abbas? D'you know, Jerry?'

'I haven't a clue,' replied the doctor, refilling Jack's glass. 'She was one of my father's patients. After he retired, I took her on but I know damn all about her personal affairs. Mind you, she was a very healthy, vigorous woman, so she hardly ever consulted Dad or me professionally.'

'Has she lived here long?'

'About four or five years, I'd say. I can look it up in my records if you think it's important.'

Jack frowned. What Jerry said rang a faint bell in his memory, but he couldn't place it. Something to do with Arthur? Perhaps. 'It might be,' he said, then let the thought go as Jerry continued.

'I remember asking what brought her here. As I recall, she didn't really like the question.' He shrugged. 'All I was doing was making polite conversation but I could tell she wasn't willing to chat about it.'

'Was she a bit of a recluse, would you say?'

Jerry shook his head. 'Not really. She took part in village activities such as the literary club and so on, but she didn't seem to socialise much. Mr Dyson might know more. She was one of his parishioners.'

'He doesn't,' said Ashley. 'I called on him this afternoon. I wanted to know if there were any relatives we should inform, but I drew a blank. Her maid says she never mentioned any family apart from her son, and we know what happened to him, poor devil.'

'I take it she was a widow?' asked Jack.

'That's what she told me,' said Jerry. 'I did wonder if there might be an unwanted husband in London.' He grinned. 'Call me a nosy parker if you like, but it struck me as a reason why she'd keep stumm. That'd explain why she buried herself in this out of the way spot.'

'You might be right,' agreed Ashley, putting down his glass

and standing up. 'Do you want to have a look at the body, Haldean?'

'Oh joy,' muttered Jack. 'What a treat. It strikes me,' he said as Jerry Lucas escorted them down the hall, 'that Mrs Martin is a bit of a mystery woman.'

'It's certainly a mystery why she was in the chapel,' said Ashley. 'As regards her keeping herself to herself, I don't find that unusual. There's plenty of people who don't want the world knowing their business.'

'But this complete silence is a bit odd, don't you think?' Ashley shook his head. 'Ah well, you might be right,' said Jack without heat.

Jerry Lucas opened a door at the end of the corridor and switching on a powerful electric light, ushered them down a short flight of stone steps into a brilliantly lit room. It was just as well the light was so good because the windows of the semi-underground room were firmly shuttered.

'I don't,' Jerry explained, 'want prying eyes when I'm conducting a post-mortem.'

'Absolutely not,' muttered Jack with feeling.

The room was fitted out with a stone table with a gully round the side. There was, Jack saw, a drain under the table. That had unpleasant connotations.

It was a cold room, but that wasn't the reason Jack shivered as he saw the sheet-shrouded form on the table. This wasn't going to be nice.

It wasn't.

Jerry took hold of the sheet with a rather morbid flourish.

'Not the whole body,' begged Jack. The poor woman was past caring but it seemed to take away her last scraps of dignity to see her unclothed.

Jerry paused and uncovered the head and shoulders. 'Fair enough,' he acknowledged. 'But as you can see, there's a massive wound to the head.'

There certainly was. Jack drew his breath in sharply as he saw that a good half of Enid Martin's face had been destroyed.

'I don't particularly want to move her,' said Jerry, 'as rigor's set in, but there's pretty extensive injuries to her shoulders and back.' He pointed to where a grey wool coat was hung up on a peg on the wall. 'As a matter of fact, looking at the body won't tell you anything much more than her clothes can.'

On a table by the wall was a neat pile of folded-up clothes and a tweed hat. A handbag sat on a wooden chair, its contents on the table. Jack took them in at a glance. Purse, powder compact, lipstick, a handkerchief, a bunch of keys – nothing out of the way.

'You can gauge how severe the injuries were by looking at her clothes and her coat,' added Jerry. 'It's a new coat,' he added with a twist in his voice. 'I don't know why that seems to make it so pathetic.'

Jack took the coat down from the peg. It was stiff with blood and hung in shreds at the back. Her cardigan and blouse were next. They, too, were ripped and matted with blood. 'Was there blood at the scene, Ashley?' he asked.

'Plenty of it,' he replied grimly. 'I've no doubt she was killed where we found her, if that's what you're getting at.'

'Thanks,' said Jack absently. He folded the clothes back up and laid them down. The tweed hat was next. He twirled it idly round his finger. 'There's no blood on the hat,' he remarked.

'No,' said Ashley. 'The hat was near her body but it either fell off or she'd taken it off. Her handbag hasn't got any blood on it, either. It had slipped under the kneeler of the pew and was shielded that way.'

Jack picked up the handbag. It was good quality navy blue leather. He smiled faintly. Navy blue was a 'useful' colour as his landlady would say and hinted at a practically minded woman.

'The contents are just what you'd expect,' began Ashley, then stopped.

Jack obviously wasn't listening. He stared at the handbag as if in a trance then, with a shake of the shoulders, seemed to come back to earth.

Moving swiftly, he walked to stand directly under the electric light, examining the bag minutely. He looked up, his face pale.

'What the devil's the matter, Jack?' asked Ashley. 'You look as if you'd seen a ghost.'

Jack took a deep breath. Waves of understanding seemed to be crashing about him. 'Seen a ghost?' he repeated eventually.

'That's what I asked Albert Burstock.' His voice cracked. 'Do you remember, Ashley? That day in the pub?'

'What on earth are you talking about?' began Ashley impatiently, but Jerry put a hand on his arm, looking at Jack in concern.

'Steady on,' he warned. 'Sit down, old man,' he said with professional friendliness. 'You look as if you've had a dickens of a shock.'

Jack sat down on the hard wooden chair, the handbag held loosely on his knees. 'Sorry,' he said after a few moments and tried to smile. 'Don't want to be dramatic. Rotten bad form.'

He lit a cigarette and pulled at it gratefully.

'So what is it?' asked Ashley.

Jack took a deep breath and pointed to the straps of the handbag. They were stitched on and, for extra ornamentation, the ends of the straps were riveted to the bag by brass buttons. The buttons had a pattern of an oak leaf and an acorn.

'Do you recognise these buttons, Ashley?'

Ashley looked at the bag, frowning. 'They seem familiar . . .' he began, then snapped his fingers. 'Got it! They're the same pattern as the button you found in the belfry!'

Jack nodded. 'That's right. And look.' He pointed to the plain brass button that secured the flap of the handbag. 'That's been sewn on recently. It's not the original. If you look, you can see the original stitch marks.'

He was trying to keep the strain out of his voice. 'If you look at it under the light, you can see that the thread has a fairly clumsy knot. It's a different type of thread and shade from the stitching round the rest of the bag.'

Ashley gazed at the bag as if thunderstruck. He took the bag and examined it under the light. 'Damn it, you're right,' he said in a dazed voice. 'But that means – it has to mean – that it was Enid Martin all along. It was Enid Martin that night in the chapel, scaring you all witless.'

Jack nodded.

'But that's incredible,' Ashley muttered. 'I knew she'd taken against the Jagos, but to go to such lengths . . . It beggars belief.'

'Look here,' said Jerry in a 'let's get to the bottom of this' voice. 'This poor woman is dead. You can see for yourself she's been killed in the most violent way. She can't be guilty of anything. I heard what happened to you, Jack, that night in the chapel. It was all round the village. But you can't honestly expect me or anyone else to believe that Mrs Martin, of all people, was behind it all.'

'But she was,' said Jack with complete certainty.

'So how did she die?' demanded Jerry. 'Are you telling me there's some truth in that wretched legend after all?'

Jack shook his head. 'It wasn't the legend that killed her.'

'Who then?' Jerry turned on Ashley. 'You said she'd taken against the Jagos. Had they taken against her? Are you saying they killed her?'

'No,' snapped Ashley. 'Of course not. They've got rock-solid alibis. You swore that Mrs Martin was killed at two o'clock.'

'So she was,' agreed Jerry. 'You saw me examine her. Damnit it, man, *you* examined her. You know she was still warm to the touch.'

'And both the Jagos had been with Mr and Mrs Stanton since about half past twelve. By your own admission they can't have hurt a hair on her head.'

'Burstock,' said Jack. He was thinking furiously about Burstock. That day in the pub Burstock had been wary and defensive, unwilling to talk. But when Jack had nettled him by dismissing the idea of seeing a ghost, his manner had changed. He'd been amused, obviously glad to put one over on the nosy, patronising Londoner. He'd been *smug*, damnit. Ridiculously smug.

'What about Burstock?' demanded Ashley.

'I don't suppose the Jagos could have . . .' began Jerry.

'No, they damn well couldn't,' said Ashley heavily. 'Look, I'm not standing here listening to perfectly innocent people being accused of a series of perfectly hideous crimes. If Haldean says that Enid Martin was responsible for all that malarkey in the chapel, then I suppose I've got to take it seriously.'

'Thanks,' said Jack absently. 'It has to be her, you know.'

'If you say so. I've known you far too long to dismiss any of your notions. Why she should do it is anyone's guess, but that's neither here nor there,' he added irritably. 'The point is, that although you were all scared stiff, no one was hurt.'

Ashley waved a hand at the body on the stone table. 'But this death and Burstock's death are different.'

'What about the other chap, Derek Martin?' asked Jerry. 'He was certainly murdered.'

'We're fairly sure it was the American, Stoker, who killed him. There's no great mystery about that. But Burstock's death . . .'

Ashley rounded on Jack. 'You were with Mr Jago, weren't you? At the fete. You were manning the rifle range and he was looking after the skittle stall.'

'And making a dickens of a lot of noise about it, too,' agreed Jack. 'When Arthur took over the rifles, Betty and I went into the tea tent.' He looked up at Jerry. 'Isabelle had been in the tea tent all afternoon along with Rosalind Jago and a couple of other ladies.'

He glanced at the sheet-covered body. 'Mrs Martin was there too. Then the Mottrams came in, horribly shocked by the noises they'd heard in the woods. Tom Jago looked in . . .'

'So you weren't actually with him all afternoon?' asked Jerry quickly.

Jack shook his head. 'Practically speaking, I was. It was only a matter of ten minutes or so since I'd left him at the skittle stall and plenty of people saw him during that time. Besides that, you know how long it takes to get to and from that ruddy chapel. I found out for the first time that afternoon because we all trooped off to find that poor beggar, Burstock.'

'Exactly,' said Ashley with satisfaction. 'So you see, Doctor, by your evidence and by Haldean's evidence, plus the evidence of a fair few men and women I interviewed after the fair, the Jagos can't have anything to do with it.'

Jerry shrugged and smiled. 'Granted, and with pleasure. I must say I've always got on with Mr Jago on the few occasions I've met him. But . . .'

He scratched his chin in bewilderment. 'It doesn't add up,' he added thoughtfully. 'However, you're quite right. I take your point that the Jagos are innocent. That's fair enough. Although I had assumed that there more or less had to be some connection. There's been two deaths in that chapel of theirs, for pity's sake.'

He looked at Jack with puzzled eyes. 'Is there a connection?'

'Oh yes,' said Jack. 'Of course there's a connection. As you say, there more or less has to be.'

'What is it, then?' Jerry demanded. 'Do you know?'

Jack hesitated and, out of the corner of his eye, saw Ashley give an almost imperceptible shake of his head. 'I've got an idea,' he temporised. 'I need some evidence to show I'm on the right lines. And, as I say, it's only an idea. I might be wrong.'

Jerry listened in silence, then looked up with a sudden grin. 'You should've been a doctor, Jack. We've got to keep things under our hat, too.'

Jack heard Ashley breath a short sigh of relief.

'Have it your own way,' the doctor added cheerfully. 'But I will say that I feel damn sorry for both Mr and Mrs Jago. I can't be the only one who's wondered where they fit into this. In fact, I know I'm not. I know our sympathies lie with old Burstock and with Mrs Martin, but the Jagos are victims too, wouldn't you say?'

'I certainly would,' agreed Jack slowly.

'Right,' said Jerry briskly. 'From now on, I'll make it my business to scotch any rumours I hear. But I must say, I'm fairly bewildered by the whole business.' He looked once more at the body on the table. 'So who or what are you looking for?'

Ashley shrugged. 'Some thing or someone else.'

'Yes,' echoed Jack slowly. 'Some thing or someone else.'

SEVENTEEN

I t was good to get out into the evening sunshine, away from the deadening atmosphere of that room with the shrouded body on the stone table.

'Hop in,' said Jack, walking to the car. 'I'll give you a lift to the station.'

'Thanks,' said Ashley, climbing into the Spyker. 'Haldean, what's your idea? I know you didn't want to say too much in front of Dr Lucas but you can tell me.'

Jack turned the engine over, pressed the self-starter and let in the clutch but said nothing.

'You *can* tell me, can't you?' Ashley added pleadingly. 'Because any idea, however outrageous, has to be worth something.'

'I'll tell you what I've got in mind,' said Jack, negotiating the big car along the narrow village street. 'That's not a problem. The problem is going to be finding enough evidence to make an arrest . . . Cindy Lyne!' he shouted.

'I beg your pardon,' said Ashley, taken aback.

Jack hit the steering wheel with a triumphant thump and, with shining eyes, spared Ashley a quick glance. 'Cindy Lyne,' he repeated with satisfaction. 'You remember. Vern Stoker's girlfriend. The rather forward young lady who Bill Rackham interviewed.'

'The hotel thief, you mean?'

'That's the one,' Jack agreed jubilantly. 'I can run up to Town tomorrow. I'm pretty sure that she can put us on the right lines.'

'But how?' asked Ashley plaintively.

'Listen,' said Jack. 'And I'll tell you . . .'

Jack stood up as the female warden showed Cindy Lyne into the room. It was a cold, depressing room, painted in grubby cream and dark green and smelling faintly, as all official institutions seemed to do, of old cooked cabbage. The sunshine coming through the windows only seemed to make the paint shabbier.

Cindy Lyne, even without lipstick and powder and with her golden hair showing dark roots, still exuded a glamour that made the room seem dingier. A cheap glamour, with a sharp, spiky core under the soft exterior, but even so, Jack couldn't help giving an appreciative smile.

Cindy Lyne caught the smile, gave a coquettish toss of her head and slowly smiled back. 'Well, I'd say you were a boy that knows how to treat a lady,' she drawled.

'I'll be outside the room, Major,' said the warden repressively. She had seen the smile too. 'I'll be able to see you but I can't hear you. And remember, nothing is to be passed between the prisoner and yourself.'

'I want to show this lady a picture,' said Jack, tapping his sketchbook which lay on the table. 'That's all right, isn't it? Chief Inspector Rackham said that would be in order.'

'Chief Inspector Rackham did give instructions,' admitted the warden grudgingly.

It was thanks to Chief Inspector Rackham that this meeting was taking place.

'You want to see Cindy Lyne?' Bill asked incredulously, when Jack breezed into his office. 'Ah well, there's no accounting for tastes. Yes, I'll arrange a meeting if you're so set on it. As a matter of fact, you're only just in time. A couple more days and that hard-bitten baggage will be on her way back to America and good riddance. You want to see her this morning?'

'I'd like to.'

'Rather you than me, but please yourself,' said Bill, picking up the telephone on his desk. 'I'll get onto Wandsworth Prison now.'

A brief conversation followed at the end of which Bill hung up the phone. 'Visit OK. You can be there by eleven, can't you? You'll let me know what she says, of course. Are you going back to Arthur and Isabelle's today?'

'That's right. There's a bit of exploring I want to do.'

'Well, drop in before you go and bring me up to date.' Bill grinned. 'And I wish you joy of Cindy Lyne, although how she's going to help you chase jaguars I can't guess.'

Cindy Lyne settled herself at one end of the table, put her fingertips together, and unleashed another dazzling smile at Jack.

He very nearly laughed. 'It's all right if I offer the lady a cigarette, isn't it?' he asked the warden. Cindy Lyne looked up eagerly.

The warden frowned. 'Chief Inspector Rackham said nothing about cigarettes.'

Jack sighed inwardly. He wanted to create as relaxed an atmosphere as possible. He took a cigarette from his case, lit it, and gave the case and his lighter to the warden. 'Would you mind giving those to Miss Lyne?' he asked with a smile. 'I'm sure the regulations don't apply to you.'

Rather grudgingly, the warden took the case and handed it to Cindy Lyne. She took a cigarette and lit it, relaxing back in the chair in a contented wreath of smoke. She tilted her head to one side and looked at the warden. 'Scram,' she said succinctly.

Greatly affronted, the warden left the room.

'You don't think much of authority, do you?' said Jack, amused.

'They can't do nuthin' more to me. You guys don't go in for the third degree and I've got nuthin' to tell, anyway. I guess I'm safe enough.'

She looked at him appraisingly. 'When I heard a Major Haldean wanted to see me, I was expecting some stuffed shirt. You came as a nice surprise.' She tapped the ash off the cigarette. 'You a dago? You look like a dago even if you don't talk like one.'

'My mother was Spanish. We can speak Spanish if you'd rather.'

'Nah. I knew plenty of dagos in Florida but I never picked up the lingo.' She looked at the sketchbook on the table. 'You want to show me a picture? I never met a guy who carried his etchings with him but you look like a boy who doesn't keep a lady waiting.'

This time Jack did laugh. 'Perhaps I should mention I'm a married man.'

Cindy Lyne raised her eyebrows. 'Buster, in my experience, that's never stopped a guy yet.'

'A happily married man.'

She raised her eyebrows still further. 'Now that is unusual. Some dames have all the luck.' She blew out another mouthful of smoke. 'Pass me the book. I'll look at your pictures for you.'

Jack slid the book across the table. The first few pages were landscapes and street scenes in a variety of watercolours and pencil drawings.

'You draw these?' asked Cindy, flicking through the book. Jack nodded. 'Pretty good,' she commented. 'But I don't know what I'm meant to say . . .'

She turned over the page, gave a little cry, then drew her breath in sharply. She stared at the pencil drawing of the man on the page and swallowed hard. When she looked up, all trace of humour had gone from her face. She suddenly looked years older.

'Do you recognise him?' asked Jack. It was, he thought, an unnecessary question. It was perfectly obvious that she did, but he had to ask.

She very nearly said no. He could see her lips framing the word but no sound came. A hard, calculating look came into her eyes. 'You've guessed it, pal,' she said at last.

She crushed out her cigarette under her foot and lit another one. 'Where d'you know this guy from?' she demanded.

It was Jack's turn to hesitate. 'Let's just say that I know him.'

She looked at him shrewdly. 'I'm gonna make a guess. It's this place that's been in the papers, ain't it? Bower. Birchen Bower.'

Jack inclined his head. 'As you know that, you might as well give me a name.'

She put her hand to her eyes. To Jack's surprise she made a sound as if she was trying not to cry.

'Miss Lyne?' he said in concern. 'I'm sorry to have upset you.'

He took his handkerchief from his pocket and was about to hand it across the table. From the door outside the warden tapped on the glass and shook her finger.

She looked up, wiping her eyes on her sleeve. 'Did you draw this from life? I mean, d'you know this guy or did you copy it from a photo?'

'I didn't copy it,' said Jack. 'I drew it from memory.'

She gave a long hissing sigh and put her hand to her eyes once more.

'Miss Lyne?' prompted Jack. He felt an absolute heel to press her, but he wanted an answer.

She looked up. 'It's Vern,' she said eventually.

'Vern Stoker?'

She nodded.

'Are you sure?'

She nodded again then, with an obvious attempt to rally herself, tried to smile. 'Sure I'm sure. How can't I be sure? I know him, don't I?' She shook herself, then stood up and beckoned the warden into the room. 'I guess we're finished here.' She swallowed. 'Nice meeting you, Major.'

*   *   *

Bill Rackham gazed at the sketchbook in blank astonishment, his smouldering pipe unheeded in his hand. 'You're telling me that Cindy Lyne told you that this was *Vern Stoker*?'

Jack picked up his cup of tea. 'I know. It's interesting, isn't it?'

'It's a bit more than interesting, it's incredible,' said Bill vigorously. 'Damnit, Jack, it can't be Vern Stoker.' He frowned at the book. 'Hang on a minute. I recognise him.'

He tapped the book with his pipe stem. 'It's that pompous Canadian bloke that came to see me last week, the one who wanted me to put the thumbscrews on Simon Lefevre.' He drummed his fingers on the desk, searching for the name. 'Thomas Jago.'

He looked at his friend. 'I'm right, aren't I?'

'Yes, you are. I felt sorry for Miss Lyne, you know.'

Bill gave a snort. 'She's as hard as nails.'

'She's a bit hard-shelled, I grant you, but I must say that I felt sorry for her.' Bill raised his eyebrows in disbelief. 'When I showed her the picture, she went from being amused and cynical and more than a bit flirtatious – which showed an almost heroic indifference to her surroundings – to being genuinely upset.'

'Actually,' said Bill, 'I felt a stab of sympathy for her, too. She obviously cared about Stoker.' He stared at the sketchbook again. 'Do you really think this could be Vern Stoker?'

'It could be,' said Jack.

'But . . .'

'But what I really think is that Miss Cindy Lyne has a very sharp mind. I presume, in view of what I've told you, you'll arrange for Ashley to interview Tom Jago?'

'I'll have to let him know. It's Ashley's case. I can't say I believe Miss Lyne, but now she's dropped this particular bombshell, we have to take notice of it.'

'And I bet she guessed that. Tell me, prisoners are allowed to write letters, aren't they?'

Bill nodded. 'Yes, of course. Why?'

'Well, another thing I'm going to bet is that Miss Lyne will write a letter to Tom Jago telling him about her interview with me. In fact,' he added, glancing at his watch, 'I wouldn't be surprised if she's already written it.'

Bill started to his feet. 'What? I'd better put a stop to that straight away.'

Jack shook his head. 'No, don't do that. Telephone the prison and, if she really has written a letter, ask them what the contents are, but let the letter go.'

'I can't allow her write to Jago, Jack. If Jago really is Stoker, then he's wanted for murder. The prison censor will take a note of the contents as a matter of course, but we can't let her warn him.'

Jack leaned forward earnestly. 'Let her send the letter. I've got a feeling it's going to stir things up.'

'Do you want to stir things up?' Bill asked doubtfully.

Jack nodded. 'That's exactly what I want. It's a bit of a long story, but I think I can explain everything, from the reason why Enid Stoker came to Croxton Abbas five years ago to her shenanigans in the chapel last week, and a good few other things as well.'

'Can you, by jingo!'

'Yes, but the problem is that I haven't any proof.' He looked at Bill with bright eyes. 'I'm sure that with all the resources of Scotland Yard behind you, you could find proof, but we're running out of time. I'd like to bring things to a head.'

Bill gave a wry smile. 'Don't you always. It's a long story, you say?'

He opened the tobacco jar on the desk and, having refilled his pipe, passed the jar over to Jack. 'Now,' he said, putting a match to his pipe, 'tell me this brilliant idea of yours.'

Jack made good time back from London. He had reluctantly decided not to tell Betty or Isabelle what Cindy Lyne had said or what was in his mind. It would be safer that way. Arthur, on the other hand, was a different matter.

'Hello, old man,' said Arthur as Jack came into the sitting room. 'Did you have a good day? Let me get you a drink.'

Jack glanced round the room. Betty, he knew, was still dressing for dinner and Isabelle was saying goodnight to Alice. 'Arthur, I need to speak to you alone,' he said quietly. 'I don't want the girls in on it.'

Arthur paused, his hand on the whisky decanter. 'Isabelle will be down in a few minutes.'

'I know. So will Betty. Look, after dinner, suggest you and I stick on in the dining room for port and cigars. I know we don't as a general rule when it's just us, but do it tonight.'

'OK.' Arthur was still for a few moments. 'Isabelle's going to smell a rat,' he said thoughtfully. 'I know! I'll break out my Trichinopoly cigars. To be fair, I grant they smell a bit ripe. Isabelle can't stand them.'

'And who can blame her?' said Jack with a grin. 'I'll make a point of asking for a Trichinopoly after dinner. That'll clear the room all right.'

It all worked out exactly as Arthur had predicted. Isabelle gazed at her cousin with a resigned expression when he asked her husband if he still had that box of Trichinopoly cigars.

'Let's leave them to it, Betty,' she said, getting up from the table. 'The room needs fumigating after Arthur's smoked one of those beastly things. At least make sure the window's open, Arthur.'

'I will,' he said with a smile. 'Don't worry.'

In the sitting room Betty toyed with her gin and ginger. 'There's something going on,' she said abruptly, cutting off Isabelle's speculations about the chances of getting a decent crop of plums this year. 'Jack never smokes Trichinopoly cigars. He prefers Havanas.'

Isabelle stopped. 'You're right,' she said slowly.

'And he was awfully vague when I asked him about today. He's planning something. I just know he is.'

Isabelle looked at her quizzically. 'You're right! He didn't want to talk about what he'd done today. He doesn't want us in on it.' She stood up with a determined expression. 'Come on, Betty. It's pointless going back into the dining room. The pair of them'll shut up like clams but if we go onto the terrace we'll be able to hear them through the window.'

'Turn the wireless on,' suggested Betty. 'They'll think we're just listening to dance music.'

As the sound of the Savoy Orpheans came faintly from the sitting room, Jack blew out a cloud of richly aromatic smoke and relaxed. 'It sounds as if they're occupied for the next half-hour or so.'

'So what's on your mind?' asked Arthur.

Jack told him.

Arthur listened intently without interruption but when Jack had finished, shook his head. 'It's all theory,' he complained. 'Even if you could get Cindy Lyne down here, she's already told you her tale and I bet she'll stick to it. You haven't got a shred of evidence to support any of your ideas apart from that brass button.'

Jack nodded. 'I know. I'm sure we'll be able to get evidence but that'll take time. I've got an idea for a short cut.'

'What's that?'

Jack tapped the ash off his cigar. 'You remember the sea cave beneath Birchen Bower woods we spotted last week?'

'Yes, of course.'

'I'm sure – more or less sure – that'll give me enough evidence to convince Ashley I'm on the right lines. If I don't find anything then I'll have to begin again. He's coming here tomorrow afternoon so I can bring him up to date.'

Arthur ignored Ashley. 'What's the sea cave got to do with it?'

'Maybe nothing but it's worth a try.'

Arthur shrugged. 'Fair enough. How are you going to get there?'

'I thought I'd hire a dingy from the harbour.'

'Oh no you don't,' said Arthur. 'The currents round there are pretty dodgy if you don't know the waters. Take the *Moonstone*.'

Jack laughed dismissively. 'Come on, Arthur. If I can't handle a dingy, I'll never handle the *Moonstone*.'

'I'll do that.' He raised a hand to quell Jack's protests. 'It'll be fine with the two of us.'

'But . . .'

'I'm coming with you,' said Arthur with an affectionate grin. 'You didn't think I'd let you tackle this alone did you? Idiot!'

'Thanks, Arthur,' said Jack, returning the grin. He knew better than to argue. 'What do we tell the girls?'

'A fishing trip?'

'A fishing trip,' repeated Jack. 'Yes, that'll do the trick.'

*   *   *

'That was easier than I thought it might be,' said Jack as the two men walked down to the harbour. 'I felt a bit rotten going on about a fishing trip, especially as we needn't have said a word.'

Mrs Dyson, the vicar's wife, had, according to Isabelle, asked her to slip over that morning to discuss the forthcoming sale of work. Betty, of course, had gone with her.

'Yes, I must say I don't like deceiving Isabelle but . . .' Arthur stopped short as they rounded the corner. Sitting on the harbour wall were Isabelle and Betty.

'Well, I'll be damned,' muttered Jack. 'Sale of work? I don't think so. We're not the only ones who can tell bouncers, old man.'

He walked up to where Betty, smiling broadly, was waiting for him. 'You knew, didn't you?' he asked resignedly.

'Of course we knew,' she said happily. 'We heard everything you and Arthur said last night.'

'But how did you guess we were planning anything?'

'Next time,' she said, taking his hand and climbing down from the wall, 'if there is a next time, don't ask for a Trichinopoly cigar. I know you prefer Havanas!'

EIGHTEEN

Sails furled, the *Moonstone* rocked gently at anchor in the shallow waters of the bay the other side of the spur of rock from Birchen Bower woods.

'We can easily get onto the beach from here,' said Arthur, hauling on the painter of the dingy.

Jack and Arthur helped the two girls into the dingy then took the oars. A few minutes later the keel of the dingy grated on the sand of the beach.

The tide was in and the beach was only a few yards wide. With the tree-fringed cliffs looming over them, shielding the sun, the meagre strip of sand was oddly forbidding. Isabelle looked up at the cliffs and shuddered. 'There's something creepy about this place.'

'You're right,' said Betty. 'I don't like it.'

'Well, you would insist on coming,' said Jack. He looked at them wryly. 'I must say I can't help wishing you two hadn't been so blessed sharp last night.'

'We're in this together, remember,' said Betty.

Jack gave a resigned smile. 'I remember. Look, I'm probably being overly cautious but it'd be as well if we kept our voices down. I think we're safe enough but we don't want to advertise our presence here if we can help it.'

'D'you know, it's remarkable,' said Arthur quietly as they crossed the sand, 'how well the cave's hidden. If we hadn't spotted it the other day, I'd never have guessed it was here.'

The cave itself was a dark gash in the chalk rock, about fifteen feet across and twenty feet high. The sand, Jack noticed, was smooth and untrodden. They were above the tideline, so it was obvious no one had been here for a long time. He found that reassuring.

'What are you hoping to find, Jack?' asked Betty as they stepped into the dark space.

'I'm hoping,' he said taking out his electric torch, 'to find a passageway. If this place really was used to land smuggled goods, it should be fairly obvious.'

'There it is!' said Isabelle.

Jack's torch shone on a dark rift in the chalk. There were steps cut out of the rock with a smooth slope inbetween.

'It's a smuggler's cave, Jack,' said Arthur with satisfaction. 'Those steps prove it.'

Isabelle looked at him quizzically. 'How?'

Arthur pointed to the smooth slope. 'That's for hauling barrels up.' He grinned at her expression. 'Smuggled brandy and so on. If you'd read the right sort of books as a kid, you'd know about this sort of thing.'

'Absolutely,' agreed Jack. 'All right, everyone. Torches on and for heaven's sake, don't make any more noise than you have to.'

They climbed the steps in single file, the sounds of the sea fading behind them.

Jack led the way. His torch, gleaming off the chalk, showed a fine layer of white dust lying undisturbed over the steps. As with the beach, it was obvious no one had used these steps for a very long time. They were in the heart of the cliff now and, although no one spoke, the sound of their chalk-muffled footsteps and steady breathing sounded loud in the silence.

They must've, in Jack's reckoning, climbed twenty feet or so before they came to a squared-out platform or landing. The steps took a sharp turn to the right.

'What's this space for?' asked Isabelle in a whisper.

'To give the smugglers a breather, I reckon,' said Arthur quietly. 'It must've been hard work, hauling barrels up those stairs.'

Another twenty feet or thereabouts brought them to another squared-out platform. This time the stairs went to the left. Jack flashed his torch on the steps and stiffened.

'Look,' he breathed.

There were footprints in the chalk.

They stood frozen, listening intently. The silence was so profound it seemed to crack their eardrums. In that intense silence, with tons of chalk and flint above, below and to either side, Jack could hear his heart beating faster.

Nothing.

Jack turned to them and gave a thumb's up, his eyes gleaming with excitement. 'We're on the right lines,' he breathed. 'Come on.'

When he reached the tops of the steps, he put his hand out behind him, palm first. Everyone stopped.

'We're at journey's end,' he whispered.

Once again, they all listened, then Jack gave a sigh of relief. 'It's safe enough,' he said quietly.

They came out of the stairway and into what was obviously a natural cave. It was about forty feet across at the widest part and, at the highest point, about ten feet high. The air, which on the stairway had been stale, was much fresher here.

At the far end of the cave, a single flight of steps led steeply upwards, while on the other side, the cave continued along a narrow passage that sloped upwards.

A stack of barrels was heaped along the wall beside the

sloping passage. They looked ancient but it was obvious the cave had been used and used recently.

Footprints criss-crossed the chalk and, on top of the barrels, was a modern oil lamp with a box of Swan matches beside it. A couple of cigarette ends were crushed out on the ground.

'Where are we, Jack?' asked Arthur softly.

Jack pointed to the single flight of stairs. 'I'm pretty certain that if we go up those stairs, we'll find ourselves in the chapel. Let's go and see, shall we?'

Isabelle looked doubtfully at the steep stairs. Running down the wall, threaded through metal loops driven into the chalk, was a thick rope, serving as a makeshift banister. Even with the aid of the rope, she didn't much fancy the climb. 'I'll stay here,' she said.

'And me,' added Betty.

'OK,' agreed Jack. With one hand on the rope banister and his torch in the other, he climbed the stairs, Arthur behind him.

Betty and Isabelle could hear their whispered comments, then came a grating noise. A shaft of weak daylight shone down the stairs.

There was another buzz of whispered comments, then the daylight was shut off. Another buzz of whispering followed, then a pause, and suddenly the daylight was back. More whispering, then the daylight was shut off once more.

A few moments later first Arthur, then Jack, came back down the stairs.

'It does lead to the chapel,' said Arthur. 'And where d'you think it comes out?'

Isabelle shook her head with a shrug but Betty stared at her husband. He was looking very pleased with himself. 'Jack! Does it come out in the tomb? The princess's tomb?'

'Got it in one,' he said.

'You knew!'

'I guessed,' he said with assumed modesty, and grinned. 'It explains quite a bit, doesn't it? Did you hear the noise as we opened it? It works on a sort of pivot. If you press it from underneath, the whole slab lifts and turns.'

'It works both ways,' said Arthur. 'Jack nipped out, shut the lid, and reopened it as easy as pie.'

'You have to know where to press down, but it's easy enough once you've seen it from underneath,' said Jack. 'It's absolutely solid if you don't know where to look.'

'Is it old?' asked Isabelle. 'As old as the chapel, I mean?'

Jack nodded. 'I'd say so. I bet it accounts for a good few stories of the hauntings that the legend records. It'd be very handy for a bunch of smugglers to have a story like that to scare off any nosy parkers.'

'It's been used recently though, Jack,' said Arthur. 'The pivot's been oiled.'

'I see,' said Betty thoughtfully. 'Or I think I see, anyway. But Jack – if the princess isn't buried there, where is she buried?'

He looked surprised at the question. 'I haven't a clue. Somewhere in here, perhaps?'

Torches in hand, they set off round the cave. They all saw it at the same time. It was a replica of the tomb in the chapel, set against the opposite wall to the barrels, a box tomb with the same inscription and the same leaping jaguar.

In this still atmosphere, which had never known wind, rain or sun, the incised writing was sharp but thick with white dust.

Betty leaned forward and blew off the dust, which made her cough. Handkerchief to mouth, she made a valiant effort to stop the noise.

'"Anna-Maria Cayden",' she read, when she'd stopped spluttering. 'It's the same as the one in the chapel. "1597 to 1638. Princess of Savages, wife of William Cayden, Gentleman. My soul is among lions, even the sons of men, whose teeth are spears and arrows. Psalm 57.4.'"

'That,' said Isabelle, after a pause, 'is just creepy. What a thing to have carved on your tombstone.'

'Well, I don't suppose she carved it herself,' said Jack.

'Why lions?' asked Isabelle. 'I thought the princess was meant to be a jaguar or a panther, not a lion.'

Arthur grinned. 'I think lion is a sort of catch-all term to describe any big cat.'

'Besides that,' added Jack absently, examining the top of the tomb, 'as far as I remember, lion in Latin is *panthera leo*, so panthers do get a look-in.'

Betty raised her eyebrows. 'Well, get you.'

'The remnants of a classical education,' muttered Jack.

There was a small thump and Arthur gave a little yelp of pain.

'Sssh,' said Jack quickly.

'Sorry,' Arthur whispered. 'I've just stubbed my toe on something.' He shone his torch down beside the tomb. 'This thing.'

He stooped down and picked up something that, at first sight, looked like a large clay cup. He grunted in surprise at the weight.

The cup – if that's what it was – was about eight inches across. Isabelle and Betty drew back in alarm. The cup was carved into the shape of a snarling jaguar head and in the sharp light and shadow of Jack's torch almost looked as if it could be alive. A hollow spout stuck out from the back of the cup.

'What on earth is it?' asked Isabelle.

'Let me see,' said Jack, holding out his hand. He took it by the spout. 'Blimey, it's heavy.'

Betty frowned at the snarling head. 'Is it a cup?'

'No,' said Jack, thoughtfully. 'No, I can't see how anyone could drink out of it.' He pointed his torch at the jaws. 'It's got holes in it, look. And,' he added, putting it down in the spot where Arthur had picked it up, 'there's no dust on it. Which means, granted that there's chalk dust everywhere else, that someone's handled it recently. What's more,' he said, turning his attention back to the tomb, 'there's not much dust on the top of the tomb, either. Nothing like as much as there was in the inscription.'

'Don't tell me this tomb opens as well,' said Betty in some alarm.

For an answer, Jack put down his torch and pressed down on one side of the solid stone slab. 'No,' he said eventually. 'It's not pivoted. If it does move, there's another mechanism at work.'

Arthur grasped the edge of the slab and pushed hard. The stone grated and, much to his surprise, moved a fraction, revealing a tiny triangle of blackness. He staggered back, hand to his mouth, retching, as a foul smell gushed out.

Choking, Jack seized the edge of the stone and together the

two men pushed the slab back. Panting, the two men rested their elbows on the stone.

'Jack,' said Arthur unsteadily. 'The princess has been buried for centuries. It shouldn't smell like that.'

'No, it shouldn't.' Jack cocked an eyebrow at his friend. 'What did it remind you of?'

Arthur breathed deeply. 'A shell hole in France. The sort that was filled with water with a couple of corpses in it.'

'Yep. Me too.'

'Corpses?' repeated Isabelle in dismay. She shuddered and turned away then, starting backwards, gave a cry that was nearly a shriek. Clapping her hand to her mouth she valiantly stifled another cry.

'Isabelle!' said Arthur, catching her in his arms. 'What is it?'

Trembling, she shone her torch into the corner of the cave. 'It's the jaguar.' Her voice was a cracked whisper. 'It's the *jaguar*!'

For a moment they stood frozen as the wavering torchlight caught gleaming amber eyes and white, bared fangs.

Arthur drew his breath in in a startled hiss then Jack shone his torch full on the snarling face and, unexpectedly, gave a soft laugh.

'Bingo,' he said with enormous satisfaction.

'What the devil . . .?' asked Arthur.

'I *knew* it had to be something like this,' said Jack triumphantly. 'I just knew it.' He turned to Betty, slipping his arm round her waist. 'It's all right, sweetheart. It's not alive.'

'Not alive?'

Jack shook his head. 'Nope. It was. Heavens knows when it was alive but it's dead now.'

He walked over to the corner and, putting down his torch, took the jaguar's head in his hands. 'Look,' he said, holding it out. 'Blimey, it's heavy.'

It was a jaguar skull, set on a metal stick about three foot long. The end of the staff was shaped into a metal claw. The skull was draped with a hood of orange and black fur.

'Its eyes,' said Isabelle unsteadily. 'Its eyes can't be real.'

Jack tapped one. 'Glass. But the effect is scary, isn't it?'

Arthur gave a low whistle. 'It's appalling.'

Jack shone a light into the interior of the skull, then, putting down his torch once more, swung the skull round on its stick. 'The inside of the skull is loaded with lead,' he said thought-fully. 'That's how the stick's attached.' He hefted the skull and brought it round in a gesture which made the others wince. 'It's beautifully weighted. This is some weapon. It'd be very easy to use.'

He leaned the skull back against the rocky wall of the cave and, picking up his torch, examined the snarling fangs. 'There's blood on the teeth,' he said quietly. 'And on the claw as well. Or, at least, I'd bet my bottom dollar it's blood.'

'No takers,' said Arthur quietly. 'What now, Jack? Do we explore further?'

Jack glanced up the sloping passage, hesitated for a moment, then shook his head. 'We'd better not. What I want to do is to get back home and then tell Ashley exactly what we've discovered.'

'Good idea . . .' began Arthur when Isabelle put an urgent hand on his arm. 'There's someone coming!' she hissed. 'Hide!'

Jack glanced up and saw, along the sloping passage, a brief flash of light as a moving torch caught a ridge of rock. 'Behind the tomb!' he whispered. 'Quick!'

Moving with incredible speed, Betty, Isabelle and Arthur got behind the tomb, but there wasn't room for Jack.

Thankful for the chalk that muffled his footsteps, he raced across the cave and wriggled himself in beside the ancient barrels. He was on the seaward side. If anyone stood directly in front of him, he was clearly visible but, with any luck, he should be able to stay out of sight.

From his hiding place, Jack couldn't see who came into the cave, but he could see the moving light of the torch. Then came the scratch of a match, and the glow of the oil lamp shone warmly.

He breathed a silent sigh of relief. The light from the oil lamp was too dim to show the box tomb. The others were safe enough.

The light moved. Evidently the lamp had been picked up. Jack watched the shadows chase across the roof. He could see the tomb now.

With a sudden jolt of dread, he could see something else, a white something, beside the tomb. Betty's handkerchief!

The light flickering on the roof halted. There was a low intake of breath, then the light jolted slowly forward towards the tomb.

There was nothing else for it. Jack walked out from beside the barrels and cleared his throat. 'Hullo.'

The man holding the light spun round.

It was Tom Jago.

He gazed at Jack in astonishment. 'Haldean? What the hell are you doing here?'

'Just having a look round,' said Jack, as nonchalantly as he could.

Jago's eyes narrowed. 'How did you get in?'

Jack pointed to the steep stairway. 'I came through the princess's tomb.'

Whatever else Jago found out, he mustn't find out about the boat. Jago had seen Arthur's boat, knew it was too big for one man to handle comfortably. If he twigged about the boat, he'd guess there was someone else here.

Jago gazed at him incredulously. 'You know about the tomb?' Then stopped. 'What about the tomb? What the hell d'you mean?'

Jack grinned. 'Come off it. You know all about that tomb. The pivot's been oiled. The mechanism's in good working order. I think it explains a lot, don't you?'

'It explains you're too damn nosy for your own good. This is my property, Major Haldean. My property and you're trespassing.'

'Granted,' said Jack with a shrug, 'but that's a fairly minor crime. Certainly compared with some others. Murder, for instance.'

'*Murder?*' Tom Jago started to laugh. 'Who's a murderer?'

'You are.'

Jago stared at him. 'Me? I'm no murderer.'

Jack smiled. 'Think again, Mr Jago. In case it'll help to jog your memory, I may say that I saw an old acquaintance of yours yesterday. A Miss Cindy Lyne.'

Jago tensed but said nothing.

'I showed her your picture. She recognised you, of course.'

Jack could see the tension in the man. Any moment now he was going to spring.

'Go on,' grated Jago. 'She's a compulsive liar. What did she tell you?'

'She told me that you were Vern Stoker.'

There was absolute silence for a moment, then the tension went out of Jago's shoulders. He threw back his head and laughed. 'Vern Stoker? Why the hell did she say I was Vern Stoker?'

'Well, it was obvious that she recognised you. She jumped six feet when she saw the picture. She knew she'd given herself away. I think – because she's a shrewd woman – she was trying to make the best of a losing hand. She's written to you, telling you what she told me. You should get the letter today. As I say, she's a shrewd woman. She wanted to do you a favour.'

'A favour? How?'

'By warning you the police were bound to investigate. They will, you know.'

Jago looked honestly puzzled. 'But this is lunacy. I can prove I'm not Vern Stoker.'

'Oh, I know that,' said Jack, as casually as he could. 'You're Derek Martin.'

Once again, the silence was absolute. Then Jago drew his automatic from his pocket. 'As it so happens, Major Haldean, you're right.' His voice changed, losing its American twang. 'Keep your hands where I can see them!'

'I'm only getting my cigarette case,' said Jack evenly. He shuffled his feet uneasily. 'D'you know, old thing, I don't much care for that gun waving about.' He turned his head away, as if to stop looking at the gun. 'It really makes me feel quite uncomfortable.' He looked up again. 'Don't do anything rash, will you? At least, not until I've had a cigarette.'

He flipped open the case, took a cigarette and lit it. 'I can't offer you one, can I?'

'You don't catch me like that,' snarled Jago. 'Have your cigarette. It's your last one on Earth.'

Jack drew on his cigarette. 'S'pity to end this conversation too soon. By the way, what should I call you? Martin or Jago or something else, perhaps?'

'Does it matter?'

Jack shrugged. 'I like to know who I'm talking to. Shall we stick with Jago? I'm used to it.'

'I don't give a damn what you're used to. Jago, for Pete's sake!' He spat the name out. 'No, don't call me Jago.'

'You resented him, didn't you?' said Jack conversationally. 'D'you know, I thought that was a probable reaction that night at the Stantons' when you told the story of your first meeting.' He blew out a mouthful of smoke. 'You remember? The ruined cottage in France with the booby trap? If it actually happened, that is.'

'It happened all right.' Martin ground out the words. 'That bastard Jago pulled a gun on me. He shot me, the son of a bitch, and made me look a fool in front of my corporal. Then wasn't he just *so* generous when he saw me in New York. It's easy enough to play the great I Am when you've got as much money to throw about as he had. He wanted to maunder on about the war and I was the only one who'd listen to him. It amused him to play God, the condescending swine, to run my life for me. He was so bloody patronising when he gave me a job as his agent and so bloody pleased with himself when I ran straight.'

'Did you run straight?' asked Jack.

Martin nodded. 'Oh yes. I made thousands of dollars for him.' He gave a wolfish grin. 'I always thought I might take his place. He didn't know about my other activities. He thought I was so damn wonderful and all the time he gave me the perfect cover. He was so rich and so respectable, that no one ever suspected me, his agent. I played him for a fool. My God, it felt good!'

He raised the gun. 'And you're another one like him, aren't you, *Major* Haldean? So bloody proud of your part in the war, so much in control, so much the bloody perfect English gentleman. Well, pal, this is where we say goodbye.'

'Just a minute,' said Jack, drawing on his cigarette. 'It might be the perfect English gentleman in me coming to the fore, but you may be surprised to hear that in a way – in a very oblique, twisted sort of way – I can see some sort of justification for you.'

The gun didn't waver in Martin's hand but there was a new wariness in his eyes.

'It was Albert Burstock who put me on the right lines,' said Jack conversationally. 'He was a smug beggar. He knew something nobody else knew. He said he'd seen a ghost. The stories say the Caydens haunt the place. When you turned up at Birchen Bower, Albert Burstock saw a ghost. He saw you. What's more, he knew who you were.'

Derek Martin started to laugh. 'He knew all right. What's more, the blackmailing little skunk, he tried to make money out of it. You know who I am?'

Jack nodded. 'Alexander Cayden's son.'

Martin stared at him, completely shocked. Then he gave a long, low whistle. 'Bloody *hell*! How did you know? You *couldn't* have known! Did Burstock tell you?'

Jack shook his head. 'I guessed.'

'Your guesses are too damn good for my liking.' Martin paused, drawing a hand across his forehead. 'I underestimated you, Haldean. I was told you were sharp. I didn't really believe it, but I was beginning to think it was time for you to have an accident.' He stared at Jack curiously. 'Let's hear it. If you guessed who my father was, what did you guess about my mother?'

Jack shrugged. 'I'd guess she was a servant of some description.'

Martin gave a crack of laughter. 'She was. His only servant. The two of them lived in that mouldering ruin of a house. She loved him, for God's sake. She thought he'd marry her, the fool!' He laughed again, a harsh, bitter laugh. 'Marry her? Not him. After he'd used her, seduced her, he sent her packing.'

He shrugged. 'When she heard he was dying, she came back. Years after, and she came back. She looked after him, hoping he'd do the right thing, leave the estate to me in his will.'

'She thought the world of you, didn't she?' asked Jack, his voice oddly gentle.

Martin laughed. 'Yeah. She thought a damn sight too much of me at times. She wanted me to have my proper place in the world, to own the estate, to be a Cayden.'

'But she didn't want your wife.'

Martin glared at him furiously. 'How the hell d'you know anything about it?'

'Well, she did try to murder her.' He nodded to where the jaguar skull stood in the corner, its glass eyes gleaming. 'I caught sight of that, that day in the woods. You shot at her.'

'I wish that bullet had gone home,' said Martin dreamily. 'Then it would all have been explained. The respectable Mrs Martin, caught in the act of complete madness. Yes, I wish I'd shot her then.'

'You did kill her though, didn't you?' said Jack evenly.

Martin seemed to swell with fury. 'Of course I bloody well killed her! No one – *no one!* – threatens my wife. While my mother lived, my wife wasn't safe. My mother wanted me all to herself. It was all her fault. If she could've persuaded my father, made him leave me the estate, none of this would've happened.' His voice grew harsh. 'But the bastard didn't! I'm a Cayden. *I was his son!* The estate should be mine!'

'And so you took it.'

'Yes, I took it.' The gun levelled in Martin's hand. 'Old man Cayden, William Cayden, was a pirate. Let's say I was following in the family footsteps.'

His finger tightened on the trigger. Jack flung himself forward as the bullet zinged off the rocky wall and Derek Martin slumped forward.

Jack lay on the floor for a few split seconds, ready to strike if Martin showed any sign of life. When he didn't, he raised his head and gave a grateful smile. 'Well done, Arthur.'

Arthur, holding the clay cup by the spout, reached down and helped Jack to his feet with a relieved grin. 'I did get your message correctly, didn't I? When you started faffing around with your cigarettes and told me not to do anything rash?'

'That's it. I saw you creep out and loom behind him. All I could think of to distract him was to shuffle my feet to cover any noise and offer him a cigarette.' He laughed. 'I suppose it was my natural politeness. Besides that, I wanted to hear what he had to say.'

Arthur looked at the still body sprawled on the ground. 'I say, I haven't killed him, have I?' He weighed the pot in his hand. 'This is a fairly meaty weapon.'

Jack felt for the pulse in Martin's neck. 'No. He'll live.'

He looked up as Isabelle and Betty emerged from their hiding place.

'Jack,' said Betty in a shaky voice. 'Thank God you're all right.'

Isabelle took Arthur's hand. 'Well done,' she said fervently. 'I don't understand,' she said, gazing down at Martin. 'How did you know he was a Cayden?'

'I'll explain everything later,' said Jack. He put his arm round Betty and hugged her. 'That's an awfully nice scarf you're wearing, darling.'

She fingered her silk scarf, puzzled. 'It's the one you gave me but why . . .?'

'Can we use it?' He glanced down. 'I'd prefer our pal to be tied up before he comes round.'

He picked up Martin's automatic. 'I'll stay here and keep watch. Ashley should be at Croxton Ferriers police station by now. If you three could telephone him, I'm sure he'll be happy to hear from you.'

He glanced up the sloping passage. 'That must lead to the house. Tell Ashley to bring a deputation to the front door. I want to get our friend here safely under lock and key.'

NINETEEN

Jack settled down to wait. What was happening up at the house? The servants would be confused – angry, even – by three unwanted guests erupting into their midst and demanding to use the telephone.

Time passed. Martin groaned and stirred. Jack hefted the pistol. Another crack on the head or a bullet through the foot? It'd have to be one or the other. That silk scarf was firmly knotted but he didn't trust it to hold a desperate man.

With a rush of relief he heard voices in the passage and saw the flashes of torch-light.

Arthur was the first into the cave, accompanied by Ashley

and Constable Catton. 'Are you all right, Jack?' he asked anxiously. 'We were as quick as we could be.'

'I'm fine but I'm glad to see you.' Jack glanced at the man sprawled at his feet. 'He was just beginning to stir.'

Ashley stepped forward and snapped the handcuffs round the erstwhile Tom Jago's wrists.

His eyes flickered open as, with the help of Ashley and Constable Catton, he was hauled to his feet. 'This is an outrage,' he said groggily.

'Less of it,' said Ashley firmly. 'You're under arrest.'

'Arrest? What for?'

'Murder.'

Derek Martin looked round, saw Jack, and let his breath out in a hiss. 'You've only got his word for it. He's mad, I tell you. Completely mad.'

'No, he isn't,' said Ashley firmly. 'Not only have we got Major Haldean's word, we also have three other witnesses. You are, so I understand, Derek Martin. Derek Martin, also known as Thomas Jago, I arrest you for the murder of . . .'

'My name is *Cayden!*' broke in Martin savagely.

'Just as you like,' said Ashley smoothly. 'I arrest you for the murder of Albert Burstock and Mrs Enid Martin. You do not have to say anything, but anything you do say will be noted down and may be used in evidence.'

Martin glared at him sullenly.

'Throw in Vern Stoker,' put in Jack. 'And Rosalind and Thomas Jago while you're at it.'

Ashley said nothing but raised his eyebrows expressively.

Jack jerked his thumb towards the tomb of the Inca Princess. 'The Jagos' bodies are in there.'

'Are they, by Jove,' muttered Ashley.

'And that,' said Jack, shining his torch into the corner where the jaguar head was propped up against the wall, 'is the murder weapon.'

Ashley started back. 'Bloody hell! So *that's* how it was done! Pick it up, constable. We'll need it as evidence.'

Constable Catton, clearly unwilling, gingerly picked up the jaguar head.

Jack tapped the clay cup beside him. 'You'll need this, too.'

'What the devil is it?' asked Ashley, puzzled.

'I think – I'm not sure but I think – it's how the growl of a jaguar was produced.'

Martin laughed cynically. 'So you don't know everything.'

'You'll find I know enough,' said Jack evenly. 'By the way, Ashley, you'd better get onto Bill Rackham. Jean Martin, otherwise known as Rosalind Jago, is at the Ritz hotel. You'd better add her to the bag.'

'Leave my wife alone!' snarled Martin.

Ashley ignored him. 'On what charge, Haldean?'

'Accomplice. Accessory before the fact. She's up to her neck in this.'

'Right,' said Ashley, rubbing his hands together. 'I'll get onto Scotland Yard right away.'

Betty and Isabelle were waiting in the house, alone. The scandalised cook and the three maids had marched off in high dudgeon. They would never, they declared, stay in a house where strangers appeared from nowhere and policemen came and went as they pleased.

Ashley had called for the police wagon from Lewes and, with Derek Martin safely stowed inside, he turned to Jack.

'Look, I know we've got the right man but I don't really understand the ins and outs of it, as you might say.' His voice took on a pleading note. 'Can you explain?'

'Come to dinner,' said Arthur. 'We haven't got time now. If we don't get the boat away soon we'll miss the tide.'

'Dinner?' repeated Ashley. 'Right-oh. Thank you very much.'

They had another guest for dinner.

After mooring the *Moonstone* at the quay, they met Jerry Lucas in Croxton Ferriers High Street.

'Jack! Arthur!' he called. 'Just who I want to see! What the devil's going on? The Jagos' servants have left the house wholesale and it's all over the village that Tom Jago's been arrested for murdering Mrs Martin.' He looked at Jack in puzzled accusation. 'You told me that Jago was innocent. You know you did.'

'Come to dinner, Jerry,' said Isabelle. 'Jack will tell you all you want to know.'

Mabel, the maid, followed them out onto the terrace with a tray of drinks. 'She's going to listen to everything we say,' murmured Isabelle as Mabel reluctantly withdrew.

'And I don't blame her,' said Jerry Lucas vigorously. He stopped short. On the table was the clay pot with the snarling jaguar face they'd found in the cave. 'What on earth is that?'

'It's what Arthur biffed Derek Martin over the head with,' said Jack. 'Ashley very kindly let me freeze onto it for the time being.'

'It's a rum sort of souvenir,' said Jerry, picking up his glass. 'C'mon, Jack. We've been ever so good and not badgered you with questions during dinner but you can't keep us in suspense any longer.'

'All right,' said Jack with a grin, taking the glass of port that Arthur handed him.

'I know when you twigged it,' said Ashley. 'It was when you saw the button on Enid Martin's handbag but what that told you, I'm blowed if I know.'

'Well, what it told me, of course, was that Enid Martin had been the one who'd given us our scare in the chapel.'

Ashley looked at him blankly. 'But that's what we said at the time. Where did that get you?'

'Well, it made me ask *why* had Enid Martin given us the fright of our lives.'

Jerry frowned. 'Because she hated the Jagos?' he ventured.

'Does that seem enough to you?'

'Well, of course it doesn't, but people do the weirdest things.'

Jack shook his head. 'You're right, of course, but it struck me there was a better explanation. Enid Martin had gone to a huge effort that night to convince us that the legend was real. Who would she do that for?'

'Her son,' said Ashley slowly. 'Her son who was supposed to be dead. Damnit, she even *told* me he was alive! I thought she was living in fairyland.'

'And I imagine that's what she and her son wanted you to think. Tell me, Ashley, were you more or less convinced that the dead man was Derek Martin after you'd seen her?'

Ashley thought for a moment. 'More. I thought she was avoiding facing facts.'

'That's clever,' said Jerry Lucas appreciatively. 'It's good reverse psychology.'

'And that's why you were so keen to see Cindy Lyne,' said Arthur. 'Obviously she'd know if Jago really was Jago or not.'

'But she told you Jago was Vern Stoker,' objected Ashley.

'So she did,' said Jack, lighting a cigarette. 'That was very quick thinking on her part. It was obvious she recognised the man in the picture. She knew Stoker had gone to confront Martin, therefore if Martin was alive, Vern Stoker must be dead.' His mouth twisted. 'I felt blinkin' sorry for her. She must've cared no end about Stoker.'

'I don't get it,' said Isabelle. 'Why didn't she just tell you the truth?'

'Because she was scared of Martin and didn't trust the police. But by saying he was Stoker, which he could easily disprove, that'd tell him we were suspicious. She was trying to do him a favour. She didn't want him gunning for her.' Jack glanced at Ashley. 'I was fairly sure she'd write to him. Did she?'

'Yes, she did,' said Ashley. 'Bill Rackham told me you wanted Martin to get that letter. Why?'

Jack laughed. 'I was being clever, or so I thought. If you'd simply interviewed Martin to find out if he was Stoker, as you were more or less bound to, that'd give him fair warning that things were hotting up. I bet the Martins have got money – Jago's money – stowed away safely. They would simply vanish. However, I was the joker in the pack. He didn't know how much I knew.'

'He asked us about you,' said Arthur thoughtfully. 'I'm afraid I told him you'd solved some fairly knotty problems in your time.'

'And if he'd got that letter, he'd definitely see me as a danger. He'd have to act. I thought he'd try and trap me somehow or other. Naturally, I was going to let myself be trapped, but with you, Ashley, in the background.'

Ashley raised his eyebrows expressively. 'I'm glad it didn't come to that. When did you work out that he was actually a Cayden?'

'When I saw the brass button on Enid Martin's handbag.'

'Get on,' said Ashley incredulously. 'You couldn't have done.'

'I know you'd had a dickens of a shock,' said Jerry. 'You looked as if you'd seen a ghost. In fact, didn't you say something about ghosts?'

'I remembered what Albert Burstock said about ghosts. He'd known Alexander Cayden. He was one of the very few who did. I don't know when he recognised the so-called Tom Jago as a Cayden, but recognise him he did. You remember, Ashley, we both thought Burstock was holding something back?'

'I remember but, even so, that's quite a leap to take.'

'Is it? I was convinced that Tom Jago was actually Derek Martin, Enid Martin's son. But who was his father? Well, Enid Martin came here five years ago.'

'That's when old Alexander Cayden died,' said Arthur.

'Exactly,' said Jack vigorously. 'All of a sudden, it all seemed to hang together. Croxton Abbas is a titchy place, an odd place to settle if you've got no connections. But if Alexander Cayden was Derek's father, then it'd make sense for Enid Martin to come and plead for what she'd see as her son's rights.'

'Yes, but even so, that's a pretty tall assumption for you to make,' said Ashley. 'You didn't have a shred of evidence.'

'No, of course I didn't. That's why I went to see Cindy Lyne. And just think about it, Ashley. Why buy Birchen Bower? If all the so-called Tom Jago wanted was a country estate, there's plenty of better prospects in England than a wilderness attached to a rundown house. No. It was Birchen Bower he wanted. He felt entitled to it. Absolutely entitled.'

'And you got all that from a brass button?'

'All the ideas seemed to strike me at once. I felt as if I'd been hit with a sledgehammer.'

'Why did he wait so long to buy Birchen Bower?' asked Betty. 'If his father died five years ago, that is.'

'Because not only was he making a very nice income from rum-running, he was making pots of money for Tom Jago. You heard him this afternoon. He intended to get his hands on that fortune. Tom Jago's desire to buy an English estate gave him the opportunity he'd been waiting for. The fight with the coast-guard made it necessary that he left Florida sooner rather than later.'

Jerry looked quizzically at Jack over his port. 'Did Tom Jago – the real Tom Jago, I mean – really want to buy a country estate?'

Jack nodded. 'I think so. I imagine Derek Martin did a real sales job to persuade him. However, the poor devil didn't live to see it.' He looked at Ashley. 'Did you open the tomb in the cave, Ashley?'

'Yes, we did,' said Ashley heavily. 'It's a nasty business. Inside, as well as the skeleton of the Inca Princess, there's the bodies of a man and a woman.'

'Tom and Rosalind Jago,' said Betty with a shudder.

'So how . . .' began Jerry, then stopped, shaking his head. 'I just don't get it. And what was all that business with the diamonds? I know Derek and Jean Martin were supposed to have pinched them, but why? If they were going to take the Jagos' place, that is. It doesn't make sense.'

'No, it doesn't,' said Jack with a grin. 'But there never were any diamonds.'

'*What?*'

Ashley choked on his pipe-stem. 'Of course there weren't!' he said, once he'd finished coughing. 'By the stars, that's smart.'

'I still don't get it,' said Jerry plaintively. 'Who's smart?'

'Derek and Jean Martin,' replied Jack. 'What must've happened is this. Tom and Rosalind Jago, prompted by Derek Martin, buy Birchen Bower. Derek and Jean Martin come on ahead, ostensibly to sort the house out. What they actually do is stay out of sight until the Jagos arrive.'

'That's when Burstock spotted them!' cried Isabelle. 'I bet it was then!'

'You're probably right, Belle,' agreed Jack. 'Burstock told me that when he'd found the house unlocked, he'd hunted around. I don't know how much hunting he actually did, but that's when he found his ghost. And, as someone who'd always been on the windy side of the law, he kept quiet and profited.'

'Blackmail,' said Ashley.

'Exactly. He wanted a price for keeping quiet. The Martins knew, of course, when the Jagos would arrive. They probably drove down to Southampton to meet them off the ship. That would've all been arranged in advance. Then back to Birchen Bower and . . .' Jack stopped and expressively drew his finger across his throat.

'That's horrible,' said Isabelle. 'Really horrible. Did Burstock know what they'd done?'

'I doubt it,' said Jack. 'The Martins would've made sure there were no witnesses. Burstock might've known a Cayden had returned to Birchen Bower, but he wouldn't keep quiet about murder.'

'I still don't understand about the diamonds,' said Jerry.

'It's simple. No one in this country knew the Jagos. As Jago's secretary, Martin knew all about Jago's affairs so could take his place without arousing anyone's suspicions. However, what had happened to the Martins? If they just vanished, there'd be an investigation. But if they'd apparently stolen thousands of pounds worth of diamonds, then it's obvious why they'd scarpered. The police could look for those diamonds until they were blue in the face, but they'd never be found – and neither would the Martins.'

'That's clever,' said Ashley appreciatively. 'Really clever. Enid Martin did her bit, of course.' He paused. 'She even gave me what she said was a photograph of her son. Not that it looks anything like him, of course. I wonder who it's a photo of?'

'Maybe it's Tom Jago,' suggested Jack. 'I can see that appealing to Martin's sense of humour. Maybe it appealed to hers.'

'Humour be damned,' grunted Ashley. 'She must've known all about the murders.'

'Absolutely,' agreed Jack. 'She was desperate for Derek to have the estate and didn't care how he got it. The fly in the ointment, of course, was Jean Martin. I got the impression that Enid Martin really loathed her.'

'I think you're dead right, Jack,' said Isabelle. 'And Jean Martin, to give the woman her proper name, returned the feeling with interest. What happened afterwards proves it.'

'It certainly does,' said Jack, refilling his glass. 'Incidentally, I think Derek embraced his heritage pretty thoroughly. He was a Cayden and the Caydens seemed a pretty unsavoury lot.'

'Everybody knows that, Jack,' said Jerry. 'That and the legend of the Jaguar Princess.'

Jack sat back thoughtfully. 'The Cayden family did all they could to foster the legend. The princess's tomb tells you as much. That ghastly chap, Lefevre, told us that the Incas believed a human could turn themselves into a jaguar . . .'

'A were-jaguar,' said Betty brightly.

'If you like,' said Jack with a grin. 'So the inspiration for the legend probably came from the princess herself. Granted that the Caydens ran a full-scale smuggling operation and didn't want anyone else muscling in, they must've found the legend very useful. Ashley, you remember the photographer, Mr Newton, swearing to us that the Jaguar Princess came back from the dead and savaged her husband?'

Ashley gave a snort of disgust. 'Yes, I do. Absolute nonsense.'

'Partly. But what's to say William's sons didn't do it? We can't know, as it's a few hundred years ago, but say William died naturally, his sons could have used his death to their advantage.'

'They mutilated their father's body?' asked Arthur, appalled.

'Why not?' replied Jack. 'Unless you want to believe the princess actually came back from the dead, it's the only explanation. And, with the help of that jaguar club we found in the cave, the family went on to keep the legend alive. It'd be worth showing that weapon to the British Museum. I know it says in the guide books that William Cayden rescued Anna-Maria Cayden from a Spanish ship. That jaguar skull was probably part of his loot.'

'"Unleash the jaguar",' Betty said softly.

'"Unleash the jaguar",' repeated Jack. 'That's in the Cayden family papers. I imagine it signifies when some poor devil was going to be attacked.'

'The mutilated animals!' asked Arthur sharply. 'Were they attacked with that jaguar club?'

'I'd say so,' said Jack. 'What's more, the attacks stopped four or five years ago. That's when Alexander Cayden died.'

Arthur smacked his hands together. 'It fits! Alexander Cayden was a recluse. He didn't want anyone on his land and used that ghastly weapon to keep them away.'

'This is fascinating,' said Jerry, strolling across to the drinks tray. He poured himself a glass of port and sat down. 'However,

I still can't figure out how Burstock came to be killed in the chapel. Both Derek and Jean Martin had rock-solid alibis.'

'As vouched for by me and Jack,' put in Arthur ruefully.

'And that really confused matters,' agreed Ashley. 'So what happened, Jack? I understand why Derek Martin wanted to kill Albert Burstock, but I'm dashed if I know how he did it.'

Jack leaned forward and tapped the ash off his cigar. 'As I said, Derek embraced his heritage. He read the family papers and explored the passage from the house to the cave. I bet he found the jaguar skull there. Burstock was a danger and had to go but Derek wanted an alibi. The fete gave him the perfect opportunity. He could, without arousing suspicion, make sure Burstock was alone in the chapel.'

'So what happened?' asked Ashley.

'Well, as we know, Derek and Jean Martin had unimpeachable alibis.'

Isabelle stirred. 'D'you know, I thought it was odd that Rosalind Jago, as we knew her, wanted to help in the tea tent. It seemed so out of character, somehow.'

'And you were dead right,' agreed Jack. 'But she needed to be seen, as did her husband. Now, I don't know this for certain but this must be what happened. Derek had hidden the jaguar skull in the chapel. It was probably at the top of the steps inside the tomb. It's easy enough to open the tomb once you know the knack. Neither Derek or Jean murdered Burstock. Enid Martin did that.'

Jerry stared at him. 'What? That old lady? She can't have done!'

'Couldn't she?' said Jack softly. 'Why not? She was a vigorous woman in her fifties. She was perfectly capable of it.'

'But . . .' Jerry struggled for expression, then gave up.

'I can well believe it,' said Ashley heavily. 'But how?'

'Yes, how, Jack?' protested Jerry. 'Burstock wouldn't have stood twiddling his thumbs while she opened the tomb and got out that hideous weapon. It doesn't add up.'

'No, of course it doesn't, put like that,' said Jack with a laugh. 'But cast your mind back. Do you remember a peculiar smell?'

Jerry frowned. 'No, I . . . Hang on! Yes, I do. It was like old socks.'

'Or nail varnish,' put in Betty. 'I said so at the time, if you remember.'

'And, correct me if I'm wrong, Jerry, but you treated Burstock for a heart condition, didn't you?'

'Yes, I did. He suffered from angina.'

'And what's used to treat angina?'

'Amyl nitrite,' said Jerry promptly, then stopped. 'Amyl nitrite!'

'Which smells like . . .?'

'Old socks! Damn me, *that's* what we could smell!'

'Exactly. It's common enough. I bet Derek Martin could've got it easily. What I think happened is that Enid Martin had a tube of amyl nitrite in her handkerchief. Somehow or other, she got Burstock to put his face close to that handkerchief – maybe she asked him if the hanky was his – and broke the tube. Jerry, what would happen next?'

'He'd collapse,' said Jerry slowly. 'With an overdose like that, his heart would race away and he'd keel over. He wouldn't be dead, though.'

'No. But a swipe with the jaguar claw would see to that.'

There was silence.

'Dear God,' said Ashley at last. 'And I suppose she made her way back to the house through the passage from the cave. It's far quicker than going through the woods.'

'That's how she could turn up in the tea tent,' said Isabelle in a small voice. 'She was there when the Mottrams came in.'

'That noise the Mottrams heard, Haldean,' asked Ashley. 'Who – what – made that?'

For an answer Jack picked up the clay pot they'd found in the cave.

'Jack!' said Isabelle. 'You'll wake the baby!' She turned to the others. 'Jack's been experimenting with the wretched thing.'

'Alice is on the other side of the house,' said her cousin soothingly. 'She won't hear a thing.' He put the spout to his lips and blew.

A hideous snarl followed by a series of growls split the night air.

A yelp sounded from behind the French windows.

Jack put down the clay pot with a laugh. 'Mabel,' he mouthed. 'I knew she'd be listening,' he added quietly.

Ashley swallowed hard. 'That,' he said with deliberation, 'is an appalling noise. I know when I heard it in the woods it gave me the willies.' He took the clay pot and turned it over in his hands. 'I suppose you could call it a musical instrument,' he said thoughtfully.

'Some music!' muttered Isabelle. 'Jack, you think it's the same vintage as the jaguar skull and claw, don't you?'

Jack nodded. 'I'd say so. But I don't think it's a musical instrument, Ashley. I think it's more in the nature of a lure for hunting.'

Ashley ran his fingers over the pot. 'What, like a duck decoy, you mean?'

'That's right. Only it's not for luring ducks, it's for hunting jaguars. I imagine Josiah Cayden, the loopy Victorian bloke, used it. We know from Sir Havelock Dane that a jaguar won't tolerate another jaguar in its territory.'

'So that's what made the noise that frightened the Mottrams,' said Ashley. 'Who made it? Derek Martin?'

Jack nodded. 'It has to be him. In the brief interval when he was supposedly looking for Burstock at the fete, he must've nipped down the path, concealed himself in the bushes, picked up this thing from where it was hidden, and blown it.'

'Just for the fun of the thing?' asked Jerry sceptically.

'No,' said Ashley. 'Martin needed Burstock's body to be discovered while everyone could swear to his alibi. Once the Mottrams had heard that ghastly racket, it was inevitable that a party would go along to the chapel. That's it, isn't it, Haldean?'

'Bang on,' agreed Jack. 'And as Derek was with us and Jean Martin was in the tea tent, it must have been Enid Martin who scared us all rigid by blowing the jaguar lure while we were on the way to the chapel.'

'Why did she do that, Jack?' asked Arthur.

'Because two groups of witnesses to something lurking in the woods – three if you include the Norris girls and their young men – are better than one.' He drew thoughtfully on his cigar. 'Derek Martin was breathing as much life into the legend as he could.' He looked ruefully at Ashley. 'I know you never believed it but I have to admit, I was shaken.'

Ashley nodded in agreement. 'As a matter of fact, so was I

when Sir Havelock Dane assured us Burstock really had been attacked by a jaguar. I suppose the tooth and claw marks are very distinctive.' He stopped. 'Here's a thought. That chap, Vern Stoker, had obviously been killed a couple of months ago.'

'That's right,' said Jerry. 'He'd been knifed. That was unmistakable.'

'So why did Martin want him found? I don't know where Martin had hidden Stoker's body previously but we weren't looking for him.'

Jack ran his finger round the edge of his glass. 'I think it comes down to the dog. Martin rang the zoo to enquire about Sir Havelock. He said as much. The zoo would've told him about Sir Havelock and his remarkable dog. I don't know where Stoker's body had been hidden, but it could've been somewhere the dog would've sniffed out. So rather than conceal it, he left it for us to find, making it seem as if a jaguar had found it first.'

'It all added to the legend, didn't it, Jack?' said Arthur. He sat up. 'There were diamonds in Stoker's pocket! I know there were his clothes and so on but it was the diamonds that made me think it was Derek Martin who'd been killed.'

'Rosalind – I mean Jean Martin – had loose diamonds,' said Isabelle excitedly. 'I remember her saying as much when they came to dinner.'

'That,' said Ashley, putting a match to his pipe, 'was very convincing.' He smiled slowly. 'That's before you had your shenanigans in the chapel. By the sound of it, that was a night and a half.'

'It was terrifying,' said Jack matter of factly. 'Yes, I know it was rigged and the next day I proved it was rigged, but it still rates as one of my worst experiences to date.'

'It was finding the dove that showed you it was rigged, wasn't it?' said Betty.

'Yes, poor little beast. By the way, you know we were puzzled about how the planks had been sawn up? That's because Enid Martin was capable of lifting a short section of planking but couldn't manage an entire length. Derek must've sawn them up beforehand.'

'It's a funny thing,' said Betty. 'I know all the creepy stuff in the chapel was faked but it's odd how sometimes I got a shivery feeling in there and other times I didn't.'

Jack looked at her thoughtfully. 'You're sensitive to impressions, Betty.'

'Was Derek Martin there when you felt creepy?' asked Isabelle.

Betty put her hand to her chin. 'Yes, I think he was,' she said eventually.

'That's it,' said Isabelle with assurance. 'You were picking up impressions from him.'

Ashley cleared his throat awkwardly. 'Be that as it may, how do you explain what happened next?'

Jack had to suppress a grin. He had a strong suspicion that Ashley would count Betty's impressions as nothing more than imagination. 'Well, what happened next is that Jean Martin wanted to leave.' He turned to Jerry. 'Tell me, Jerry, would you say Enid Martin was entirely sane?'

Jerry raised his eyebrows in surprise. 'To be honest, I don't really know,' he said slowly. 'She always seemed sane enough.'

'She can't have been,' said Isabelle. 'For a start she spent goodness knows how long in that crumbling ruin with Alexander Cayden, and she was cracked about her son. She committed murder so he could have what she saw as his rights.'

'That's right, Belle,' agreed Jack. 'And when it looked as if she was going to lose Derek once more, I think it sent her over the edge. It's got a horrible twisted logic to it. Jean insists Derek should leave so, if Jean is dead, Derek will stay.'

'She must've been mental,' said Arthur. 'I know she was, Jack. I heard Martin in the cave this afternoon. Enid Martin tried to murder Jean and Derek Martin murdered his mother in response. However' – he leaned forward and took a cigarette from the box – 'I don't know how.' His face clouded in a puzzled frown. 'Isabelle and I were with both Derek and Jean Martin until we found the body.' He glanced at Jerry. 'Unless you were wrong about the time of death.'

'I can't have been,' protested Jerry. 'You can't judge the time of death down to the minute, but she must've been killed about two o'clock, give or take twenty minutes or so on either side.'

'It was ten past two when we found her, Jack,' said Arthur. 'I checked my watch.'

'Go on, Haldean,' said Ashley. 'I know Martin did it because he said as much, but how?'

'Remember the twenty minutes leeway Jerry gave us,' said Jack, drawing on his cigar.

He looked at Isabelle and Arthur. 'You all had lunch together, didn't you?'

Arthur nodded.

'What happened after lunch?'

Isabelle frowned. 'Martin – it's hard not to think of him as Jago – took us out to inspect the estate. Mrs Jago – Martin, I mean – stayed in the house to pack up some clothes. She was there when we got back.'

'Right,' said Jack. 'But as we know, there's a shortcut to the chapel. What I think happened – what must've happened – is that after you'd left to look round the estate, Jean Martin shot down the passage and came out in the chapel. Now Enid Martin's coat was new. I remember you saying so, Jerry. What's the betting that Derek bought it for her? And, at the same time, bought another one for Jean?'

Ashley stared at him. 'I'm beginning to see where this is going. Did she have a hat and wig as well?'

Jack snapped his fingers. 'Got it in one! What's more, I bet you can probably trace the shop who sold Jean Martin that wig.'

'I'll do that,' said Ashley with satisfaction.

'You'll have to chuck in a few more explanations,' said Jerry plaintively.

'I know what happened,' said Isabelle. 'I can't believe we were taken in, but it looked so *real*, didn't it, Arthur?'

Jerry looked at her enquiringly. 'Go on.'

'Well, as I see it, Jean Martin had the coat but she'd previously ripped it up as if she'd been attacked and spilt blood on it.' She stopped. 'Where did the blood come from, Jack? Because there was blood. And slivers of bone.'

Jack shrugged. 'It was probably a rabbit. It wouldn't stand analysis, but all that was needed was to create an impression. Martin knew that you wouldn't examine the body closely, Arthur, not with Isabelle there.'

'He was right about that, damn him. I didn't go near it. Poor Isabelle was terribly upset. I wasn't feeling any too bright.'

'And I don't blame you. What happened after you found the body?'

'We went back to the house to ring for the police and Jerry.'

'Exactly. In the meantime Jean Martin scoots back to the house via the passage ready to be horrified when you arrive.'

'But Enid Martin was murdered,' protested Jerry.

'Of course she was. Derek must've arranged to meet her in the chapel at, say quarter to two. He could've given any reason but if I was him, I'd say I'd discovered something amazing, something really important, in the chapel that he had to show her. He'd also warn her that he might have visitors with him – an engagement he couldn't get out of – and to stay out of sight, perhaps behind the belfry door, until he called her.'

'And then, when he did call her . . .' finished Betty. She shuddered. 'That's absolutely horrible, Jack.'

Jerry gaped at him. 'You mean she was killed *after* Isabelle and Arthur found her?' He shook his head impatiently. 'You know what I mean.'

'That's right,' agreed Jack. 'I'd say twenty past two would be about right. And, of course, it looked absolutely right because it was, in a sense, absolutely right. Arthur, you and Isabelle had seen the dead body of Enid Martin, who'd obviously been savagely attacked, and when you, Ashley, and you, Jerry, turned up there was the dead body of Enid Martin, exactly as Arthur had seen it.'

'I was beginning to suspect him,' said Ashley after a pause. 'However,' he added with a shrug, 'their alibis seemed absolutely unbreakable. What do you think they intended to do? After Enid Martin was out of the way, I mean?'

Jack took a long pull on his cigar. 'Vanish. I think Derek really cared about Birchen Bower but Jean Martin hated it. I think she'd have won.'

'She wanted to go back to America,' said Isabelle. 'She told me as much.'

Jack nodded. 'So that's what they'd probably have done.'

'But they couldn't,' said Betty with a frown. 'Not as Tom and Rosalind Jago, I mean. Too many people would've known they were phoney.'

'That's true,' agreed Ashley. 'And as Derek Martin was wanted for murder, that was out as well.'

'I know,' said Jack. 'But d'you remember I said I wanted to bring things to a head? Because otherwise our precious pair would simply disappear? Well, I think that's what they would've done. Tom and Rosalind Jago would have an "accident" – perhaps a boat trip that went badly wrong – and, armed with fresh identities, they could go wherever they liked. They had plenty of money, after all.'

Jerry shook his head. 'Surely someone would recognise them.'

'Maybe. They'd probably be safe enough as long as they kept out of Florida. And what if someone did recognise them? As we know from what happened to Albert Burstock, they had a fairly short way with anyone who had an inconvenient memory for faces.'

Arthur raised his eyebrows. 'Blimey, Jack. It sounds as if you might have prevented yet more murders.'

'It does indeed,' agreed Ashley heartily.

'What's going to happen to the estate?' asked Jerry.

Ashley shrugged. 'We'll have to positively identify Tom and Rosalind Jago. Once we've done that, the estate belongs to whoever their heirs are.'

'Surely they wouldn't want it,' said Betty with a shudder. 'I know I'd hate to live in a house with that history.'

'They'll probably put it up for sale,' said Arthur. 'In fact . . .' He broke off, his eyes abstracted. 'It'll go for a song. We could buy it! Get the land cleared. I've always wanted to do that. I don't know who'd want the house, though.'

'I'll tell you who would want it,' said Jack, struck by a sudden memory. 'Sir Havelock Dane! He thought the house was more or less perfect. How would you like him for a neighbour, Belle?'

She grinned. 'You liked him, didn't you, Jack?'

'Very much. And he's got a marvellous springer spaniel.'

'That's good,' she said happily. 'I like spaniels.'